"Perhaps you could move over and stop crowding me."

"No, I prefer to sit close enough so I can easily take back the reins if necessary." He leaned forward and placed his lips near her ear again. "Besides," he said in a low, silky, voice, "We present such a cozy image this way. Anyone seeing us would certainly believe we are eager to wed."

"Too bad there are so few around to see us."

"We'll get to a more populated section of the park eventually. And anyway, sometimes it's enough if the right people see us."

"The right people?" Since the horses continued to plod on placidly, she chanced a look at Lord Norwood.

He moved back, but they were still only inches apart. A lazy smile played around his mouth. "The right people. Gossipy people, who will spread the word about seeing you and me looking besotted with each other." His blue-gray eyes glowed warmly as he studied her, his gaze so intent and focused it was as if there was nowhere he'd rather be than here by her side. "Infatuated. Completely captivated with each other," he whispered.

Her mouth fell open slightly as she tried to regain her breath and overcome the strange dizziness that scrambled her thoughts. That jumbled her emotions.

He moved in closer still as his gaze traveled down to her mouth.

Charlotte's breath now came in little huffs, and she wasn't sure which scared her more: that he was going to kiss her, or that she wanted him to.

Not
the
Kind of
Earl You
Marry

An Unconventional Ladies of Mayfair Novel

KATE
PEMBROOKE

FOREVER

New York Boston

Copyright © 2021 by Kate Pembrooke

Cover design by Daniela Medina. Cover illustration by Alan Ayers. Cover photography by Shirley Green Photography.
Cover copyright © 2021 by Hachette Book Group, Inc.

Forever
Hachette Book Group
1290 Avenue of the Americas, New York, NY 10104
read-forever.com
twitter.com/readforeverpub
First mass market edition: July 2021

Forever is an imprint of Grand Central Publishing. The Forever name and logo are trademarks of Hachette Book Group, Inc.

The publisher is not responsible for websites (or their content) that are not owned by the publisher.

The Hachette Speakers Bureau provides a wide range of authors for speaking events. To find out more, go to www.hachettespeakersbureau.com or call (866) 376-6591.

ISBNs: 978-1-5387-0375-5 (mass market); 978-1-5387-0376-2 (ebook)

Printed in the United States of America

CW

10 9 8 7 6 5 4 3 2 1

To my parents for instilling in me a deep
love of books
and
To my husband, with much love

Acknowledgments

I owe a huge debt of gratitude to all the people who've helped me turn a story with great potential into a great story. Thank you to my wonderful agent, Rebecca Strauss for her enthusiastic support and her unfailing ability to brighten my day. You are the best.

Thank you to Junessa Viloria, my amazing editor, for loving this story as much as I do. Your insightful guidance has been invaluable. And a huge shout—out to my team at Forever: Jodi, Daniela, Tareth, and Shelley. You guys rock!

I wouldn't have the opportunity to be writing these acknowledgments if not for my critique partners. Thank you to Teri Anne Stanley, who read the earliest versions of William and Charlotte's story. Many thanks, also, to the Sunshine Critique Group who have helped me hone my writing skills and who never complained when I asked "Could you look over this chapter again?"

Thank you to Cathy Maxwell, who took an aspiring writer under her wing and generously offered advice and encouragement.

Thank you to Janet Raye Stevens, who judged my manuscript in a contest and then introduced me to her agent, who is now (I bet you guessed it!) my agent.

And finally, my deepest thanks to my husband, who didn't bat an eye when I told him I was going to write a book. Thanks also to my kids who've cheered for me each step of the way on this journey to getting a book published.

Thank you all from the bottom of my heart.

Not
the
Kind of
Earl You
Marry

Chapter One

London, 1817

The morning began tranquilly enough. Finished with her breakfast, Miss Charlotte Hurst reached for the neatly stacked pile of correspondence beside her plate, when the doors to the dining room unexpectedly flew open and the butler entered, his normally impassive face flushed, his mouth pinched into an uncharacteristic frown.

Standing just inside the doorway, Hopkins turned toward Charlotte's brother, Phillip Hurst. "My lord, there's a man who insists he must see you. I explained you don't receive visitors before breakfast, but he said he couldn't wait, that the matter was urgent."

"Did he now?" Phillip cut a bite of ham before spearing it with his fork. "Did this man give you his name? Or explain the nature of this urgent business?"

"He gave his name, sir. He said it was—"

"Norwood."

A tall, dark-haired gentleman strode into the room, finishing the butler's sentence in a commanding, lord-of-the-manor voice.

Startled, Charlotte dropped her correspondence, scattering the pages in an untidy disarray upon the table. Drat the man and his unheralded appearance.

"Don't blame your servant, Hurst," the gentleman said, coming to a halt beside Phillip's chair. "He made it quite clear you don't take visitors during meals. However, this cannot wait."

Phillip laid down his fork. "You may go, Hopkins. I'll attend to this."

"Very well, sir." With a nod, the butler departed.

"I can scarcely imagine any business between us that couldn't wait, Norwood," Phillip said.

"Can you not?" The man slapped a newspaper down on the table in front of Phillip. "Then read this. Perhaps it will jog your memory."

Charlotte blinked, her interest sharpened. So this was the Earl of Norwood. She'd certainly heard of him, although they'd never been introduced. His social set and hers didn't have much in common. Her brother knew him, since they were both peers in the House of Lords, but this hadn't led to any sort of acquaintance between Charlotte and the earl.

Still, all of London knew Lord Norwood was a rising star in the world of English politics, and that among his greatest political assets, aside from his impressive family and social connections, were his poise and unflappability, though he seemed to have only a tenuous grip on those traits this morning. He was angry, that much was clear. Less obvious was how it concerned Phillip.

Her brother ignored the earl's command. "Since Hopkins is usually allowed to usher in our guests, I must presume you have a singular reason for interrupting our meal in this irregular way."

"I do." If Lord Norwood noticed the hint of censure in Phillip's voice, he gave no sign of it.

Phillip glanced at his unfinished breakfast, then picked up the paper and began to read. The earl's gloved hand slapped softly against his thigh, producing a rhythmic *tap, tap, tap* that sounded unnaturally loud in the otherwise quiet room.

Since Charlotte remained an invisible entity—Lord Norwood had not yet spared a glance in her direction—she took the opportunity to study him. His manners left a great deal to be desired, but she couldn't say the same for his looks. He was undeniably handsome with dark brown hair that showed a tendency to curl, and well-appointed features. His lips were firm and finely molded, his nose straight and patrician, and his slate-blue eyes, framed by dark lashes, had faint laugh lines at the corners. However, no hint of humor showed on his face at the moment. Instead, his gaze was stern and unwaveringly fastened on Phillip as he bent over the newspaper.

After a moment, Phillip pushed the paper aside. "I'm as mystified as you are. I've no idea how that came to be published."

Lord Norwood gave her brother a hard, assessing stare. "Then perhaps she does," the earl said tightly. His gaze swung for the first time to Charlotte, with a look so scorching she had to stifle the impulse to place more distance between them.

"If you think that, you're barking up the wrong tree." For some reason, Phillip looked amused rather than affronted by the earl's angry insinuations. "However, Charlotte can speak for herself." He slid the newspaper across the table to her. "Have a look at this."

She hesitated, wishing the earl's attention hadn't shifted

away from her brother. Lord Norwood glared at her as if she were an annoying insect he'd like to squash. For one defiant moment, she considered refusing, if for no other reason than she didn't care for his rude, high-handed manner, but her curiosity surpassed this rebellious urge.

"If I must," she said, deliberately keeping her tone cool and disinterested. She moved her neglected correspondence out of the way, then unhurriedly reached for the paper and drew it over, aware that her lack of haste was fanning the flames of the man's wrath, and yet unable to behave otherwise. Her dislike of him had overruled any spirit of cooperation.

She read through the offending item, then once more, slowly this time, to make sure she hadn't misunderstood. Cold tendrils of apprehension swirled through her, settling in a tight band around her chest as the implications of the brief paragraphs sank in. No wonder the man was so angry.

It was the announcement of her betrothal to the Earl of Norwood.

Shocked, she looked back at the earl, blinking stupidly. How had it come to be in the newspaper? It was false and utterly ridiculous. For heaven's sake, she wasn't even acquainted with the man. But true or false—it hardly mattered. This announcement could still ignite a firestorm of gossip that would upend her quiet, well-ordered life.

"Well?" Lord Norwood demanded.

The blood pounded in her ears at his accusatory tone. *Her* actions required no defense. On the contrary, if anyone had behaved indefensibly, it was the earl. Even now, apparently convinced of her guilt, he looked as if he'd like to leap over the table and shake a confession out of her.

"If by 'well' you mean to imply I have any knowledge of who published this"—she gestured toward the paper with a dismissive flick of her wrist—"disabuse yourself of the notion right now. I didn't have anything to do with this, and I welcome it no more than you."

A look of utter incredulity crossed Lord Norwood's handsome face. "Forgive me if I sound conceited, Miss Hurst, but there are any number of young ladies who would more than welcome the chance to align themselves with my fortune and title, and—"

"And I assure you I'm not one of them," she cut in coolly.

His lips pinched together for a second. "Furthermore, this wouldn't be the first time a lady tried to entrap a gentleman by dubious methods." He leaned forward and placed both hands on the table, his face so close to hers she could see the darker band that rimmed his blue eyes and smell the spicy scent of his shaving soap. "But make no mistake, I've not offered for you, nor shall I feel bound to honor a nonexistent engagement just because our betrothal announcement appeared in the *Morning Post*. It seems to me the *only* party who would benefit is you."

They remained nearly nose to nose, Charlotte smarting from the sting of his last words. She searched her mind for a suitably scathing reply, but the perfect set-down eluded her. She settled for meeting his angry gaze with a defiant one of her own.

At last, he straightened and crossed his arms. "So, Miss Hurst? Do you still deny you had anything to do with this?"

It was his impossibly haughty expression, coupled with that presumptive *I-know-you're-guilty* tone that loosened her tongue at last.

"I've already denied it," she replied, "but you, with your colossal arrogance, have determined I must be guilty because of your faulty assumption that I'd welcome an alliance with you." She paused and took a deep breath, determined to maintain control of her temper, especially since he seemed to have such a fragile grip on his. "However, nothing could be further from the truth. Most of society may put a premium on a man's fortune and title when weighing his worthiness as a prospective husband, but I do not. I'm much more interested in the content of a man's character than the contents of his purse."

Her verbal slap hit the mark. The color rose on his face as he drew in a sharp breath.

"To put it plainly," she continued, "I may not know you very well, but I'm completely sure you're the last man I'd want to marry." She shook her head. "No, not even the last man, because that implies a circumstance in which I'd agree to marry you, and I can say with great certainty you're not a man I would *ever* choose to marry."

He scowled at her in disbelief for a long, thunderous moment. Charlotte watched with a certain fascination as he struggled to control his emotions. A vein throbbed at his temple, his jaw tightened like a vise, and the muscles in his throat worked furiously, though no words slipped through his tightly clamped lips.

Once more she resisted the urge to put more space between them. Her rational side insisted his gentlemanly instincts would prevail over any murderous impulses he might presently harbor. And if not, surely Phillip's phlegmatic nature wouldn't prevent him from leaping to her defense if necessary.

After several seconds of glaring at her in strained silence, something in the depths of Lord Norwood's stormy gaze shifted and the rigid lines of his shoulders relaxed ever so slightly. He'd become, once again, the unflappable aristocrat.

William Atherton, the Earl of Norwood, realized a few things in those moments he stood speechless before the Hursts. For one, they hadn't appeared guilty when he'd challenged them on their knowledge of the engagement announcement. Confused, yes. And in Miss Hurst's case, severely affronted. But culpable? No. It was now clear to him they'd had nothing to do with it.

But if they hadn't submitted that false betrothal announcement, who had? A new possibility suddenly popped into his mind. One he ought to have seen earlier, and would have if he hadn't let his emotions overrule his reason. But no, he'd been so angry at the notion that some girl he'd never met would try to entrap him into marriage—and so eager to give her the dressing-down he thought she so richly deserved—that he hadn't stopped to consider anything else.

He was one of a half dozen or so candidates being considered for an important post in the prime minister's government. It wasn't at all far-fetched that one of his political rivals had tried to bolster their chance for the appointment by stirring up a scandal through a false claim that he and Miss Hurst were engaged.

He should have known easygoing Phillip Hurst was an unlikely accomplice for an entrapment scheme. As for Miss Hurst's fiery denunciation of him, he had to admit it wasn't how a lady reacted if she harbored ambitions of becoming the next Countess of Norwood.

In fact, if looks could kill, he'd be lying on the ground mortally wounded because Miss Hurst was currently shooting daggers at him with those fine blue eyes of hers. Not that he blamed her. He wasn't such a boor that he didn't realize he owed her an apology. A very pretty apology, and if she made him grovel a bit, it was probably no less than he deserved. He took a deep, fortifying breath and exhaled, prepared to do what it took to set things right between them. He'd need her cooperation if they hoped to minimize the damage.

"I owe both of you my deepest apologies. I had no right to invade your home as I did, much less make accusations for which I hadn't a scrap of proof. I'm sorry. Deeply, deeply sorry."

Miss Hurst's eyes widened slightly. No doubt an apology was the last thing she expected from him. She'd probably pegged him a pompous ass after his performance and with good reason. After all, he'd informed her practically every unmarried female in the kingdom desired him for his title and fortune. And worse, accused her of doing so as well.

"Apology accepted, Norwood," Phillip Hurst said. "Any man would be rocked to the core in similar circumstances."

"You're remarkably forgiving, Phillip," his sister said. "I, however, am not."

"I understand your reluctance to forgive me, Miss Hurst." William gave her what he hoped was a charming (and conciliatory) smile. "Nonetheless, I ask you to forget the last few minutes and let us begin our acquaintance from this moment instead."

"Would you like to go out and come back in again?" Phillip asked in an amused voice. "It might help Charlotte to erase the drama of your first entrance from her mind."

"If only it were that easy," William said. Miss Hurst, with her flashing blue eyes and stubbornly set mouth, didn't appear as if she'd let go of her first impression of him too readily. "Naturally, we'll carry on as if the betrothal were real. For the time being, at least."

"Naturally?" She gave him a look that questioned his sanity. "You made it abundantly clear how you feel about that false betrothal announcement, not to mention your belief I was the scheming mastermind behind it."

"A grave error on my part," he assured her. "But you were

also quite explicit in expressing your opinion of me. I admit your set-down of me was well-deserved. However, now that I realize you weren't trying to carry out an entrapment scheme, a temporary engagement between us seems the best solution. I won't let you suffer from a plot aimed at me."

"A *plot*?" she asked, again looking as if he were touched in the upper works. "You make it sound as if we're characters in a gothic novel. Surely this is nothing more than someone's notion of a bad joke. But whatever the motive behind it, we need only insert a retraction into the next issue of the *Morning Post*, endure the inevitable tempest in a teapot, and get on with our lives. There's no need to pretend we're engaged."

She spoke of an engagement to him with about as much excitement as one might use when mentioning a visit to the tooth-drawer, though he could hardly fault the absence of enthusiasm on her part. He didn't deserve her approbation, given the way he'd confronted her so rudely and with such an appalling lack of tact and diplomacy. Which was all the more ironic, given that he routinely relied on both to win over his political opponents.

"I must respectfully disagree," he said. "There is every need to protect you from nasty gossip. And believe me, simply inserting a retraction wouldn't prevent the sort of tongue wagging that could ruin your reputation, and by extension, your marital prospects."

"I hope my *marital prospects*, as you put it, aren't so delicate that they can't weather the storm."

William didn't miss the sarcastic inflection she gave to his words, and recognized it as a subtle rebuke for using such a sterile phrase to sum up her value on the marriage mart. Still, they couldn't ignore reality. "In a perfect world perhaps, but society can be an unforgiving place, especially toward an unmarried female. I can't let you risk your future."

"But it's *my* future, is it not?"

"It is, but you see, it's not only *your* future that's at risk."

"Ahh, yes," she said. "I assume you refer to the afore-mentioned plot because the title of earl ensures your marital prospects are ever safe from the potential taint of scandal. Unlike mine, being merely a female of little consequence." Her gaze sparked with a martial light, as if she dared him to contradict the truth of her statement.

An admiring smile tugged at his lips, but he wasn't fool enough to take her bait. "You know I'm just stating a fact when I refer to the precarious state of a lady's reputation when gossip begins to work its mischief."

"If I may interrupt," Phillip Hurst cut in. "This may take a while, Norwood, and I'm getting a crick in my neck looking up at you standing there. Have a seat. Help yourself to some breakfast, if you wish. I'm going to get a fresh plate myself."

"Thank you, but I'll decline the offer," William replied, though he did take a seat. He'd begun to feel awkward carrying on the conversation standing over the Hursts while they remained seated. Furthermore, Miss Hurst wasn't likely to adopt a cooperative attitude if she felt he towered over her.

"Honestly, Phillip, how you can you still have an appetite?" Hurst's sister remarked, eyeing him as he heaped food onto a plate.

"I can't accomplish anything on an empty stomach."

"What else is there to accomplish?" she asked, her gaze resting on William though ostensibly she was responding to her brother's last remark. "I still say we insert a retraction and hope it blows over quickly."

"You're very willing to sacrifice your interests if it means you needn't endure a temporary betrothal with me," William said.

"If I am, haven't you given me ample reason to be?"

"To my abundant regret I have, but surely that shouldn't trump your good sense, which would argue that a temporary betrothal is the best way to protect your reputation."

"That might persuade me if I were currently interested in making a match, but I didn't come to London because I'm looking for a husband, nor am I in any hurry to do so. When I am, I trust my character will speak for itself and I won't suffer any ill effects from whatever gossip arises from this."

"All right, since that line of argument isn't persuading you, let me offer another. You wouldn't be the only one of us adversely affected by this. That false announcement may be a device to discredit me by a political rival. A scandal could destroy my chances of obtaining an important chairmanship on a commission the prime minister is forming. While this may not sound terribly important to you, it is to me, and possibly to the people of England." There. He'd laid his cards on the table.

"My, my," she said, tilting her head to one side. "It sounds as if we've circled back around to that plot you spoke of earlier. Do explain how our engagement, or lack thereof, could affect the people of England."

He ran a hand through his hair impatiently. "It's... complicated."

"Then enlighten me."

"Very well," he said, hoping a brief summation would convince her. "The prime minister is creating this commission to address a number of issues, including the pain the Corn Laws are inflicting upon the general populace. Rising food prices have led to unrest, and several riots have broken out across the country. Former soldiers are struggling to find work, now that Napoleon is no longer a threat. The prime minister believes these issues should be addressed before things take a turn for the worse. He wants this new commission to study the problems facing England in these postwar years and to suggest ways to alleviate people's suffering. Unfortunately, not every candidate being considered for the chairmanship is interested in effecting change. Some support the status quo, while some, I suspect, see it as a means to reject real reforms, and instead use it as a way to line their own pockets. Needless to say, I'll do everything I can to prevent that from happening."

"Including, so it would seem, becoming engaged to me," she murmured.

"Yes, because to do otherwise could cost us both dearly. It need only last long enough for the prime minister to name a chairman and for us to become yesterday's news. Society's attention is fickle. Once it's turned elsewhere, we can quietly and discreetly end our engagement."

She remained silent for several moments. Hurst was busy consuming his new plate of food and William didn't speak either, giving her an opportunity to think about what he'd said.

"Even if I agree to go along with your plan," she said, "and I'm not saying I will—but *if* I did, I don't see how it could possibly succeed. Nobody is going to believe it. There's been no courtship, or any other connection between us."

"None of which truly matters. If we behave like an engaged couple, people will believe we're an engaged couple."

She lofted a skeptical brow. "Don't you think it stretches credulity that an earl who most often escorts the crème de la crème of fashionable society is suddenly enamored with the unexceptional daughter of a mere baron?"

"I think you rate yourself much too lightly, Miss Hurst." She might not be a diamond of the first water, but she was quite pretty, with those lovely blue eyes of hers, and a rosebud mouth that looked soft and inviting when it wasn't pinched into a frown of disapproval.

She blinked and drew in a quick breath. "Be that as it may, there's still the fact that we've never spoken to each other before today. I don't think the *ton* is so gullible as to believe that two strangers would suddenly decide they should marry."

"Nonsense, Charlotte," Phillip Hurst said. "Put aside such romantic notions. Slight acquaintance has never been a hurdle to an aristocratic marriage."

She didn't look pleased with her brother's observation, but she didn't challenge it either. Instead, she turned her attention back to William. "Wouldn't it bother you to perpetuate such an out-and-out lie?"

"Yes, to be honest, it would, since I'm not in the habit of telling them. On the other hand, it seems the best solution to a problem that has landed in our laps and needs to be dealt with quickly."

"Don't try to make mountains out of molehills, Charlotte," Phillip Hurst said. "Norwood's generously offering the protection of his name and position until this blows over. At a more auspicious time, you can have the pleasure of jilting him." He paused, frowning. "Unless, of course, you don't jilt him. Then he'd have to marry you. You have considered that, haven't you, Norwood?"

"It didn't escape me that your sister would hold all the power," William said dryly. "However, I'm confident she'll cry off when the time comes, seeing as I'm...how did you put it?" he asked, turning to Miss Hurst. "Not a man you'd ever choose to marry. I believe that declaration followed an unflattering comparison between the quantity of my fortune versus the quality of my character." Her mouth twisted slightly, though whether this indicated amusement or chagrin, he couldn't tell.

"That does capture the gist of what I said," she affirmed.

"Then I have no hesitation in considering us betrothed for the time being."

She appeared to mull this over. "So how long would this betrothal need to last before I could cry off?"

He honestly had no idea how to answer that. Much depended on Liverpool, and how soon he made his decision. And then there was her reputation to consider. "That's difficult to predict. As long as it takes for the right moment to arrive so that's it safe for you to cry off."

She looked alarmed, and he hastened to add, "Perhaps not that long at all. I promise we'll keep it as short as possible."

She let out a long exhale. "I suppose I could agree to a very temporary, *very brief* betrothal." Again, she had that *going-to-the-tooth-drawer* intonation.

"Excellent. Then I'll call on you this afternoon. We'll take a carriage ride in the park, and let London get a look at us as a newly engaged couple."

She frowned. "A carriage ride together? Is that really necessary?"

"Yes. I can't think of a better way to kick off our charade than to ride through Hyde Park during the fashionable hour. We'll be seen by dozens of people who will then have no reason to doubt the veracity of our betrothal. That is, provided you can manage to look appropriately infatuated with me."

"When I agreed to this plan, I didn't realize it would include flirtatious carriage rides. I'm not confident I'm *that* good of an actress." She pursed her lips and gazed at him thoughtfully. "Although, if you let me drive, I think I could manage to look reasonably happy."

"That, Miss Hurst, sounds suspiciously like blackmail."

She gave a saucy little shrug. "In acting, I believe it's known as *motivation*. And it's the price you must pay to have a flirtatious fiancée by your side this afternoon."

Her brother choked back a laugh. "Capitulate, Norwood. She can be stubborn when she gets her heart set on something."

"Imagine that," William murmured. He decided he might as well accept this defeat with good grace. "Have you ever driven a curricle before, Miss Hurst?"

"No, but under your tutelage, I'm confident I'll do quite splendidly." She gave him a bright smile.

"I'm not sure *I'm* that good of a tutor."

She looked amused. "We'll find out then, won't we?"

"I'll expect a performance worthy of Covent Garden if I'm to let you handle the reins," he warned.

She dipped her chin and looked at him coquettishly through her lashes. They were dark and long and perfect for throwing flirtatious glances at a man. He was astonished by this transformation. She could be a stunner if she wished to.

"Will this do?" she asked, before dropping the pose and replacing the come-hither look with a faintly challenging one.

"Er, yes," William replied after a beat of silence. "Send those looks my way during our drive, and we'll have no trouble succeeding with our charade."

"Good Lord, Charlotte, where have you been hiding those feminine wiles?" her brother asked in amazement.

"I haven't been hiding them." She directed an exasperated look at her brother. "I just haven't had any reason to use them."

Phillip Hurst grinned. "I guess the opportunity to drive Norwood's bang-up equipage gives you sufficient reason to trot them out."

"And that, dear brother, just proves my point about motivation."

William pulled out his pocket watch to check the time. He had other business requiring his attention this morning and now that he'd secured her cooperation, it might be wise to depart before she could reconsider. "I see the day is getting on, so I'll bid you adieu now that we've settled things between us." Since neither of the Hursts offered any objection, he rose to his feet and bowed. "Until this afternoon."

He'd reached the doorway before something prompted him to turn and look back at Miss Hurst. "You won't renege on your promise, will you?"

"About being engaged, or about driving your curricle?" she asked, an arch smile playing about her mouth.

Her reply caught him off guard. He'd meant his question to refer to the planned drive this afternoon, but he could see how it could be taken both ways. "Either. Both," he said.

"I won't change my mind about this afternoon with a chance to drive your curricle on the line, and I suppose that commits me to the other, doesn't it?" She spoke flippantly, but her expression was one of…of something hard to describe actually. A mixture of uncertainty, caution, doubt, defiance even, and somewhere in all those layers of emotion, he thought he detected a small gleam of something else. Not anticipation, exactly, more like a stirring of interest.

Whatever it was, he didn't have all day to stand there and figure it out. But it was encouraging, given the intense dislike he'd seen in her eyes earlier.

"Until this afternoon then," he said again, giving the Hursts a brief nod of farewell.

Miss Hurst's voice followed him into the hallway. "I'll see you later, Lord Norwood," she called after him. "In the meantime, don't forget *your* promise to let me drive."

He smiled to himself. As if he could. Despite their short acquaintance, Miss Hurst was proving to be a surprisingly unforgettable girl.

Chapter Two

Charlotte spent the rest of the morning in a fever of indecision. She'd agreed to go along with Lord Norwood's plan even though, despite his assurances to the contrary, she thought it a mad—and quite probably doomed—scheme. How did they hope to make people believe that a quiet, ordinary girl like herself had caught the attention of one of London's most eligible bachelors? Just because they acted as if something were true, would society actually *believe* it was true? That's where her doubts crept in.

She could well imagine what people must be saying about their sudden engagement:

"Hurst? I'm not acquainted with the family."

"Nor am I. She must be no one of consequence."

"Her brother's a baron. They lead a quiet social life from what I understand."

"I heard she's a bluestocking. Pretty enough, but really,

what's the attraction on his part? Especially when he's so far above her touch." Here she imagined an exchange of raised eyebrows and sly looks.

And so it would go.

Unfortunately, she knew all too well how deeply words could wound. A familiar churning began in the pit of her stomach.

It wasn't too late to call it off. She could send a note to Lord Norwood informing him she'd changed her mind. But then what of her reputation and his chances for that political appointment? Would either emerge unscathed if she broke her promise?

Maybe. But then again, maybe not. Was she willing to make that choice? Live with those consequences?

Her thoughts circled back and forth, unable to arrive at a satisfactory decision.

Despite this inner turmoil—or perhaps because of it—when it came time to dress for the outing, she donned her prettiest gown suitable for a drive in the park. Her dress, a deep blue lutestring with a matching spencer, nicely emphasized her eyes, arguably her best feature. With it, she would wear her favorite bonnet, a smart little number trimmed with a spray of silk flowers and a few jaunty feathers.

If she had to participate in this charade, she'd do it looking her best. She wouldn't give the gossips any reason to make unfavorable comparisons between her and the handsome earl.

By half-past two, she and Phillip were in the drawing room awaiting the earl's arrival. Phillip was engrossed in reading an agricultural journal and her attempts at conversation had gone nowhere. She chewed her lower lip as she flipped through the pages of a recent issue of *Ackermann's Repository*, trying to find an article of interest, but none seemed capable of capturing her attention enough to prevent her thoughts from wandering back to her bargain with Lord Norwood.

Her gaze repeatedly flitted to the front window, which was opened to admit the mild afternoon breeze, tempting her to watch for the approach of the earl's carriage, even though the last thing she wanted was to appear anxious. With a sigh she turned back to the magazine lying across her lap and tried once again to concentrate on the improbable, but true, account of a cook's daughter who became one of Italy's most celebrated singers.

"For heaven's sake, Charlotte. Stop fidgeting," her brother said, not taking his eyes off the page he was reading. "You've never been the nervous type of female."

"I'm not nervous."

He raised his gaze just enough to give her a dubious look.

"Well, I'm not. I'm..." She paused, searching for a word that would adequately sum up the stew of emotions that simmered within her. "...Disgruntled." She waved a hand in a circular motion. "I'm thoroughly disgruntled by this whole scheme, and I regret that I agreed to it."

"Oh, I shouldn't fret over that if I were you." He laid his periodical aside and clasped his hands, resting them against his waistcoat, the pads of his thumbs bouncing against each other. "Have fun while Norwood squires you about town. The man commands entrée to the kind of functions we're rarely invited to, so you might as well enjoy yourself."

She stared at him, amazed that he was missing the point entirely. "You know very well I've no desire to become a social gadfly, and especially not on the arm of some idle aristocrat." Nor did she wish to subject herself to the whispers and conjectures of London society as to just how she'd come to be upon said aristocrat's arm. She remembered what it was like to be the social outsider during her years at finishing school, and it wasn't an ordeal she was eager to repeat. She'd arrived at Portney's School for Young Ladies eager to make friends with girls her own age, since much of her childhood had been spent in the relative isolation of Chartwell, her family's estate in the countryside of Berkshire, with Phillip as her closest companion.

With that background, Portney's had beckoned Charlotte with the prospect of girlish friendship. Instead, it had been a rude awakening to the difficulty of insinuating oneself into social circles that were well established. Particularly when one was quiet and bookish and unprepared for the cruelty that existed in cliques populated by girls who were already connected by family and social ties. She feared this pretend betrothal might resemble those months at finishing school in more ways than she wished.

"He's not some idle aristocrat, whiling away the hours at social functions or gambling hells or"—Phillip stopped abruptly, giving her the distinct impression he'd checked his words—"or wherever else you might imagine him idling away his time."

"You can't deny he's mentioned a great deal in the society papers, so he's clearly indulging in his fair share of London's social whirl."

"I suppose he is," Phillip said. "My point is that's not *all* he does. He takes his parliamentary duties very seriously, and no one's better than Norwood when it comes to working out compromises with those on the opposite side of the political aisle." Her brother's expression turned into one of mild reproach. "You really shouldn't be so hard on the man, Charlotte. I know he put your back up, and I don't entirely blame you for holding on to your initial dislike of him, but give him a chance, and you'll discover he's a decent enough fellow."

"I still think the whole thing is a preposterous plan, and I'm sorry I let myself get talked into it."

He gave her a pointed look. "In the first place, no one talks you into something you're truly opposed to, and in the second, it really is the best solution for the both of you." With that pronouncement, he picked up his periodical, but before he could resume reading, Hopkins appeared in the doorway and announced Lord Norwood's arrival.

Charlotte rose from her seat on the sofa as the earl strode over to her. He bowed and with a flourish, presented her with a bouquet.

"Thank you, but you needn't feel obligated to make such gestures." Despite her words, she was pleased by his thoughtfulness. Taking the ribbon-tied flowers from him—they were quite lovely, pink roses in the first flush of bloom mixed with fragrant, white lilies—she laid them upon a side table before resuming her seat. One of the maids could put them in a vase later.

"Think of it as a peace offering then." He crossed to the mantelpiece and carelessly leaned one shoulder against it.

"In that case, you should have brought an entire hothouse."

One side of his mouth quirked up and his eyes gleamed with humor. "No doubt I should have. Still, I'm letting you drive my curricle. Surely that earns me a bit of your favor."

"*That* earns you my coquettish smiles," she said archly.

"Ah, yes." He turned to Phillip, who was seated in a large armchair. "Your sister drives a hard bargain."

"Don't most females?" Phillip asked, earning him a swift, scathing glance from Charlotte. Her brother tossed his periodical onto a side table. "I've been thinking about that pair of bays you drive. They seem a good deal too spirited for a novice."

"They *are* too spirited for a novice," Lord Norwood agreed. "I brought a dappled gray pair that I used to teach all my sisters to drive. They're familiar with a lady's touch on the ribbons. You needn't worry about your sister's safety."

"Knowing Phillip, he was more worried about the bays," Charlotte said dryly.

"Not true," her brother replied. "I'm concerned for you *and* the horses. But it sounds as if Norwood has things well in hand."

"You mention 'all my sisters' as if you have a great quantity of them," Charlotte said, suddenly struck by the fact she knew nothing about his family. "Just how many sisters do you have?"

"Four. Two older, two younger."

"And brothers?" she asked.

"Didn't bother to read up about me in *Debrett's*, eh, Miss Hurst?" Lord Norwood flashed her a teasing grin.

She gave a guilty-as-charged shrug. It hadn't even occurred to her to consult *Debrett's*, the authority of everything aristocratic, since she didn't pay much heed to the intricacies of the *ton*'s social hierarchy.

"As it happens, I'm the only son. The coveted heir, doted upon by my parents. I might have turned out quite spoiled, but my sisters, particularly the older ones, refused to let that happen. My oldest sister, Elizabeth, still seizes every opportunity to take me down a peg or two, when she thinks it's warranted." His ironic tone implied his sister frequently *did* think it warranted.

Charlotte couldn't help but smile at that. "I hope I get the chance to meet her. I think I like her already."

"No doubt you'll get along famously with each other. Libby would've looked on approvingly had she been witness to that peal you rang over my head this morning." He pushed away from the mantel. "However, we should be going if we want to get in a driving lesson before the paths become clogged with the late-afternoon riders."

"Of course," Charlotte agreed, coming to her feet. "My bonnet and gloves are on the table in the front hall."

Once she was properly accoutered, and he'd donned his hat, Lord Norwood took her arm, and they walked outside to his waiting curricle. It was a very smart vehicle, gleaming black with dark forest-green trim and matching green leather seats. He helped her in, then went around to the other side and climbed in himself. The groom handed him the reins and the carriage lurched forward.

A thrill of excitement shot through her. *She* would have a chance to drive this sporting vehicle. It almost made this crazy alliance with Lord Norwood worth it.

Almost.

She was still terrified of making a fool of herself posing as his fiancée.

No sense worrying about that now, she thought.

Traffic was fairly heavy this afternoon, but the earl expertly maneuvered the curricle through the streets of Mayfair. He made it look so effortless, the way he held the reins in his left hand, making only the slightest adjustments as he directed the horses. It was impressive, and for the first time, she felt a smidgen of doubt in her own ability to master this skill.

Oh, for heaven's sake. That's why he's giving you a lesson. To learn how to do it.

She tried to study his technique, but more often than not, she found herself studying him. He cut a very dashing figure beside her in a navy-blue jacket that set off his broad shoulders to perfection, buff trousers that hugged his thighs, and tall, gleaming black Hessian boots. Perhaps she wouldn't have found all this sartorial splendor so distracting if the man

wearing the clothes weren't so devastatingly handsome. It was
no wonder he was considered such a brilliant catch. Even without a title and fortune, he would draw the ladies' attention.
With them...it became even less believable that she'd been the
one to reel him in.

Chin up, Charlotte. The die is cast.

Appearing with him in public like this meant there was no
going back. A wave of uneasiness washed over her. Would
she come to regret her decision to take part in this charade
and possibly expose herself to the *ton*'s ridicule? Her throat
tightened and her hands felt clammy as her mind considered the
possibility of failure.

Determined not to let her fears get the better of her, she
shoved these thoughts aside and watched the city slide past as
they made their way to the park. They drove along residential
streets filled with rows of stately town houses, and slowly made
their way through commercial districts crowded with vehicles
of every description. Even though she'd been in London for two
months, she still marveled at the sheer variety contained within
the city, whether one considered the people, or architecture,
shops, or entertainments. Even she, who preferred the quieter,
open spaces of England's countryside, had to admit it was an
endlessly fascinating city. A good place to visit, just not one in
which she'd choose to live.

After several minutes, Lord Norwood broke the silence.
"You're very quiet," he said, regarding her with a quizzical look.

"I'm sorry for being a dull companion. The truth is I don't
have much talent for making small talk, so usually I don't."

"I wasn't complaining about the silence. There is only so
much one can say about the weather, and personally I've never
been a fan of society gossip, so let's dispense with the small
talk and speak of more interesting topics."

"Such as?" she asked. Since she didn't know him, it was difficult to gauge what he might consider of interest. Politics, probably, but that seemed a weighty topic for a drive in the park.

"Putting me on the spot, are you?"

"Well...yes," she said. "I thought perhaps you already had something in mind."

His sideways glance was assessing. "Not really, but give me a moment."

"Or we could go back to silence," she suggested. "You did say you didn't mind it."

"That's true, but so far our conversations have proved most...diverting."

"By my reckoning, we've had only two conversations. If you found this morning's conversation diverting, you hid it well behind that angry scowl, and as for this afternoon, it's been a rather ordinary discussion, I would say."

"About this morning...Initially, I *was* angry, but once I discovered my wrath was misdirected, I respected the way you didn't allow me to get away with my unpardonably rude behavior toward you." His mouth twisted into a wry smile. "I assure you, I was raised to behave better than that. And as for whether you have a talent for making idle chitchat, I'd say your ability to deliver a clever riposte is far more entertaining. You're not a predictable female, Miss Hurst, and *that* is quite intriguing."

"Which just goes to show, you don't know me very well, because I doubt anyone who does would characterize me as an intriguing sort of person."

"Ah, but see, you've gone and done it again," he said. "Intrigued me," he added, when she directed a questioning look at him.

"I can't imagine why," she said.

"You have a tendency to downplay yourself, while most ladies of my acquaintance, the unmarried ones, at least, are more likely to try to find ways to catch my attention. That sets you apart, marks you as different, makes you"—he lowered his voice—"intriguing."

She felt her jaw slacken a little at the way he pronounced the last word, imbuing it with a certain seductive quality, but she managed to pull herself together enough to say, "What a faradiddle."

"On the contrary. I'm completely serious."

He did appear serious. She had to give him that. He was smiling at her, but it was friendly, rather than teasing. "In that case, I won't argue the point further, since doing so would probably serve to deepen this misapprehension of yours."

"So true." He threaded the team past a moving dray that had lost part of its load, and then the curricle executed a neat right turn onto Oxford Street and they were nearly to their destination. Hyde Park was just a short way ahead.

"I assume you haven't changed your mind about driving," he said when they turned onto Park Lane a few minutes later.

"At the risk of being predictable, I have not."

"Yes," he murmured. "I rather thought that would be the case."

"You know, I threw out the idea of your letting me drive on a whim. I didn't really expect you to agree."

He gave her a sidelong look that seemed to say *I wish I'd known that earlier.*

"Although, I'm glad you did," she continued. "I've wanted to learn for some time now. It seems quite practical, don't you think? Being able to drive."

"If one doesn't question the practicality of the expense that goes with owning a carriage and a driving team."

"Well, yes, there is that consideration. I was speaking more to the practicality of being able to go where one wished, without having to depend on someone to take you there."

"Ah, yes, the lure of independence," he replied.

She couldn't tell from the tone of his voice whether he thought that was good or bad. If he were like most men, he wouldn't approve of a lady asserting her independence. Not that society gave females very many opportunities to do so. Regrettably.

"I like to be able to do things for myself. Surely that's not an unreasonable desire on my part," she said, suddenly feeling a bit defensive.

They entered the park through the Stanhope Gate and he turned the curricle onto a path that led toward the Serpentine.

"I find it perfectly reasonable," he said equably. "If I didn't, I wouldn't have taught my sisters to drive."

"So you think it's a good thing for a lady to be independent?"

"Is that a trick question?" he asked.

"No. Why would it be?"

"I don't know." He gave her an assessing glance. "It seemed like it might be."

"You still haven't answered it," she prompted.

"I suppose it depends on what you mean by independent. If you mean, able to drive herself around in a carriage, you already know the answer to that. If you mean able to form her own opinions, yes, I agree with that also. I'm not one of those men who wants females to agree with my every utterance, and heaven knows my sisters disagree with me often enough. If you're talking about women being able to retain ownership of property when they marry, I don't oppose that in principle, but I'd hesitate to support a change in the law until society embraces the notion of educating females in a manner similar to males. An uneducated mind can be taken advantage of too easily. For now, I think the answer must be found in drawing up marriage settlements that keep the wife's property separate from the husband's control."

"There exist educated men who foolishly squander their property," she pointed out.

"That's very true, and unfortunate. But not a reason to bolster a married woman's property rights without laying the groundwork first." He turned toward her with a slightly apologetic look. "Rome wasn't built in a day, you know."

He wasn't entirely wrong. But Charlotte had been fortunate enough to receive a thorough education, thanks to her father, who'd been something of a gentleman scholar, and it still chafed that, merely by virtue of her sex, she was prohibited from being granted many of the rights enjoyed by men—even those considered fools.

"Have you ever met Lady Serena Wynter?" he asked.

"No, but if she's part of your social circle, that shouldn't come as a surprise. After all, *we* never met before today."

"I'll introduce the two of you. Serena has very decided opinions about a great many things, and she's very independent-minded. I think you'll like her."

There was a lull in the conversation as they skirted the northern edge of the park. Tall trees edged the path, birds flew and swooped above them, and the last of the golden daffodils swayed gently in the breeze. Charlotte found it difficult to properly pay attention to the loveliness around her though. Her impatience to take the reins began to grow, now that they were in the park. Finally, when they hadn't passed another soul for at least five minutes, she said, "Couldn't we begin the driving lesson soon? Surely this is a good time since there's no one else about."

"I'm coming to the same conclusion." He brought the team

to a halt and turned to her with a grin. "Actually, I came to that conclusion about three minutes ago. I was just waiting to see how long it took you to say something."

She gave him a pointed look. "Your sisters, I presume, thought you a pesky brother."

He blinked at this non sequitur, then chuckled. "I'm sure at times they did." He grinned cheekily. "And you know what they say?"

She shook her head.

"Old habits die hard."

"While that's undoubtedly true," she said primly, "perhaps you could squelch your annoying habits for the duration of the lesson."

He laughed at that. "Most ladies would hasten to assure me I have no annoying habits, while you're more likely to start enumerating them."

"Would you like me to?"

He shook his head. "No, your earlier tongue-lashing was sufficient."

"Another day then," she said, folding her hands in her lap.

"Talk like that, and I may change my mind about our lesson."

"You wouldn't!" she gasped.

He smirked. "I wouldn't. I'm only teasing. Old habits, you know."

"Don't you have enough sisters to tease that you needn't torment me as well? I have a brother of my own, thank you very much." Not that she found Lord Norwood at all brotherlike. It might be better if she did.

He grinned. "It's true I have plenty of sisters, but it's also true your eyes sparkle most becomingly when you're provoked."

"A poor excuse," she said. Still, she couldn't help being pleased by the compliment.

"I suppose it is," he agreed. "Let's begin then. Here's how we'll proceed. As I'm sure you noticed, I drove with the reins only in my left hand. That's the correct way to drive so that the right hand is free to employ the whip."

"Hence, its name, the whip hand," Charlotte said, trying to contain her impatience. "I do know a little bit about driving, even though I've never had the opportunity to do so myself."

"Yes, well, it's good you're not entirely ignorant of the process. However, for our purposes today, I'm going to have you take the reins, one in each hand, while I retain hold of them just behind your hands. Then we'll start the horses in a walk, and when you feel comfortable, say so, and I'll let go. The horses know what to do, and will remain in a walk as long as you hold the reins steady. Any questions?"

"It sounds simple enough," she said. "But shouldn't we trade places first so that I'm on the right?"

"Not this first time. Once we're both confident in your abilities to handle them, we'll move you to the driver's seat. For now, I want you to get a feel for how to hold the reins. We've got a long straight stretch of path here. All you need to do is hold them steady while the horses walk. This exercise is less about driving and more about you and Zeus and Apollo getting acquainted."

"All right." She held out her hands. "Show me how to hold the reins."

He studied her gloved hands a moment, a small crease between his brows. She was just about to ask him if there was a problem when he said, "Pray don't misconstrue this, Miss Hurst."

Before she could question what he meant, he slid across the seat until they sat pressed against each other. While she sat frozen, too shocked to protest the way his body fitted flush against her side, he transferred the reins to his right hand, slipped his left arm around her, then repositioned the reins, so that he now held one in each hand.

She gasped. No man had ever held her like Lord Norwood was holding her now. His arms wrapped around her in something very like an embrace, and she could feel the heat from his body where the solid wall of his chest met her shoulder and the firm length of his thigh rested against hers. The closeness was such that the layers of their clothing seemed woefully inadequate for maintaining any semblance of propriety between them.

The contact was shockingly improper, and if she were being truthful, shockingly pleasant.

"Couldn't you have warned me?" she managed at last, annoyed at the breathless quality in her voice that betrayed her ruffled emotions.

"No, as I was fairly certain you'd object, and I didn't want to waste time debating my methods."

His warm breath disturbed the loose tendrils of hair lying against the back of her neck. A shiver chased along her skin, and she struggled to focus on something—anything—besides his unsettling masculine presence.

She stared hard at the horses' swishing tails for a moment. "Is it absolutely necessary that we sit this way?"

"As a matter of fact, it is." They were so close she could feel the words rumble in his chest. "Now reach up and grip the reins just behind my hands. Hold them exactly as I am."

She did as he instructed.

"Perfect." His voice came warm and deep right next to her ear, and she swallowed hard as a swarm of butterflies began tickling her insides. "Now hold them firmly while I move my hands just behind yours. Ready?"

She managed a nod.

"Here we go."

She felt the horses pull slightly, before they obediently began a sedate walk along the path. Charlotte kept a light grip on the reins, aware of the earl's hands right behind hers. On this straight stretch, it took almost no effort to guide them. A good thing, since the distracting nearness of Lord Norwood continued to wreak havoc on her equilibrium.

"Ready to try solo?" he asked, his lips still disturbingly close to her ear.

She nodded again, not trusting that her voice wouldn't betray her. He'd rattled her, but once he removed himself to his side of the seat she'd be fine. More than fine because she'd be in control of his magnificent carriage.

His arms dropped away from her as he leaned back, but he still sat much too close for her comfort. One arm rested on the top of the seat, mere inches from her back, impossible to ignore. She worked to hold the reins steady, feeling the horses pull at the bits, ready to set a faster pace at a sign from her.

"You're doing very well," Lord Norwood said after a few moments. "But then you do have an excellent tutor, though I say it myself."

She didn't dare take her eyes off the empty driving path, afraid that a lapse in her attention would somehow lead to a mistake. But though she couldn't see him, she felt his amusement, and she couldn't let his self-congratulatory statement go by unanswered.

"Or I'm an exceptionally talented student," she suggested.

He laughed. "Let's agree it's a bit of both. Shall we?"

She pursed her lips and cocked her head as if considering this. "All right. I can agree with that, and since you just admitted I'm a good student, perhaps you could move over and stop crowding me."

"No, I prefer to sit close enough so I can easily take back the reins if necessary." He leaned forward and placed his lips near her ear again. "Besides," he said in a low, silky voice. "We present such a cozy image this way. Anyone seeing us would certainly believe we are eager to wed."

"Too bad there are so few around to see us."

"We'll get to a more populated section of the park eventually. And anyway, sometimes it's enough if the right people see us."

"The right people?" Since the horses continued to plod on placidly, she chanced a look at Lord Norwood.

He moved back, but they were still only inches apart. A lazy smile played around his mouth. "The right people. Gossipy people, who will spread the word about seeing you and me looking besotted with each other." His blue-gray eyes glowed warmly as he studied her, his gaze so intent and focused it was as if there was nowhere he'd rather be than here by her side. "Infatuated. Completely captivated with each other," he whispered.

Her mouth fell open slightly as she tried to regain her breath and overcome the strange dizziness that scrambled her thoughts. That jumbled her emotions.

He moved in closer still as his gaze traveled down to her mouth.

Charlotte's breath now came in little huffs, and she wasn't sure which scared her more: that he was going to kiss her, or that she wanted him to.

Chapter Three

$\mathcal{H}$e shouldn't do it.

He shouldn't kiss her.

But devil take it, he wanted to.

For the second time that day, William struggled to regain his self-control. He slid along the seat to place a more respectable distance between them.

"You were going to kiss me," she accused, her eyes now filling with indignation.

"Now, Miss Hurst, if I'd kissed you, this would no longer be a temporary betrothal, and I don't think either of us is ready for that."

Her eyes narrowed. "Then what were you doing, leaning in, looking like you were intent on seduction?" She glanced at the horses, who were walking along the bridle path as if nothing untoward had happened. "What could you possibly have been thinking?"

That was just it. He hadn't been thinking. Bewitched. Beguiled. Mesmerized by a pair of lovely eyes. He'd been responding, not thinking. Caught up in her gaze, which had turned soft and dreamy and filled with hesitant yearning, drawn in by her rosy lips, so beckoning, tempting, inviting, that he'd nearly thrown caution to the wind and given in to yearnings of his own.

None of which excused his behavior, even though it did, to a degree, account for it.

He'd never lost his head over a lady before. Never even come close. Why had he done so now? He couldn't explain it to himself, much less provide a reasonable answer to Miss Hurst, though it was clear she expected one.

"In the first place, I would hardly seduce you in a public park, particularly when you were in control of my cattle. In the second place, I was just illustrating how convincingly I can play the besotted suitor." True enough, but it still didn't explain why he'd gotten carried away. To his chagrin, he'd momentarily forgotten one of the most basic tenets of gentlemanly behavior drummed into him by his father, and nearly turned what had begun as a bit of stupid teasing into something that had almost ended in... disaster.

Her mouth turned down at the corners. "You're not auditioning for a part on Drury Lane," she said in a cool, reproachful voice. "There's no need to inhabit your role so completely, and I'll thank you to remember that in the future. What if the horses had taken off while I was distracted by your playacting?"

"They're too well trained to do that unless you direct them to." Though she was in profile, he saw her eyes widen. Just a bit and just briefly, but enough that a tiny seed of suspicion took root in his mind. "You *were* going to set the horses off," he accused.

This surprised him. He'd barely managed to pull himself back from the brink of making an irretrievable mistake, and he'd assumed she'd been equally focused on that almost-kiss. Evidently, she hadn't been as caught up in the moment as he.

"No, I wasn't," she said, not sounding entirely convincing.

"You were."

She shook her head. "I really wasn't. But when you looked like you were about to kiss me, the thought entered my mind to give the reins a brisk slap." She glanced at him. "It seemed easier, you see, with both my hands occupied with driving. There didn't seem to be a good way to slap *you*."

He stared at her profile with a mixture of vexation and grudging respect. "You might have caused an accident," he muttered.

"Do you think so?" she asked, a little frown wrinkling her brow. "You said yourself this pair is well trained and used to novices. I just intended to create a distraction."

He sighed. "You probably wouldn't have caused an accident, but for the duration of our lessons, I want you to promise you won't do anything to risk your safety or that of my cattle."

"If we're making rules, then I want you to promise you won't try to kiss me."

"Very well," he agreed. "Though as I explained, that was an exercise in looking besotted." It might have started as that, but for a moment, the temptation to kiss her had been all too real. In the future, he wouldn't underestimate the power of her captivating blue eyes.

"Ummhmm," she said skeptically. "Then you should know your version of appearing besotted looks very much like *I'm-going-to-kiss-you*."

"Duly noted," he said. "Now let's mix up the lesson a bit. This stretch is perfect to practice starting and stopping." He explained to her that stopping the horses required only the slightest pull on the reins as one said "halt." And to restart the pair, she need only say "go" while easing up on the reins until they took the bit in their mouths.

As he expected, she mastered these quickly. Fortunately, they'd reached a meandering section of the driving path. The horses didn't really need instruction to go around the curves, but William taught her to bear right by tipping her right hand forward and drawing it slightly toward her until she felt the bit engage, and a similar maneuver to turn left.

"I'm impressed you taught all four of your sisters to drive. Not many men would take the time to do so," she remarked.

"That sounds dangerously close to a compliment, Miss Hurst."

She dipped her chin slightly, her lips pursed into a reluctant smile. "I suppose it does."

"Don't worry." He lowered his voice conspiratorially. "I won't let it go to my head."

"Phillip says he isn't brave enough to teach me, but it's a moot point, since we don't have a proper carriage for me to learn on. My brother owns a town coach, but our coachman holds sway over it."

"I'm surprised Hurst doesn't have a curricle or phaeton. Those are the vehicles of choice for squiring ladies around town."

"If that surprises you, then you don't know him very well. Phillip doesn't squire ladies around. For one thing, he's taciturn by nature, and wooing a lady generally requires a certain amount of talking. And for another, and this is really the clincher, he gets hopelessly tongue-tied around females." She tilted her head to the side. "At least, the ones he's not related to," she amended.

"So he's a determined bachelor then."

"Not so much a determined bachelor as a tentative suitor. If he's ever to get married, I'll probably have to manage it for him."

He laughed. "Spoken like a sister."

She smiled at that. "I suppose you'd know. Though speaking of sisters, I'm curious what yours had to say about our predicament."

"I'll tell you when I find out. I've been too busy with other matters today to have a chance to speak with them. However, I can safely predict they were surprised."

"That hardly qualifies as a prediction. Who *wasn't* surprised? Do you think they were outraged? Or delighted? Or somewhere in between?"

"That will depend upon the sister. Lydia will be delighted for me no matter what. Elizabeth will demand to know why she wasn't apprised of this ahead of time. As for my other sisters, I doubt they've even heard about it yet. Cecily is currently rusticating as she awaits the birth of her second child. Amelia is sixteen, and too caught up in her own concerns to pay much attention to mine."

Ahead of them, a carriage turned onto the path. Miss Hurst glanced uncertainly at him. "Do you wish to take the reins now?"

"No. Steady on, Miss Hurst. I'm confident you can handle this, but I'll be right here, should you require assistance."

The carriage contained a group of young ladies and one harried-looking chaperone. As the two carriages drew closer to each other, William raised his hat in greeting. An eruption of giggling came from the occupants of the other vehicle, followed by a few audible sighs as they passed.

Miss Hurst shook her head and muttered something under her breath.

"What was that you said?" he asked. "I didn't quite catch it." He knew good and well it hadn't been meant for his ears, but that only made him all the more curious.

"Just expressing my amazement at their reaction to you. Do you often encounter similar expressions of... I don't know what to call it. Silly admiration, I suppose."

"Only occasionally, but it does happen," he admitted. "Usually it's confined to the girls just making their come-outs. The ones I find too young to catch my interest no matter how much sighing they do."

"If it's any consolation, I promise never to sigh over you."

"Yes, I rather assumed you wouldn't," he said dryly.

Although a sigh from her would be sincere, at least. Her judgment of him was based solely on himself as a man. Not his title, not his possessions, not what she could gain through acquaintance with him, none of the measures by which society usually judged him.

Her words this morning had pricked him, but they'd also made him aware of a complacent arrogance he hadn't real- ized he'd acquired. But years of being fawned over, deferred to, flattered, praised whether he deserved it or not... all had added up to instill a certain expectation within him of his own worth.

He was glad she'd made him aware of this defect in himself, even if he hadn't particularly enjoyed her blunt assessment of his character.

"Lord Norwood?"

Her question brought his attention back to the moment. "Sorry. I was woolgathering. Did you say something to me?"

"It wasn't important."

"No, no," he said. "We've already established you don't indulge in idle chitchat. If you said something, it's bound to be worth hearing. So pardon my inattention and tell me again, please."

"If you insist. I merely suggested that you *not* smile so flirtatiously at the young ladies if you don't want them making spectacles of themselves over you."

"That wasn't a flirtatious smile on my part," he objected. "Merely a polite one. Definitely not one intended to draw *that* sort of reaction."

"If that's the case, perhaps you should be a tad less polite. And it wouldn't hurt to tone down the charm when you smile."

He really couldn't resist. "So you think I have a charming smile, do you?"

"That's *not* what I said."

"Oh, but I think it was. I definitely heard the word *charm* and a reference to my smile paired up in your sentence. You can't deny it."

"I certainly can when you're twisting around the meaning of my words."

"Zeus and Apollo heard you. I'd bet they'd agree with me."

"Well then, it's too bad for you that horses can't speak, isn't it?" Her glance was smug.

"It is rather, since you're being so stubborn. Can't you throw me a bone, Miss Hurst? A sop for my pride which you so thoroughly demolished just a few hours ago."

"I doubt your pride was so easily trampled," she said. "But if it was, I expect a few more instances of young ladies giggling and sighing over you will restore it. No need for me to feed it. Surely you receive so much feminine approval wherever you appear that my good opinion is of negligible importance."

"You might be surprised," he said dryly. "As for all that 'feminine approval,' dare I risk being called conceited for saying I could behave as a complete curmudgeon, and they'd still react that way. They respond as they do because I'm an unmarried earl. That I have all my teeth and I'm under the age of thirty is of small significance. They'd smile and flutter their eyelashes at me regardless."

⌒

Charlotte knew what he meant, though she thought him mistaken to believe his looks were of no significance to those sighing girls. She was struck by his tone of weary resignation though, and a pang of empathy tugged at her. It wasn't an enviable position to be in—always questioning the sincerity of those around him.

She wasn't sure how she felt about this glimpse of a vulnerable Lord Norwood. There'd been no danger of falling for the rude, overbearing man she'd initially thought him, whereas the more likable version of him...that would require her to keep her guard up.

Forewarned is forearmed, she told herself.

Because while a likable Lord Norwood would help make this whole betrothal scheme more bearable, it didn't change the fact that they led very dissimilar lives, inhabited very different social circles, and held vastly disparate aims in life, he obviously wanting to live his life in a more public sphere than she could ever be comfortable with. Charlotte wasn't fool enough to think those differences would magically disappear in the unlikely event an attraction sprang up between them. And no matter how pleasant his company might prove to be, she was still wary of becoming the target of the *ton*'s vicious-tongued gossips.

"What? No argument, Miss Hurst? No admonishment for possessing an overweening vanity?"

To her relief, his voice held a wry, teasing quality once

again. Best to keep things light between them. She could feel his gaze upon her, waiting for an answer, but she didn't dare take her eyes off the road. They were nearing the Serpentine and traffic had picked up a bit.

"If you already recognize your overweening vanity, then how effective would a reproof from me be?" she asked.

"And who's twisting words now?" he said. She imagined him raising one dark aristocratic brow while making this remark. He often did when he was being ironic. "I wasn't admitting I have an overweening vanity, merely acknowledging *you* think I do. So I was surprised you passed up an opportunity to take me to task."

"I did so with great reluctance because it's always tempting to prick that conceit of yours," she said, indulging in a little teasing of her own. "But I'm concentrating on my driving."

"Ah, Miss Hurst, what will I do without you to keep me in check when this betrothal ends?" He sounded amused, and she pictured him with one side of his mouth quirked up in a careless smile, a glint of lazy good humor in his eyes.

"Become even more insufferable?" she suggested, softening the words with a smile.

He chuckled and gave a rueful shake of his head. She could see the gesture from the corner of her eye. She liked that he didn't take himself too seriously.

"More likely I'll hear that tart tongue of yours chiding me in my mind, and keeping me in line, even from afar."

"I doubt you'll even think of me once we've parted ways," she said. "What with all the eager hopefuls rushing to fill my vacated spot as your fiancée."

"I don't think I'll find you so forgettable." There was no bantering tone in his voice now, and she wished she could see his face to gauge his mood. Did he mean he wished he could forget her, but couldn't? Or that he didn't want to forget her?

A small tingle flared in the pit of her stomach, but she ruthlessly squelched it.

It doesn't matter, Charlotte.

"We're getting close enough to Rotten Row that traffic will be picking up. I can take over now if you'd like."

"That's fine with me," she replied. "My arms are getting tired anyway."

He placed his hands in front of hers on the reins. "You can let go now." She did, and he transferred both lines to his left hand. "And lest you've forgotten, you promised to look properly infatuated in exchange for a driving lesson. I've kept up my end of the bargain."

The path was indeed becoming more crowded with riders and carriages. They were nearly to Rotten Row, the wide, graveled path that traversed the southern section of Hyde Park where much of London's upper crust congregated on fine afternoons. The part of the drive she'd been dreading was upon them, but she'd given her word, and she wouldn't go back on it.

"And I'll keep up mine. I'll flutter my eyelashes and look like a smitten idiot," she said, though admittedly she didn't sound very enthusiastic about it.

He glanced at her. "If it makes you feel any better, you won't be the only one in this carriage looking like a lovesick nitwit." He guided the horses toward a gap in the line of vehicles and riders already promenading along the Row, placing the curricle between a pair of bucks on horseback ahead of them, and a stately barouche behind.

Ironically, his attempt at being reassuring fell short of the mark. Because while no one would question her desire to marry him—He's wealthy, titled, handsome! What more could a girl want?—everyone would be questioning his interest in her. So, of course, he must look like a man in the throes of infatuation. Otherwise, they had little hope of convincing people they were happily engaged.

But she was suddenly having second thoughts about her ability to remain unmoved by his warm, speaking glances, his secret smiles just for her, his appearance of being captivated with her. Heaven help her, if she'd learned anything on this drive it was that he was too appealing by half.

You're a sensible girl, Charlotte. You know this is only playacting.

"Smile," he murmured as he tipped his hat to the occupants of a carriage passing them from the opposite direction. "Cue the smitten idiots."

Charlotte forced her lips into a stiff smile, hoping it appeared genuine to the trio of ladies parading past. Thankfully, their attention seemed to be mostly on Lord Norwood. "By all means. Let the performance begin."

Chapter Four

~

William pulled up to the front of his London town house after seeing Miss Hurst to her home. They'd spent an hour driving along the Row pretending to be enamored with each other, a performance that hadn't required much effort on his part. Miss Hurst had turned out to be a diverting companion, who, true to her word, played her part to perfection.

There'd been an awkward moment when they passed a carriage containing the Duchess of Maitland and her daughter, Lady Jane. They'd returned his and Miss Hurst's polite nods of greeting with frosty stares of acknowledgment. He could tell Miss Hurst had been taken aback by their response, though she didn't say anything, and thankfully no one else had displayed such obvious hostility.

Climbing down from his curricle, he handed the reins to a waiting groom and made his way up the front steps, taking them two at a time. Once inside, he deposited his hat and gloves on the hall table and turned to his butler, who stood in the entryway.

"Lady Peyton called on you, my lord. She left ten minutes ago."

"Should I be glad I missed her?" William asked. His sister must have been in high dudgeon over his lack of communication today.

"I really couldn't say, sir. But she instructed me to give you these." He handed William several notes. A quick glance revealed all but one were addressed to him in Elizabeth's handwriting. The lone exception bore his sister Lydia's girlish script.

"Did she write all these while she waited for me?" William asked in amazement. There were at least seven missives from Libby.

"No, those arrived earlier. She came herself when she didn't receive any response from you. I explained you'd been out all day and hadn't seen them. She said to tell you she wanted a reply immediately upon your arrival home." Coates paused before adding, "Her ladyship placed special emphasis on the word *immediately*."

"Very well, Coates. Please have a light dinner sent to my office. I will see to this *immediately*." William headed for his study. He settled himself at his desk and scanned the notes from his sisters. Lydia's was full of congratulations and good wishes, while Libby's progressed from annoyed, but congratulatory, to just highly exasperated with him in the final note, which according to the opening lines had been written at half-past four this afternoon. It was a short note, the gist of it contained in the next-to-last paragraph...

Honestly, William, you might have seen fit to make us acquainted with her before news of your betrothal got splashed across the pages of the newspaper. I had so many callers today, bombarding me with questions, and what could I tell them? That you'd gotten yourself engaged to a girl whose existence I knew nothing about before today? Hardly! I hope you plan to introduce her to us as soon as possible. I can't rely on fobbing off people's inquiries with vague generalities forever! I must say, William, you've managed this badly so far. I can't imagine what got into you to bungle things this way. Did you not realize the amount of gossip you would stir up by going about it like this?

He folded the note and laid it on top of the others. He couldn't blame Libby, really. He'd send her a reply, explaining what he could, which presently wasn't much more than his conjecture that a political rival was behind it. He glanced through the stack of correspondence that Stevens, his secretary, had placed on his desk, looking for a reply to an inquiry he'd sent out earlier in the day. Finding it, he broke the seal and read.

The message from the *Morning Post* stated they could offer no information about the identity of whoever had inserted the fake betrothal notice in that morning's paper. After questioning their staff, they'd ascertained it had been delivered by a man attired in neat, but nondescript, clothing and who'd given the impression he was his lordship's secretary. Naturally, the description they'd supplied of a short, stocky man did not match the build of William's actual secretary, Mr. Stevens.

So, nothing truly helpful like a messenger wearing an identifiable servant's livery. William wasn't surprised by this. It was precisely the method someone wishing to cover his tracks would use. Still, the inquiry had been worth raising, even if the answer was what he'd expected. He doubted further investigation would turn up much, but he'd put out some more feelers, and keep his ears open for any gossip that might provide clues to the culprit's identity. Not that identifying him would necessarily help at this point. The mischief had been unleashed. Now it was a matter of trying to contain the damage.

Which meant planning another outing with Miss Hurst. He leaned back in his chair, contemplating the possibilities. He imagined she'd jump at another chance to drive his curricle, and while he wasn't opposed to letting her drive again, he thought they ought to vary up a bit. What else would allow them to be seen by a lot of people, and yet was an activity to which she'd readily agree? His fingers drummed on the arm of his chair as he considered various ideas.

A dinner party was too limited in scope. He received invitations to any number of routs and soirées, but he suspected she'd object to attending any of those unless she'd also gotten an invitation, and given how their paths had never crossed before now, he thought it unlikely there'd be much overlap.

The theater. *Perfect.*

A night at the theater would offer an excellent opportunity for them to be seen by a large number of people, and his sisters could easily join them. A show of family solidarity could help erase any lingering questions in peoples' minds.

But first, he needed to write to Libby and explain the nature of his engagement. Persuading her to attend a performance at Covent Garden would be easy. All his sisters adored the theater. He reached for a pen and some stationery. Forty minutes later, the note to his oldest sister was sanded, sealed, and entrusted to a footman for delivery. He dashed off a shorter note to Lydia, before turning to the plate of food, which had been brought in nearly thirty minutes ago. He lifted the silver cover and began to eat the roasted chicken and potatoes.

As he ate, his thoughts turned to Miss Hurst. Charlotte. It was a pretty name, but not fanciful. It suited her. And although he suspected whoever had paired them in that fake betrothal announcement had chosen her because she was such an unlikely candidate for his fiancée, he was unexpectedly pleased with the selection of Miss Hurst. She had a sharp wit and a sense of humor not unlike his own.

That he found her attractive was without question, since he'd nearly acted upon that ill-advised impulse to kiss her earlier, an action so out of character he was still taken aback by it. What was it about her that provoked such a strong response in him? Maybe nothing more than that he still hadn't recovered from the shock of seeing that announcement in the morning paper, since angrily storming over to the Hurst residence had been an equally uncharacteristic response for him.

It was nearly eight o'clock before he went upstairs to dress for the evening. He planned to stop at his club before heading to a standing engagement at the residence of Lord and Lady Millhouse. They hosted a weekly political salon, which William was in the habit of attending when he didn't have other plans. He was particularly keen to go tonight. These gatherings were a good place to pick up gossip. Maybe he could glean some clue as to who had placed that betrothal announcement.

It was the wee hours of the morning when he returned home. He'd gained no further information as to the origin of that false report of his betrothal. Disappointing, but like the dead end he'd encountered with his inquiry to the *Morning Post*, not particularly surprising.

A sleepy-eyed Coates was waiting to give him another note from Libby. William sent the butler off to bed, then read Libby's note as he climbed the stairs. He was forgiven (mostly), although Libby strongly felt she should have been consulted straightaway. But she agreed showing Miss Hurst as a member of the family circle at the theater would help calm the gossip mill.

It wasn't until after his valet, Thompson, had finished helping him out of his evening clothes that he realized a glaring oversight on his part. He hadn't yet invited Miss Hurst to accompany him to the theater. He cast a longing glance at his turned-down bed. He was exhausted, but he shouldn't leave this task until the next day. He had an early meeting with his solicitor, which he suspected would last most of the morning, after which he must head to the Palace of Westminster for an afternoon meeting with some members of the House of Commons. He crossed over to the small writing desk in the corner and, once seated, drew out a sheet of stationery from the drawer. After a moment's thought, he dipped his pen in ink and began writing.

My dear Miss Hurst…

By half-past seven the next morning Charlotte was at her desk in the sitting room attending to household matters when Hopkins brought in a note for her.

"This just arrived for you," the butler informed her. "I was instructed to see you received it straight away."

A strange foreboding gripped her as her mind immediately leaped to the idea that some sort of disaster concerning her betrothal had occurred. Had their deception come to light?

"Not bad news, I hope." She took the missive from the servant.

"I can't really speculate as to that, miss," Hopkins responded.

"I'm sure I'm being silly and overreacting," she assured Hopkins. "Just because this came so early, doesn't automatically mean it spells doom."

Brilliant, Charlotte. Bad news and doom. Why don't you mention a catastrophe, too, and really give the servants something to chew over belowstairs?

Though she trusted the discretion of their servants, the suddenness of her betrothal had to have raised a few eyebrows. No need to raise their curiosity even more.

"Thank you, Hopkins. That will be all." Charlotte nodded a dismissal.

She stared at the note a moment. The handwriting on the outside of the folded sheet was unfamiliar, but her name was written across it in a bold scrawl that was unmistakably masculine. Since she had no beaus who might be penning her billets-doux, it wasn't hard to guess who had sent it.

She broke the wax seal and unfolded the single sheet of expensive paper, the weight and feel of it indicating it had come from one of the more exclusive stationers. A glance at the signature proved her suspicion correct—it was from Lord Norwood.

My dear Miss Hurst,

She frowned. My dear? *My* dear? That seemed unnecessarily familiar to her. She gave a little shake of her head and resumed reading.

My dear Miss Hurst,

I'm writing to request your company at Covent Garden Theatre tonight. It should be a packed house as Mrs. Siddons has been persuaded to come out of retirement and reprise her role of Lady Macbeth. If you've never seen her perform, you're in for a treat. I'll call upon you at seven o'clock sharp. It goes without saying your brother is welcome to come along as well. I don't know if he routinely acts as your chaperone, or whether you employ someone else in that capacity, but either way, my town coach can accommodate us.

It will be an excellent time for you to meet some of my family, as two of my sisters will also be attending tonight's performance, and they are, understandably, eager to make your acquaintance. My eldest sister, Elizabeth, will be there and I expect she will coerce her husband, Robert, Lord Peyton, into attending. My younger sister Lydia will also be present (she's fourth in the birth order of the five of us, in case you wish to keep track of such things), as will Lydia's husband, Lord Chatworth. They've been married only a few months, and are still in that honeymoon phase of inseparability.

Since you've never met them, let me give you some idea of what to expect. Both of my sisters are fair-haired and similarly featured. In terms of personality, though, they are quite dissimilar; Elizabeth is prone to managing those around her, the bossy one you might say (and I do), while Lydia has a sweet, gentle nature. You will adore

Lydia. Everyone does, and don't be surprised if she considers you one of her bosom bows right away because I know my sister, and this is simply how she would treat my fiancée, even one who only intends to occupy the position temporarily.

As for the men, Libby's husband is dark-haired, while Chatworth has chestnut hair. Both are pleasant fellows. I hope this helps you sort them out, as it would be best for our charade if you act as if you're already acquainted with them.

Until we meet again, I remain
Your most humble and devoted servant,
Norwood

So, not news of a disaster, but rather an invitation.

A flutter of nervousness ran through her at the thought of meeting his family. She supposed it was inevitable she do so, but she hadn't expected it would happen at Covent Garden in front of a multitude of theatergoers.

"Let's hope all eyes are on Mrs. Siddons," she muttered to herself.

She set the note on her desk. His plan to call upon her so they could ride to the theater together wouldn't work. A maid was sufficient to accompany her on errands, but not for an excursion to Covent Garden Theatre.

Phillip had other plans for the evening, and even if he didn't, her brother was no fan of theater, be it plays or opera. However, since there was no one besides her brother to act as her chaperone, she'd arrange to have Lord Norwood meet the Hurst carriage at the entrance.

While engaged couples might have a bit more latitude in

these matters, since they intended to call their betrothal off at some point, it was especially important to adhere to the strictest propriety so there would be no reason for anyone to question her virtue when she did cry off. However, meeting him in the presence of their fellow theatergoers was akin to having dozens of chaperones.

She drew out a sheet of her stationery and began to write.

Lord Norwood, she penned. Would he notice the lack of *dear* in the salutation, and understand her reproof of his earlier familiarity? Or was she being too subtle?

> *I am anticipating with pleasure the performance of Macbeth tonight. However, I must decline your offer of transportation. I haven't hired a chaperone for my sojourn in London this Season. Phillip, who could normally function in that capacity, is otherwise engaged for the evening. If you could apprise me of the time I should arrive, I'll simply meet you at the theater.*
>
> *I look forward to making the acquaintance of your sisters, and never fear, I will be sure to pretend I've a prior familiarity with them. All this subterfuge, however, brings to mind the following quote:*
>
> *"Oh, what a tangled web we weave, when first we practice to deceive." Are you familiar with Scott's poem? Don't you think this line is apropos of our charade? Until this evening, I remain*
>
> *Your humble servant,*
> *C. Hurst*

Charlotte rang for Hopkins, who promised to have her note delivered with all haste. One hour later, while she was still laboring over the household accounts, Hopkins brought in a reply.

My dear, dear Miss Hurst,

No chaperone? How shocking. While I admit, I find their presence is often more annoying than not, I'm surprised you're willing to let your brother fill that role. Or rather, that he is the only option you have for someone to fulfill the role. Then again, perhaps he enjoys the ever necessary trips to the modiste or the milliners or the myriad of other shops that provide all the sundries you ladies seem to need while in Town. (And yes, I speak from personal knowledge with those four sisters of mine, which is why I've always employed the necessary chaperones for them.)

This leads me to the crux of this note. My great-aunt is willing to function as your chaperone tonight. We will call for you, as originally planned, at seven o'clock.

Ever your most devoted servant,
Norwood

P.S. Naturally I am familiar with Sir Walter Scott's work. Have you read Waverley yet? A rousing good story. I highly recommend it.

P.P.S. I hope you don't object to the presence of a cat during the carriage ride. Aunt Florence is quite devoted to her pet and takes him everywhere.

Charlotte reached for a sheet of stationery.

Lord Norwood,

There is no reason to disturb your aunt's (and her cat's) evening. I am perfectly capable of getting myself to Covent Garden Theatre by my own means. However, I sense that you will insist I arrive there via your carriage, so I will offer no further objections on the matter. I will be ready at seven o'clock as requested.

As for my lack of chaperone (beyond having Phillip or my maid act in that capacity), there is nothing shocking about it. I originally arranged for my former governess to act as such during my time in London. However, just prior to our coming, she met with an unfortunate accident while trying to rescue a kitten from a tree. Miss Holmes is currently recovering from a broken leg.

I decided to forgo trying to find someone else to come in her stead. It seemed possible to spend these months in London sans chaperone since neither Phillip nor I are social gadflies, and besides, I'm practically on the shelf. I didn't think a lack of formal chaperonage would prove injurious to my reputation. Although, I confess I find attitudes in London toward unaccompanied females to be much stricter than in the country. Which is funny considering one might expect Londoners to be more permissive about it, since things, in general, seem to be looser here, and vices are more readily tolerated. Not that I'm suggesting being an unaccompanied female is a vice of any sort. Still, it does seem unfair, given all that men can get away with, and no one blinks an eye. But I am rambling…

Your humble servant,
C. Hurst

P.S. The feline in question is friendly, I hope.

P.P.S. I haven't read Waverley, but I shall see about obtaining a copy.

A bit later, while Charlotte was having a light repast, a footman delivered a reply from the earl. Charlotte easily recognized the bold strokes of his handwriting by now. She couldn't help smiling in anticipation.

My dear, dear, dear Miss Hurst,

She rolled her eyes. Clearly, he was funning her with his ridiculously effusive salutations.

Practically on the shelf? There's no reason to make yourself sound like a dried-up spinster. I'd never characterize you thus, and as a man, my opinion should carry some weight when it comes to a lady's looks.
In answer to your inquiry, the feline in question

is most friendly. Perhaps too much so, but if he is overly enthusiastic in his attention toward you, I will (manfully) deal with him, risking an injury from tooth or claw to protect you from the rascal. He has (or so my aunt claims) a weakness for pretty ladies. You are forewarned.

And at the risk of also rambling, I agree that society unfairly places more strictures on the female than the male. I sympathize with you at the rules that frown upon an unmarried female being able to run simple errands without someone accompanying her. Social mores are slow to change, but take heart, at least chastity belts are no longer in fashion.

I remain your most devoted servant,
Norwood

P.S. No need for you to buy a copy of Waverley. I'll lend you mine.
You are forewarned.

So his aunt's cat supposedly gravitated toward pretty ladies, and he felt the need to warn her? Did he think her pretty? His statement seemed to imply as much. It was silly, but she couldn't help feeling a flush of pleasure at the thought. Especially since Lord Norwood was capable of choosing from the loveliest of society's unmarried females, those diamonds of the first water in whose company Charlotte most definitely did not rank.

Apparently, she had her own streak of vanity.
You are forewarned.

The man wasn't without charm, that much was certain. She hurriedly finished her meal, then hastened to her writing desk, and once again pulled out a sheet of stationery.

Lord Norwood,

Your sympathy is appreciated. However, I can no longer remain silent. (I mean this figuratively, of course, since I'm writing these words rather than speaking them.) I must object to the overly familiar tone of the salutations and closings of your notes. Were we to correspond often enough, you would eventually need to cover an entire page with "dears," requiring a second sheet for the body of your message. Ridiculous, but I wouldn't put it past you! And my "most devoted" servant? Really? Need I remind you this is only a pretend betrothal? I know we must put on a show in public, but surely there is no need for a display of such excess of feeling in our private notes.

Your humble servant,
C. Hurst

My dear Miss Hurst,

First, let me say your notes have been an unexpected bright spot in what has proved to be an otherwise tedious day. Therefore, I'll acquiesce to your wishes and confine myself to one "dear" in the future. (I presume you would also object if I switched to my darling Miss Hurst.) Perhaps you can find it in your heart to address me with at least one "dear" in our correspondence. Even though I am only a temporary fiancé, it wounds my vanity that I don't rate even one "dear" from you. As for the closing, I'm afraid I do consider myself...

Your most devoted servant,
Norwood

P.S. I wouldn't object if you changed your closing to "your obedient servant" in lieu of being a humble one, since I imagine obedient fiancées are the most manageable type to have.

Dear Lord Norwood,

Are you happy now? (Although I have grave reservations about feeding your vanity! I fear it is much too big already.)

As for the suggestion in your postscript...ha!
Your humble servant,
C. Hurst

She sent off the note and went back to her work, but every time Hopkins or a footman was in her vicinity, she looked up expectantly, and every time felt a small stab of disappointment when she realized they weren't delivering a reply from Lord Norwood. Well, she reasoned, he had work to do, just as she did. Her brother's household didn't run by itself. She still needed to go over next week's menu with the housekeeper, Mrs. Bridwell, and she ought to write an advertisement for a new upstairs maid, since the current one had just given notice.

Still, she wondered if he'd found her last note amusing, and if he had, what he might have written back in reply. Not that it mattered, except she was curious. It felt a bit like missing the last part of a serialized story.

At any rate, she blamed this unsatisfied curiosity for the sense of breathless anticipation that dogged her through the rest of the day as she counted the hours until the planned excursion to Covent Garden.

Chapter Five

*P*recisely as the clock chimed seven, Hopkins announced the arrival of Lord Norwood. Charlotte's breath caught in her throat as the earl walked through the doorway. Resplendent in his evening clothes, he was even handsomer than she remembered. Had it just been yesterday when he'd stormed into her life? In some ways it already seemed a lifetime ago, and in others, so recent she almost felt like pinching herself to make sure this wasn't all a dream.

"Miss Hurst," he said, striding toward her, reaching for her hand as she rose from her seat. He clasped her fingers in a warm grip. "You're ready with admirable punctuality. Dare I hope you've been as eager for my company as I have yours?" he murmured, bending over her hand, and brushing her fingers lightly with his lips.

"You may dare anything you like," she said, deliberately

keeping her tone light despite her quickening heartbeat. "Who am I to stop you?"

"Who indeed?" He grinned cheekily. "As my betrothed, I thought you knew it was your bounden duty to manage me and keep me in line."

"If you'd mentioned *that* yesterday morning, I'd have agreed to this engagement with a good deal more alacrity."

He laughed. "Ah, Miss Hurst, you never disappoint. Always with the clever comeback."

"I was simply stating the truth."

"I know, which only makes it more refreshing."

Their gazes caught and held for a few seconds until Charlotte, suddenly skittish of her own emotions, blinked and looked away. It was then she noticed he carried a small squarish package wrapped in brown paper.

Seeing that it had caught her attention, he presented it to her. "I brought you this."

Charlotte took it from him. "Should I open it now or later?"

"Open it now."

She undid the neatly tied bow, wondering if he'd wrapped it himself or given the task to a servant. He'd done a very creditable job if he had. The corners were crisp and the paper was tucked around the ends with smooth efficiency. Very unlike the carelessly done-up packages she received from Phillip on her birthday. Freed of the confining ribbon, the wrapping fell away to reveal a book.

It was a copy of *Waverley*. A very fine copy. The cover was made of dark brown, fine-grained leather, soft and smooth to the touch. She traced a finger over the gold embossed lettering on the front, then raised her gaze to his and smiled. "Thank you for delivering it so promptly. I'll start it tonight. I always read before bed. It helps me sleep better." She felt her cheeks warm as she realized her bedtime habits weren't an entirely suitable topic to discuss with the earl. To hide her embarrassment, she ducked her head and opened the book, slowly turning the pages.

"Open to the flyleaf," he said.

She did as he requested. A bookplate had been pasted in. William Atherton, she read, somewhat surprised he'd written his given name rather than his title. Then she saw the inscription on the inside cover.

> *To C. Hurst,*
>
> *I hope this gives you as much enjoyment as it did me.*
>
> *Warmly,*
> *Norwood*

Glancing back toward him, she saw he was regarding her with an almost boyish expectancy. He meant it as a gift. A strange warmth flooded through her at the thoughtful gesture, but this was quickly followed by an instinctual reluctance to allow things to get too cozy between them.

"Oh, but…you shouldn't," she demurred. "This is your copy. I wasn't expecting you to *give* it to me."

"I know, but I'd like you to have it."

It was a very ordinary statement, and yet a prickle of excitement chased along her skin. Was it her imagination, or had his voice held a hint of something else, something beyond the simple meaning of the words?

It's your imagination, Charlotte. What else would it be?

Honestly, she needed to get hold of herself, but she'd turned into a quivering mass of feminine sensibilities ever since he'd bowed over her hand and kissed it. No doubt such gestures were second nature to him, but she was unused to receiving those sorts of gallantries from a man, and clearly it had affected her good sense. Trying to regain some semblance of her usual nonquivering self, she placed the book on the nearby sofa table, then busied herself with carefully folding the wrapping paper and the satin ribbon.

"If you're ready," he said when she finished her task, "we should go. My aunt is waiting in the carriage."

"Yes, of course." She'd momentarily forgotten about his aunt who'd come along to perform the duties of a chaperone. "I never meant to keep her waiting. Let me call for my cloak, and we can be off."

They met Hopkins in the entry hall, where he stood holding the satin garment, ready to help her into it. Lord Norwood looked on as Hopkins draped it around her shoulders. Charlotte reached up to fasten it, but aware of the earl's gaze, she found herself fumbling with the metal clasp.

"Would you like assistance, miss?" Hopkins asked.

"Yes, I believe I would," Charlotte said, feeling quite foolish that she let herself yet again become so discomposed by the earl.

"Allow me," Lord Norwood said, stepping forward and gently pushing her fingers aside. He leaned in slightly as he peered at the closure. Only inches apart, Charlotte caught the masculine scents of sandalwood and clean linen that clung to him.

"Ah, I see how this works," he said. Charlotte swallowed hard. His fingers brushed the skin at the base of her throat as he worked the halves of the clasp in place. "There you are," he said, stepping back.

"Thank you," she said, hoping he didn't notice the slight trembling of her hands as she drew on the elbow-length gloves

Hopkins handed her. She was reacting like a green girl of sixteen, rather than what she was—a levelheaded woman of three
and twenty, who (up to now anyway) had never been susceptible
to bouts of feminine nerves in the presence of a gentleman.

Once outside, she drew in deep breaths of the evening air,
trying to cool her response to the earl. By the time he helped her
up into the carriage, she'd regained her equilibrium enough to
barely notice the warm clasp of his gloved hand about hers.

William climbed in after Miss Hurst and wasn't at all dis-
pleased to see that his aunt's pampered pet, a large ginger cat,
was sprawled across the leather seat next to its owner, forcing
him to sit next to Miss Hurst. He'd barely taken his seat when
the coachman directed the horses to "walk on," and they took
off with a lurch.

While William performed the necessary introductions, the
cat raised up and stretched its legs, before perching itself on
the edge of the seat, its large green eyes staring intently at Miss
Hurst, who gave the creature a tentative smile. The cat reached
out with one paw and lightly batted at Miss Hurst's knees.

"He wants to get to know you," his aunt said. "He does like
the ladies, my Harry does."

"Harry?" Miss Hurst said. "That's a very appropriate name
for him. He possesses such a luxuriant coat of fur, and he's
quite friendly, isn't he?"

Harry, whose balance was amazingly unaffected by the
movement of the carriage, was now resting his front paws
against Miss Hurst's knees while his back legs remained
planted on the seat across from her. She reached out to pet the
cat under his chin.

"Aye, that he is. Furry and friendly is my Harry," Aunt Florence said. "He's named after a former beau of mine, the Honorable Henry Albers, a ginger-headed rascal who went off to fight in the American colonies. We had an understanding before he left England, but he was wounded and captured at the Battle of Yorktown..." She shook her head and let out a long sigh. "Alas, he didn't return, and I never gave my heart to another."

"Oh, how tragic," Miss Hurst said.

As if sensing his mistress's melancholy, Harry turned and jumped onto the older lady's lap, rubbing his face against her shoulder. The sound of the cat's purring filled the coach as his owner began crooning over him and scratching his head fondly. She reached for a small pouch on the seat beside her, pulled out a few yellow morsels, and fed one to the cat. "You do love your cheese, don't you, my boy?" The purring increased in intensity.

"Aunt Florence's tale of lost love isn't quite as tragic as you may be imagining," William murmured into Miss Hurst's ear, feeling compelled to set the record straight. "Her feckless beau survived the war, married the daughter of a wealthy Bostonian merchant, and as far as we know, is still a hale and hearty citizen of Massachusetts."

"It's still tragic for her either way, don't you think?" she whispered back. His aunt was too occupied with her pet to notice this side conversation.

"Perhaps, though I suspect she's well rid of such a fickle beau. One has to wonder if he proved an equally faithless husband," he observed.

"I take comfort in the fact I have my memories of him," Aunt Florence said, still feeding Harry, who was greedily gulping the pieces of cheese. A fond smile wreathed her face. "You couldn't trust that rapscallion in a closed carriage. My maid was suspiciously unaware of Harry's wandering hands. I suspect he bribed her not to notice his liberties." She let out a cackle of a laugh. "Not that I minded. I always preferred a man with a robust appetite." She peered closely at Miss Hurst. "Girls today are so missish."

Miss Hurst blinked, and it was clear that she wasn't quite sure what to make of this statement. Nor was she the only one. Was his aunt hinting that girls ought to allow gentlemen liberties? He was beginning to rethink the choice of Aunt Florence for a chaperone. But he'd had no idea she had such...radical notions of what constituted acceptable behavior.

"Aunt Florence, you're going to give Miss Hurst a poor impression of us, talking like that." He turned to Miss Hurst. "My family doesn't, as a rule, condone fast behavior."

"Speak for yourself, Nevvy," his aunt retorted. "Times were different in my youth, to be sure. Then no one minded a bit of slap and tickle, as long as the gentleman intended to come up to scratch in the end."

"Yes, well..." William cleared his throat uncertainly. "I don't really know how to respond to that," he muttered under his breath.

Miss Hurst offered him a sympathetic smile.

Harry chose that moment to disentangle himself from his owner's affectionate embrace and jump across the gap between the seats, landing squarely on William's lap, precisely in that area of a man's anatomy that was sensitive to blows of any kind.

He couldn't quite stifle his gasp of pain. Harry was fourteen pounds (give or take), thanks to Aunt Flo's habit of frequently feeding her darling tidbits of his favorite foods. Without a word, since he was suffering through the pain with a clenched jaw and tightly pressed lips, he brushed Harry off his lap onto the leather seat in the space between them. Miss Hurst, to her credit, pretended not to notice his obvious discomfort.

"Harry," Aunt Florence scolded. "Be nice. You know better than to jump on people."

Unperturbed, Harry bumped his head against Miss Hurst's right arm. He continued to meow and bump against her arm until she reached over and scratched between his ears. Once again the sound of Harry's purring filled the carriage.

No one spoke for a few minutes. Miss Hurst's attention was solely focused on the cat, which he suspected was her considerate way of allowing him time to recover from Harry's unexpected leap onto his groin. Aunt Florence appeared to have dozed off, and before long, she began to snore, the sound mingling with Harry's contented purring. The carriage ride, William noted with irony, was not precisely unfolding as he'd envisioned it, and he couldn't decide whether he preferred his aunt's company when she was awake or asleep. He could only imagine what Miss Hurst's impression of all this was.

After a while, William felt more himself. Miss Hurst was no longer petting the cat, who was now busy giving his chest a tongue bath. Less preoccupied with his own discomfort, he noticed with some concern that Miss Hurst seemed to be suffering from some discomfort of her own. Sitting quite stiffly, her hands clasped tightly in her lap, she reminded him of his youngest sister, Amelia, who suffered bouts of stomach sickness during carriage rides. Perhaps Miss Hurst also suffered from that malady, although she'd seemed fine riding in his curricle yesterday. Or maybe she only became sick while riding in a closed carriage.

Just then, an odd hiccup-like sound escaped her, deepening

his suspicion that she did suffer from the same condition that plagued his sister.

"Are you all right?"

"I'm fine," she replied. But since the declaration was obviously pushed through clenched teeth, he didn't believe it for a moment. The last thing this evening needed was for Miss Hurst to cast up her accounts in the carriage.

"If you're going to be sick, I keep a basin in the carriage for that purpose. My youngest sister, Amelia, can't ride in a carriage without one."

At his words, a peal of laughter burst from her before she could clap a hand over her mouth, and he watched in bemusement as she bent forward in convulsions of muffled laughter. Apparently they wouldn't need the basin stowed under the seat.

Finally, wiping the tears from her eyes, she straightened. Across from them, Aunt Florence, her head lulled back against the seat, snored on, and between them, Harry continued with his cat toilette, twisting himself around in an attempt to bathe his back.

"Oh my goodness," she said. "I thought for certain I'd wake your aunt. I apologize for making a spectacle of myself. I couldn't help it."

"So I gathered," he said.

"If you're wondering what was so funny, it was a series of things."

"Was I included in this series of funny things?"

"To a degree," she admitted. "Mostly it was the noise being made by your aunt and her cat. One doesn't typically hear those sounds on the way to the theater, and it struck me as funny. And then you were sitting there so stoically, which wouldn't have seemed so amusing, except that you maintained your stoicism amid the racket. And then when you offered me a basin...not that I didn't appreciate your solicitude, but..." She paused, and he suspected she was fighting the urge to giggle again. Finally in command of herself once more, she continued. "I don't know why, but for some reason those elements added together just struck me as hilarious."

"I can see where they might," he said. "Once I wasn't so busy being...stoic, I became aware of the more...farcical qualities of this ride."

Harry leaped across the seats and settled himself next to his mistress, and began to lick his foreleg with vigorous motions.

"I'm beginning to rethink my aunt's suitability as a chaperone," William said dryly.

"It's a moot point, don't you think?" Charlotte asked. "It's not as if you're planning to take any liberties."

He shot her a droll look. "It's the principle of the thing. I assumed, given my aunt's age, and her status as a spinster, that she'd be a stickler for propriety. Instead, she all but encouraged me to ravish you, and now she's fallen asleep, giving me the opportunity to do so."

"True, but I'm sure she trusts that you will behave as a gentleman."

"Does she? Apparently, the Honorable Henry didn't all those years ago."

"But you're not the Honorable Henry, who, from what I know of the man, didn't live up to the honorable part of his name. It sounds as if he treated your aunt quite shabbily, having an understanding with her and then marrying a girl from the colonies without breaking it off first."

"It's possible the understanding only existed in Aunt Florence's mind." He let out a dry chuckle. "You know what's funny? Funny in the absurd sense, that is."

She shook her head. "What?"

"I just remembered that my aunt, on occasion, acted as a chaperone for my married sisters when they were being courted by their husbands. Which makes me wonder if any of my brothers-in-law ever took liberties with my sisters." He wasn't outraged exactly, but at the same time, he wasn't entirely comfortable at the thought of this potential misconduct.

"I don't suppose it really matters now, does it? Since they're respectably married."

He shrugged and sighed. "It would have been so much easier if I'd had only brothers. Thank God, Amelia is the last one left to launch into society. When she makes her come-out, I'll be sure to employ a proper dragon to watch over her. A real fire breather to keep her in line," he added.

"But you're the third child. Would you be satisfied living the life of a younger son?"

Would he? Even though he felt the burden of carrying on the family legacy, and of stepping into the shoes of his father, whom he'd idolized, would he truly prefer things to be different than they were?

If he were honest, the answer would be yes, at times. But the yearning for a more carefree existence came less frequently, and he liked to think his father would be pleased with him, with his efforts to manage the family estates, ensure the welfare of their tenants, take an active role in politics.

"I have moments when I envy younger sons, but I don't guess I'd wish for a life other than the one I have," he said at last.

"There are times I envy sons, younger or otherwise," she said. "Men have so much more freedom and choice."

"True, but freedom often comes with the burden of greater responsibilities."

"Then perhaps," she said, giving him an arch smile, "you

gentlemen should hurry up and support legislation that gives us a more equitable legal standing, so we ladies could help you shoulder those burdens. As it is now, I have more legal rights as a single woman than a married one. It's shameful that a female's identity, legally, at least, is subsumed by her husband's the minute the wedding vows are finalized."

"You aren't talking politics with the girl, are you?" Aunt Florence demanded, evidently having wakened from her nap. "Good heavens, boy! Is that the best you could come up with while I was dozing?" His great-aunt gave her hair a pat, then ran a hand across her chin. "No drool, thank goodness. Are we almost there? I hope so if you're going to foist political talk on us."

"In my defense, Auntie, I don't think Miss Hurst minds." He glanced toward Miss Hurst, who looked as if she wanted to start laughing again. "In fact, nearly from the moment we met she's been quite emphatic about expressing her opinions."

His aunt frowned. "Really? She seems like a nice girl. Too pretty to be a bluestocking, I should have thought." She shrugged. "Well, no wonder you two paired up. Birds of a feather, and all that."

William wasn't sure what to say in response to his aunt's observation, which managed to both compliment and insult Miss Hurst. Since he had the distinct impression that she was amused by his aunt's pronouncement, he decided the best course would be to say nothing at all.

"Norwood," his aunt continued, "since your sisters are joining you tonight, I hope you don't mind if I spend the evening in Fanny Walpole's box. I haven't seen her in a donkey's age."

"I've no objections," he said. "Provided you rejoin us for the ride home."

Aunt Florence waved her hand dismissively. "Well, naturally. I'll need you to take me home, won't I?"

"And Miss Hurst needs a chaperone, Auntie," he reminded her.

"She only needs the appearance of one. You're no Henry Albers, Nephew, and that's a fact." The old lady gave a sad little shake of her head. "If you were, that girl"—she gestured toward Charlotte with a bony hand—"would look well-kissed right now. Henry would have taken advantage of his opportunities if my maid had nodded off like I did."

"This is the first time I've been lectured for *behaving*," William said. "But despite your opinion, Aunt Flo, I'm quite sure Miss Hurst appreciates my restraint."

"Certainly, I do," Miss Hurst murmured.

"Maybe she does, or maybe she doesn't." His aunt chuckled. "Sounded like a pretty lukewarm response to my ears."

He'd also been struck by the lack of conviction in Miss Hurst's voice, but he blamed it on his aunt's embarrassingly *outré* attitude making Miss Hurst uncomfortable. Which was why he felt compelled to say, "I'm sure you misread the lady, Aunt."

"Maybe so. You know her better than I do." She turned toward Miss Hurst. "My girl, I apologize if I'm the reason for that pretty blush you're sporting."

"Truly, no apologies are necessary," Miss Hurst said.

William had to agree with his aunt—Miss Hurst blushed most becomingly. Their gazes met, and to his amazement, her blush deepened and for a brief moment he caught a flicker of something unexpected in her eyes—an echo of that yearning he'd seen in them yesterday—making him wonder if Aunt Flo's observation didn't have some merit to it after all.

Was she blushing because his aunt had hit on the truth of it?

William would have dismissed the notion if not for that flash of emotion he'd seen in her eyes. Did Miss Hurst feel the same tug of attraction for him that he felt for her?

The carriage drew to a halt outside the theater, effectively putting an end to the conversation, but not his curiosity. Whatever the truth of her feelings, this pretend betrothal would afford the perfect opportunity to uncover them.

Chapter Six

*O*nce inside the theater, they parted company with Aunt Florence, who went off in search of her friend. It took Charlotte and the earl quite some time to work their way to his theater box because they were frequently stopped by acquaintances of his who wished to offer congratulations on their recent engagement. Despite this, the earl somehow managed to steer them inexorably through the crowds, and Charlotte let out a small sigh of relief when they finally reached the entrance to his box.

She disliked being the center of attention, and particularly scrutiny of this kind, where one felt rather like a specimen being examined under a magnifying glass. She'd expected to be an object of curiosity tonight, and tried to prepare herself for it, but the truth was her natural inclination ran more to avoiding the glare of attention than seeking it.

They stopped in front of a tall door that divided the hallway from the interior, and Lord Norwood helped her out of her cloak, handing it to the attendant standing nearby.

He gave a brief bow and swept his arm out gallantly. "After you," he murmured.

Upon entering his box, Charlotte spied a gentleman and lady who already occupied a pair of the ornately carved, gilt chairs. Before Lord Norwood could even announce their arrival, the woman stood and, wearing a bright smile, began to make her way toward them.

She was dressed in the latest stare of fashion in a mulberry-colored silk gown. Her blonde hair, flawlessly curled and coiffed, framed a beautiful face, delicately featured, with slate-blue eyes startlingly like Lord Norwood's. It wasn't hard to deduce she was one of his sisters. Since the gentleman following in the woman's wake possessed thick chestnut hair, Charlotte surmised this must be the Chatworths.

"William," the lady said. "And Charlotte, my soon-to-be sister." She reached out and took Charlotte's hands in her own, and gave them a friendly squeeze, her gaze resting on Charlotte with an expression of genuine delight. "I can't tell you how thrilled I am to welcome you to our family. William is the luckiest of fellows. And I'd be entirely remiss, dear Charlotte, if I didn't say how lovely you look tonight. That blue gown sets off your eyes so beautifully. I do hope my brother remembered to pay you a pretty compliment."

Charlotte blinked, rendered momentarily speechless by the effusiveness of this greeting, not to mention the uncertainty of how to frame an answer that didn't cast the earl in a bad light, and also didn't sound as if she wished for a compliment.

"Well, actually...that is to say—"

Before she could devise a satisfactory reply, the earl cut in, "I was regrettably neglectful in expressing my admiration for

Miss Hurst tonight." He turned to Charlotte. "I hope you will accept it now though. You look quite captivating." He leaned in and added in a low voice. "And I'm not just saying that. I mean it. I should have told you earlier."

Lady Chatworth slipped her arm through Charlotte's and began drawing her toward a seat. "Come," she said, smiling prettily. "We'll have a cozy chat, you and I." She turned to her husband and William. "You can entertain yourselves for a bit."

Lord Chatworth's eyes lit up. "So you won't mind if we pop over to Reggie Dermont's box? I hear he's thinking of selling Golden Shamrock."

"If you fancy a chance to add him to your stables, Chatworth," Lord Norwood said, "he'll cost you a pretty penny. I heard Dermont won't let him go for less than six hundred pounds."

"Six hundred pounds is a bit high for my blood," the other man replied, sending a hesitant glance in his wife's direction. "But I wouldn't mind feeling him out, all the same."

"Go." His wife made a shooing motion with her hand, and having secured her approval, the gentlemen bowed and departed.

Lady Chatworth's mouth drew into a fondly indulgent smile. "I'm counting on William to provide a restraining hand and keep my husband from making any rash expenditures. His stables are his weakness." She laughed. "Well, along with me, of course." They'd reached the front of the box, where three chairs were placed in a row. Lady Chatworth sat in the one farthest left and patted the velvet-covered seat of the middle one.

"I understand you haven't been married very long," Charlotte said, settling into the chair Lady Chatworth indicated.

"Only six months. Six blissful months." Her eyes brightened with a merry, almost mischievous gleam as she leaned toward Charlotte. "I *highly* recommend marriage."

"You do present a compelling picture of wedded bliss."

Lady Chatworth's face dimpled adorably. "My sister Elizabeth always teases me about it. She says it's the height of bad taste to look so obviously happy, but I can't help it." She tilted her head and studied Charlotte a moment. "I think the two of us shall get on famously, don't you?"

"I sincerely hope so," Charlotte said, warmed by Lady Chatworth's easy friendliness. Lord Norwood had been right about his sister. With her sweet nature you couldn't help but like her.

"So, tell me about yourself, Charlotte. You don't mind if I call you, Charlotte, do you?" Her brows lifted uncertainly. "I don't want to be annoyingly forward, but calling you Miss Hurst seems so frightfully formal. We tend to be more casual within our family circle."

Charlotte refrained from pointing out that she wasn't in the family circle, nor was she likely to be.

"I don't mind at all," she assured her. "My family's never been high sticklers for that sort of formality, either. I don't call my brother by anything but his given name."

"Oh, excellent." Lady Chatworth clasped her hands before her briefly. "And you must call me Lydia. And now that's out of the way, let's get to know each other better. What sorts of things do you like?"

"Goodness, that's a very broad question." Charlotte gave a little laugh. "Where should I start?"

"What's your favorite thing to do? Mine is dancing. I *adore* dancing."

"I like dancing well enough," Charlotte said, "though I can't say it's my favorite thing. But then again, I've spent most of my life in the country, and local assemblies didn't happen with great frequency, so it's just as well I never came to like it as much as you. My favorite pastime is probably going to sound rather dull to you," Charlotte warned, "but I like to read. It's generally what you'll find me doing when I have a free moment."

She considered adding that she also liked to putter about in the flower gardens, go for brisk walks, and manage her brother's household for him, but decided those *would* make her seem hopelessly boring.

"You sound like my sister Cecily. She always had her nose in a book, and if you ever had a question about anything, she knew the answer, or where to find it. She speaks four languages, can recite lines and lines of Shakespeare, and most amazingly, she can work mathematical calculations in her head faster than anyone I know. Even William, and he's no slouch when it comes to maths. I'm not that brilliant, but I love knowing people who are."

Aware that Lydia was probably crediting her with a great deal more knowledge and talent than she actually possessed, Charlotte said, "I'm not that brilliant, either. I only speak English and French, and while I like arithmetic, I prefer to work out my calculations on paper."

Lydia gave her a look that implied she thought Charlotte was being modest.

"Actually," Charlotte said as a thought occurred to her, "there *is* something else I enjoy. Quite a bit. Driving your brother's curricle might be my new favorite thing to do."

"How lucky for you. William has never let me drive his curricle."

"But how can that be? I thought he taught all of his sisters to drive," Charlotte said in some confusion. "That's what he told me."

"Oh, he did, but it was with an old gig. Nothing as sporting as his curricle. That's an honor he's bestowed only on you, dear Charlotte."

"I rather forced his hand," Charlotte demurred.

Lydia shook her head. "I doubt that. William can't be forced to do anything he doesn't want to. You must rate high in his opinion if he allowed you to take the reins of his curricle."

Charlotte knew better, but she didn't wish to contradict her new friend. "Not high enough to drive his bays, however."

"Men are *so* particular when it comes to their horses," Lydia agreed. "Although, I can understand Will's reluctance to let a novice drive them. James says those bays are one of the finest driving pairs in London. Maybe even in all of England."

"James being Lord Chatworth?" Charlotte asked.

"Yes, although I'm the only one to address him so. *His* family doesn't embrace informality. Even his mother calls him Chatworth. Not that that's so very unusual, but she tries to make me feel gauche for using his given name." She smiled and gave a dainty shrug. "I risk her frowns and do it anyway. I refuse to let her cow me into doing otherwise."

"Mothers-in-law can be terrifying, or so I've heard."

"Mine is, but we seldom see her except during the Season. Since James's father died, his mother spends the rest of the year in Scotland, the land of her birth." Lydia lowered her voice confidentially. "The chilly weather suits her chilly personality."

"What are the two of you whispering about?" a feminine voice asked from behind them.

Charlotte started in surprise. She hadn't heard anyone enter the box. She twisted around to face the speaker, and Lydia did likewise.

"Elizabeth!" Lady Chatworth greeted the newcomer. "I was just telling Charlotte about James's mother."

Charlotte started to come to her feet, but the lady waved away the gesture. "No need to stand. I'll just slip into this chair." She chose the unoccupied chair to Charlotte's right, so Charlotte scooted her chair backward, enough so that their seats formed a slight semicircle more conducive to conversation.

"It appears you and Lydia are already on a first-name basis." Lady Peyton's cool blue gaze studied her a long moment. "In that case, please call me Elizabeth."

"You're very kind," Charlotte murmured, suspecting that this sister didn't make such concessions as easily as Lydia did.

"We seem to be attracting a great deal of attention this evening," Lady Peyton said. "Which isn't surprising given the circumstances, and advantageous for our purposes, I should think."

For the first time since entering the theatre box, Charlotte looked around at the audience. Unfortunately, it took only a brief glance to confirm Lady Peyton was right. Heads craned in their direction, and dozens of pairs of eyes curiously studied them. In any other context, such unabashed scrutiny would be considered rude, but at the theater one came to see and be seen. Watching the onstage performance was only a secondary consideration, if it were a consideration at all.

"Don't let them bother you," Lady Peyton said, evidently sensing Charlotte's dismay. "You're this week's curiosity, but with luck, something else will come along soon and grab people's attention. Believe it or not, there are some in London who are positively green with jealousy at your sudden notoriety. Not to mention that you've—as far as they know—nabbed my brother. So chin up."

"I don't think I have any alternative at this point," Charlotte said dryly.

"In the meantime, Miss Hurst…Charlotte, if I may…are you free tomorrow? Lydia and I would like to invite you to spend the afternoon with us."

Charlotte's social calendar wasn't so clogged that she had any difficulty recalling that she was perfectly free the following afternoon. Most of her afternoons were open, since she usually finished any household tasks in the mornings. The copy of *Waverley* that Lord Norwood had given her came to mind. Evidently, she wouldn't be spending tomorrow afternoon reading it.

"I'm perfectly free, and I'd welcome the opportunity to get to know you better."

"Wonderful," Lady Peyton said with an approving nod. "Then Lydia and I shall call for you after luncheon. It's never too early to begin trousseau shopping."

Trousseau shopping? Charlotte stared at Lady Peyton, trying to gauge whether or not this was a joke. To her dismay, it was clear it wasn't, but why would Lady Peyton even suggest trousseau shopping when there wasn't to be a wedding? And then it occurred to her that perhaps the earl's sisters didn't know that yet. She'd assumed their brother had told them this, but maybe he hadn't. In which case, she needed to set them straight immediately.

"You do know, don't you," she began in a low voice, not wanting to be overheard by anyone nearby, "that your brother and I don't actually intend to marry. This betrothal is temporary, just for show as a means of avoiding any scandal that might arise because of that betrothal announcement in the *Morning Post*."

"Oh, we do know," Lady Peyton said, keeping her voice

equally low. "Which is exactly why you must shop for a trousseau. Perception is *everything* in this case."

Lydia nodded in agreement.

"But we won't actually make any purchases, will we?"

Lydia eyes widened and she looked as if Charlotte had just made a heretical pronouncement.

"Who would go trousseau shopping, and then not purchase anything?" Lady Peyton asked. "That's sounds nonsensical."

"Does it? More nonsensical than buying items for a trousseau I don't need?" Charlotte asked.

"You'll need one eventually," Lady Peyton pointed out matter-of-factly. "But that's neither here nor there. We must act as if you have an immediate need for one. So while *we* know there's no actual betrothal, and no actual wedding planned, we must still act as if those things *are* real."

Charlotte took this to mean that yes, she'd have to purchase some items for her fictional wedding to Lord Norwood.

"But I wouldn't even know where to start," Charlotte said, knowing that argument was likely to prove futile given the very determined light shining in Lady Peyton's eyes, but not willing to give in too easily.

"Exactly. Which is why we will take you in hand." Lady Peyton's voice was crisp and decisive. She knew she'd won this skirmish.

"It shall be great fun," Lydia chimed in. In contrast to her sister, she sounded bubbly with anticipation. A fact that amazed Charlotte, who rated clothes shopping only slightly above being dosed with bitters.

She threw up her hands in surrender. "What time must I be ready?"

William found his attention wandering. He couldn't muster up much interest in the potential sale of Golden Shamrock. Dermont obviously intended to drive a hard bargain, and Chatworth was fooling no one in his attempt to appear only slightly interested in the horse. Like a hound on the scent, Dermont sensed Chatworth's weakness for fine horseflesh and the deep pockets that allowed him to indulge it.

William glanced toward his theater box. He'd been doing this frequently, checking to see how Miss Hurst was getting on with his sister. As he'd predicted, Lydia had immediately taken to her, and Miss Hurst looked equally delighted to make his sister's acquaintance, and to anyone watching the pair, it didn't appear they'd met for the first time this evening. They just might be able to pull this off successfully.

Peyton strolled into Dermont's box, and came over to William's side. The other two gentlemen, caught up in their discussion of all things equine, barely acknowledged his presence. "My wife sent me to drag Chatworth back before he makes an expensive mistake," the viscount drawled. "I'm not too late, am I?"

William shrugged. "Chatworth's a big boy, and he's got the blunt to afford the Shamrock if that's what he wants to do. He'll need to outbid Lepley though. Dermont claims he offered six hundred and seventy pounds. At that price, I don't see Chat making a competing offer." He shrugged again. "But then again, he might. As far as I can tell, they're currently debating the merits of pairing the Shamrock with various dams. I confess, though, I haven't been paying close attention."

Peyton grinned. "Good time to draw him away then, and

dance attendance on our wives. Or in your case, wife-to-be. *Macbeth* will be starting soon."

William knew what this meant. Libby preferred they take their seats before the main performance began. She disliked having her enjoyment of the play interrupted by the comings and goings of others in the box. His gaze traveled once again toward his sisters and Miss Hurst. "Past time," he said grimly. "It appears Lady Bohite is paying them a visit." He came to his feet. "Make my farewells to Dermont for me. That harridan's tongue is sharper than a razor, and she delights in flaying people with it."

He departed before Peyton could reply. He could only imagine what venomous insinuations Lady Bohite was spewing at Miss Hurst. She was a mean-spirited woman who searched for the worst in everyone and everything, and she had, at one time, harbored hopes for a match between her youngest daughter and William. For an entire Season, she'd seized every opportunity to push the girl at him, seemingly oblivious to his polite rebuffs and complete lack of interest. She'd held a grudge against him ever since.

He sped through the hallways, discouraging conversation by nodding curtly to acquaintances as he walked past them. He reached his destination just in time to hear Elizabeth say coldly, "Lady Bohite, that is quite enough. You will apologize to Miss Hurst and then leave my brother's box immediately."

"Don't think people won't remember the hasty way this came about in a few months when the truth will be apparent for all to see," Lady Bohite replied.

"*Don't* say another word that isn't an apology to my fiancée," William said in a steely voice, coming up behind the group.

All four ladies jerked with surprise. Lady Bohite turned to face him, her eyes glittering with malice, but one look at his face was enough to cause a note of fearfulness to creep into her expression.

"Apologize," he continued, his voice low and furious. "And then you will take your malicious self away from here. You won't repeat this scurrilous and completely untrue accusation or, so help me, I'll make sure you regret your words. Do I make myself clear?"

Lady Bohite swallowed. "I'm sorry if I gave offense," she said, not quite meeting his eyes.

"Now apologize to *her*," William ordered, nodding toward Miss Hurst, who looked pale, and as if she'd like to be anywhere else but here.

Lady Bohite swiveled toward Miss Hurst. "I'm sorry if I maligned you." She fled as soon as she delivered the apology.

William went to Miss Hurst's side. "Are you all right?"

She drew in a shaky breath and gave a weak nod. "I just need a moment to recompose myself."

"Come on then." He took her arm and began steering her toward the back of the box. "Let's withdraw to the hallway for a moment." They met the returning Chatworth and Peyton just as they were exiting. His brothers-in-law gave them puzzled looks, but didn't ask any questions. His sisters could fill their husbands in on what had just occurred.

Once out in the hall, Miss Hurst let out a long breath. "That was quite…unpleasant," she said quietly.

"I imagine it was." He led her over to a cushioned bench nestled between some classical statuary, thinking she might wish to sit down, but she shook her head.

"Let's stroll the hallway, if you don't mind. No one's around to think it odd, and I feel more like moving than sitting."

"As you wish," he said. They headed for the far end of the spacious hall where a large fireplace was flanked by a pair of tall marble columns. "I'm sorry I wasn't there to protect you from that woman's viciousness."

"Your sisters came to my defense. I was too stunned by the woman's sudden verbal attack to say much of anything." She gave a little shake of her head. "One minute I was being introduced, and the next she was unleashing her vitriol. I simply wasn't prepared for it."

"Now that surprises me, considering how admirably you put me in my place yesterday morning."

"You were angry, but not vicious like she was, and instead of coming to my own defense, I just retreated inside myself, like I used to do at finishing school."

"I'm sorry to hear you were ill-treated at school," he said, wishing there were some way to avenge those old wrongs, but knowing there wasn't. "It's an unfortunately all-too-common aspect of life during one's youth." There'd been bullies at Eton, but William had been able to use his fists to defend himself. That wouldn't have been a solution open to her, since girls tended to fight with words alone.

"It was a long time ago. There was a group of girls who tried to make me miserable, and largely succeeded, I suppose. I was quiet and bookish and an easy target because I never knew how to respond to them, so I didn't. Just pretended I didn't care what they said or did."

"I can't tell you how much I wish you hadn't had to endure that," he said.

She shrugged. "Like I said, it was a long time ago."

Maybe so, but he still heard the pain in her voice. "And yet I think it still continues to haunt you."

"Not really. Not unless something brings it to mind. The truth is I hadn't thought of those days in quite a while. But then that engagement announcement suddenly appeared, and I knew the gossip it would stir up wouldn't always be kind." Her mouth twisted into a rueful smile. "As Lady Bohite proved tonight."

"About Lady Bohite," he said. "You should know that while she may have directed her ire at you, her words were more likely aimed at me. She's harbored an intense dislike of me since I failed to fall madly in love with her daughter when she continually threw her at my head a couple of Seasons ago."

"Was her daughter named Jane?"

"No, it was Delia or Dorothea or Delphinia, something along those lines, but definitely not Jane. Why do you ask?"

She studied him a long moment, those fine blue eyes of hers intent and probing. "Then I don't think it was about her daughter because Lady Bohite mentioned an interest on your part for someone by the name of Lady Jane."

"Did she?" he asked with some irritation. He could guess what Lady Bohite had intimated about himself and Lady Jane, and while it had no merit, he wasn't sure Miss Hurst would be easily convinced of that. "Well, that's quite remarkable, considering the woman has never been a confidante of mine."

They reached the end of the hall and turned around, heading back in the direction of his box. A pair of elderly ladies exited the stairwell and walked down the hall toward them, before veering into the box located next to William's.

"She seemed very confident that a match between you and this Lady Jane was in the offing until I devised some wicked scheme to catch you myself." She frowned, and her mouth pressed into an unhappy line before she fixed him with a slightly accusing glare. "You might have mentioned it before I agreed to participate in our little charade."

"I didn't because there's nothing to tell. I assume she's referring to Lady Jane Crowley, the Duke of Maitland's daughter. Some time ago the duke vaguely hinted that he wouldn't oppose a match between us. I did give it a brief consideration because her father is a powerful man, a close friend of the prime minister, and it could have been an advantageous match for those and many other reasons. However, I never pursued the idea further, never courted the girl or showed any more interest in her than I have in any other young lady before you. That Lady Bohite claimed it to be so is preposterous."

Her brow furrowed briefly as she digested this. "Then how do you explain that she seemed to genuinely believe her claim?"

"I've no idea why she would believe it. Perhaps she was led to think so by someone. Possibly Lady Jane's mother, the Duchess of Maitland. She and Lady Bohite are cousins. It could be the duchess convinced herself there was still a chance for a match to come about between me and her daughter, and she refuses to let go of the notion."

"So her claims are baseless?"

"Completely. And you needn't worry that she will continue to repeat them. I will see that she doesn't."

Once again, they'd paced the length of the hallway. They turned around and William was surprised, but pleased, to see Lady Serena Wynter coming toward them. He'd been eager for Miss Hurst to meet her, and the timing couldn't be better—a friendly face to counterbalance the unpleasant confrontation with Lady Bohite.

"Thank heavens I caught you before the performance began," Serena burst out before he had a chance to make the introductions. "I gave Papa my solemn promise I'd be in my seat before Mrs. Siddons takes the stage. She's a great favorite of his, and he's quite excited about her special appearance tonight. But when I heard you'd arrived in the company of a lady, I knew it had to be your fiancée. So naturally I was eager to meet her and extend my warmest congratulations on behalf of Papa and myself." She gave him a pointed look as if to say *Well, get on with the introductions*.

Which William did with alacrity, glad to see that Miss Hurst wasn't at all taken aback by Serena's somewhat forward manner, since he hoped a friendship would blossom between them. Serena's father, Lord Huntington, was his political mentor, and more than that, had become like a second father to him since his own father's unexpected death shortly after William turned eighteen. He held a great deal of affection and esteem for both of them.

After exchanging pleasantries, Serena pulled out a small notebook and pencil from her reticule.

"So, this isn't just a social call," William said with a wry smile. Serena had a penchant for involving herself in a variety of charitable projects. "What worthy endeavor have you embarked upon now?"

"It's the same one that's occupied me lately. Helping destitute war widows. The Duke and Duchess of Rochester are hosting a subscription ball to raise money for the cause. Can I put you down for two tickets?"

"Of course." His reply drew a swift glance from Miss Hurst. No doubt she didn't like the idea of attending a ball with him. "We wouldn't want to miss the chance to support a worthy cause, would we?" He slanted her an innocent look.

"No, we wouldn't," she said, putting an ever-so-slight emphasis on the word *we*. "I adore worthy causes, even ones that involve a ball."

Touché, Miss Hurst.

Serena scribbled a notation in her notebook. "I knew I could count on you to support us. Especially now that you have a fiancée to accompany you." She turned to Charlotte. "If you meant what you said about worthy causes, there's a great deal to be done yet to help these women who lost their husbands on the battlefield. Perhaps we could get together one afternoon and discuss it further."

"That would be lovely," Miss Hurst said, sounding sincerely interested now.

A theater attendant hurried over to them. "They're getting ready to raise the curtain, my lady."

"Thank you for letting me know. Well! This has been a disappointingly short chance to talk, but I must fly if I'm to make it back to our box in time. Au revoir then. Miss Hurst, I'll be in touch very soon."

"I look forward to it," Miss Hurst said.

"We'll walk with you to the stairs," William said firmly, "and then the attendant can see you back to your father's box."

"That's completely unnecessary. I know the way back and I'm perfectly capable of seeing to myself."

"Indulge me. Even at the theater, an unaccompanied lady can attract unwanted attention."

"Sometimes, William, your gentlemanly instincts are a little *too* finely honed for my taste."

"As I'm well aware, Serena." They exchanged a look that acknowledged past differences. "But I have to live with my conscience." It was a lesson his father had drilled into him from a young age—to always do what was right; that a man must satisfy the dictates of his conscience.

"All right, you win this time." Serena rolled her eyes at him, a gesture that made him laugh. "Anyway, you know I don't have time to debate with you."

When they parted ways at the stairs, William paused before continuing down the hallway in the direction of his theater box. "Are you ready to return to our seats? Or would you like some more time to compose yourself?"

"I think I'm about as composed as I'm going to be. But even if I weren't, I don't want to miss the play. I've looked forward to it so much. I'm not going to let that dreadful Lady Bohite completely ruin the evening for me." There was an almost defiant tone to her voice now, and her eyes held a spark of determination.

This was the Miss Hurst he was coming to admire, the quiet bluestocking who sparked to life when the occasion called for it.

"Then let's go in there and show them a happily engaged couple enjoying a night at the theater." He smiled and leaned toward her in a conspiratorial manner. "It will drive Lady Bohite crazy."

Chapter Seven

It was long after midnight when Charlotte finished getting ready for bed. She didn't normally keep such late hours, but instead of being sleepy, she felt oddly restless. She'd seen no sliver of light at the bottom of Phillip's bedroom door when she'd passed it earlier. Normally she appreciated that he was the sort of brother who didn't believe it necessary to monitor her comings and goings, but tonight she'd have welcomed his company.

She sighed. If she wanted companionship, it looked like she'd have to find it in a book. Her gaze fell upon the copy of *Waverley* on the bedside table.

Perfect. She'd read until sleepiness overtook her. She climbed into bed, plumped the feather pillows into place behind her, and finally satisfied with the arrangement, reached for the book. She leaned back into her cozy nest, taking a moment to study the cover, to run her fingers over the leather, to feel the weight of it in her hands as she imagined *him* holding it thus.

Her fingers tingled.

She was being foolish. There was no reason to go all tingly over a man's book, for heaven's sake. Clearly the late hour was affecting her even if she didn't feel tired.

The late hour, Charlotte? some corner of her conscience taunted her. *Couldn't those tingles be the result of spending the evening in the company of a handsome, charming man? A handsome, charming man who's also your betrothed?*

She dropped the book like it was a hot coal.

It sat on her lap until, with a heavy sigh, she picked it up.

No tingling. No shivers running up and down her spine. No heart palpitations. *Thank goodness and hallelujah!*

She turned to the first chapter, determined to lose herself in the story. This resolution lasted only for a few pages. Because now, with the copy of *Waverley* open, she could catch the faint scent of sandalwood. Just barely, but it was there.

His book. His scent. Lingering within the pages.

A melting warmth flooded through her.

She was reading *his* book in *her* bed.

It felt intimate, and a bit wicked.

You are being a complete ninnyhammer! she scolded herself. She took another deep breath, trying to regain some semblance of the levelheaded sensible girl she usually was.

But tonight her sensible self was nowhere to be found.

Instead, some impish, indecorous girl had taken her place.

And *that* girl lifted the book to her face, buried her nose right in the middle of the open spine, and inhaled.

Images of him flashed through her mind. The way his finely molded lips quirked into an amused smile. The intensity of his grayish-blue eyes looking into her own when they spoke, as if what she had to say was of the utmost interest to him. The way his dark wavy hair, with its unruly tendency to stray from its carefully brushed perfection, tempted her to forget herself and smooth it back into place.

Well, all right then. He was a very good-looking man. It would probably be odd if she *didn't* feel some sort of attraction to him.

It meant she was human, but it didn't mean she was fool enough to start believing the lie. This betrothal was only a means to an end—a political appointment for him, an intact reputation for her. No matter how much he sent her pulses racing, it would never become more than that for any number of reasons.

There was too great of a divide between them socially and temperamentally. His family background and political ambitions would dictate the type of life he'd lead, and by extension, the type of wife he'd choose—one like him, who belonged to the elite social circles of the upper crust, whose connections would enhance his desire for a career in politics, not hinder it. Someone who would be comfortable acting as a political hostess in addition to the usual social demands placed upon the wife of a prominent peer. Someone nothing like her.

Unlike the earl, Charlotte didn't have grand ambitions for her life. Her preference would be for a quiet life in the country, well away from London with its gossip and rumors and people like Lady Bohite. Her tastes were simple, and her interests, which would be considered dull by many, gave her a great deal of pleasure, whatever they might lack in excitement.

None of that was going to change just because the earl had a handsome face and a winning manner. For the two of them, this engagement was a means to an end. Nothing more.

She closed the book and set it back on the nightstand. Her

life had been turned upside down in the past two days, she'd been thrust into a role she was reluctant to play, and then to top it all off, she'd been verbally assaulted at the theater tonight. Naturally she was overset, and not reacting as she normally would. What she needed more than anything was a good night's sleep.

She threw back the covers and swung her legs over the side of the bed. Perhaps some warm milk would make her drowsy. She could always throw in a splash of whisky. Her former governess, Miss Holmes, always swore by the efficacy of either warm milk or a bit of good Scotch whisky to cure insomnia. The two in tandem should do the trick, so wrapped in her dressing gown, she headed for the kitchen.

The next morning, she was still tired when she headed down to breakfast.

"Late night?" Phillip inquired, looking up from his plate. "You could've slept in, you know."

"I planned to, but I was wide awake by a quarter of seven," she said, filling a plate with toast and some stewed fruit.

She didn't add that her early awakening had been the result of a dream. One in which she and Lord Norwood had been at the theater. There had been a number of books scattered around his theater box, some on the seats and some piled on the floor. She and the earl had each picked a book, then seated themselves in the front row of the box just as they had the night before, except instead of watching the play, they'd begun reading.

When one of them came upon a particularly clever passage, they read it aloud to the other, and it had actually been a pleasant dream up to that point. But then the earl, after reading a snippet to her, had said, "Do you mind if I kiss you?" And she'd replied, "Oh, I wish you would."

Then he'd leaned in much as he had on the carriage ride,

and just before his lips touched hers, she'd awakened, heart pounding and disappointed that the dream had ended when it did. There'd been no possibility of sleeping after that, so she'd gotten up.

Taking a seat, she reached for the pot of black currant jam, and spread some on a slice of toast. She yawned widely, then took a bite, tiredly glancing at the large stack of correspondence next to her plate.

What she needed was a good, strong cup of tea. She started to take a sip from her cup, and then realized she hadn't poured any yet. So she reached for the teapot and remedied this oversight.

She and Phillip ate in silence, which was very much to his preference. Her brother wasn't a great believer in mixing conversation with the act of eating one's meal, and this morning Charlotte was inclined to go along with him.

Happily the food and the hot, sweet tea had the desired effect of perking her up and making her feel much more able to face the day. She poured another cup, mixing in the milk and sugar with a liberal hand, then turned to the letters, invitations, et cetera. that Hopkins had set at her place. The pile was much bigger than normal. Not surprisingly, her social standing as the fiancée of Lord Norwood appeared much greater than it had ever been pre-engagement.

She pulled out a few of the invitations and glanced through them. Three were invitations to balls, one to an evening soirée, another to a musicale, another to a poetry reading…and this represented a mere dent in the quantity of stiff, creamy cards in the pile. Furthermore, of those she'd opened, she recognized the names of only two of the hostesses, and she really had no idea which invitations she ought to accept and which she should decline. As Lord Norwood's fiancée, she suspected the act of choosing what to attend involved more than merely following one's own inclination. She decided to change tack and move on to the letters.

The first was a note from Lady Peyton informing Charlotte that she would come by at two o'clock with her carriage for the planned shopping trip. She set this aside and was breaking the seal on another when Hopkins entered bearing a small package, which he handed to Charlotte. "This just arrived for you. I was instructed to place it into your hands right away."

She took the proffered package. "Thank you, Hopkins."

"Looks like a jewelry box," Phillip remarked. "Must be from Norwood."

Charlotte refrained from delivering a sarcastic reply. *Really? And not from one of my other suitors? Oh, that's right. I don't have any other suitors. Although when you come right down to it, he doesn't really count as one either, does he?* It wasn't Phillip's fault she'd gotten such a poor night's rest. Nor was it his fault she felt ill at ease with all that had transpired in the last two days.

Instead, she said doubtfully, "I can't imagine *why* he'd send me jewelry." She balanced the box on her palm, raising and lowering it as she considered its weight. A small brooch perhaps?

If not jewelry, what could it be? She couldn't think of many other things that might fit in the box. A seashell? A pretty pebble? A small flower? But why would he—?

"You might try opening it," Phillip suggested, interrupting these internal speculations. "Saves the bother of endless guessing."

"Yes, right," Charlotte replied, pulling on one end of the thin ribbon that tied it. The bow unraveled and the brown paper wrapping fell away. She drew off the snug-fitting lid, and there, nestled in the folds of a piece of white satin, was a ring.

She swallowed, or tried to. Her throat had suddenly gone dry as a stale biscuit. Not a brooch, nor any other ordinary item.

A ring.

A very fine ring. And the last thing she would have guessed it to be, even though a ring ought to have been the obvious choice, given that a betrothal ring was the usual symbol of one's engagement.

He'd chosen this one to symbolize theirs.

She took it from the box, holding it gingerly as she examined it. The gold band had a delicate filigree pattern engraved upon it, while a modest sapphire resided in the setting, with a pair of small, sparkling diamonds on either side. It was lovely without being too showy, and exactly the sort of thing she would have picked out for herself.

"Do you like it?" Phillip said. "Norwood asked me about your taste in jewelry, but I'm afraid I wasn't much help. Truth is, I wasn't any help, since I've no idea what you like when it comes to jewelry and feminine gewgaws like that. But I must say what he chose looks like something you might like."

She didn't reply, just continued to study the ring as thoughts tumbled through her mind. Thoughts which boiled down to one thing—wearing his ring would make this charade seem uncomfortably real.

"Well, dash it. *Don't* you like it? Looked like you did when you pulled it out of the box."

"Yes, I like it. Of course. It's lovely." Too lovely. She wished she didn't like it because then she wouldn't mind so much that she had to give it back. "I can't accept it, though it was very thoughtful of the earl." At her brother's perplexed expression, she added, "You didn't think I'd keep it, did you? It would be completely inappropriate for me to accept such an expensive—and very personal—gift from him."

Phillip continued to look at her as if she were speaking gibberish.

"That is to say, we're not *really* engaged. And this is clearly meant to be a betrothal ring. I can't accept it under those circumstances."

"Under what circumstances?"

"False pretenses. A pretend betrothal. Those circumstances."

"First of all, it's temporary, not pretend. You always ignore that distinction. But either way..." He spread his hands wide. "I fail to see what's the problem here."

Of course Phillip didn't see a problem because from a logical perspective there wasn't one. The idea of wearing this ring scared her for reasons she didn't particularly care to delve into, and which she could hardly explain to her brother.

She drew in a long breath. "The problem is," she repeated after a moment, "that I can't keep this ring. It's much too fine, and obviously, it's a family heirloom, since the style, while beautiful, is rather old-fashioned. I'm sure he didn't just pick this out at Rundell and Bridge. But even if he had, I couldn't accept anything so...so..." *Meaningful.* "...irreplaceable."

"Try it on, Charlotte," Phillip urged. "Norwood requested I send over one of your rings so he could have this one sized to your finger."

"Didn't you hear a word I just said? There's really no point," she objected, even as a tiny part of her wished that there were.

"Maybe not," Phillip agreed. "But he went to enough trouble that you should try it on anyway. Makes his effort seem less of a waste if you at least try it on your finger to see if it fits."

Charlotte wasn't entirely convinced by this reasoning, but

she supposed it couldn't hurt to put it on. Just for a minute. It really *was* a lovely ring.

She slipped it onto her finger and held her hand out at arm's length, turning it to admire how nice the ring looked, with the gemstones sparkling in the morning sun that streamed through the windows. The earl had impeccable taste.

"How does it fit?"

"Perfectly," she admitted.

"Seems a shame to give it back then."

She shook her head. "Even if I felt right about keeping it— only for the duration of the betrothal, of course—I don't want the responsibility of having it in my possession. I'd be terrified of losing it." She didn't add that losing the ring was the least of her fears.

"I don't see how you would be in danger of losing a ring that fits you well," Phillip pointed out.

"Because I'd only wear it when I went out in public. The whole point of my wearing it is to give credence to the story of our engagement. But what if I mislaid it in between times?"

"Seems to me you could just wear it all the time. Then you wouldn't have to worry about it."

She didn't wish to discuss the issue anymore so she merely said, "I'll give it some thought."

Her brother's eyes narrowed as he shook his head and pushed back from the table. "I can see you're going to do what you're going to do. No sense in trying to talk you out of it." He walked to the open doorway, then turned back to her. "I'll just say this. He's behaving quite decently. Least you could do is cooperate and wear his ring for a few weeks."

He didn't wait for an answer, just left her to stew over his words. She studied the ring on her finger and mulled over what to do. In one sense, Phillip was right: wearing the ring should be a simple matter, an easy gesture of cooperation. Sending it back would look petty and ill-humored, and completely ungracious in the face of his gestures of goodwill: letting her drive his curricle, giving her his copy of *Waverley*, and now sending over the ring, obviously a family heirloom, and probably of sentimental value quite apart from its worth as an expensive piece of jewelry.

Charlotte slid it off her finger, then back on again. It fit so perfectly it might have been made for her. Would it really be so difficult for her to wear it? It was just metal and stone. She knew quite well it didn't symbolize anything *real*.

And in the meantime, she could enjoy wearing a beautiful piece of jewelry. Why was she trying to overcomplicate it? This ring shouldn't make any difference in her feelings toward him. As long as she relied on her good sense to keep her emotions in check, she would be fine. She could manage that, couldn't she?

She studied the ring, sliding it up and down the length of her finger as she pondered what to do. Lord Norwood would probably object if she tried to give it back to him, and there was a distinct possibility he wouldn't give up on the matter as easily as Phillip had. Did she really want to get in a debate with him over it?

"To wear, or not to wear. That is the question," she muttered to the empty room. To her chagrin, the soft sound of someone discreetly clearing his throat told her she wasn't alone after all.

She looked up from her contemplation of the ring on her finger and saw a footman standing just inside the door. He hesitated a moment, then came over to her, holding out a note.

"Mr. Hopkins asked me to give this to you."

She took it and nodded her thanks. She recognized the handwriting. It was from Lord Norwood.

How ironic, she thought, breaking the wax seal, the movement causing the sapphire to wink in the light. And odd, since he hadn't sent it with the ring.

My dear Miss Hurst,

I trust this note finds you well this morning. By now, you've (hopefully) received the package I instructed the jeweler to send to your residence.

I took the liberty of selecting a betrothal ring without consulting with you about your preferences. Forgive me, but I wished to have it prepared for you to wear as soon as possible. Let anyone dare question our betrothal with it on your finger!

I hope it meets with your approval, but even if the style is not to your taste, I think you'll agree its history is remarkably appropriate. My grandfather presented it to my grandmother upon the occasion of their engagement… after she'd turned him down twice. The first time she refused him she told him he was a very frippery fellow, and not worth her attention. The second time, she said that, despite improvement, she still found his character lacking.

As you can see, my grandmother was a believer in speaking her mind plainly. I think the two of you would have gotten on well if you'd had the opportunity to know each other.

As always,
Your most devoted servant,
Norwood

P.S. I have it on good authority that Liverpool intends to appoint the committee chair within the month. I thought you'd be happy to hear this.

Charlotte considered this last bit of information. One month was longer than she preferred, but *within the month* could indicate an even shorter period. She'd feared the engagement might drag on much longer than that. But one month? That was manageable. That she could do.

She could wear the ring for one month.

But once that appointment was made, she intended to end this arrangement between them immediately. Before her lamentably susceptible heart had a chance to convince her otherwise.

Chapter Eight

That afternoon Lady Peyton's carriage drew up to an un-prepossessing storefront on Bond Street, and a ripple of unease skipped through Charlotte as she peeked out the window. In her experience, the more discreet and nondescript a shop's exterior, the more expensive were the goods inside. She hoped it wouldn't prove true today, but the only thing that marked this as a place of business was a modest brass plaque next to the front door with *Mme. Rochelle, Modiste* engraved in a neat script.

She ought to have anticipated this. Last night at the theater, both sisters had been exquisitely attired in gowns obviously created by skilled—and probably outlandishly expensive—modistes. She hadn't questioned Lord Norwood's sisters about which shops they planned to visit, preferring to leave those details in their hands. Now she regretted not speaking up sooner and making clear her shopping habits didn't include purchasing garments from such a high-end modiste.

Aggravated with herself, Charlotte stepped out of the carriage and followed Lydia and Elizabeth to the shop's entrance. If the prices at this modiste proved as expensive as she expected, she could order nothing and request they visit a different dressmaker. Mrs. Wickersley, from whom Charlotte had bought a few items earlier in the spring, was an excellent seamstress who kept a small shop just off Bond Street. The location was less fashionable than this, but her prices were quite moderate. She'd suggest her if this Madame Rochelle charged outrageous prices.

They entered a small anteroom furnished with comfortable-looking chairs and a sofa, all elegantly upholstered in soothing hues of cream, sage green, and soft rose, such as one might encounter in a tasteful drawing room in Mayfair.

The only item to indicate this was a place of business was a long counter of polished wood, which ran along the entire length of one wall. A pretty young woman stepped from behind the counter and came toward them. Her fair hair was swept up in an elegant chignon, her dress an exquisite confection of pale yellow muslin embroidered with sprays of blue and purple flowers. Charlotte wondered if the gown was an example of Madame Rochelle's workmanship.

"Lady Peyton, Lady Chatworth, how may I be of service to you?" the shop girl greeted them, her voice a charming mixture of perfectly enunciated English with just a hint of a French accent. Her gaze turned to Charlotte, her eyes making a quick head-to-toe sweep, as if sizing her up as a potential client.

"We have an appointment with Madame Rochelle because we need several garments for the trousseau of our brother's intended," Lady Peyton said, gesturing to Charlotte with a wave of her hand.

The modiste's assistant nodded her head in a businesslike manner. "But, of course, we can provide those items. Please." She gestured with her hand toward a curtained doorway that led farther into the shop. Charlotte followed the earl's sisters through the velvet drapery into a larger, but more sparsely furnished, room.

A Persian rug in muted tones of rose and green covered the center of the floor, while a row of dressmaker's dummies graced one side of the room. Surprisingly, only two displayed evening gowns, while the rest showed off some of the loveliest undergarments and nightgowns Charlotte had ever seen.

These were made of a sheer, gauzy linen, with delicate embroidery and a liberal use of lace. The petticoats and chemises looked as insubstantial as cobwebs and so beautiful it would be a shame to cover them up.

Charlotte fingered the smooth fabric of one of the garments, imagining how wonderful such finely woven material would feel against her skin. Wonderful, but impractical, and probably insanely expensive.

"Madame Rochelle is gifted with a true artistry, isn't she?" Lady Chatworth murmured close to Charlotte's ear.

Charlotte nodded, since it was impossible not to admire the quality of the workmanship. "They're quite exquisite," she agreed, then lowering her voice, said, "but does she make less beautiful, more serviceable items? I don't need anything so fancy that will just be covered up by my outer clothing."

Lydia shot her an amused glance. "Keep in mind it's your trousseau we're purchasing today, and throw considerations of practicality out the window. If it makes you feel better, people will expect William's bride-to-be to order such items from Madame Rochelle."

"But who will know of our visit here?" Charlotte asked. "It's not as if it's likely to come up in conversation over a cup of tea."

"By this evening, it will be known across London that you've ordered your trousseau items from here," Lady Peyton said, joining the conversation. She'd been conferring with the shop assistant, but the girl had returned to the entrance area, leaving the three of them alone. "Any modiste worth her salt makes sure the *ton* knows when she caters to prominent customers, and now that society believes you to be the future Countess of Norwood, you have become a prominent customer. From now on, your business will enhance the cachet of any shop."

Charlotte blinked. The idea that, by virtue of her association with Lord Norwood, she'd become influential in any way and that something as mundane as where she shopped would be of interest to the *ton*, was rather unbelievable.

And silly, she reminded herself. The world had much bigger concerns than where she shopped for her unmentionables.

Before Charlotte could offer any comment, a tall, dark-eyed woman swept regally into the room, followed by two girls, one carrying a sheaf of papers and a pencil, the other, a wooden sewing box. The woman inclined her head ever so slightly to the earl's sisters in a movement that was simultaneously deferential and haughty, and so quintessentially French that there was no question in Charlotte's mind this must be Madame Rochelle in the flesh. The imperious modiste barked out some words of rapid-fire French too quickly for Charlotte, who spoke the language fairly fluently, to understand all that the modiste said. She recognized the terms "delicate bones," "slim-hipped," and something about her bosom, although whether the observation had been complimentary or unflattering was unclear, as Charlotte hadn't quite caught the adjective Madame had used.

The assistant with the papers busily transcribed this torrent of French, while the girl with the box stood nearby in a posture of stiff attention. Charlotte presumed her job was to hold the seamstress's tools at the ready should the woman decide she needed them. What she might need presently beyond a tape measure, Charlotte couldn't imagine.

At last, Madame fell silent, and with one finger tapping thoughtfully against her lips, she walked in a full circle around Charlotte. When she regained her starting point she stopped, gave a dismissive flick of her hand, which sent the two girls scurrying out of the room, and with an acquiescing nod of her head toward the earl's sisters, said, "It will be a pleasure to provide the necessary garments for Lord Norwood's bride-to-be." Her words were heavily accented, unlike her shop assistant's nearly flawless English. "With her figure, the earl will find her most *délicieuse* and *charmante* in the items we make for her. Angelique is writing up the bill of sale now. Once you've approved the order we can take measurements."

Perhaps this was the French way of shopping, but to Charlotte's mind, it seemed to be all backward. One took measurements and chose garments before a bill of sale was written up. A shop existed to serve the customer's needs, after all, not the other way around.

And how could Madame Rochelle know what she needed before Charlotte told her? Besides, there was her budget to consider. A seamstress of Madame Rochelle's caliber could command a high price for her work even if said work would never be seen outside the confines of one's private quarters. Even a few pieces would likely come at a dear price. Charlotte had no intention of presenting her brother with an outrageous bill simply because the audacious modiste expected it.

"But I haven't given you an idea of what I want," Charlotte objected.

Madame's brows quirked ever so slightly. "But, of course, you have. You are shopping for your trousseau, yes?"

Charlotte nodded.

Madame shrugged. "Then that tells me everything I need to know."

Charlotte blinked several times, not sure how to argue her case in the face of the woman's unshakable conceit that she knew best what Charlotte needed, as well as her complete unwillingness to consult Charlotte's wishes, even if she ultimately intended to ignore them. Madame Rochelle's talents might be with a needle, but she had the unmistakable aura of the prima donna about her.

Charlotte looked to the ladies Peyton and Chatworth for support, but they weren't by her side any longer. They now stood near the doorway, engaged in conversation with a newcomer to the shop. Her back was to Charlotte, but her dress and bearing indicated she was a lady of means. So a client of the modiste, not an employee.

"Well, it certainly gives us a starting point," Charlotte said, turning her attention back to Madame Rochelle. "But you can't know *specifically* what I want."

"Mademoiselle, this is my business, my livelihood, my passion, if you will. I guarantee you, I know better than yourself what you want when it comes to garments of an intimate nature." Her lips curled in Gallic disdain. "You English misses are kept wrapped in cotton wool before marriage, and then thrown into the intimacies of the wedding night...the wedding bed...with scant foreknowledge of what to expect. How can you possibly anticipate what you, or perhaps I should say, what your earl might want in terms of your wardrobe?"

Charlotte felt a hot, furious blush sweep across her face. Thanks to her innate curiosity, and the discovery of some rather prurient books in her late father's library, she had a very good idea of the sorts of bedroom activities that went on between men and women. And Madame Rochelle's words brought to mind images of herself and Lord Norwood tangled together in the same manner as some of the illustrations in those books.

"Aaaah." A smug—and rather admiring—smile played around Madame Rochelle's lips. "I see you are not completely unfamiliar with the *affaires de coeur*. The earl must be a man of strong passions."

"I've no knowledge of his passions, nor he of mine," Charlotte said, thinking if it were possible for a body to spontaneously combust, she'd be a pillar of fire right now. The only saving grace was that Lord Norwood's sisters were still engrossed in conversation with the newcomer, and so were oblivious to her embarrassment.

The modiste gave her a doubtful look, then shrugged. "If that's the case, then more than ever I must insist that you trust my judgment in this."

"But you don't even know what colors I prefer, or what styles," Charlotte said, unwilling to concede defeat yet.

"Would you dictate to a painter the colors he must choose for his painting? As for style, that is determined by your figure, your carriage"—Madame Rochelle waved her hands about as she searched for the right word—"by your essence. There is no *choice* to it."

This attitude was a far cry from Mrs. Wickersley's more collaborative approach. At least, she listened to Charlotte's ideas, even if, after discussion, they settled on something different.

"I have a list," Charlotte continued doggedly, determined to prevail in the types of garments purchased, even if she had to allow the modiste latitude in the details of style. She reached into her reticule and pulled out a folded paper. "These are the only things I require. I know it's not a great many items, but I suspect my clothing budget won't cover much else." She glanced toward the dressmaker's dummies displaying night-gowns that were composed of as much lace as they were fabric. "Furthermore, I must insist that the nightwear be substantial enough to provide some warmth for sleeping."

She handed her list to Madame Rochelle, who had scrunched her face into an expression of artistic outrage. "Mademoiselle, you miss the point. My creations aren't made with sleeping in mind, therefore considerations of warmth are irrelevant."

"Surely they can serve a dual purpose," Charlotte said firmly.

"*Mais non*, mademoiselle. Let me suggest you add an extra blanket to the bed. Or better yet, curl up in the arms of your lover."

Unfortunately, this statement caught the attention of the others, who had drifted closer at some point during the conversation with the maddening Frenchwoman. The earl's sisters wore similar expressions of wide-eyed surprise, while the other lady, whom Charlotte now saw was Lady Serena, looked amused and—somewhat unexpectedly—approving.

"I don't have a lover," Charlotte declared, not wishing for anyone to get the wrong idea, and not entirely certain whether or not they'd heard any of what had preceded this talk of a lover.

An awkward beat of silence followed before it was broken by Lady Serena. "Goodness, don't let us interrupt such a deliciously improper conversation," she said, beaming a bright smile at Charlotte. "How delightful that our paths cross again,

Miss Hurst. Rest assured, I would never stand in judgment if you *did* have a lover, since I've long decried the societal double standards that demand virginity in unmarried females while nothing of the sort is expected from the male sex." She turned to the modiste. "We English and our peculiar traditions, eh, Madame?"

Madame Rochelle bestowed the lady with a look of genuine welcome. "As you say, Lady Serena. I have long found the English peculiar."

Lady Serena laughed good-naturedly. "Some would say the same of the French, but we won't debate the eccentricities of our nationalities today."

"Before we leave the subject entirely, I'd still like to make it clear there is *nothing* improper about my relationship with Lord Norwood," Charlotte replied.

Lady Serena's eyes twinkled merrily at Charlotte. "Never fear. I know William too well to think there was."

"Yes, but I'm not sure about the rest of London," Charlotte said, with a rueful smile, thinking of Lady Bohite and her ilk.

"If there's one rule I live by, it's don't let the opinions of others bother you. Gossip and scandal are the meat and marrow of London society. And there are always those who will draw the worst conclusions, but even among those who don't, the suddenness of your engagement has the town buzzing. You and William are the current *on dit*."

"My brother didn't manage this very well, I grant you," Lady Peyton said. "But what man lets his head rule his heart? Once he settled on Charlotte, he saw no reason to wait simply to accustom people to his choice."

"And I for one applaud his impetuosity *and* his choice of fiancée." Lady Serena gestured to Charlotte's hand. "May I take a look at your ring? It is your betrothal ring, isn't it?"

"Yes," Charlotte said, feeling self-conscious as she held out her hand for Lady Serena to get a better look at it.

"Very nice." Lady Serena nodded approvingly. "Is it a piece with sentimental value?"

"It belonged to his grandmother," Charlotte said, keeping her answer deliberately vague. Since it was a family ring, she presumed it held sentimental value, but the earl's note hadn't explicitly communicated this to her. She glanced toward Lydia and Elizabeth. "I hope your family doesn't mind if I wear it." She stopped abruptly, fortunately catching herself before she voiced the rest of her thought aloud. It would have been hard to explain to Lady Serena why she hoped the family wouldn't mind if she wore it *for a little while*.

"Mind?" said Lydia, almost indignantly. "Why we're delighted Will chose it for you."

"It does suit you," Lady Peyton added.

Madame Rochelle, who had been standing silently in their midst while the conversation swirled around her, spoke abruptly. "I'm sorry to interrupt, but I must see if Angelique is done writing up the bill of sale. My next appointment will be here in thirty minutes, and my assistant still needs to take the measurements. While she's doing that, you and I, Lady Serena, will discuss our business." The modiste looked toward Charlotte with an ironic smile. "I'll have Angelique add a few"—she glanced down at the list Charlotte had given her—"flannel nightgowns, mademoiselle. But with the proviso that you tell your Lord Norwood that I objected most strenuously to them."

"I certainly will," Charlotte agreed, shocked at this concession by the modiste but happy to comply with her condition. It was a moot point anyway, since the topic would never come up in the first place.

Madame Rochelle departed through a curtained doorway that Charlotte supposed led back to the working areas of the dress shop.

Lady Serena raised an amused brow. "She must like you, Miss Hurst. I can only imagine how it must grieve her artistic soul to make something so mundane as flannel nightgowns. I don't think she would agree to make them for many of her customers."

"I am all astonishment," Charlotte said. "Particularly, since thus far, the capitulation has been one-sided."

"She can be a force to be reckoned with," Elizabeth observed.

"And then some," Charlotte replied. It was on the tip of her tongue to ask Lady Serena what business brought her to Madame Rochelle's, but the modiste returned and handed the bill of sale to Lady Peyton, who looked briefly at it. "Yes, that looks about right."

"I beg your pardon," Charlotte said. "But you've given that to the wrong party. Lady Peyton isn't responsible for the bill."

Madame Rochelle sent a questioning glance in Lady Peyton's direction.

"I insist on handling the expense," Charlotte said firmly.

"No, dear Charlotte." Lord Norwood's eldest sister shook her head. "Lydia and I will take care of this. It's our gift, to welcome you to the family."

Before Charlotte could mount a protest, Lydia said, "You must allow us to do this to celebrate our new sister."

A small lump formed in Charlotte's throat at the genuine affection she saw in Lydia's eyes. She'd always wished for a sister, and she couldn't imagine a finer one to gain than the sweet Lady Chatworth. Even the more reserved Lady Peyton— no, Elizabeth, she corrected herself—even Elizabeth would make a wonderful (albeit more exasperating) sister.

"That is much too kind … and generous," she began, stopping when her voice cracked on the last word. She swallowed past the lump in her throat and tried again. "Really, I couldn't."

Accepting such a gift would not be a wise move. She needed to keep her distance, to keep herself firmly rooted in the reality that she wasn't joining this family. It was all playacting, a performance, nothing more.

"If it will assuage your conscience, I promise you Peyton won't bat an eye at the total. It's a great deal less than I usually spend when shopping for clothes." Elizabeth folded the bill and tucked it into her reticule. "Now let's allow Madame to take your measurements."

"Angelique, Gabrielle," the modiste called. The two girls reappeared and stood at attention on either side of their employer. "Well, mademoiselle? Shall we proceed?" the modiste asked, giving Charlotte the last word on the matter.

Charlotte hesitated, conflicted. Refusing the gift was, in a way, tantamount to refusing their friendship, and she was loath to do that. But accepting would be crossing a line she wasn't sure should be crossed. She felt the eyes of every person in the room on her, awaiting her decision.

"There *will* be some flannel nightgowns?" she said at last, forcing a smile to her lips to cover her precarious emotions.

"*Oui*," said the modiste with a faint smile. She signaled to Gabrielle, who opened the box. Madame selected a tape measure and said, "Angelique will take you back to our changing area and help you undress. You must strip to your shift."

Angelique led Charlotte to a curtained-off corner of the room, where the modiste's assistant busied herself with the fastenings at the back of Charlotte's gown. The curtain protected Charlotte's modesty but didn't prevent her from hearing the conversation taking place.

"How is Mrs. Bright working out for you?" Lady Serena said. "Are you satisfied with her workmanship?"

"Mrs. Bright is a most welcome addition," the modiste replied. "Her workmanship is par excellence; she's industrious and reliable. I could take more like her, if you can find others so skilled with their needle."

Charlotte listened with interest, feeling like an eavesdropper, even though she wasn't eavesdropping exactly. After all, it wasn't a secret she was behind the curtain.

"I'm so happy the placement is satisfactory, and that you're interested in employing more of these women," Lady Serena said. "I brought some embroidery samples for you to evaluate."

Angelique began to undo the lacing of her stays. Charlotte could hear low murmurs of approval, and then Lady Peyton said, "This one is exceptionally fine." Charlotte presumed they were passing the embroidery samples around for all to see.

"Yes," Madame Rochelle agreed. "She is an artist with her needle, that one. These others are quite well done also. I'd be willing to give all these ladies positions. How soon can they start?"

"In a fortnight. Possibly sooner, depending on how well some last-minute details fall into place," Lady Serena said. "All currently reside outside the city, but if you're willing to employ them, we'll move them into new lodgings close to here."

"It is a good deed, you do, Lady Serena, giving these women a chance at an honest living."

"Well, someone has to," Lady Serena replied dryly, "since our government hasn't seen fit to address the problem by supplying them with a widow's stipend. I appreciate your willingness to employ them and not take advantage of their desperation."

"I pay fair wages for a fair day's work," Madame Rochelle said. "I will not profit off of another's misery."

"If only everyone shared your attitude," Lady Serena said.

"I know what these women face. My family fled the terror in France and came to England. Life became very difficult for us after my father's death. We nearly starved before a kind innkeeper gave my *maman* employment. So I'm glad to do something similar for others."

"I'll be in touch once we're able to bring these women to London and get them settled. And, ladies, thank you for your support of our subscription ball."

Charlotte surmised this last was directed to the earl's sisters. Lady Serena must have sold them tickets when they'd been talking together while Charlotte had been wrangling with Madame Rochelle.

To Charlotte's relief Angelique finally began taking her measurements. Listening behind the curtain had its drawbacks, namely that it made participating in the conversation awkward.

"Miss Hurst," Lady Serena continued. "So nice to see you again. As I promised last night, we shall have a nice coze soon and get better acquainted."

Despite her current state of undress, Charlotte thrust her head out from between the curtains. "Yes, we must. I very much want to hear more about your efforts on behalf of the war widows."

Lady Serena smiled and inclined her head. "Au revoir to you all then."

Madame Rochelle waved a hand indicating Charlotte should step out from the sheltering curtain. She hesitated, her innate modesty making her uncomfortable with stepping out before Lord Norwood's sisters while wearing only a shift.

Lydia must have sensed the reason for her reluctance because she said, "We'll wait for you in the anteroom." The sisters departed, leaving Charlotte alone with the modiste and her assistants, and in quick order she was measured, and then Madame had a selection of fabrics draped across Charlotte's shoulders. The modiste stood and studied the effect of each of these with pursed lips and a thoughtful look. And no explanation.

Charlotte assumed it was to ascertain how the various colors looked on her, but she wasn't sure. It wasn't as if she'd ordered gowns, which naturally would have a varied palette. Undergarments usually came in shades of white and cream, although the trimmings might incorporate different colors. At any rate, Charlotte didn't question the modiste, having by this point decided to take the easiest course and let the Frenchwoman go about her business unimpeded. So it was with no small relief that she rejoined the earl's sisters.

Lady Peyton gave her an understanding look and said, "I think we could all do with some tea."

Chapter Nine

*I*n short order, Lady Peyton's coachman whisked them to her residence on Grosvenor Square. As soon as the carriage came to a stop, a footman in forest-green livery hurried over to open the door and help them down. Charlotte took a brief look at the brick exterior faced with tall white columns spaced between the front windows before she followed the earl's sisters up a set of marble steps.

The butler met them in the spacious entryway and took their hats and gloves. "Shall I have tea sent in, my lady?" he inquired.

"Please do, Ridley," Elizabeth replied. She led the way across the black-and-white parquet flooring of the foyer to a door that opened into a sunny sitting room. The color scheme suited Lady Peyton: The pale yellow walls echoed the tint of that lady's fair hair while the furniture, upholstered in blue and green florals, provided a pleasing counterpoint. The effect was feminine without being cloying. She waved Charlotte toward a small sofa, while she and Lydia settled into matching armchairs.

As they waited for the tea to arrive the conversation turned to their recent shopping trip.

"It was an excellent start," Lydia said. "Except for stockings, Charlotte is set as far as lingerie goes. We should order her new gowns next, and then tackle the question of millinery and shoes. I was thinking—"

Start? Good heavens, she'd assumed they were finished, but apparently in the minds of the earl's sisters they'd barely begun. "Oh, no, no, *no.* What we ordered at Madame Rochelle's should be enough to satisfy the pretense of preparing a trousseau. It will have to be, because I've no intention of purchasing more items I don't need. My present wardrobe is sufficient to see me through to the end of the betrothal." Lydia's expression dimmed at Charlotte's mention of ending the betrothal.

"I understand your reluctance to incur unnecessary expenditures," Elizabeth said. "However, there is the matter of a ball to celebrate your engagement. You'll want to order a special gown for that, at least."

"I'm afraid I consider a ball as unnecessary as an expanded wardrobe," Charlotte said, feeling that things were spiraling out of control and not confident she could stop it. Nonetheless she had to try. "Please view this from my perspective. I agreed to an engagement with your brother only as a means to an end, and making all this fuss…" Charlotte raised her hands in a gesture of helplessness. "Don't you agree that, under those circumstances, acquiring a wardrobe I don't need, or hosting a ball to celebrate an engagement that isn't really an engagement, is taking things too far?"

Elizabeth shook her head. "The ball isn't really negotiable.

We must act as if your betrothal is real, and that means we must have a ball to celebrate it."

"But in the time it takes to plan and finalize the arrangements and send invitations, the betrothal may well be over, which would be awkward to say the least," Charlotte argued.

"That is something to consider." Elizabeth tapped one elegant finger rapidly on the arm of her chair as she thought about this. "I think the easiest solution is for you and William to remain betrothed until after the ball, even if it could be ended earlier."

"No!" Charlotte blurted out the single word with more force than she intended. "No," she repeated, softening her tone in response to the frowning expressions of concern worn by both of Lord Norwood's sisters. "Dragging out the betrothal isn't an option. It's best to be done with this business as quickly as possible so your brother and I can resume our normal lives."

"We simply won't refer to it as an engagement ball and we won't characterize it as one on the invitations," Lydia said, leaning forward excitedly. "Everyone will assume that's why you're giving it, Elizabeth, but it's a way to save face if the betrothal ends before the ball takes place."

"That's rather deviously brilliant," Elizabeth praised her sister. "I like it."

Lydia turned to Charlotte with an apologetic smile. "I know you aren't keen for Elizabeth to hold this ball, but it's the expected thing to do. People will think it odd if we don't mark the occasion with a grand to-do of some sort. You do understand that, don't you?"

Before Charlotte could reply, a maid entered bearing the tea tray, and fast on her heels were Lord Peyton and Lord Chatworth, which effectively put an end to the discussion. Charlotte supposed the interruption hardly mattered, since it was unlikely she would have prevailed anyway. The maid set the heavily laden tray on the low table in front of the sofa on which Charlotte was seated.

"Just in time for the food," Elizabeth said, giving her husband an arch look.

"As is my usual habit," Lord Peyton agreed with a cheeky grin. "I'm glad to see you requested a substantial repast." He plucked a carved wooden chair from its spot along the wall and placed it next to his wife's armchair. Lord Chatworth walked over to Lydia and kissed the top of her head, then stood next to her, one hand resting fondly on her shoulder.

"Ridley deserves the credit. He ordered the tea, not I." Lady Peyton busied herself serving the cups of tea and passing around plates of food. The conversation lulled as the gentlemen busily devoured several of the tea sandwiches while the ladies showed a preference for the sweeter items.

Charlotte nibbled on a lemon biscuit as she studied the two couples. Lord Chatworth hovered beside his wife, solicitously refreshing her plate when she expressed a desire for some more of the sugared fruits. She found it touching that he was so obviously enthralled by his wife, eager to please her slightest whim. The Peytons, well past the honeymoon stage in their marriage, seemed amused by it.

Charlotte idly wondered what sort of husband the earl would make. She couldn't picture him as slavishly devoted as Lord Chatworth. He didn't strike her as the type to wear his heart on his sleeve, though she could imagine him covertly bestowing warm, speaking glances on the object of his devotion. Or bringing a blush to her cheeks as he whispered teasingly improper suggestions in her ear.

Caught up in these speculations, she was startled when Lord Norwood unexpectedly appeared in the doorway. So startled that she choked on a bite of biscuit and coughed out a fine dusting of biscuit crumbs onto the front of her bodice. Honestly, had she been trying to make an inelegant spectacle of herself, she couldn't have done a much better job. But then, to her continued chagrin, she couldn't stop coughing as some biscuit crumbs still tickled her throat and windpipe. The Peytons and Chatworths watched her with a mixture of uncertainty and concern.

Lovely, Charlotte. Just lovely. She held up a hand to indicate she was fine, but her continued coughing seemed to contradict her message.

To his credit, Lord Norwood crossed the room with commendable haste. He handed her the teacup sitting on the table beside her.

"Take a drink," he said. "It will help." His mouth twitched slightly. "And if it doesn't, I can slap you on the back a few times if necessary."

She shot him a *don't-even-think-about-trying-that* look, and then did as he suggested, taking several soothing sips of tea. "Thank you," she said, suddenly feeling flustered. He often had that effect on her, even when she wasn't making a spectacle of herself.

William might have teased her a bit more, but since they had an audience, he refrained. "Always at your service," he murmured, coming around to settle himself beside her on the sofa.

"So you were able to come," Libby said. "I wasn't sure you would."

"I promised to try, and here I am."

From Miss Hurst's questioning glance, he surmised Libby hadn't mentioned the possibility of his joining them. No wonder she'd looked faintly shocked at his arrival.

"Was the shopping successful?" he asked.

"I suppose so," Miss Hurst said, setting her cup down.

"You don't know?" he asked. He leaned forward to accept a cup of tea from Libby.

"Well, I didn't actually see the written order. Your sister Elizabeth immediately took charge of it." She gave him a meaningful look.

"Ah," he said. "Don't let her bossiness bother you. That's just Libby treating you like family."

Lord Peyton let out a bark of laughter, which earned him a withering look from his wife.

Libby turned to William. "Would you like a sandwich or some biscuits?"

"No, thank you. The tea will be sufficient." He crossed one leg over the other, then balanced the cup and saucer on his thigh.

"Made any headway in discovering who was behind that betrothal announcement?" Lord Peyton asked.

Miss Hurst looked surprised by his brother-in-law's question.

"Not really. Whoever did it made an effort to cover their tracks. I'm almost positive it's a political rival. Is it absolutely critical I know which one?" He shrugged. "I'd like to know who's behind it, but it's not as if I'd demand a dawn meeting on the green even if I discovered the culprit's identity."

"Naturally not," Peyton replied. "But if I were you, I'd still want to know. It's no small thing that this mischief led to you and Miss Hurst becoming engaged, even if it is just until this all blows over. Although, as a man of honor, there really wasn't any other course open to you."

"Fortunately for me, Miss Hurst has turned out to be the most delightful of fiancées. And the truth is, she's protecting my interests just as much as I'm protecting hers."

Her expression turned skeptical, and he suspected she wanted to dispute these statements, though she didn't. Instead she said, "I hope you aren't just letting the matter drop. I don't like the idea of an unknown enemy lurking in the background."

"I've hired an investigator, a former Bow Street Runner, to do some digging, but so far he's turned up nothing. Admittedly, his efforts are hampered by our need for the strictest discretion. He doesn't know about the false betrothal announcement, only that I suspect a political rival is trying to undermine me in some way."

"Oh," she said doubtfully. "That doesn't sound very promising for producing results."

"Perhaps not, but the fewer who know the truth about our betrothal, the better. For now, we'll wait and see what he can find out. Although I can tell from that frown forming on your brow this doesn't meet with your approval as a plan of action."

"Because 'wait and see' seems less of a plan of action and more a plan of giving up."

He laughed at that. "Would you be happier with it if we scheduled a driving lesson to break up the tedium of sitting and waiting?"

"I would, though you could double my happiness by making it two lessons," she suggested, giving him a saucy smile.

"Two, then." William shook his head in mock resignation. "Thank heavens I don't have to meet you across the negotiating table." He found it hard to deny her anything when those blue eyes of hers softened and lost some of that aloofness she was so fond of cloaking herself in.

"We'll leave the two of you to work out the details of your driving plans," Libby said briskly, coming to her feet. She turned to Peyton, who was polishing off the last of the sandwiches. "Robert, come along. I need to consult with you on some household matters."

"Yes, dear." Peyton shot William a look as if to say *Be warned. This is what marriage does to a man.*

They'd barely exited the room before Lydia said, "I hope you don't mind, but James and I should be going. We're dining with his mother and she insists on keeping country hours even when she's in town."

"I should be getting along as well," Miss Hurst said, coming to her feet.

"Oh, no." Lydia waved a hand indicating Miss Hurst should re-take her seat. "William can keep you company for a bit. I'm sure Elizabeth will be back shortly. No need for you to rush off yet."

"Well, I'm not sure—" Miss Hurst began. He could tell her desire to wait politely for Libby's return was at war with her suspicions about his sisters' true motives.

"No." Lydia again gestured for Miss Hurst to sit back down. "You and Will need to...to discuss your plans for the up-coming lessons," she said, her words tumbling out in a rush. And before Miss Hurst could protest further, she and Chatworth departed.

Miss Hurst sank back onto the sofa. She stared at the empty doorway a few seconds before turning to William with a perplexed look. "Am I being overly suspicious, or did they just leave us alone together on purpose?"

"From the way they practically bolted from the room, I'd say it was definitely on purpose."

She frowned at that. "Well, it's rather odd, don't you think?"

He leaned forward and deposited his empty cup on the tea tray. "No, I don't find it odd. A little unexpected, but given that it's my sisters, I don't find it odd at all." Her mouth pressed into an unhappy line, and though she didn't say anything, he had the distinct feeling she wanted him to do something about his sisters' obvious attempt at matchmaking.

"There's no point in telling them not to meddle, because they'll do it anyway," he said.

"Well, no matter their motivation, you needn't feel obligated to keep me company," she said.

"I don't feel it's an obligation." He gave her a lazy smile. "A challenge maybe, since you seem eager to be rid of me, but not an obligation."

"I didn't mean to give you the impression I don't welcome your company. Merely giving you an out if you didn't wish to go along with your sisters' scheming." She smoothed the fabric of her skirt, then folded her hands in her lap. "You know, in case you had something else you needed to attend to."

"Very thoughtful of you." He reached for a biscuit. "But I'm at loose ends for the next few hours. Which means I'm all yours for the moment." He grinned and popped the shortbread into his mouth.

"Lucky me." She smiled as she said it though.

"Since we have a moment of privacy..." He looked at her hands primly clasped in her lap. "I hope you liked the ring I sent."

"I...yes. It's very lovely." She held out her hand so he could see the ring on her finger. "It's much finer than anything I own, which makes me nervous to have it in my possession. Be assured that I'll do my best to keep it safe until I return it to you."

"I'm not worried about that," he said. "I just hoped you liked it well enough that you wouldn't mind wearing it." She drew in a sharp breath as he took her slim hand in his, holding it lightly, pretending to study the ring, but really admiring her slender, tapered fingers, enjoying the warm feel of her skin against his. "I like the way it looks on your hand." He met her gaze. "Almost like it belongs there."

He wasn't sure why he had added that last part, except he was curious to see how she reacted to the idea. Her response was much as he expected.

Her eyes turned wary and with a shaky laugh, she pulled her hand away. "It would look good on anyone. It's a beautiful piece of jewelry."

"Not on anyone," he murmured. "Not in my opinion."

Her lips parted and for a moment he saw the same yearning in her eyes he'd seen on their carriage ride when he'd nearly given in to the impulse to kiss her. He fought a similar urge now, but he hesitated to act on it, caught between the dictates of prudence and desire.

The sound of children's voices drifted in from the hallway, interrupting the moment and effectively ending the opportunity to kiss her. Miss Hurst turned toward the doorway.

"Libby's children must be returning from an outing," William said. They couldn't see them yet from their vantage point, but the increasing volume of the young voices indicated they were coming nearer.

"I didn't realize your sister had children," she responded. "Although if I'd thought about it, it seems logical. After all, she's older than you, and I presume has been married to Lord Peyton for a while."

"For eight years," he told her. "She has three rambunctious boys."

He'd no sooner finished saying this when cries of "Uncle William, Uncle William, you've come to visit" filled the sitting room as two of his three nephews surged in and ran up to him like a couple of eager puppies. A harried nursemaid followed them, issuing an apology for their behavior. She was accompanied by his youngest nephew, a sturdy toddler who had a thumb firmly planted in his mouth.

"Peter, Henry," William said sternly. "There's no need to act like ruffians. Mind your manners now, and bid Miss Hurst a 'good afternoon.'"

"Sorry, Uncle William," Peter said. He and Henry turned contrite gazes toward Miss Hurst and said in unison, "Good afternoon, Miss Hurst."

"Good afternoon," she replied. She smiled as she took in their disheveled appearance. Grimy streaks marked their clothes, their legs, and their faces. "From the quantity of dirt you've accumulated, I'd say you've had a fun outing."

They nodded enthusiastically. "We threw rocks in the pond," said Peter, as if imparting a fascinating fact.

"And sailed our boat in it," Henry said. He leaned forward and rested a grubby hand on her knee. "I almost fell in," he added, half whispering this confidence to her.

"Really." She widened her eyes and spoke in a voice meant to convey the appropriate amount of awe and reverence that the boy seemed to expect from sharing this revelation. "You *have* had an adventurous afternoon."

Their heads bobbed in agreement, and he could see that they were charmed by her.

His youngest nephew came to stand next to her, staring at her with large solemn blue eyes. He pulled the thumb out of his mouth. "Up, pwease," he said.

"You needn't—" William began, because the toddler was as grubby as his brothers. She ignored him and lifted the little boy onto her lap.

"I don't mind," she said. "I like children." She turned back to the boys. "Now which one of you is Peter and which is Henry?"

"I'm Peter," the elder boy informed her. "And he's Henry," he added, pointing to his middle brother.

"What's your name?" she asked, addressing the chubby youngster perched on her lap.

He blinked at her a moment, then without extracting the thumb he'd reinserted in his mouth said something that sounded like "Wiwa."

Not surprisingly, Miss Hurst glanced toward William with a confused expression. "I'm afraid you'll have to translate for me."

"William," he supplied. "His name is William."

"Your little namesake," she murmured.

He rather envied his namesake just then, for young William had snuggled against her cozily, and rested his head on her shoulder.

"Uncle William, won't you please give us a horsie ride?" asked Henry. "Pleeease," he wheedled, leaning toward William with a wide-eyed hopeful look.

William let out an exaggerated sigh and grimaced. "Haven't you outgrown my horsie rides yet? You have your own ponies to ride now."

"No!" "No, sir!" The denials were swift and emphatic.

"Here goes the last shred of my dignity," William said wryly. "Provided you're not too missish to view me in only a shirt and waistcoat."

"I think I can withstand the sight of you so casually dressed," she said, looking amused at this turn of events. "I'd say it's more a question of whether your pride can absorb the blow."

"We're about to find out." He stood and tugged at the sleeve of his jacket. It proved stubborn, a result of the fashionable styling that required the garment fit him like a second skin. "Do you mind?" He stuck out an arm toward her.

"Perhaps I should ring for help," Miss Hurst said, blinking

up at him innocently. "I'm not sure I'm up to the challenge of divesting you of Weston's immaculate tailoring."

He gave her a sardonic look because she'd guessed correctly. He did indeed get his jackets from London's premier tailor. "Just give my sleeve a brisk tug, will you? One good pull to get it started and I can manage the rest."

"I hope so," she murmured. She hesitated, then reached for his cuff with both hands, little William sitting placidly between her outstretched arms. She gave a firm pull on the garment and it shifted slightly. His cuff now rested halfway along his hand, and the effect was almost as if she cradled his hand between hers. She frowned and gave it another tug, and this one freed enough of his arm so that he was able to shrug it out of that sleeve. After that, it was an easy matter of loosening the jacket's grip on his other shoulder so he could slide it off. He draped the garment over the sofa back and turned to his nephews.

"Coin flip to see who goes first?" he asked, reaching into his waistcoat pocket and drawing forth a guinea. The boys nodded. "Call it, Peter," he said, flipping the coin high in the air.

"Tails," Peter replied.

They all watched as the coin arced through the air. He deftly caught it, and slapped it on the back of his hand, displaying it to them all. Even little William leaned forward to take a look. "Heads," William called out. "Come on, Henry. You go first." William went to his knees, then crouched low on all fours, hoping he didn't look like too great a fool to Miss Hurst.

His nephew clambered onto his back and clutched his cravat. "Giddyap, Uncle William."

William shot a quick glance at Miss Hurst, who was smiling at the spectacle of him playing horse for the boys, but—and this heartened him—it was a friendly smile, not a derisive one. He proceeded to caper about the room on all fours, bucking and weaving and jouncing young Henry, who laughed and squealed with merry delight. Peter sat beside Miss Hurst on the couch, laughing as he shared in the fun.

When he finally arrived back at the sofa, William was breathing heavily from his exertions. He was sure his cravat was worse for wear, he suspected his cheeks were reddened, and his hair was falling over his forehead in a manner he knew would displease his valet.

He lifted his hands from the floor and balanced on his knees, then reached for Henry's shoulders, and flipped the boy over his head and onto the sofa by Peter. "Next," he said, dropping back to all fours.

Peter climbed onto William's back and they were off, "galloping" and bucking around the room, until, breathless and sweaty, William delivered him back to their starting point. As he'd done with Henry, he flipped his nephew over his back and onto the sofa. He came to his feet, flexed his spine a couple of times, and reached for his jacket. "Looks like I can skip my session at Gentleman Jackson's this week," he joked, referring to the popular London boxing establishment visited by many men of the peerage.

"Horsie, pwease," young William said, reaching his arms up to him.

He studied the boy a moment, then said, "Why not? As long as Miss Hurst is willing to help hold you on." He turned to her. "Do you mind?"

Little William turned and patted her cheek with a chubby hand. "Pwease," he coaxed.

"How can I resist such a sweet request?" she said, nodding her acquiescence.

Once again William went down on all fours. He looked over his shoulder at her. "I'm ready for you to lift him on."

She stood and set the boy in place, gently holding her hands under the boy's arms to keep him from falling during the ride. They circled the sitting room at a relatively sedate pace, but it was enough to make the little boy gurgle with delight.

William was keenly aware of the way her legs brushed against his ribs as they made their way around the room, of the scent of roses that filled his nostrils with her every step, of the tantalizing glimpses of trim ankles he had as she walked beside him. It was easy to imagine that this could be the two of them with a child of their own.

He wondered, *did the same thought occur to her?*

"Oh, for heaven's sake!" Libby's voice came from the doorway. "What are you children doing in here?"

The young nurse who'd been watching them from a chair by the door jumped up. "Oh, my lady, I apologize, but the children ran in before I could stop them and—"

Lady Peyton cut her off. "Leave aside the explanations for now, Mary. Please take the boys to see their father in his study, and after that, see that they get a good wash before they eat."

Mary curtsied and went to do her mistress's bidding. Miss Hurst lifted young William off his back and passed him to the girl's waiting arms. Peter and Henry offered quick farewells, then followed Mary from the room.

"I'll be back shortly," Lady Peyton said in a distracted voice, and then she too swept out of the room in a rush.

He and Miss Hurst both stood where they were, eyeing the nearly closed door.

"It seems Libby does expect me to get on with the task of courting," William said thoughtfully.

"Let's not jump to conclusions," Miss Hurst said. "Maybe it was an unconscious action on her part to nearly close the door."

He shook his head. "My sister is nothing if not deliberate, and she's perfectly aware that strictly proper behavior requires that door to be wide open, since there is no one here to perform the duty of chaperone."

"But your sisters know the truth. It doesn't make sense that they would encourage a match between us."

"I don't know about that. I can tell they like you. I know they think I've evaded parson's mousetrap far too long." He gave a nonchalant shrug. "I suppose they consider that reason enough. They must, since they're blatantly pushing us toward one another."

She frowned. "The idea is preposterous."

"Is it?" He took a few deliberate steps in her direction.

"Y-yes." She raised her chin a notch. "Absolutely it is. How can you not see that?"

He moved closer still until there was less than a foot separating them. "I admit the idea would have seemed far-fetched just three days ago when we were glaring at each other over your dining table, but we've gotten along rather well since then, don't you think?"

"That's only because this charade would be impossible to carry off if we didn't make an attempt to be cordial to each other. Don't make the mistake of reading more into it than that."

"And here I thought I was growing on you," he teased. "I'll have to try harder." Her cheeks pinkened becomingly, but the wariness returned to her eyes.

"That would be wasted effort," she protested. "We're ill-suited for each other."

"My sisters evidently don't think so."

She gave a huff of impatience. "Your sisters don't know me well enough to make that judgment."

"All right. Then you enlighten me. Why are we so ill-suited?"

"Because I wouldn't be the sort of wife you're looking for."

"Ahh." He nodded and clasped his hands behind his back. "And pray tell, what sort of wife do I want?"

"Someone like you."

His brows shot up. "I can't even begin to guess what you mean by that. You'll have to be more specific."

She let out a frustrated exhale. "Someone from a prominent family like yours, who's adept at playing the social games the Beau Monde is so fond of playing. Someone who wouldn't rather stay at home curled up with a book, who would make a good political hostess, who could further your political ambitions and not hinder them. Someone who would look good on your arm while you attend the endless parade of social events. Someone more like Lady Jane."

"Lady Jane wouldn't have picked up a grubby little boy and cuddled him on her lap." The words came out more harshly than he intended, but it aggravated him that she couldn't—or wouldn't—grasp that he didn't want someone merely because she had an attractive face or an enviable social status. "Do you really think I'm that shallow?"

She had the grace to look as if she regretted her words. "I didn't mean it quite the way it sounded."

"Let's put aside any notion that Lady Jane, or someone like her, is a rival to you. I've fixed my interest on no particular lady to date. But when I do, I promise you she won't just be a pretty ornament on my arm."

"I'm sorry. It was wrong of me to suggest you would choose a girl only because she was beautiful, but you do have to admit that would be true of many men."

"But not true of me. It might interest you to know, that like you, I place more value on a person's character than on looks or a family name." They stared at each other through a long beat of silence, before he reached out, placed one finger under her chin, and gently tilted her face up. "Besides, you underestimate your charms, Miss Hurst." His gaze took a leisurely perusal of her face before settling on her mouth. "I find you very attractive. Very attractive indeed." Slowly, he bent his head closer, giving her the chance to draw away if she chose to.

She didn't.

So he leaned in closer and closer until his lips touched hers, tentatively at first, then exploring with a more determined purpose. His hands came up to cradle her cheeks as he deepened the kiss, coaxing and teasing, and at last tasting as her lips parted beneath his. Her mouth tasted like tea and lemon, and felt like heated satin. She raised herself up on tiptoe, and wrapped her arms around his neck as she kissed him back. Her enthusiastic participation prompted him to lower his hands, sliding them around to the small of her back, drawing her flush against him.

She felt so good in his arms, so right. The way she fitted against him, the way she met him kiss for kiss, not shyly, and yet not boldly either. Each of them equally taking and giving, exploring and discovering, sliding toward a delicious oblivion of desire.

He was vaguely aware that his hands had slipped down to cup her sweetly curved backside, and that she offered no protest he'd done so, and then his ability for rational thought faded away as the passion of the moment overtook him. Overtook them both as notions of propriety were cast aside.

Until a voice from the entry hall brought them back to their senses.

"Ridley, see that the carriage is brought around," Libby instructed the butler.

They both stiffened guiltily, and Miss Hurst moved back as

far as his embrace allowed, which wasn't far at all, since she was still pressed tightly against him, chest to thigh.

"*Now* she comes back," William muttered, his arms falling away. He stepped back, ran a hand through his hair as he eyed her with a rueful expression.

Miss Hurst's hands moved to her hair, checking it for signs of disarray, adjusting a few hairpins.

"Don't worry. Your hair looks fine," William assured her before his sister re-entered the sitting room. Now her lips . . . they were another matter altogether. They had the telltale signs of having just been thoroughly kissed.

"Charlotte, I called for the carriage. William can see you home," Libby said brightly. Her gaze sharpened as she took in Miss Hurst's appearance, but she only said, "One of the maids can serve as a chaperone."

A guilty flush stained Miss Hurst's cheeks. "Thank you, but that's not necessary. I'm sure your brother has more pressing matters to attend to. I can certainly ride home alone."

"If that's what you wish," Libby said, glancing uncertainly at William.

"I assure you, Miss Hurst, I am at your service should you wish my company, but I shall accede to your wishes regardless." He wasn't completely surprised that she'd rejected Libby's offer that he see her home. She'd retreated behind that aloof demeanor again.

"It's been a lovely afternoon, but I don't wish to impose any further. Thank you for everything though, your earlier generosity, a delicious repast, the way you've welcomed me into your lives."

Libby reached out and took Miss Hurst's hands in her own. "The pleasure has been all ours."

Ridley returned and informed them the carriage was waiting.

William had to satisfy himself with taking his leave of Miss Hurst with Libby looking on. He wished they'd had a moment of privacy, because the matter of that kiss still hung between them. But evidently his sister deemed she'd given them more than enough privacy already.

Settling things between them would have to wait. Knowing Miss Hurst, she'd probably want to ignore that kiss, to act as if it had never happened.

But it had happened, and William was determined to know what it meant—if it meant anything at all—about their future together.

What had she been thinking?

Charlotte had asked herself that question repeatedly since leaving Lady Peyton's residence. It had filled her thoughts while she dressed for dinner, and then kept her so preoccupied and quiet during the meal that Phillip had inquired—with some concern—if she was feeling all right. She'd blamed a headache and used it as an excuse to retire early to her room, preferring solitude while she grappled with her emotions.

Even now as she finished preparing for bed, her cheeks still grew warm whenever her thoughts returned to that kiss and the memory of the way his lips felt—so warm and right against her own. Of how it felt to be held in his arms, of the way the feel of the firm masculine planes of his body against her had ignited a warmth right down to the very marrow of her being.

Gah! She had to stop dwelling on it. Much easier said than done, and yet after expending all this mental energy she was no closer to understanding her actions than she had been six hours ago. With a heavy sigh, she sat at her dressing table, picked up her silver-backed hairbrush, and drew it through her hair. She studied her reflection in the looking glass, a bit surprised that she didn't look a jot different from how she had this morning. Which was silly, of course. It's not as if being kissed marked you somehow.

And yet she felt different... changed... not the same girl she had been a mere twelve hours earlier. And *that*, she supposed, was the reason for all this self-inspection. She didn't want to let a man affect her like this, to rattle her, to make her question what she knew about herself. On some level, it was precisely what she'd feared before she agreed to go ahead with this betrothal—that she'd become so enmeshed in the pretend she'd forget what was real.

In truth she still wasn't sure why she'd let that kiss happen. And she couldn't chalk it up as merely the natural curiosity of a spinster who'd never been kissed, because it wasn't her first kiss. Not that she had a vast body of experience when it came to kissing, but she'd received a few mistletoe kisses in her youth, and at sixteen, Johnny Martin, the squire's youngest son, had pulled her behind the refreshments' tent during Fair Day and planted his lips on hers in a relatively chaste kiss, though Charlotte had found it thrilling at the time. Poor Johnny later died at the Battle of Waterloo, and she hadn't been kissed since.

Hadn't even come close to being kissed.

So was it any wonder, when Lord Norwood had signaled his unmistakable intent to kiss her, and given her the opportunity to object, that she hadn't?

Not only had she *not* objected, she'd encouraged him. A hot flush swept over her at the memory. For heaven's sake, she'd curled her arms around his neck and snuggled against him with greedy wantonness.

What *had* she been thinking? It would be one thing if they

truly intended to marry, but as she frequently reminded others, theirs was a sham engagement. How had *she* lost sight of that fact?

It might have had something to do with that moment he took her hand in his to inspect the ring on her finger. She'd briefly let herself imagine what it might be like if things between them were real. It almost definitely had something to do with him capering about the sitting room on his hands and knees. It had been impossible not to admire his broad shoulders as he easily gave the boys their rides, and equally hard not to notice the way his trousers stretched tightly over a very finely shaped derriere.

He hadn't been the only one left breathless after those rides. How could she have known that the sight of him clad in shirt-sleeves and waistcoat would send her pulse racing? Or that it would take all her strength of will not to smooth back his dark, unruly hair when it fell over his brow while he entertained his nephews?

Something about seeing him relaxed and disheveled...she'd let down her guard, failed to remember the demarcation between pretense and reality, and had been swept up in a kiss that never should have happened.

All because she'd allowed her thoughts to roam down paths better left untrodden.

She wouldn't—wouldn't, wouldn't, *wouldn't*—make that mistake again.

Chapter Ten

~

The next day shortly before noon, William was working in his study when Stevens poked his head around the door. "I believe you'll wish to see this, sir." His secretary held up a note, and at William's nod, walked over and handed it to him.

"Thank you, Stevens." The secretary went back to the small office he occupied just off William's study. The wax seal bore the imprint *PH*. William had sent a draft of the marriage settlements to Phillip Hurst, advising him to look them over and then contact William when he was ready to discuss them. He'd been waiting for Hurst's reply. He broke the seal and unfolded the single sheet of paper.

Norwood,

Charlotte plans to run errands this afternoon. Could you come over at half-past one? Our business

*shouldn't take long to discuss. I haven't mentioned
this to Charlotte. I think it's best that way.*

Hurst

William smiled at Hurst's reluctance to tell his sister they
were having the marriage settlements formalized, although he
acknowledged the man was likely right. She wouldn't be happy
about it if she knew.

"Stevens," he called.

A few seconds later Stevens appeared in the doorway.
"Yes, sir?"

"Please send a reply to Lord Hurst telling him I'll arrive at
half-past one per his request."

"Very good, sir."

William turned back to the report he was preparing on ways
to fund England's lingering war debts. He'd like to finish it
before heading over to see Hurst.

So it was that an hour and a half later he was mounting the
front steps of the Hurst residence. Hopkins answered his knock,
inscrutably correct as befit his station.

"Good afternoon, Hopkins," William said. "Would you
inform Lord Hurst that I've come to call?"

"If you will follow me, my lord. I've been instructed to take
you straight up." Hopkins led the way upstairs to a modestly
sized room with a pair of tall windows that overlooked the back
gardens. Phillip Hurst sat at his desk, where a maid was just
laying out an afternoon repast of sandwiches and fruit.

"Norwood," he said in greeting, as both servants exited the
room. "Perfect timing. Sit down and help yourself to a bit of
sustenance." He indicated a chair in front of the desk. William
pulled it out and settled himself into it.

"I always seem to catch you when you're eating," William said with a grin.

The other man waved a careless hand through the air before reaching for a sandwich and setting it on a plate in front of him. It wasn't the dainty type of sandwich often served with afternoon tea but a substantial concoction made of thick slices of bread, meat, and cheese. Surprisingly, Miss Hurst's brother maintained a slim build despite an apparently hearty appetite. "This is just a snack to see me through to dinner," Hurst continued. "Going over the estate ledgers makes me hungry. Have some if you like." He pushed the platter of food closer to William's side of the desk.

"Thank you, but I ate before coming here. I'm eager, though, to hear your thoughts about the settlements. I'd like to have them finalized as soon as possible."

Hurst nodded and finished chewing his bite of sandwich. He wiped his fingers on a napkin and drew out a sheaf of papers from a stack sitting on his desk. "That makes two of us. Very good of you to have it drawn up so quickly. I've read through everything, and have no objections to what you've outlined in it. I added a few notations, just minor details. The exact sum of Charlotte's dowry, the amounts of a couple familial bequests she'll come into on her twenty-fifth birthday. Nothing that changes the document substantially."

"Good enough then."

"I'll send this on to my solicitor for him to go over," Hurst said. "Just to make sure everything's right and tight, as it were."

"Naturally. I would expect you to." William nodded approvingly. "If he has any suggestions, I'm amenable to hearing them. At this point, it's really an exercise in form more than anything else, since as things stand, your sister intends to jilt me when it becomes convenient to do so."

"True," the other man agreed. "But Charlotte ought to be protected in case a marriage does occur between the two of you."

"A highly unlikely event, unless you know something I don't?"

Hurst chuckled. "I'm not implying anything. If I were a betting man, I wouldn't put my money on Charlotte becoming Lady Norwood. No offense to you, of course, but she is quite adamant this isn't a real betrothal." He gave William a pointed look. "You and I know it is real, even if temporary in nature. For some reason, Charlotte doesn't want to acknowledge that."

"She has made her views clear," William agreed.

"This is just so we can cross our *t*'s and dot our *i*'s." Hurst indicated the document he held. "Without a serious intent to marry, it's essentially meaningless. Even so, I'm not going to mention we're having it drafted."

William lifted a brow. "You think it's going to upset her that much?"

Hurst scrunched his face into a thoughtful grimace. "Don't get me wrong. My sister is one of those rare females who isn't prone to fits of drama. She's remarkably calm and rational most of the time. Clearheaded, logical, doesn't bend a man's ear with idle chatter." He gave William a frank look. "It's a shame you created such a bad impression the other morning because she'll make some man a fine wife."

"I do regret that mightily," William said.

"You'd have a heap of work to do, to get her to regard you in a favorable light. Every once in a while, she digs in her heels and there's no changing her mind." He shook his head. "Not to belabor the point, but I think we'll all be happier if we don't enlighten her." He emphasized this by waving the document in the air, before setting it to the side.

"All right, I won't bring it up, but neither will I deny its existence if she somehow tumbles onto the fact I had it drawn up."

"Fair enough," her brother said. "It's possible I'm wrong to anticipate her wrath. I mean she *did* agree to wear your betrothal ring, and I wouldn't have expected her to do that."

She kissed me passionately yesterday, and I didn't expect that either.

"She presents a worthy challenge to a man," William said. A challenge he found harder to resist the more time he spent in her company.

Phillip Hurst gave him a sharp look. "I'm not sure of your meaning, but I caution you to take up that challenge only if you *do* mean to marry her. I won't have you trifling with her affections."

"I'd never trifle with a lady's affections," William assured him. True, he *had* kissed Miss Hurst and, in turn, been quite pleasantly kissed by her. Surely it couldn't be considered trifling if they'd both wanted those kisses, and if he was willing to do the right thing in the event those kisses gave rise to a growing affection between them.

Devil take it, affection or not, he'd do the right thing should the lady demand it. When a man kissed a woman he'd better be prepared to face the consequences. Which was why he didn't make a habit of kissing anyone. Certainly not marriageable females, and, for the past few years, not even those with whom gentlemen of his class often dallied. Casual liaisons had never held much appeal to him—probably because of his own parents' example of marital devotion and faithfulness.

"Didn't think you would," Hurst said. "But felt it was my brotherly duty to warn you, in any case."

William crossed one knee over the other. "I admire your

devotion to your sister's interests. With four sisters of my own, I'd personally eviscerate any man who treated them in a less than honorable manner. Let me assure you again, I'd never do anything to hurt your sister."

"Thank God," Phillip Hurst said with heartfelt sincerity. "I'm not the sort of fellow who relishes a dawn meeting on the park green."

"Nor am I," William said with a wry grin.

"Why on earth are the two of you discussing fighting a duel?"

William scrambled to his feet and turned toward the doorway. Miss Hurst stood there, surveying them with narrowed eyes.

Phillip Hurst, who'd also come to his feet, said, "Oh, you're back, Charlotte. We were just saying that neither of us was the sort of chap who relished dueling."

"So I gathered," she said, entering the room and coming toward them. William gestured to his recently vacated seat, indicating she might sit in it if she wished. She waved off the offer with her hand. She'd obviously just returned from her outing, as she still wore her bonnet and gloves, and she carried two wrapped parcels under one arm.

"The question is," she continued, her curious gaze traveling between the two men, "how the subject of dueling came up in the first place."

There was a long beat of silence before Hurst said, "Dash it, Charlotte. Who can say? It just came up is all, in the normal flow of conversation."

"You're just trying to evade my question by posing one of your own. Now out with it, Phillip. I know by that guilty look on your face that there's something you don't want to tell me, and that it somehow concerns a duel."

"Actually," William said, stepping forward and relieving her of the packages, "we were discussing the marriage settlements I had drawn up. We veered onto the topic of dueling because your brother made it clear that if I didn't toe the line where you're concerned, he'd have to defend your honor."

She surveyed them coolly for a moment. "You do realize, don't you, Phillip, a duel at dawn would interfere with your breakfast habits."

"It would likely interfere with a great deal more than that," her brother retorted. "Norwood is a crack shot."

She began to draw off her gloves. "As for marriage settlements, there's no need for them *since there's not going to be any marriage.*" She frowned as she untied her bonnet. "Honestly, does no one besides me remember this is only a *pretend* engagement?"

She went over to a mahogany half-cabinet and placed her bonnet and gloves upon it. William held out his vacated chair, and this time she accepted the offer and sat down in it. There were a pair of empty chairs near one of the windows. William fetched one and placed it beside Miss Hurst for himself to sit on.

Phillip frowned. "The engagement is real but temporary. There's nothing pretend about it." He shot a look at William that seemed to say *See what I mean? Denial.*

"Think of it how you will. Marriage settlements are still unnecessary," Miss Hurst said, her words clipped, her voice tight with irritation.

"It's for your protection," William said. "Just in case."

"Just in case, what?" she asked, her blue eyes flashing at him with aggravation. "It's hardly likely that I'll find myself accidentally married to you."

William suppressed a grin. He *did* find her attractive when she sparked up like that. "True enough. You make your dislike of the notion of being married to me abundantly clear. However, it lends credence to our charade. If we truly intended to tie the knot, we'd draw up marriage settlements. And more importantly, it benefits you. Just in case."

Phillip nodded. "Norwood's terms are quite generous, Charlotte."

"I don't care. I'm *not* marrying him," she said, making another thing very clear to William. Even if she'd enjoyed his kisses, she remained stubbornly opposed to the idea of a match between them.

"Of course not," Hurst said placatingly. "But he's stipulated your dowry monies are to remain yours to do with as you see fit, as well as any family bequests you're to receive. The provisions he made for you from his own funds are quite generous as well. Pin money, a quarterly allowance, access to an account with additional funds should you need them." He nodded his head. "Very magnanimous if you ask me."

His sister gave him a look that said quite clearly she *hadn't* asked him. "That's all well and good, but as I said, it comes to nothing in the end." After a moment, she added, almost tiredly, "We aren't marrying."

Phillip Hurst shrugged and reached for a peeled orange from the fruit plate. "That's up to you, isn't it? If you don't jilt him, the settlements will be binding. You might give some consideration to the fact that, aware of this, he still had them drawn up that way."

Charlotte Hurst's mouth pressed into a thin line. Clearly, she was less delighted by these facts than her brother. William decided the sooner the topic shifted to something else the better.

"I brought my curricle," he said. "Would you like to have another lesson?"

Chapter Eleven

∽

*C*harlotte stared at Lord Norwood, who looked utterly cool and collected. And too impossibly handsome for his own good. Or hers.

Butter wouldn't melt in his mouth.

She knew what he was doing by posing that question—dangling a carrot in front of her, trying to distract her and divert the discussion away from marriage settlements.

I brought my curricle. Would you like to have another lesson?

He'd dropped it in the conversation so casually, so offhandedly...a verbal sleight of hand if she'd ever heard one. The question was, would she take the bait?

She rather thought she would.

She'd been itching to take the reins again since their first driving lesson. And she ought to make the most of these opportunities. Heaven knew when she and Lord Norwood parted ways, Phillip wouldn't be eager to take over as her driving instructor. However, she might be able to persuade him to if she'd already attained a basic level of competency.

"I didn't see it parked on the street," she said, hedging a bit before she capitulated.

"My groom was instructed to walk the horses around the block until I'm ready to depart." He gave her a lazy smile that made her heart do funny things in her chest. "Shall we?"

"Give me a moment to freshen up, and we can be off," she said.

"I'll be waiting right here." He paused, then added, "However many 'moments' it takes."

Ha! She'd show him she could defy the notion that ladies always kept gentlemen waiting too long. Charlotte hurried to her room. She wouldn't mind running a cool cloth over her face and neck, and she ought to let her maid attend to her hair. On impulse, she'd ducked into a milliner's shop while she was out and ended up buying a very modish bonnet, although not until she'd tried on several others, and her coiffure had suffered in the process.

Ah, vanity, thy name is Charlotte. After all, she would have to wear a bonnet during their drive, so did the state of her hair *really* matter?

Yes. Yes, it did.

And what's more, if her maid, Sally, helped her change into her fawn-colored gown with cobalt-blue trim, it would be the perfect foil for her new bonnet trimmed with ribbons and silk cockades in the same bright shade of blue.

Fortunately, the indefatigable Sally proved up to the challenge, quickly stripping Charlotte down to her undergarments, laying out the new outfit while Charlotte took a quick sponge bath. The efficient maid then spritzed her from head to toe with rosewater before helping her into the other dress and, finally, redoing Charlotte's hair in a smooth chignon.

A mere twenty-five minutes later (a miraculously short time, considering), she rejoined the gentlemen. Phillip sat hunched over an open ledger while Lord Norwood, who looked very much the gentleman at his leisure, was reading a newspaper. On catching sight of her, he came to his feet, then cocked his head and regarded her with an admiring expression, making the whirlwind effort worth it.

Doubtless, the rush to get ready was why she felt a little breathless in his presence now. It had nothing to do with that warm intent gaze of his.

"That"—he motioned up and down with his hand to indicate her person—"is nothing short of astonishing. I know to accomplish a similar transformation, my sisters would have required double that amount of time, if not triple." He came to stand before her. "You've even changed your hairstyle," he murmured.

She blushed at the compliment and at the way his eyes continued to steadily regard her with undisguised admiration. "I'm surprised you even noticed," she said, self-consciously reaching up to smooth her hair.

"It's very becoming," he said, his voice a quarter-tone lower and vastly more intimate.

A frisson of excitement chased up her spine and she felt a familiar tingling in her fingers and toes. She swallowed hard, trying to regather her wits. "Th-thank you," she said, hoping he didn't notice the breathless quality of her words. "Shouldn't we be going?"

"After you." He made a sweeping gesture with one arm, indicating she should exit the room first. They took their leave of Phillip and made their way downstairs. Once they reached the front entryway, she stopped to don her new bonnet. He watched her in the mirror as she settled the bonnet on her head and began tying the ribbons.

"Very fetching," he commented.

She eyed his reflection as she worked to get the bow just right. "I bought it today."

One corner of his mouth quirked up. "I'd say it's money well spent."

"Flatterer," she murmured. Finally satisfied with her efforts, she turned and faced him. "I trust you'll behave yourself today."

He offered her his arm and they proceeded out the front entrance, where a groom stood with the horses. "Come now, Miss Hurst. Where's the fun in that?"

Where indeed? Nonetheless she gave him a quelling look before climbing into the curricle.

They spent the next two hours driving in Green Park before taking a turn through the neighboring St. James's Park. Lord Norwood taught her how to handle the reins in her left hand alone, and she proved fairly competent at this, though admittedly her efforts were helped by the scarcity of other vehicles in their vicinity. She was sure that's why he'd chosen these less-fashionable parks for today's drive.

Finally, at her request, Lord Norwood retook the reins. He grinned. "Feeling it in your driving arm?"

"My arm, my shoulders, my back. For something that looks so effortless, it's quite tiring."

"Endurance comes with practice," he said. "Let's celebrate your progress with a visit to Gunter's. An ice sounds good right now."

"An ice sounds heavenly," she said. "You must be burning up wearing that dark jacket." The sunny afternoon had grown warmer, and while he didn't appear to be suffering from the heat, she had to believe he was, given that her own lighter-colored garments were becoming uncomfortably hot.

He chuckled. "In hindsight, midnight blue wasn't the best choice for such a summerlike day."

This was true as far as comfort went, but—and she had no intention of informing him of this—it was an outstanding choice for emphasizing his good looks, deepening the color of his eyes to a dark sapphire, reminding her (not that she needed a reminder) that the man could break a girl's heart without even trying.

They arrived at their destination in short order. The corner of Berkeley Square that housed the popular tea shop was a beehive of activity, with waiters hustling between the shop and the many carriages parked in the vicinity. A waiter hurried across the street to take their orders—a lemon ice for Charlotte, mint for the earl—before dashing back inside to collect the sweet treats.

While they waited, Charlotte studied their surroundings. Plane trees shaded the curricle, parked as it was on the side of the street opposite the buildings. Trees, shrubs, and tall planters of flowers grew within the wrought iron railing that encircled the oval-shaped private gardens in the middle of the square. The only access to the parklike space was through a gated entrance, and only the residents of Berkeley Square had keys to unlock it.

"I wonder if the people who live here take advantage of having a miniature park just for their pleasure," she mused. "A wonderful oasis just beyond one's doorstep." The Hurst town house wasn't located on a square with a keyed garden in the middle, but if it were, she'd have availed herself of it.

"They do," Lord Norwood said, "I occasionally see people

entering or exiting it." He shrugged when she turned a questioning glance in his direction. "I know because I live on the opposite corner over there." He gestured to a spot located diagonally from where they sat, but the square's greenery prevented her from being able to catch a glimpse of his residence.

"So you're one of those lucky enough to be able to enjoy it," she said, not surprised to discover that he lived in one of the most fashionable areas in Mayfair. "I confess I'm a little envious."

"I'm fortunate enough to have access, although"—he grimaced slightly—"I may be risking your censure by admitting I almost never take advantage of it."

"Heavens, do you think me such a scold that I can't make allowances for a busy man like yourself?" She hoped he didn't, but she supposed she couldn't really blame him if he did.

He chuckled. "It's probably just my own guilty conscience thinking I deserve a scolding, and knowing you're one of the few bold enough to give it to me."

"Only when I think you truly need it," she said, giving him a pert smile.

"A debatable point. However, you'd better be on your best behavior. Lady Jersey is one of my neighbors at number thirty-eight. She might rescind your vouchers to Almack's if you're not nice to me. I'm a great favorite of hers, you see."

"I never obtained a voucher to Almack's, although honestly, it's never held much appeal for me anyway." She tilted her head to the side and smiled. "I've never met any of the patronesses of Almack's, much less earned their favor so that I could attend dances in the assembly rooms."

"I have vouchers, but rarely attend." He gave a careless shrug. "The refreshments are dreadful—warm lemonade and unfrosted cakes—and on the whole, it's a dull way to spend an evening. None of which," he added dryly, "seems to dampen people's fascination with it."

Charlotte arched one brow. "Careful. That's a heretical speech to deliver so close to Lady Jersey's residence. You may be placing your vouchers in danger voicing those opinions."

"Only if I'm overheard, and perhaps not even then." His gaze grew teasing as he leaned over and said conspiratorially, "I'm a very eligible *parti* despite your own reluctance to have me."

"Whoever does eventually catch you will have to check that monstrous conceit of yours," she said in mock seriousness, trying to ignore the way her skin prickled with awareness and failing miserably.

He gave a short laugh. "No one will do it so well as you, my dear Miss Hurst."

She was saved from having to answer by the return of the waiter. He carried a tray with a pair of crystal goblets and silver spoons. Lord Norwood gave the man some coins before reaching for the refreshments. He handed Charlotte a spoon and her goblet containing the lemon ice, which appropriately enough, had been molded into the shape of a lemon. Lord Norwood's had been molded into the shape of a frog—a nod, obviously, to the green color of his ice and not the flavor.

They ate in silence, the warm afternoon forcing them to eat quickly before the frozen shapes melted into colored pools of liquid. As she consumed her treat Charlotte became aware of the undisguised curiosity directed at them from the occupants of the nearby carriages. How long would it take, how many public appearances must they make, before people lost interest in them? Or did Lord Norwood always attract interest simply by virtue of who he was? He appeared oblivious to all the attention they were attracting. Or, at least, unbothered by it. She wasn't sure which.

The only other thing drawing people's attention with an equal intensity was the front window of an establishment a few doors past Gunter's. What was so interesting in that window? Nearly everyone strolling down the street stopped to take a look, and quite a few passersby proceeded to go inside. Her curiosity was piqued.

She finished her ice just as the earl finished his. He took her goblet, then hailed a waiter to collect them.

"What sort of business is that?" she asked, motioning with her head toward the area where a knot of people congregated on the walk.

"I don't know." Lord Norwood glanced in the direction she indicated. "But it's entertaining the masses, and doing a brisk business to boot. I've seen several people exit carrying packages. Do you fancy taking a look?"

"I think I might," she said.

The waiter came to collect their empty dishes, and Charlotte asked him about the establishment.

"I believe, madam, it's an artist's shop," the waiter replied before hurrying away.

Well, there was hardly anything unusual about that. Artists' shops were scattered about town as profusely as daisies along a country lane.

"Must be new," Lord Norwood remarked after the man left. "I don't recall exactly what used to occupy that spot, but I know it wasn't an artist's shop."

"I'd like to know what it is about that shop that's drawing so much attention," she said. "Would you mind helping me down?"

"Certainly. Let me summon someone to tend the horses while we're gone." He exited the curricle and walked to her side to help her alight.

"If you prefer to stay with the curricle, I'm capable of visiting the shop by myself," she said. "I'd be in your sight the whole time."

He shook his head as he again waved over a waiter. "It could draw unflattering comment if you went unattended. Besides, you've got me curious now." He produced more coins and offered them to the man who'd answered his summons, instructing him to hold the reins until they returned.

They crossed the road, walked past Gunter's, and joined the crowd in front of the shop window. Charlotte noticed that they received a number of sly glances from those around them. A prickle of unease flitted across the back of her neck, and she gave herself a mental shake. Honestly, she was letting all this attention turn her into someone scared of her own shadow.

The wares displayed in the window looked innocuous enough—a series of small seascapes done in watercolors, a few miniatures rendered in oil, a large painting of a horse with a pack of hounds milling about it. Nothing very remarkable, and she chided herself for allowing her imagination to run riot. People were simply reacting to seeing her with the earl in the wake of that betrothal announcement and nothing more.

If Lord Norwood hadn't leaned in for a better look at a framed print in the lower corner of the large front window, she might have missed it. But he did, and her gaze traveled to the spot as well.

It was a cartoonish drawing of the sort created by caricaturists and sold in shops all across London, but in this one, she recognized the exaggerated figures of herself and Lord Norwood, though not that of a third figure, a modishly dressed lady with blonde curls, pink cheeks, and a disgruntled countenance.

Was it meant to represent young ladies in general who were disappointed the earl was no longer on the marriage mart? Or one in particular? The golden-haired Lady Jane, for instance.

The artist had pictured Lord Norwood in the middle, wearing a leering grin and looking toward the "Charlotte" figure, although the likeness to herself was tenuous at best. Still, it resembled her enough that there was no question in her mind who it was meant to represent in this little trio, even though the artist had chosen to depict her wearing a smug expression on her face and cradling a gently rounded abdomen. The caption read *Beware of Man Traps*.

Her chest tightened as a strange numbness began to work its way along her limbs. Here was the artistic representation of Lady Bohite's accusations and yet another confirmation of what she'd feared when she had agreed to this mad engagement scheme—that no one would believe she'd won Norwood on her own merits. Instead, she was portrayed as a lady of loose morals who'd caught him by playing on his sense of honor. Unfortunately, she found no satisfaction in being correct. Seeing a piece of gossip rendered into a picture and set up for sale was even more mortifying than she could have imagined.

"Don't let it bother you," Lord Norwood murmured. "These things come and go, and you know there's not a grain of truth in it."

"Would that were true of more people," she muttered, then compelled by a desire to know the worst added, "I'd like to see what else they have for sale."

"That's not a—" Lord Norwood began, but she'd already headed for the door.

Once inside she quickly spotted a table displaying several similar caricaturist prints. To her relief no others lampooned her and the earl. The majority of them poked fun at Prinny, the high-living Prince Regent. A few were political in nature, a pair of prints seemed to be making fun of a beleaguered gentleman who appeared to have inspired (according to the print's caption) *An Epidemic of Swooning Ladies in London This Season* and another that proclaimed *Feminine Faints or Feints?* This one depicted the gentleman standing in a ballroom, the ground at his feet littered with unconscious young ladies. The rest of the offerings for sale appeared to be mocking society in general.

She let out a long exhale, only then realizing she'd been holding her breath. Lord Norwood, who'd followed her inside, watched her with a concerned frown.

He leaned close and spoke softly, "I know it's small comfort, but take heart that we were only featured in one of them. It means we aren't interesting enough to merit more."

She gave him a tight smile. "Thank heavens for Prinny and his antics." Nonetheless, the earl had the right of it being small comfort to be featured in only one of the prints for sale. And who could say there wouldn't be more in the future? To distract herself, she glanced around the shop's interior. It was mostly devoted to the sales of framed oils and watercolors, with a few displays of art supplies. The table of prints, however, appeared to draw the most attention from the shop's customers.

"Seen enough?" Lord Norwood asked.

"Yes." She turned to exit and that's when she saw a pile of printed papers on a shelf next to the exit. A large sign was propped next to them. GET THE LATEST EDITION OF *Tattles and Rattles About London,* it read. A pair of matrons each dropped some coins in a basket before grabbing copies of the scandal sheet.

"I wouldn't bother," the earl said, anticipating her intention.

Charlotte steeled herself, since she knew her willpower wasn't sufficient to simply walk past and ignore it.

WHO IS SHE? teased a bold headline.

Who is she, this mysterious miss who has captured the heart of Lord N? As far as can be gathered Miss H is newly come to London, but she certainly hasn't let the grass grow beneath her feet, has she? She has achieved what countless others have failed to accomplish, including (if our source is to be believed) the beauteous Lady J, daughter of the Duke of M. What a coup for Miss H! One can only guess how she managed such a feat—an unknown miss capturing the hand (and heart??) of one of the most eligible bachelors in London. Tongues are wagging and speculation is rife. Time will tell whose guess turns out right!

Their lovely outing was quickly becoming a nightmare. She didn't get the chance to read more, because Lord Norwood's hand clasped her elbow and he gently pulled her out the door. As they headed back to the curricle, he leaned close and spoke into her ear. "Can you manage a smile?"

"What?"

"Smile as if I'm whispering lovers' nonsense to you," he said, still speaking close to her ear. So close, his warm minty breath stirred tendrils of her hair, tickling her cheek and neck. "As if we've already forgotten that load of claptrap they published about us."

Like an automaton, she managed to curve her lips in a stiff smile, then rallying her mettle, said, "Lovers' nonsense? How *un*romantic you are."

He continued to lead them back to the curricle. "Oh, I can be plenty romantic." They reached the carriage and he clasped her hand to help her up. "Do you wish to see a demonstration of my romantic nature sometime?" He tilted his head to the side and regarded her with a challenging light in his eyes.

Her mouth suddenly felt dry, and for a moment she couldn't breathe, couldn't think, couldn't move as the seconds lengthened and she remained frozen, pinned in place by his steady blue gaze, which seemed to suggest possibilities too dangerous to contemplate. But oh so tempting all the same.

Finally, she said, "That's not necessary. I'll take your word that it exists." And anyway, what had that kiss in his sister's sitting room been if not a demonstration of... well, his passionate side if not his romantic one? Quickly, she climbed into the curricle, but he still clasped her hand though it was no longer necessary he do so.

"What...?" she began, but the words died away as he lifted her hand to his lips, placing a lingering kiss on her knuckles before giving her a look so smoldering it made her toes curl. Then, as if the last few moments hadn't somehow tipped her world out of kilter, he dropped her hand without a word and casually strode around the curricle to the waiter patiently holding the reins. He gave the man another coin for his services, then climbed up beside her and chirruped the horses.

Berkeley Square was well behind them before Miss Hurst spoke again. "Was that *really* necessary?" she demanded. "I told you I didn't need any romantic demonstrations."

William kept his eyes on the road, but he could feel her gaze upon him, and could imagine the spark of aggravation in their blue depths. "Oh, that wasn't for you. *That* was for our audience back there, a dramatic exit to give them something to talk about besides that silly print. Was it necessary...?" He lifted one shoulder. "I suspect our opinions differ on that point, but I figured it couldn't hurt."

From the corner of his eye, he could see the movement of her bonnet as she slowly shook her head. "If that print in the window is anything to go by, your efforts were in vain."

He frowned. *That damned print.* He hated that it had upset her, but she was giving it entirely too much weight. "That print only proves people love mean-spirited gossip, and there are some who are happy to profit off that side of human nature. Anyway, in the end it doesn't matter what people think."

"Easy for you to say," she muttered. "But I can't wait for all this to be over. How am I supposed to go about in public holding my head high knowing that prints like that exist and that people are influenced by them?"

"Because appearing in public is the best way to refute that rubbish. Do you think I enjoy seeing myself portrayed as the leering despoiler of innocents? But since I can hardly control what others think, I don't dwell on it. It doesn't change who I am. And whatever they choose to think about you, it doesn't change who you *are*."

"I know that," she said swiftly. "But it's different for someone like you, who's already so well-known, whose...whose place in society is well established...people aren't going to form their opinion of you based on a print like that. But it isn't the same for me. They *will* believe that unflattering portrayal because they don't know anything about me beyond what they see in that print, and I'm skeptical there's much I can do to change that no matter how many carriage rides we take, or plays we attend, or...or anything else we might do together."

"You're right," he said quietly. "I do have a certain advantage when it comes to people knowing more about me. I'm so sorry you were hurt by what you saw back there. You have a right to be upset. The first time I saw myself lampooned in a print, I wasn't able to dismiss it too easily either."

"The first time? How many times have you been the subject of a satirical cartoon?"

He gave her a wry smile. "A half dozen, at least."

"How awful."

"I've become indifferent to it. Even that print today—nasty as it was—only bothers me because it hurt you."

"Those other prints depicting you…what were they? Political in nature? Or personal?"

"Political mostly. Though there was one that showed me in a group of bachelors running down the street pursued by several wild-eyed young ladies. I think the caption was something like *The Ladies' Yearly Hunt Commences*."

"That one doesn't sound too horrible," she said.

He grinned at her. "I found it amusing. Unfortunately, so did my sisters. They *still* tease me about it every year when the social Season starts. And then there was the one Libby had framed and gave to me for my birthday."

"Oh no, she didn't," Miss Hurst said.

"Oh, but she did. I have it hanging in my study. It's titled *A Lot of Hot Air from the Silver-Tongued Orator of Berkeley Square*. The artist drew me with a large cloud of words floating above my head in front of a dozing audience."

"I'm surprised you didn't chuck it in the dustbin."

"It's a good reminder not to be a prosy old bore."

"Do you need such a reminder?"

He laughed, because something in her teasing expression suggested that he probably *did* need such a reminder. "No more than any other man, I hope." He paused, then added, "It's good to see the sparkle back in your eyes."

"If your objective in telling me about these prints is to cheer me up, I admit it has. But I'll still be glad when this betrothal is behind us and I won't be fodder for the satirists. Obscurity has its advantages."

He didn't reply right away. For some reason, her comment bothered him far more than the caricaturist's print had. "So you're still eager to jilt me?" he said at last.

"Why, yes. Nothing has changed in that regard." She sounded surprised that he might think otherwise.

"I see. If nothing's changed, then what was that kiss?" He gave her a questioning sideways glance.

"A mistake," she said firmly. "One that we won't repeat."

He hoped she was wrong about that. Not that he necessarily *planned* to kiss her again, but he hadn't planned *not* to, either. She might put the possibility of another kiss between them in the *definitely not* category, but he preferred to keep the option open.

"So it didn't persuade you that we might be better suited than you previously thought?"

"No," she said. "Not at all."

"Hmm... now that is disappointing." He wasn't quite sure what their kiss meant, but he wasn't willing to dismiss it as easily as she was.

"Disappointing... how?"

"I thought I might have been promoted from fake fiancé to real suitor. Or at least a potential suitor."

She shook her head. "That would not be a good idea."

"Pity, that," he murmured.

"You know I'm right. The differences between us are too glaring."

"But are they?" he pressed. "You can't deny we enjoy each other's company."

Not to mention they'd both enjoyed that kiss. That was equally undeniable.

"If we do—and I don't dispute that we do," she added quickly, perhaps sensing he'd object if she didn't concede the point. "That simply means this betrothal, while it lasts, won't be as unpleasant as we might have expected, given that initially we didn't like each other too well."

"What are these glaring differences you base your conclusion on?"

"Well, if you need them spelled out . . . for one thing, I prefer a quiet life; you enjoy the hurly-burly world of politics. Here in London, hardly anybody knows who I am, and practically everybody knows who you are. I like to read books—"

"Ha! I like to read books, too," he said, his voice triumphant.

"Yes, but to finish my sentence . . . I like to read books more than going out to parties. Somehow I don't think that's true of you."

"It depends on the party," he said, giving her an amused sidelong glance.

She let out a long sigh. "You're not taking this very seriously."

"One could say you're taking the differences between us *too* seriously."

"You know what I think?" She twisted around on the seat, angling herself so she could study him with a serious expression. He slowed the horses' pace to a slow walk. The residential street wasn't busy; he could give her the bulk of his attention.

"I think the reason you're so willing to entertain the thought of a match between us is because you know I have no interest in one. Ergo, your pride is behind this notion"—she twirled a hand in the air—"that there could be something between us."

"That's ridiculous," he said flatly.

"Is it?" Her blue eyes stared into his, intent, probing, looking for confirmation that she was right.

"Yes. Absolutely. It's ridiculous." Would a prideful man practically beg a girl to give him consideration as a suitor? Granted the circumstances of their relationship were highly unusual, but even if he hadn't pursued her in the beginning, he didn't think the idea of doing so now was as outlandish as she evidently did. *Pride, indeed.* She'd been shredding his pride from the moment they'd met. "I suppose, though, it's good to know where things stand between us," he said at last.

"Exactly where they always have. That kiss didn't change anything."

He might have argued the point further, but they were nearly back to the Hurst residence. They rode in silence until he pulled the curricle up in front of the town house on Berners Street. His groom, who'd been lounging on the entrance steps, scrambled to his feet. William climbed down and handed the lad the reins before helping Miss Hurst descend from the curricle. Again, silence prevailed as he walked her to the front door.

"Thank you," she said. "For the driving lesson, and for treating me to an ice at Gunter's. I can see myself inside." She smiled, but her expression was guarded. She'd retreated behind those walls again, the emotional barriers she erected to keep him at a distance.

One part of him wanted to insist on taking his leave of her in the entryway, rather than here on the doorstep, but he quickly decided the better choice was to let her have her way. In the art of persuasion, sometimes being agreeable was the more effective course. He'd give her the victory this time.

"I *will* see you at the Huntingtons' dinner party tomorrow night?" he asked.

She nodded. "Phillip and I will both be there."

"Until tomorrow then." As he'd done outside of Gunter's, he reached for her hand and brought it to his lips for a longer-than-strictly-proper kiss.

"Was that another performance?" She glanced behind him toward the street. "For the neighbors, this time?"

He looked down at their still joined hands, before reluctantly releasing hers. He smiled, lifting his gaze to meet hers. "No. This one was for me."

Chapter Twelve

∼

The next day seemed interminable to William. Partly, he imagined, because he'd spent too much of the night tossing and turning with insomnia as he pondered the conundrum of his relationship with Miss Hurst. Was she correct in thinking his pride was the reason he wished to consider the possibility of being more than...than whatever the hell they were. Allies, he supposed.

Female approbation, as he'd once complained to Miss Hurst, was all too easily gained when one possessed the title of earl. *Was* he so eager to win her simply because she hadn't fawned over him from the beginning like almost every other female of his acquaintance? He didn't think so, but then one's faults were rarely self-evident.

Still, his pride could hardly explain the electricity of that kiss in Libby's drawing room. Miss Hurst might claim that kiss hadn't changed anything, but he begged to differ. A kiss like that—an *attraction* like that—didn't come along every day. He had the experience to know this, even if she didn't.

He was willing to concede she might be entirely correct when she said their differences were too great for anything of a permanent nature to blossom between them. But he found it maddening that she refused to even *consider* exploring the possibility of turning their pretend betrothal into a real one.

Because, really, where was the harm in that? If they truly didn't suit, then they'd go back to their original plan, she'd jilt him when the time was right, and they'd go their merry ways. He wasn't sure how to overcome her resistance on this point, but he'd like to try.

He'd spent too much time during his meetings today thinking about her objections, and how to counter them. Truth be told, he hadn't landed on any good ideas, but he remained optimistic that he would. In the meantime, he looked forward to seeing her tonight at the Huntington dinner party.

Unfortunately, the evening didn't go quite as he'd hoped. First, he'd been seated across from Miss Hurst at the dinner table. The dictates of good manners prevented him from engaging her in conversation, while the placement ensured he had a perfect view for watching Lord Wellcott, a randy widower, try to flirt with her all through dinner. And leer at her bosom when the old goat thought she wouldn't notice.

After dinner, the ladies moved on to the drawing room while the gentlemen smoked, drank port, and jawed over political matters. William didn't smoke, and he'd never cared for port, but he impatiently endured this habit of aristocratic males, biding his time until the men rejoined the ladies. But once again he was thwarted in his objective, when he was detained by Huntington, who wished to discuss his latest efforts to persuade Liverpool's advisers William was the man to head the reforms commission.

When he and Huntington finally made it to the drawing room, they'd immediately been drawn into a group debating the issuance of government bonds to pay off lingering war debts versus finding ways to increase tax revenue. Normally William loved these sorts of evenings, but tonight he had one goal, and so far he'd been frustrated in achieving it. His patience was at a low ebb.

So low, in fact, that he was currently fighting the strong inclination to cross the room and warn Charles Townshend that if he didn't quit monopolizing Miss Hurst's attention, he'd draw his cork for him. To William's great annoyance, she didn't seem to mind the way the man stayed plastered to her side. On the contrary, she appeared to enjoy Townshend's company a great deal. She laughed at something he said, her mirth turning her cheeks a becoming pink, while the soft curve of her lips brought to William's mind thoughts of kissing.

Not that there would be any more kisses between them. Not unless he convinced her they could be more than just friendly allies.

Townshend leaned in cozily and said something to her that made her laugh again. Someone needed to tell the blighter to keep his distance from her. Why was Townshend so intent on keeping her to himself? And where was Serena? William had long suspected she harbored a secret tendre for the man, for all that air of cool disdain she put on whenever Townshend was around. She couldn't be liking this cozy tête-à-tête.

An acid-like burn simmered in his gut. Jealousy—particularly jealousy over a lady—was a foreign emotion for William, but he had it in spades tonight.

"I say, Norwood, you're awfully quiet," a gentleman named Rayburn said jocularly. "Cat got your tongue?"

"Yes," William replied. "I'm afraid I'm going to have to

leave it to you gentlemen to solve England's problems tonight," and to the astonishment of his companions, he stalked across the room to Charlotte's side.

She looked at him in surprise, and some of the laughter faded from her eyes. "Is something wrong?" she asked.

"No," he said, trying to reorder his expression into something more pleasant than the scowl he suspected graced his face.

"You look like you've had enough politics for the evening," Townshend said, with a nod to the group of gentlemen William had just left.

"I've had more than enough political talk, and not enough of enjoying my fiancée's company." He positioned himself closer to Miss Hurst's side, sending a clear message to the other man.

Townshend shot him a quizzical look, then said, "I, uh, believe Weatherby is signaling to me." He turned to Charlotte and bowed briefly. "If you'll excuse me, Miss Hurst."

"What's the matter?" Charlotte asked after Townshend departed. "You looked upset a moment ago."

"Nothing. I'm just not in the mood to discuss the government's finances tonight."

"Is that what you were talking about over there? I wondered why you were glowering."

"I'm surprised you noticed; Townshend was keeping you well entertained."

"You say that like it's a bad thing."

He'd sounded more disgruntled than he'd meant to. He took a deep breath and smiled at her, trying to look less like a jealous suitor, despite still feeling like one. "What was so entertaining?"

"He told me about a funny happening he witnessed from his club last week. A gentleman named Gilbert Ogilvy lost a bet and had to parade down St. James's Street in a skirt and bonnet."

"I heard about that," William replied, chuckling in spite of his lingering jealousy. "Gilly is an inveterate gambler and merely an average card player, who has—as usual—outspent his quarterly allowance paying off his bets. I expect he'll have to carry out any number of outlandish stunts until the next quarter day."

"According to Mr. Townshend, he will. Apparently, Mr. Ogilvy recently lost another wager and has to interrupt a performance of *The Marriage of Figaro* by standing up and singing all the verses of 'God Save the King.'"

"I pity the operagoers that night. Gilly has a god-awful singing voice."

"That's precisely what Mr. Townshend said." She smiled and jealousy speared him again. He didn't want her smiling fondly like that over another man's words.

"Come along," he said abruptly. "I want you to see something." He clasped her elbow and led her over to Serena, who was deep in conversation with two ladies, who, like Serena, often involved themselves in charity work and championed various social causes.

"Duchess, Lady Beasley, Serena." He nodded and gave the ladies a smile meant to charm them into doing his bidding. "I beg pardon for the interruption, but I need to steal Serena away for a moment, if I may. It's urgent."

"Certainly, Norwood." Lady Beasley beamed at him fondly. "Felicitations to the both of you, by the way."

William inclined his head slightly. "Thank you." He hoped his impatience with this small talk wasn't obvious, because the truth was, after waiting all day to enjoy Miss Hurst's company, he wasn't willing to share it. Hence, the need for Serena's help.

"Yes, congratulations, Norwood," the Duchess of Rochester said with a gracious smile. "With such an enchanting fiancée, you ought to purchase tickets to our subscription ball, if you haven't already."

"Serena made sure that I did," he said. "Now if you ladies will excuse us...this won't take long."

"Oh, it's quite all right," Lady Beasley assured him. "Grace and I've been monopolizing Serena too long anyhow. Go. Take care of your urgent business."

William led the way out of the drawing room into the empty hallway beyond. "I'd like you to accompany Miss Hurst and myself to the roof. I want to let her look at the stars through the telescope your father keeps up there."

Serena gave him a strange look. "It will have to be set up first," she said, "which I can certainly have done. But the viewing won't be very good, since the moon is nearly full. It would be better to wait for the new moon. Unless the moon is what you wish to view, but then that would be even better at the full moon."

"The moon will be fine," William said, with a touch of impatience. He should have remembered that the telescope would need to be uncovered and positioned. He chalked this lapse up to the fact that his mind was chiefly occupied with finding a private moment with Charlotte, the better to assuage this burning desire to kiss her again. "Actually, don't bother with the telescope. I have a better idea. I'd like Miss Hurst to see the library. Your father's Shakespeare folios are particularly fine."

"All right then," Serena said, once again looking at him as if she wasn't quite sure what to make of his requests. Miss Hurst stared at him with a perplexed, slightly suspicious expression, but she didn't offer any objection, so Serena led them down the hall, and into a moderately sized room with floor-to-ceiling bookshelves along two walls, several comfortable-looking chairs, and a large marble fireplace at one end of the room.

Before she could unlock the cabinet where the folios were stored, however, William said, "No need to get out the folios. What I'd really like is a private moment with Miss Hurst. If you could just wait here to lend countenance to our absence from the gathering, she and I will duck out onto the terrace for a few moments." Serena glanced at Miss Hurst, as if trying to ascertain what she thought of this idea.

"There *is* something wrong, isn't there?" Charlotte said. "I knew it. You're acting so strangely."

"No," he said, turning to her and keeping his voice low. "Nothing's wrong. I just need a few minutes with you."

She frowned and studied him a few seconds as if trying to figure out what was on his mind. "I don't know..." she began.

"Please," he said.

"Is it really necessary that we go outside?"

He nodded and glanced at Serena, who shrugged and said, "I'll wait here, and get out one of the folios to show you. Charlotte looked rather keen to see them when you first suggested it. And I find it's best to stick as closely to the truth as possible, so we shall have a look."

"I would like that." Miss Hurst was forced to throw these words back over her shoulder because William, already intent on getting her outside, was pulling her toward the French doors that led out onto the terrace.

"Hurry back," Serena called after them. As William pulled the door shut behind them, he saw Serena's knowing smile. She knew what he was up to.

Miss Hurst, on the other hand, didn't seem to have tumbled

onto what was behind his urge to get her alone because her expression, illuminated by the nearly full moon, was one of bemusement.

"Well?" she asked. "What's so urgent that we had to come out here?"

"I've barely seen you this evening," he said, taking her hand in his and pulling her farther along the flagstones of the terrace right up to the verge with the gardens beyond.

"Why, you've seen me quite a lot," she contradicted. "We sat across from each other at dinner, and we were in sight of each other after that in the drawing room. The only time you didn't see me was when you gentlemen remained behind in the dining room to have your port and cigars."

He gave a brief shake of his head and smiled wryly. "If you're being strictly literal, then yes, I've seen you quite a bit. I watched you converse with the gentlemen on either side of you through dinner, while I was prohibited to do so without appearing rude for speaking across the table. And in the drawing room, I watched Townshend monopolize you until I thought I should go mad with frustration."

He saw confusion chase across her features. "Is it because he's a Whig, and you have Tory leanings? I didn't think that would be a problem since he's a guest of Lord Huntington's. I thought he was very nice—"

"My frustration stems from the fact that you obviously found him very nice."

"But I..." She stopped and eyed him uncertainly. "I wasn't *flirting* with him, if that's what you thought. Oh, but perhaps others would think that," she said consideringly. "I suppose that's not good when we're trying to make people believe we're—"

She didn't get the chance to finish her sentence because

William had drawn her into his arms and lowered his mouth onto hers. This wasn't like their first kiss, tentative and exploring. This was about possession, claiming her as his, and easing the flame of desire that had been building within him throughout the evening. His kiss was greedy and demanding, and for the first second or two, one-sided. But only for a second or two, because then, to his immense satisfaction, she was kissing him with just as much ferocity as he was kissing her.

Tongues tangled and danced as he held her so close against him that she was in danger of having the buttons of his waistcoat imprinted on her front. She didn't seem to mind this though. Her hands crept around his neck, her fingers buried in his hair, pressing into his scalp, as if to say *More. Don't stop. I want this*.

So he didn't stop, and neither did she until several breathless minutes later both seemed to remember Serena waiting in the library, and beyond that, a drawing room full of guests who would surely begin to wonder if they didn't return soon.

"Charlotte," he breathed as they drew back from each other, both struggling to regain their breath. Her eyes were large and liquid in the moonlight, her face pale and guarded. Her hands slid down to rest lightly on his shoulders for a second before she snatched them away.

She raised her chin. "You seem to think that kiss gives you the right to use my given name."

"I think after that kiss it would be ridiculous for us to fall back on formality. In private, at any rate."

"I think after that kiss it becomes more important than ever that you address me as Miss Hurst, the better to ensure we don't make a habit of this."

He brushed his knuckles along her cheek. Her skin was warm and satiny. He gently cradled her jaw, and ran his thumb along her bottom lip. "Whether I call you Miss Hurst or whether I call you Charlotte, it won't change my desire to kiss you. As far as habits go, I'm afraid it's one I've acquired already, and there's no use in pretending that I haven't."

She didn't say anything, didn't step away from his caress. She closed her eyes for a second and he sensed she was fighting some internal battle.

"Charlotte," he whispered, "tell me you don't like my kisses."

She let out a long sigh. "It doesn't matter if I like them or not. What matters is keeping things in perspective and not getting so caught up in our roles that we forget what's real."

"And that, according to you, is that we have so little in common it doesn't matter if we're attracted to each other, in the end this betrothal will be over and we'll go our separate ways."

She nodded. "The problem is when you kiss me I have trouble remembering that."

"When I kiss you, I have trouble *believing* that." He glanced back to the French doors. He could see Serena through the glass, her back to them as she appeared to study the library shelves. "If I had more time, I'd attempt to convince you on precisely why we should continue to indulge in this habit." He emphasized this by pulling her close again, and giving her one last quick kiss before letting her go. She took a step back, and then another, placing some distance between them.

∽

"And just how do you plan to convince me? By kissing me some more?" she asked coolly, trying mightily to maintain some emotional distance. No easy feat when she'd just been kissed so thoroughly and held so closely that it was as if their two bodies were trying to meld into one.

"Yes, since I can hardly do more than that in Huntington's garden, much as I'd like to."

Her breath caught at his words.

Since I can hardly do more... much as I'd like to...

More... more... more...

The words echoed in her mind, setting off a warm tingling from her head to her toes.

Don't refine upon it over much, Charlotte. He's a man. Of course, he wants to do more if you're ninny enough to let him kiss you like that in a dark garden. Be sensible!

She was trying to be sensible, truly she was, but her heart pulled her in one direction, her mind in another, and on top of that William was able to breach her defenses with almost no effort.

She pretended to be unaffected by his statement though, deliberately smoothing the front of her gown, then checking her coiffure for any loose pins or wayward tendrils. Satisfied that her outward appearance was tidy, whatever the state of her inner turmoil, she said, "That would be a mistake, and we both know it. In any case, this isn't the time or place to argue over it. We should be getting back. Lady Serena will be wondering what happened to us." She turned toward the French doors.

"Serena is too worldly to think we were doing anything other than what we were doing, but she's discreet and won't say anything."

When they re-entered the library Lady Serena greeted them with a knowing smile. "How was the moonlight?" she said.

"Illuminating," William said, flashing an irritatingly roguish grin at her. Honestly, men could be such insufferable creatures.

"I shouldn't be absent from the drawing room much longer," Lady Serena continued, "but if you'd like to take a quick look at this folio, you may. It's not the finest of the four Papa owns, but it's in quite good shape nonetheless."

Charlotte examined the book, turning the pages carefully, respectful of its prized place in Lord Huntington's book collection. It had that old book smell, not exactly unpleasant, but distinct, a mix of leather, paper, ink, and for lack of a better word, age. It took Charlotte back to her youth, and long afternoons spent reading in her father's library, happily curled up in an overstuffed armchair before the fireplace, lost in a book.

"I can tell you're a bibliophile from the reverent way you handle the pages," Lady Serena said.

"I do love books," Charlotte replied, "but I'm being careful mostly because I don't want to damage one of your father's valuable books. It's a treat to see it though."

"I'd be happy to show you the others sometime, if you'd like. They'll be plenty of opportunities. William is a frequent visitor, and now you will be, too."

This comment, innocent though it was, produced a sharp little ache in Charlotte. Ending the betrothal would impact more than just her relationship with William. It would affect all the friendships she'd made with people she'd met through him. She forced a smile. "I'd like that." She glanced around the room, at the shelves filled with books, which beckoned so enticingly. "Spending an afternoon in here would be a bit like going on a treasure hunt."

Serena laughed. "Oh, I do like you," she said, linking her arm with Charlotte's. "We bluestockings must stick together since we're largely unappreciated by the rest of society."

On that note, they made their way back to the other guests.

No one seemed to take much notice of their return to the drawing room. Card tables had been set up in their absence. There were now several games of whist and piquet in progress.

Phillip, who was seated at one of the whist tables, glanced up as Charlotte walked past. He looked at her a moment, his gaze one of mild inquiry, although he didn't say anything to her.

She couldn't tell if he suspected what she'd been up to, although if he did, he could hardly ask her about it in the middle of the drawing room. Besides, Phillip wasn't the sort to meddle in her business, believing that Charlotte was a grown woman capable of managing her own life. It was one of the traits Charlotte most appreciated in him. But even her easy-going brother might draw the line at her wantonly kissing a man in a garden.

Mr. Townshend approached, and after one long look at the earl, during which some unspoken message seemed to be communicated between them, he said, "Would you care to form a table, Norwood? Lady Serena and I against you and your lovely fiancée."

"I'm agreeable, but I'll leave the decision to the ladies."

"I'm in," Serena said. "Are you up for a few rounds of whist, Charlotte?"

"Certainly."

"Shall we play for money?" Serena asked brightly. "Make it a bit more interesting?"

"No," William said dryly. "I prefer a friendly game. You're too much of a cutthroat when you play for stakes."

They chose an empty table in the corner of the room. It was decided that Lady Serena would deal first. The first game ended quickly. Lady Serena and Mr. Townshend won handily by taking all the tricks for a grand slam.

"I should have warned you from the outset what we were in for," Lord Norwood drawled from across the table as Charlotte, who was the next dealer, shuffled the deck. "Card sharps, the pair of them."

"So I see," she replied, dealing the cards. She was no slacker when it came to whist, but Serena and Mr. Townshend were in a different league.

Mr. Townshend gathered up his cards and arranged them to his satisfaction in his hand. He led, playing the ace of hearts. "Lady Serena and I mix about as well as oil and water in most matters, but when it comes to whist"—he flicked a veiled glance at Lady Serena—"we make a formidable pairing."

Lord Norwood then played the four of hearts, Lady Serena the two, and Charlotte the seven.

"That's true," Lady Serena said with a touch of impatience, "but I hope you're not going to turn chatty during the play. You know I hate that."

"Breaks her concentration," Mr. Townshend said *sotto voce*. Having won the last trick, he led again. This time with the king of hearts. "So, Miss Hurst, don't think my silence means I'm unsociable. It just means I must keep my favorite whist partner happy."

Lady Serena rolled her eyes. "So much for being your favorite partner. You chose Kingston as your partner the last time we played."

"That was only because you wanted to play for stakes that were far too rich for my blood." He turned to Charlotte and added, "My blood is not as blue as the rest of yours, and my money is hard won through my own labor."

"I'm surprised you haven't emigrated to America yet with their more egalitarian society," Lady Serena snapped, her cheeks flushing a delicate pink and her gray eyes sparkling ominously in that gentleman's direction.

"But then I would miss all the fun of being a thorn in your side," he replied, his voice calm, but with a steely edge to it.

William won the trick, and Lady Serena's mouth pinched

into a tight line. "Oh, for heaven's sake. *Will* you quit talking? Look what I did. Led off with a king when I should have known better."

"You know better than to do a great many of the things you do," Mr. Townshend replied. "But that never stops you."

Lady Serena did not answer him this time, just gave him a withering look, and they played in silence until Charlotte and Lord Norwood lost the game and the rubber.

"Shall we play another rubber?" Lady Serena asked gaily, her good humor apparently restored by the victory. "Give Norwood and Miss Hurst a chance to redeem themselves?"

"Regretfully, I think I must call it a night," Mr. Townshend said. He rose, bowed to the ladies, and left.

"I swear, he is the *most* aggravating, annoying, *impossible* man in London," Lady Serena muttered, watching his retreating back. "Makes me wish he weren't my best whist partner."

To Charlotte, this seemed a bit excessive, since Mr. Townshend had struck her as very amiable, but it was clear there was some history between him and Lady Serena. She couldn't tell if they actually disliked each other, or merely acted like they did.

"You're too hard on him, Serena," Lord Norwood said.

"Pfft" was her answer. She gathered the cards and absently shuffled them a moment, then said, "Charlotte, if you're free tomorrow afternoon, why don't you come over here at two o'clock? We can have a nice visit, I'll tell you all the embarrassing stories I know about William, and then I'll fill you in on what we're doing to help war widows."

"I'd like that," Charlotte said. "I can't wait to hear the embarrassing stories."

Serena shrugged and made a face. "I regret to say I was only funning. I don't actually know any embarrassing stories about William, because he's such a goody-goody." She gave Charlotte a mischievous smile. "It's up to you to corrupt him a bit."

"I'm the wrong person for that job," Charlotte said firmly.

"I wouldn't be so sure," Serena murmured.

"I'm incorruptible, Serena. You know that."

"So you are, which, I hold to be a very good thing, since Papa has grand plans for your political future. *Corrupt* was a poor word choice. What I meant was you need to unbend a bit, and be a little naughty once in a while."

William's gaze flicked over to Charlotte and she knew he was thinking about their kisses. "I don't have your penchant for breaking rules, Serena."

"I try to confine myself to breaking only the stupid ones," Serena said. She plunked the cards down on the table. "I should get back to my duties as hostess, though, and mingle with the other guests."

"By all means," the earl said. "I can keep Miss Hurst entertained."

"I'm sure you can," Lady Serena replied with a knowing look. She rose and drifted over to a group of young matrons.

"No need to entertain me," Charlotte said. "It's getting late. My brother will be ready to leave soon."

"You won't get rid of me that easily," he said, giving her an endearingly lopsided smile. "I'm at your disposal."

"Don't you still have politics to discuss?" she asked, motioning with her head to a cluster of men gathered near the fireplace. It was the same group he'd been a part of earlier.

"They've probably moved on to discussing horses and hounds by now. Or the latest farming techniques."

"If they're discussing farming techniques, they're doing so with quite a bit of animation," she observed.

"You have a point," he agreed. "Which reinforces my inclination to stay here with you."

A footman bearing a silver tray of drinks paused beside them. Charlotte selected a glass of lemonade; William chose sherry.

Charlotte slowly sipped her lemonade, turning over in her mind a comment Serena had made about William. She wanted to ask him about it, and at the same time she wasn't sure she wished to have an answer because she feared it would confirm what she already knew. But not asking seemed cowardly, and anyway she preferred facing things head-on.

"What plans does Lord Huntington have for you?" she blurted out.

He tilted his head to the side with a bemused expression. "I'm not sure I understand what you're asking."

"Serena said something about her father having grand plans for your political future. What did she mean by that?"

"I think she's referring to the fact that Huntington believes I have an affinity for, I suppose you could say, political discourse. And because of that, he encourages me to step up in the political arena."

"That is a politician's answer," she said, "because I have no idea what it means. And it doesn't really address my question. What *plans* does he have for you?"

"Let me assure you that the term 'plans' in this context has a very nebulous meaning. It would be more accurate to say he harbors ambitions on my behalf. He thinks I could work my way up in Liverpool's administration, should I wish to."

Was he trying to offer obtuse answers? Or did it just come naturally?

"So do you wish to? Work your way up the ranks in the prime minister's government, I mean. And please, just answer the question clearly," she said, suddenly feeling weary.

"I'm open to the possibility of serving the country in some official capacity." His answer came out slowly, almost tentatively. "I want to head the reforms commission because I feel so strongly that England needs to make progress in ways this commission can shape. As a peer, I already have a duty to sit in the House of Lords, but beyond that, I don't have any *specific* goals for political office."

"Except for heading the commission," she said flatly.

"Yes, but that's only because I know some of the men who want that appointment, and if one of them gets it, I guarantee you nothing good will come of it."

"But in the future, you would be amenable to accepting other posts. Am I understanding you correctly?" she pressed. Because he still hadn't answered the question with full clarity. Not in her mind, at least.

"I might be," he said. "Depending upon the post."

She didn't reply, just looked around the room at the other guests. Some still played cards, but more than half of the guests were scattered about the room in small groups, largely divided by gender, although Serena seemed to be attempting to draw some men and women together. But if the evening had a predominant theme, it was one of lively discussion and political debate.

And this was his world.

"I hope you get the chairmanship of the reforms commission," she said at last. He was the sort of man England needed among the ranks of its leaders.

"Thank you," he said. He looked pleased at her words. "Let's hope that the powers that be come to the same conclusion." He lifted his glass slightly, as if making a toast. Charlotte matched his gesture, and finished the last of her lemonade. He drained the rest of his sherry.

She rose from the table. "I'm going to collect my brother. It's nearly midnight, and he gets grumpy when he's up too late."

"You're joking," he said, coming to his feet as well.

"Actually, I'm not." This was true, as far as it went, though she didn't make it a practice to oversee her brother's bedtime. It was merely an excuse to leave, since she couldn't admit the real reason—their discussion had left her blue-deviled and she craved solitude.

In a stroke of good timing, Phillip's card game had just ended as she reached his chair. He stood, yawned widely, and said, "I hope you've come to tell me you're ready to head home." He yawned again, and Charlotte, who was a bit tired herself, couldn't quite stifle an answering yawn. That prompted another head-splitting yawn from Phillip.

"Dash it, Charlotte, don't start that. I'm tired." Phillip opened his eyes wide and gave his head a little shake.

She shot a pointed look at William before turning back to her brother. "I didn't start it. You did. We'd best be going before you fall asleep on your feet."

They bid good night to their hosts, and Lady Serena reminded Charlotte about their meeting the next day. William accompanied them to their coach.

"Good night, Charlotte." He bent over her hand and pressed a kiss against her knuckles, and when he straightened his gaze held hers a long moment before sweeping down to linger on her mouth. "Sweet dreams," he said huskily.

"Good night, Lord Norwood."

He handed her up but didn't release her hand right away. "Parting with you, Charlotte, *is* a sweet sorrow," he said in a low voice. "Since we must, I hope I dream of you till it be morrow."

Charlotte blinked at this unexpectedly romantic rephrasing

of the quote from *Romeo and Juliet*, too surprised by it to think of any good reply. He smiled and stepped back so that Phillip could climb in.

He raised a hand in farewell as the coach pulled away. It wasn't until he was out of sight that Charlotte breathed normally again.

Phillip loosened his cravat. "Gad, I'm done in. I hate these affairs where the main entertainment is talking, talking, and more talking. Can't tell you how glad I was when Huntington suggested bringing out the card tables." He gave Charlotte a keen look. "Where did you go off to with Norwood?"

"He and Lady Serena showed me the library," Charlotte said. "I got to see one of Lord Huntington's Shakespeare folios."

Phillip made a face. "I guess if anyone enjoys perusing old books, it would be you."

"You make it sound like a moral failing," she said, giving a little laugh.

"Didn't mean to if I did. Just thinking that Norwood could go about it better when it comes to wooing a girl."

"Since he isn't wooing me, I fail to see your point."

"Don't have one really," he said, turning toward the window. "Although I thought Norwood might have taken you out for a moonlight stroll. Seems the sort of man who wouldn't let a night like this go to waste."

Was Phillip probing because he suspected something had gone on in the moonlight? Or was he, like the earl's sisters, trying to push a match between the two of them? She couldn't decide which. It was unlike him to be suspicious of her actions, although in this instance he would have reason to. But the last thing she'd expect from her brother was a spot of match-making.

"No moonlight stroll," Charlotte said, wondering what Phillip would say if she admitted there'd been a fair amount of kissing in the moonlight. Not that she intended to admit this. He was a forbearing brother, but even he would object to her kissing a man in a garden with no intent to marry him.

"Pity," her brother said, leaning his head back against the seat, as if intending to doze off in the carriage.

"For heaven's sake, do you want me to *marry* Lord Norwood?"

"You could do worse," he replied. His still-reclined head rocked slightly side to side with the movement of the carriage. He sounded sleepy, enunciating the words in a less-than-precise manner. "And it would save a deal of trouble. Wouldn't have to go through all this again."

"Go through all *what* again?"

He yawned. "Negotiating marriage settlements. Accepting invitations like tonight. Having Norwood come to call on you."

"In the first place, you will recall *I* protested the need for a marriage settlement. And anyway, it didn't appear you did much negotiating beyond having your solicitor look over the contract Lord Norwood supplied. And in the second—"

Phillip waved a hand in the air. "Too tired to debate it tonight." He yawned again. "We can discuss it tomorrow if you want."

"I don't want," Charlotte said. Her brother just nodded tiredly.

They rode on in silence. Or near silence. Phillip breathed deeply and audibly in his sleep.

Charlotte fixed her gaze out the window and tried *not* to dwell on that kiss in the garden, or to imagine what William might dream if he *did* dream about her.

She sighed. She doubted she was going to sleep well that night.

Chapter Thirteen

ere we are. Number Six, Red Lion Square," Serena announced as the Huntington coach rolled to a stop. "I hope you don't mind that I'm dragging you about town rather than serving you tea and biscuits in a drawing room."

"Heavens, no. Nothing against tea and biscuits, of course," Charlotte said, smiling. "I wanted to know more about your work with the war widows. It's more interesting to see things firsthand than simply be told about them."

A footman opened the carriage door, lowered the step, and they exited. Number 6, Red Lion Square, turned out to be an unremarkable multistory building in the southwest corner of what was one of the more unremarkable of London's garden squares, having faded from fashionability sometime in the last century. It still retained a measure of shabby gentility and was known as a favorite location for aristocratic gentlemen who wanted a convenient love nest to house a mistress.

The few people walking along the street looked respectable enough, though one well-dressed gentleman seemed to take an unusual interest in them, staring in their direction rather rudely. Charlotte didn't recognize him, but since Serena hadn't noticed him, she didn't bother asking if she knew him.

They were met at the door by a maid wearing a large pinafore. She bobbed a curtsey to them, before addressing Serena. "Lady Beasley is inspecting the kitchens. The workmen just left, and we've been trying to clear out the mess and dust. If you'll follow me, I'll take you to her."

It was obvious the house was undergoing renovations. Furniture was stacked in the foyer under protective dustcovers, rolled carpets were tilted against the walls, and a number of dust motes hung in the air, illuminated by a broad shaft of sunlight that slanted in from a large fanlight over the front door. Charlotte and Serena picked their way around the obstacles as the maid led them to a flight of steps that descended to the lower level of the house.

The kitchens were in a similar state of disarray, and somewhat gloomier because they lacked natural light. The only windows were against the back wall, small and at ground level. Charlotte could see a bit of grass and shrubbery through them. Argand lamps had been lit to provide additional light.

Lady Beasley turned from a large stove that she'd been inspecting. "Serena, Miss Hurst," she greeted them, a smile wreathing her face. "The workmen just finished installing this range from Walker's on Bridge Street. It's the latest in modern cookery, or so they assured me. I've never even warmed milk for myself, although there's a similar contraption in my own kitchen." The newfangled stove was nestled within an old brick cooking hearth, its black finish and nickel trim gleaming dully in the low light of the room.

"We'll have to make sure the kitchen maids know how to use it," Serena said. She turned to Charlotte. "Inspired by our success of placing several war widows in domestic service in London households, we've employed some of them as staff to run this house. Even so, Lady Beasley, the Duchess of Rochester, and I have loaned some of our own servants to help get things ready. We should be ready for occupants in two weeks at the most."

"But aren't some of the war widows, like Mrs. Bright from Madame Rochelle's shop, already in London? Where are they staying presently?"

"Not far from here actually," Serena replied. "There's an inn one block away on Eagle Street. They're lodging there for the time being."

"This will be a vast improvement from a public inn," Charlotte said, looking around the kitchen. A series of washtubs had been installed under one of the windows, and cupboards were hung along one of the walls. A large wooden worktable stood in the center of the room, piled with crates stamped with FORTNUM & MASON.

"Come, let me show you the rest of the improvements," Lady Beasley said. She led them back upstairs. The ground floor had two sitting areas, a large dining room, and a water closet with a copper hip bath as well as a portable bath-shower that could be placed over the copper tub and would allow a bather to pour water over herself from the elevated receptacle.

The bedrooms, which occupied the next two stories, each contained six narrow beds, two dressers, each with a porcelain pitcher and basin, four nightstands, and small flat trunks that easily fit beneath each bed for additional storage. Flowered wallpaper decorated the walls and bright chintz curtains framed the tall windows.

As they toured the upstairs rooms, Serena and Lady Beasley described their vision for helping the war widows. This house, they informed Charlotte, would be devoted to women without children, but they planned to lease a larger building—one they could use to house widows along with their children. This, they explained, was the reason for the subscription ball. Combined with the monies they'd already raised through other means, they could afford to sign a three-year lease on a building only three blocks away. A property that at one time was used as a small inn, so the renovations necessary to make it suitable for housing women and their children were fairly minor.

"What you see here is only the beginning," Serena explained. "The new property will allow us to do so much more than what's possible here."

"One of our biggest goals for the new place," Lady Beasley chimed in, "is to build a schoolroom for the children. We believe education is one of the keys to lifting people from a life of poverty."

"Education for the girls as well as the boys," Serena added. "Our ultimate goal is to put these women and their families in a position to help themselves."

Charlotte was impressed by the extent of their vision, as well as by what they'd managed to accomplish so far. "I'd no idea of how big a project you'd undertaken," she said. They'd finished inspecting the bedrooms and stood at the landing in the upstairs hallway. "It's incredible how you saw a need and found a way to do something about it."

"We've made a good start," Serena said, "but there's much work ahead of us. Work you can share in, if you're interested."

Charlotte didn't even hesitate. "Well, of course, I'd be happy to help, but I'm not sure exactly what I can do besides going through my linen cupboards for items you could use."

She didn't have the London social connections that they did to help with raising funds or securing donations of furnishings, nor did she know how to help find employment opportunities, but if they could use her assistance in any way, she'd be glad to lend it.

Because the truth was she found the idea that she could make a difference in the lives of others very beguiling. And not only that, it was something she could be a part of once her betrothal came to an end. Because while she'd never want to change her life to the degree she'd have to if she were to marry Lord Norwood, she didn't want her life to completely return to its former state either. She liked a quiet life, but she was coming to realize she'd been living too quietly, too... *narrowly* to be truly happy, and though it had satisfied her in the past, it wouldn't in the future.

Meeting Serena had made her aware she could *do* more and *be* more, that a lady needn't always wait meekly for opportunity to come along, that she could make her own opportunities if she set her mind to it. And *that* was an intoxicating truth.

"Don't discount any effort, however small you think it to be," Serena said. "All together, they add up to accomplishments."

"There might be one other thing I can do," Charlotte said, remembering what they'd told her in the kitchen about placing some of the women on household staffs. "I'm looking for an upstairs maid, since one of ours recently gave her notice. If you have someone capable of serving in that position, I'd be willing to take her on."

"I do have someone," Serena said. "A young widow newly arrived in London. I'll arrange for you to interview her."

"Please do. It's another small way I can contribute, since I need a replacement maid."

"Are you free tomorrow morning? I can send her over and let you decide if you wish to employ her."

"Yes, tomorrow morning will be fine. Say at half past ten?" Charlotte suggested.

"Half past ten, it is," Serena replied.

"Let's have some tea in the finished sitting room," Lady Beasley said. "We can talk there in a great deal more comfort than we can here in the hall."

They trooped back downstairs to a back sitting room decorated in shades of tan and rose. A maid brought in the tea tray and Lady Beasley poured for them all.

"This room is actually restful now," Lady Beasley remarked. "A vast improvement over the garish red, purple, and gold that exemplified the taste of my late husband's last mistress." She handed a cup of tea to Charlotte. "I do hope I'm not shocking you, Miss Hurst, but this house used to be where my husband tucked away his mistresses. Now I have unfettered use of it during my lifetime." Her lips curved into a self-satisfied smile. "I think we're putting it to much better use. Not that I minded my husband's infidelities. Oh, but now I *have* shocked you, Miss Hurst," she said, giving Charlotte an apologetic look.

"Not shocked so much as surprised. I don't think I could adopt such a tolerant attitude," Charlotte said. She paused before adding, "Even though I know many ladies do."

"I didn't. Not at first. As a bride, I was a wide-eyed idealist, hopelessly in love with my husband, and I thought his affection for me was similar to mine for him." She lifted a slim shoulder in an indifferent shrug. "I quickly had the blinders lifted from my eyes, and after the first few hurtful years of our marriage, came to appreciate my husband's roving ways, since it kept him busy elsewhere. He wasn't, if I may be candid, the most skilled when it came to lovemaking."

"Charlotte won't have that problem with William," Serena said.

Charlotte was sure her surprise at Serena's comment was evident on her face because Serena let out a laugh before she added. "Well, that could be taken the wrong way, considering your last comment, Edwina. I meant, Charlotte, that you won't have to worry about William straying. He's much too honorable to treat you so shabbily."

"No, I shouldn't expect she would," Lady Beasley agreed. "Norwood is not at all like my late husband, who was a notorious womanizer well before our marriage. Still, I'm not complaining though I sound like I am. Beasley, for all his faults, left me *very* well-provided for, and I will tell you quite frankly, I'm enjoying my widowhood. Too much to ever marry again."

"I doubt I'll ever marry," Serena said. "I can't think of one man for whom I'd be willing to give up my freedom, and what legal rights I have as an unmarried woman. Can you believe it's 1817 and a woman's legal identity disappears when she marries? It's medieval!"

"It is," Lady Beasley said. "One of the reasons a girl can't be too careful when choosing a husband."

They all nodded their agreement to this statement.

"It's disheartening that Mary Wollstonecraft wrote *A Vindication of the Rights of Woman* twenty-five years ago, and very little has changed since then," Charlotte said. "I was fortunate that my parents believed a daughter deserved as good an education as a son. Naturally I couldn't attend Eton like my brother did, but I had an excellent governess, and my father tutored me in advanced mathematics and astronomy."

"It's up to us to persuade the men in our lives to push for our legal rights in Parliament." Serena's smile turned a bit saucy. "My father has heard many a lecture from me on this topic."

"Thank heavens *my* father protected my interests, even though I was too naive and too in love to consider those things at eighteen," Lady Beasley said. "Papa stipulated in the marriage settlements that the property I brought into the marriage reverted back to me in the event Beasley predeceased me, which he did, obviously. Or our children, if he didn't. Either way, he only had control of them during the marriage, and even then I had claim to a quarter of the income from them." Lady Beasley's eyes twinkled mischievously. "But I'm afraid we'll give Charlotte second thoughts if we keep talking in this vein. I do hope you don't mind if I call you Charlotte as Serena does."

"I don't mind at all," Charlotte replied. She felt a twinge of guilt as she recalled how dismissive she'd been regarding William's generosity in the marriage settlements. True, they didn't really mean anything unless they married, but she should have shown more appreciation for the gesture. He was, after all, depending on her to cry off. If she didn't, those provisions, which granted her a great deal of financial independence, would be binding.

"Good. I do prefer to be on a first-name basis with my friends, so you must call me Edwina," Lady Beasley said. "I was Edwina before I took the name Beasley, and I've reached a point in my life where I like being just Edwina once again."

"Charlotte, you've gotten very quiet. William will be most put out with me if we cause you to reconsider the engagement," Serena said.

"No, I'm not reconsidering," Charlotte replied with a wry smile. Although Serena could hardly know this answer meant she would indeed cry off and end the engagement.

"Let me ring for a fresh pot of tea," Edwina said. "Mine has already cooled to a tepid temperature." She rose and went over to a velvet bell pull and gave it a tug. "I got so busy talking, I quite forgot to drink it while it was hot." She collected Serena's and Charlotte's cups, and set them back onto the tray. A pretty young maid arrived, and upon receiving instructions to bring them some fresh tea, she gathered up the old tea things.

The servant had no sooner departed than the same maid who'd answered the door for their arrival entered the sitting room. With her was the Duchess of Rochester, accompanied by a young lady of about eighteen who bore enough resemblance to the duchess that there must have been some family connection. Charlotte knew the relationship couldn't be one of mother and daughter. The duchess had been speaking of her children the prior evening at the Huntingtons', and she'd mentioned her oldest was but twelve years old.

"Ah, Grace, you were able to join us after all." Edwina waved a hand toward the tan-and-rose-striped sofa, indicating that's where the newcomers should take a seat. "I hoped you would."

"We finished our errands in good time." A swift glance passed between the duchess and the girl. "Though I think Phoebe would have preferred to browse a bit longer in the bookseller's shop."

"I don't blame her," Serena said, and Charlotte nodded her agreement.

"Nor do I," the duchess replied as she settled on the sofa. "But I imagine the six books we purchased will keep her busy until we return next week." She gave the girl a fondly indulgent smile. "Although she devours them so quickly I suspect she keeps the candles burning into the night far later than she ought."

"And yet there's always a plentiful supply of candles in my bedroom, Aunt Grace." Phoebe's eyes held a mischievous twinkle, and when she smiled a lone dimple appeared in one of her cheeks.

"Of course there is," her aunt replied with a saucy tilt of her head. "I can't bring myself to discourage a love of reading, and anyway your mother wouldn't like it if I allowed you to strain your eyes reading in poor light. Next year, when you have your come-out, there will be less opportunity for late-night reading because social events will keep you out until the wee hours of dawn, so I may as well allow you to indulge yourself now."

"She looks well-rested enough," Edwina remarked as a maid returned with another tea tray. "I, for one, envy the energy of youth. Nowadays I read only late at night when I need help falling asleep."

Once fresh cups of tea had been handed out, and a belated introduction made between Charlotte and Phoebe when it was realized they'd never met, Serena asked the duchess for the latest tally regarding tickets sold to their subscription ball.

"Providing neither of you have new ticket sales to report, we only have seventeen unsold tickets, but even if they remain unpurchased, we've met our monetary goal."

A broad smile came over Serena's face. "I was confident we would. So much so, that in a few days Papa's solicitor and I have an appointment with the landlord to sign a three-year lease." Her gaze swept among the room's occupants, pausing briefly to study each lady's face in turn. "And with this success, I think it's time to embrace the sentiment that many hands make light work and create a more structured group of ladies who share our vision."

No one said anything for a moment as they let the idea

sink in, but Charlotte could tell Edwina and the duchess liked this idea.

"We could have regular meetings," Serena continued, "to keep everyone informed about specific ongoing projects, or about what needs to be done. We could still use some items for this place, and the new property will have to be supplied with furniture and linens, which we hope to do solely through donations. Given what it took for the three of us"—she nodded toward Edwina and the duchess—"to secure what we have here, furnishing a bigger place will require a great deal of effort. We're going to need help. Not to mention we'll have to devise various ongoing ways to raise funds to pay the household expenses for two places."

"We could hold the meetings at my house on Upper Grosvenor Street," Edwina said. "I've plenty of room and no man in my life to raise any objections."

"I second that," the duchess said. "Should we meet weekly or on a biweekly schedule?"

"Weekly, I think," Serena said. "Although, if you feel that's too frequent, we could plan on biweekly."

"I tend to think weekly would be best for our purposes," Edwina said. "And I don't mind hosting a gathering once a week. The question is do you think people would be willing to come that often?"

"A fair point," the duchess said. "I expect they would, particularly if there's a social element to our meetings."

"Good refreshments couldn't hurt," Charlotte offered. "My brother says good food and good brandy can lure a man to the dullest of gatherings. I imagine we can apply that principle to ladies as well. Not," she added hastily, "that I'm implying your gatherings would be dull."

Edwina smiled impishly. "Offering brandy might hold the

appeal of novelty, not to mention it's deliciously improper. For ladies, at any rate."

"Why don't you make it the female version of a men's club?" Phoebe asked. "You could still keep people apprised of whatever is going on with your projects, but it wouldn't be only about that."

"I like the idea of making it a mix of social club and social causes," the duchess said. "Though I'm not *exactly* sure what Phoebe means by suggesting it be a female version of a men's club."

"Just that men use their clubs as a place to eat, drink, smoke, play cards, place wagers, gossip, discuss business, and get away from the ladies in their lives. While we"—she made a sweeping gesture with her arm—"have nothing quite like it. *I* think it would be nice if we did."

"To be clear, dear, you're not suggesting we take up drinking and smoking and gambling, are you?" the duchess asked. "Because your mother would have my head if I allowed you to do any of those things, and you'd find yourself back in Spinneymead in a trice."

"Not precisely. What I really mean, I suppose, is that it would be nice to have a place to be free from the usual strictures imposed upon the female sex. So, for example, if I wished to slouch on the sofa..." She let her back rest against the sofa before sliding forward on the seat, and letting her head loll to one side. "...like my brothers do sometimes, I could. Or having the freedom to say what I'm really thinking, and not be confined to those sorts of topics considered suitable for a lady. Or maybe..." She came upright again and animatedly leaned forward. "*Maybe* we wouldn't just have the freedom to talk about unsuitable topics, we could *learn* about them, too. There's nothing more frustrating than asking a question about something and not receiving an answer because whatever the answer might be it's deemed too inappropriate for a young lady's ears. Or too complicated for the female brain. Or too unfeminine for a lady to be concerned about."

There was a moment of silence as they all looked at one another. Finally, Edwina spoke up. "From the mouths of babes. Now I'm a bit embarrassed that a similar idea never occurred to us."

Serena nodded as she idly traced the rim of her teacup with a forefinger. "Phoebe raises some interesting possibilities. It would certainly expand the idea of the group beyond merely a philanthropic one."

"If we're going to be a group that casts aside social conventions," the duchess chimed in, "I vote we allow breeches be worn during the meetings." She smiled at her niece, who looked surprised at her aunt's suggestion. "What? Before I became a duchess, I was, much to my mother's chagrin, an incorrigible hoyden. I frequently borrowed castoff breeches from one of my brothers for riding about the countryside."

"Brandy, breeches, and taboo topics. It sounds as if the only convention will be an adherence to unconventionality," Charlotte said. "So count me in, please."

"We'll have to be circumspect, though," Serena warned. "I like these suggestions, but we don't want to put our main goal at risk."

"That's true," the duchess said. "And we don't have to decide anything today. Let's all give it some thought."

"Why don't we reconvene here next week at this time?" Edwina suggested.

They all agreed to this plan, and for the next three quarters of an hour the conversation drifted among a variety of topics, until the lateness of the hour brought an end to their gathering.

Serena and the duchess were attending a ball that evening, and needed to get home to begin getting ready.

"Will we see you at the Vandeveres', Charlotte?" the duchess asked.

"I'm afraid not. I'm attending a poetry reading with William," Charlotte replied.

"Well, I expect our paths will cross again before long. I'll see you here next week, if not sooner."

"Oh, absolutely. I'll be at the next Wednesday Afternoon Social Club," Charlotte said, referring to the name they'd jokingly dubbed the group.

Chapter Fourteen

W ell, you're going to have to do *something*," Charlotte said.

Her maid, Sally, shrugged. "Unless you wish to wear a damp chemise, you must don this one. Or one of the others in those parcels over there." She gestured toward the boxes sitting on the foot of Charlotte's bed, part of the order from Madame Rochelle.

Charlotte felt a throb starting in her temple. She hadn't arrived home from the tea at Red Lion Square until nearly four o'clock, and she hadn't even had a chance to divest herself of her bonnet before Hopkins handed her a note. Recognizing William's writing, she'd torn it open.

> *My dear Charlotte,*
>
> *I apologize for the last-minute nature of this note. I'm expected to attend the Vandevere ball tonight;*

it's a long-standing engagement, but one which had slipped my mind until I received a note from Lady Vandevere this afternoon. I know we'd planned to attend a poetry reading tonight, and while I like poetry as well as the next person, I'd far rather have the chance to waltz with you. Besides, Lady V is my godmother, so I can't back out at the last minute. She is, according to her note, most eager to meet you. I'm sure you see where this is going...

Lydia and Chatworth are also attending. We'll come for you at half-past seven.

Your devoted servant,
William

P.S. Since I'll obviously be in your debt, I won't blame you a bit if you extract the promise of a dozen driving lessons from me.

She'd turned to the butler. "Hopkins, please have a light repast sent to my bedroom, and instruct a maid to draw a bath for me."

Then Charlotte had hurried upstairs where she'd found Sally unpacking the newly arrived parcels from Madame Rochelle.

She'd apprised her maid of the change in plans and the need to rush if she was to be ready on time. Sally helped her out of her day dress, and Charlotte went to take her bath while her maid readied a ball gown.

And now, still flushed from her warm bath, she was having a standoff with her maid.

"You put all my old chemises in the wash?" Charlotte asked with no small exasperation. "*All* of them?"

"I did, even the one you took off before your bath," Sally said. "How was I to know, miss, you'd want to wear an old one? With the arrival of the garments from Madame Rochelle's, I decided to give those older chemises an overnight soak in water mixed with lemon juice to brighten them."

"Oh, very well." Charlotte slipped off her robe and Sally lifted a new chemise over her head, helping Charlotte thread her arms through the armholes. The material was soft and feathery light against her skin.

A maid arrived with a plate of cheese and fruit, a slice of buttered bread, and a pot of tea. Charlotte would have to eat while Sally helped her get dressed. She nibbled on a piece of cheese while her maid fetched a pair of pale blue silk stockings from the dresser. Sally helped Charlotte put them on, before kneeling in front of her to tie on a pair of delicately embroidered garters. Next Sally fastened her into her stays, then helped her into a new petticoat. Charlotte refrained from asking if her old petticoats had also been sent downstairs to be laundered.

"All right," Sally said. "Now let's tackle that hair of yours, miss." Charlotte seated herself at her dressing table and popped a slice of apple into her mouth. Sally plucked the hairpins from Charlotte's hair, brushed it, and then stepped back, studying the long brown strands in much the same manner a painter studies his canvas. She glanced at the mantel clock and muttered, "Yes, yes, I think I can do it."

Charlotte finished eating while Sally braided and coiled sections of her thick hair, pinning them into an elaborate coiffure, before she heated the curling tongs to create a fringe of loose curls framing Charlotte's face.

"And now the dress," Sally said. She helped Charlotte into an ice-blue satin ball gown. The silvery spangles sewn onto the gauzy overskirt of net twinkled in the light whenever she moved.

Finally, as the mantel clock struck seven, her maid spritzed her all over with a light spray of rosewater.

"And now the final touch," Sally said as she clasped a strand of creamy pearls around Charlotte's neck. "He won't be able to keep his eyes off you."

"If that's the case, you'll deserve all the credit."

Sally blushed with pleasure. "You'd best go on down." She bustled over to the bed and began putting away the items from Madame Rochelle's. "You can tell me all about it later."

∽

Their arrival at the Vandevere ball was much like their arrival at the theater the other night—a blur of faces and names. The only ones who stood out were their hosts, Lord and Lady Vandevere, whom Charlotte found charming.

Lady Vandevere was an older version of Lydia, a sweet-natured lady you couldn't help but like, and who obviously regarded her godson with a great deal of affection.

"Oh, my dear," Lady Vandevere said, taking Charlotte's hands in her own for a moment. "I can't tell you how happy we are at this news. Why, I positively shrieked with delight when I read about it in the *Morning Post*."

"A very piercing shriek," Lord Vandevere cut in with a twinkle in his eye. "It startled the footman, who dropped a pot of jam. I thought my wife had found an insect in her eggs or something equally disastrous."

"Don't be ridiculous. As if Cook would allow bugs in our food," Lady Vandevere declared, lifting one haughty brow to underscore the point.

"Of course not, dear, but I couldn't think of anything else that would provoke such an earsplitting sound from you." He smiled and bowed over Charlotte's hand. "Delighted to meet you, Miss Hurst. I wish you both every happiness."

"Thank you," Charlotte said.

Lady Vandevere playfully tapped her godson on the arm with her fan. "Now, William, I've instructed the musicians to lean heavily toward waltzes tonight, so don't squander one of your dances with Miss Hurst on a country dance."

"Your thoughtfulness is appreciated." He glanced at Charlotte with a roguish look that set off a flutter of anticipation.

Once past the receiving line, they slowly made their way to the edge of the dance floor. Just like at the theater, they encountered a steady stream of William's acquaintances who wished to meet Charlotte.

The musicians began tuning their instruments for the opening dance. "If this is a waltz…" William murmured, giving her a meaningful glance.

But it quickly became apparent that they were opening with a country dance, so when a young viscount, a cousin of Lord Chatworth's, requested her hand for the first dance, Charlotte accepted. She took her place opposite Viscount Hall in the line of couples. William joined a different group of dancers, but while he was tall enough to be seen through the crowd, his partner was not. She spied Chatworth standing on the perimeter and wondered if William's partner could be his sister Lydia. She hoped so, because when she'd first seen he was dancing, she'd been seized with an irrational pang of jealousy.

The Sir Roger de Coverley was a lively dance, and Charlotte was a little breathless when the viscount returned her to the sidelines where Lord Chatworth chatted with a gentleman as he waited for his wife to come off the dance floor. He introduced her to his companion, a tall, dark-haired marquess by the name of Farrars. As the musicians began the familiar three-quarter tempo of a waltz, Charlotte looked around for William but didn't see him anywhere. So when the marquess asked her to dance, she couldn't refuse unless she wished to refrain from dancing for the rest of the evening.

Lord Farrars was an excellent dancer, though he admitted he rarely frequented balls if he could help it.

"I'm only here tonight at the request of my sister," he said. "Although with Caroline, you could probably use the word *request* interchangeably with the word *command*."

Charlotte thought him quite amusing and she enjoyed waltzing with him, even though she couldn't stop herself from looking to see if William was also out on the dance floor. She thought she spotted him on the far side of the ballroom, but she wasn't sure, since it was only a fleeting glimpse.

Lydia and Chatworth waltzed past. Lydia wore a dreamy look as she danced in her husband's embrace, and Chatworth gazed at his wife with undisguised adoration. A pang of regretful longing shot through Charlotte at seeing them so blissfully happy together.

It was silly of her, she knew. At twenty-three, she'd accepted the idea of a comfortable marriage, if she even married at all. Ladies her age were flirting with spinsterhood, and pining for a marriage like Lydia's was setting oneself up for disappointment.

The waltz had barely ended when the musicians swung into a quadrille. Lord Farrars led her back to the edge of the ballroom where a rakishly handsome gentleman requested an introduction. The marquess obliged, and Charlotte gained a new dance partner.

Mr. Miltner was the younger son of the Earl of Ryland, an

inveterate flirt and quite amusing, although Charlotte didn't put a great deal of stock in the flattery and compliments with which he plied her during their dance. But if she was unaffected by Mr. Miltner's chatter, she was very much affected by the sight of William standing on the side lines.

He watched her with what could only be called a brooding look, leaning against the wall, arms crossed, his heavy-lidded eyes following her progress through the dance with an intensity that belied his casual posture.

It was a very convincing show of jealousy, and although she knew it was only for appearance's sake, she couldn't help feeling a strange thrill at his possessive gaze.

As soon as the music ended, he pushed off from the wall and stalked toward them. Charlotte's heart thumped hard in her chest. They were still on the dance floor when he reached them.

"Miltner." He nodded at the man, then turned to Charlotte. "I believe this dance is mine."

Mr. Miltner looked surprised at his curt manner, but he smiled good-naturedly. "Of course, Norwood. Miss Hurst, it was a pleasure."

"Shouldn't you have waited to see if it was a waltz?" Charlotte asked, lightly gripping his arm as they waited for the music to start again.

"It will be," he assured her. One corner of his mouth tipped up slightly and his gaze contained hints of emotion that sent shivers racing along her skin. "I made sure of it. I was determined to have a waltz with you. Do you know how interminable a quadrille can be when viewed from the side lines? Especially when I have to watch Miltner plying you with those charming smiles of his, blast the man. He knows you're taken."

Of course, she wasn't. Not really. But she loved hearing him say it.

Moments later the musicians began to play again—a waltz, just as he'd predicted. He took her into his arms and it was a far cry from what she'd experienced earlier with Lord Farrars. Every part of her thrummed with awareness. The small of her back where his hand rested, her gloved hand clasped in his, the front of her body mere inches from his, everywhere they touched, or almost touched, tingled and burned with a sweet, aching desire.

You are on a dance floor in the middle of a crowded ball-room, Charlotte. Pull yourself together!

An impossible task when he held her like that, and his eyes, darkened to the blue of a midnight sky, studied her with an intensity that melted her insides and took her breath away.

They danced in silence. Charlotte couldn't think of anything to say. Her brain didn't function much better than her lungs when he watched her like he was starving and she was a morsel he wished to devour.

"Actually, I do know how long a quadrille seems from the edges of a ballroom," she said at last, finally bringing her rioting emotions under control, "since I'm usually among the ranks of the wallflowers. Becoming your fiancée has had a miraculous effect upon my popularity, even though the truth is I'm just as unremarkable as I ever was."

"Men are idiots," he said. "And I find you quite remarkable."

A warm wave of pleasure washed over her at the way he leaped to her defense. "I won't argue that men are idiots," she said.

He laughed. "Of course you won't."

"I will concede, however," she said, glancing up at him

through her lashes, "that both genders have their fair share of idiots."

"Very generous of you."

"Isn't it?" she teased.

His gaze dropped to her mouth and once again he looked hungry. Desirous. Predatory.

She turned away, looking over his shoulder to distract herself. It was a matter of self-preservation. He slipped past her defenses too easily. With one look, he could turn her all fluttery again, a quivering mass of feminine sensibilities, her hard-won calm disappearing like dew on a warm summer morning. Avoiding his gaze was her only defense at the moment.

And that's when she saw the gentleman from Red Lion Square who had stared at her and now was staring at them.

William had been forced to wait far longer than he liked to finally waltz with her. But the jealousy he'd felt watching her with Miltner, and before that Farrars, faded when he'd clasped her hand in his and placed his other hand on the small of her back. Some primal sense of male possessiveness was satisfied by holding her in his arms, feeling her body sway in time to his.

Even so, he still wished he could defy conventions and pull her tight against him and kiss her rosy mouth well and thoroughly.

He frowned. Something had caught Charlotte's attention. She tensed in his arms, her eyes narrowed in concern, and a crease appeared between her brows. For one second, he thought she'd spied Lady Jane or her waspish aunt, but he'd had the foresight to ask his godmother if they planned to attend, and been told they hadn't been invited. Which didn't prevent someone else of their ilk from making her uncomfortable, but by damn, they'd answer to him if they did.

"There's a man wearing a heavily embroidered yellow waist-coat standing beside the middle set of French doors," she said, her voice tinged with urgency. "Can you see him?"

William looked in the direction she described. The move-ment of the waltz now placed him in a position that allowed him to look in the direction she'd faced moments earlier.

"Yes," he said. "I see him. What's more, I know him. His name is Pemberton. Why do you ask?" The man in question was no friend of William's, but he knew him tolerably well.

"He was staring at us, and not a curious stare. I don't know ex-actly how to describe it—not malevolent exactly, but definitely not friendly either. When I caught his eye, he looked away. But the odd thing is he directed a very similar look at Serena and myself when we went to Red Lion Square this after—"

"What were you doing in that part of town?" he asked. That area wasn't quite genteel anymore and not a place he wanted her to frequent without some sort of protection. "I suppose it's too much to hope that you were accompanied by a pair of brawny footmen."

She lifted her chin slightly. "It's not *that* sort of neighbor-hood. And we had the coachman with us."

"Who would have to abandon the horses and carriage to see to your welfare," he said, unable to keep the anger and frustration out of his voice. It was one thing for Serena to visit that part of town. She often visited questionable neighborhoods, despite William's frequently expressed displeasure at her careless lack of regard for her own safety. But it was quite another for her to put Charlotte in jeopardy as well. "Now, just what were you doing in Red Lion Square?" he asked again.

"You needn't go all glaring eyes and clenched jaw on me. Serena and I met Lady Beasley at a home she owns there."

"Beasley's love nest," he said flatly. "Not an entirely appropriate destination for a lady."

"You know of it?"

"It was hardly a secret. Everyone knew he kept his mistresses there. Even his wife."

"Well, it's acquired a better purpose these days."

"And that would be...?"

"You mean you don't know?"

"I wouldn't ask if I did," he replied, wondering what Serena was getting her involved in.

"They're turning it into a home for women left destitute when their husbands died fighting Napoleon's armies."

"And while you were there, you ran into Pemberton," he said, somewhat relieved. He knew when it came to Serena, her desire to help the less fortunate wasn't tempered with prudence for her own safety. Or her reputation. Which was the reason she wasn't invited into the houses of society's highest sticklers, although her family's standing protected her from outright ostracism.

"We didn't run into him precisely. He was there, in the vicinity, and the way he watched us struck me as odd at the time. I don't think Serena noticed him though, and I didn't give him another thought until just now when I saw him staring at us. It doesn't necessarily mean anything, but..." She gave a little shake of her head. "It just seems odd that I've caught him staring at me twice in one day."

It struck William as a little odd, too, though he wasn't quite sure what to make of it. "If he pesters you, let me know, and I'll take care of it," William assured her. "But you should know he is a long shot to head the reforms commission. That might explain his interest in you. In us, especially if..."

He didn't articulate the rest of his thought, but Charlotte's eyes widened as she caught the implications of this statement.

"You think he...?"

"I didn't before tonight. His style is more along the lines of insinuating himself into people's good graces by flattery, not underhanded tricks. But I can't say I'd put *it*"—he gave her a significant look—"past him."

"Do you think he's plotting something else? Something that could hurt your chances?"

"I doubt he's the type to quit the field quietly just because his first plan failed. Assuming he *is* the culprit. I'll have my investigator look into it. In the meantime, must we ruin a perfectly good waltz talking about Pemberton?" Etiquette dictated they dance together only twice in one evening. He didn't want Pemberton to intrude on this one any longer.

"If he's plotting to take away your chance for that chairmanship, then yes," she said, her eyes snapping with indignation. Oh, but he wanted to kiss her just then. He loved to watch her eyes flash with emotion, and the fact that she was riled on his behalf was damned appealing.

"*What* are you smiling about?" she demanded. "I don't see how you can find it amusing this man could be undermining you."

"If I'm smiling, it's because you look adorable right now." Her eyes narrowed suspiciously. "It's true," he insisted. "I find you utterly adorable. Not to mention, temptingly kissable, though there's nothing I can do about *that* at the moment."

Her gaze faltered and cut away. When it met his again, he saw she'd erected that wall of reserve once more. Why did she insist on holding him at arm's length? In the figurative sense, naturally, because he held her as closely as he dared. Any closer, and they'd set tongues wagging.

Somehow he managed to breach the wall when he kissed her. Afterward, she'd summon that cool reserve and lock it back into place, but not during. During she was warm and pliant, seeking and passionate. His blood began to heat just thinking of it.

The string quartet began playing the closing bars of the waltz. He wasn't ready to relinquish his time with her, but he'd have to unless...

When the music stopped, he clasped her elbow, but instead of leading her back to her place at the perimeter of the room where another man could swoop in to claim her for the next dance, he kept right on going to a doorway in the back corner of the room.

"Where are—" she began, her steps faltering as they reached the threshold of the open door.

"The library," he said curtly. This hadn't been his original intention. His original destination had been a quiet alcove, one that could provide the necessary privacy to steal a kiss or two. Or, given the desire coursing through his veins, a few dozen kisses. But he was afraid her hesitation at leaving the ballroom could turn into a flat-out refusal if he didn't provide her with a bit of motivation, as she'd once put it.

Evidently a visit to the Vandevere library was motivation enough, because she exited the ballroom at his side without protest. Well-acquainted with his godmother's residence, he led her down the narrow hall, past the secluded alcove, shadowy and empty, perfect for trysting.

"Why are we going to the library?" she asked. "Is there something else you wished to tell me about Pemberton? Something you didn't want others to hear?"

"I've simply had enough of the ballroom." *And not enough of you.* "Since you like books, I thought you'd like to explore my godmother's library." He stopped before a paneled door and opened it. "After you."

She gave him an appraising look before entering. He followed, closing the door behind him, which earned him another close look, but she didn't protest. Instead, she walked to the center of the room and slowly turned in a full circle, studying the shelf-lined walls, her lips curved in a slight smile of pleasure. The sight of her taking in the contents of the library did nothing to quell the desire roaring through his veins. Who knew watching a girl survey a room filled with books could be so arousing?

She turned back to him, one brow raised impudently. "I don't suppose the Vandeveres own some fine Shakespeare folios you wish to show me."

"I'm sure they do, but I didn't bring you here to show you any folios." Still, he made no move to proceed with the reason he'd brought her here, instead maintaining a circumspect distance between them.

"Then why are we here?" she asked. "The real reason why we're here"—her gaze flicked to the closed door—"alone."

He gave a careless shrug. "Isn't it obvious? Our dance was ending, and I wanted more time with you. Why did *you* come?"

There was a hint of self-mockery in her eyes. "Because you offered to show me the library."

"Then let me point out the fine Turner over the fireplace," he said. "And over in that alcove is a Vermeer that Lord Vandevere gave his wife as a wedding present."

She walked over to the Vermeer, leaning forward as she examined them. "I've never been a great fan of the Dutch masters," she said at last. "Although I admire their skill, they've never held any appeal for me."

"I'm rather partial to Italian paintings myself."

"For me, it depends upon the Italian. I like Botticelli, but I find some of the Caravaggios quite nightmarish." She crossed the room to take a closer look at the Turner. It was bucolic in nature, a river wending through a path of tall, almost languid trees. "I like this. It's very restful."

He came to stand beside her. "It is that." He breathed in her scent—a mix of roses and the clean lemony scent of soap. He ignored the inclination to draw her into his arms, strong though it was. Instead, he let himself study her as she studied the painting.

His eyes traced the slender curve of her neck, the graceful slope of her shoulders. He imagined kissing the spot where a curly tendril of her hair rested against her shoulder just below her ear. He allowed his gaze to linger on the creamy pearls resting against her skin, warmed by her body. He felt his own body tighten in response.

But still he didn't reach for her. He was waiting for a sign from her, for some indication that she ached for him the same way he ached for her.

Or was he simply ignoring her signals? This was Charlotte. The fact that she'd come here with him, that she hadn't moved out of his reach...Given how she stubbornly tried to maintain an emotional aloofness, that might be all the sign she was willing to give.

She sighed, and turned to him. "Is that the end of the library tour, or is there something else you wish to show me?"

"What would you like to see?" he murmured.

She blushed prettily. "I thought there might be some books you intended to point out."

"Well..." he said, trying to remember the more interesting items contained in the Vandeveres' library, and not coming up with much, mainly because he was distracted by the pulse in her throat, which caused her pearls to jump and shift slightly with each heartbeat. "Umm...my godmother has a selection of novels you might like to browse. They're over here."

He led her to an area of the room that had a decidedly more feminine flavor. The winged armchairs were upholstered in a pale blue damask and a large vase of cut flowers sat on an end table, next to a pair of reading spectacles.

"Here," he said, gesturing to the bookcase in front of them. "In addition to novels, there are some books on household management, horticulture, and, well, you can see for yourself what else she has."

"You must be close with your godmother to know precisely where her books are located in the library," she said.

He shrugged. "I am. She was my mother's dearest friend. When my father died, Lord Huntington stepped into that role, providing much needed guidance for the green boy I was then. When my mother died only a year after Papa, Lady V took me under her wing. She oversaw Lydia's come-out three years ago since, as a twenty-two-year-old bachelor, I was hardly qualified to do so."

~⌒~

"I'm so sorry," Charlotte said. She knew he'd lost his father when he was eighteen, and then to lose his mother so soon after that...She laid a hand on his arm. "You never quit missing them. I know I haven't."

"When?" he asked, his tone gentle. Just one word, but she knew what he meant.

She drew in a deep breath. "Mama died a year and a half ago. She was in ill health the last few years of her life. It's the reason I never had a London Season. She urged me to come to London when I turned eighteen, had even arranged for a school friend of hers to sponsor my come-out, but I refused to leave her."

"And your father?" he said.

"Papa died when I was sixteen," she said. "He caught a severe cold that turned into an inflammation of the lungs."

"I'm sorry." His eyes were kind and filled with concern. They didn't say anything more. They didn't need to. Each understood the other's sense of loss.

She wasn't sure when he drew her into the shelter of his arms. It wasn't until her mind registered the sound of his heartbeat that she realized he held her cradled against him, one side of her face resting on his chest, the smooth fabric of his evening jacket touching her cheek.

His chin brushed her forehead, and she felt the faint scrape of whisker stubble against her skin, the stirring of her bangs with his every exhalation. She hadn't known until this very moment how deeply she'd been wanting to be held just this way, hadn't realized how she craved this sort of closeness with another human being.

With him.

Why was she fighting this?

He seemed to like her, to find her amusing. Unquestionably, he liked kissing her.

Lust isn't the same as love, Charlotte. Don't confuse the two.

With a little encouragement on her part, could it turn to love?

If she stopped tamping down her emotions every time they tried to stray outside the boundaries she deemed acceptable, she could very easily fall in love with him.

And what if you did? she asked herself. What if *he* did? What then?

But then again, what if he *didn't*? Did she really want to be that pathetic girl pining over a man she couldn't have?

"Are you all right?" he asked. "That was a very heavy sigh."

She lifted her head. "Yes, of course. Just lost in my thoughts."

"You can stay lost in them as long as you wish." He leaned his head back to smile down at her. "I'm in no hurry."

She mustered her resolve. "We've been absent from the ballroom too long. And there's no Serena here to mitigate the damage if we're discovered together."

"And what if we are caught?" She could feel his chuckle rumbling in his chest. "What can they do to us? We're already betrothed."

"Yes, but you're forgetting one crucial detail. My reputation will be in tatters if I cry off after being caught in a compromising position with you." She brought her hands up and gave his chest a light push. "It's time to get back."

He stared down at her, his eyes dark and unreadable, and if he'd told her that he no longer wanted her to jilt him, she might have been tempted to consider changing their agreement, even though she had grave doubts about the wisdom of choosing such a course.

But all he said was "I suppose you're right." His arms fell away and he stepped back, running a hand through his hair, mussing it adorably. "You know I intended to kiss you. Thoroughly, so that when we returned to the ballroom anyone paying attention would know I'd kissed you. I don't want Miltner or Farrars or any other gentleman to get ideas about stealing you away."

"I don't think you have any reason to worry about that," she said.

"As I've told you, you rate yourself too lightly. Maybe gentlemen didn't notice you before, but they're noticing you now, and I assure you, they like what they see. Now, let's go before I forget my good intentions."

Charlotte swallowed hard. Her heart rather wished he'd chuck his good intentions out the window, but her head knew every stolen kiss was a dangerous mistake. No matter how much she wanted his kisses—and she craved them, desperately, fiercely—in the end she needed to be able to walk away, to free him from their betrothal. And she preferred to do it with her heart intact. Or as intact as it could possibly be.

To her mingled relief and disappointment, he remained true to his word, and they left the library, retracing their steps back to the ballroom. They'd nearly reached it when she asked, "What if Pemberton approaches me tonight? Should I talk with him, subtly question him to see if there's any reason to think he's the culprit?"

"If he tries to interact with you, and it's possible he will, just let any conversation with him unfold naturally; don't try to force the issue. If he's the one behind that false betrothal announcement, we'll leave it to my investigator to find evidence of his involvement. If he says anything you think is important, send a footman to find me, and I'll come to you."

"Where will you be?" she asked, confused by his statement. Was he leaving the ball?

His mouth twisted into a rueful grin. "I intend to visit the card room for a while. I'll rejoin you in time for the supper dance, so don't be promising that to anyone else."

"Won't you be disappointing the ladies? Absenting yourself from the ballroom?"

"I shouldn't think so. As far as they're concerned, I'm taken."

He clasped her elbow and they made their way back to the ballroom, where they met Lydia and her husband, who were just finishing some flavored ices supplied by Gunter's for the occasion. When William inquired if Charlotte would like one, she nodded.

"Lemon flavored, like the last time?" he asked.

"If they have lemon, yes," she said, pleased that he remembered. The same day they'd spotted that awful caricature in the artist's shop. "If not, I'll be happy with whatever you choose for me."

He soon returned with a dish of lemon ice, which he presented to her with a flourish.

"Didn't you want any?" Lydia asked, looking surprised. "It's so stuffy in here. James has already had three."

"I'm off to the card room for a bit. Keep an eye on Charlotte for me," William said, giving his sister a wink. He turned to Charlotte. "Don't forget. The supper dance is mine." He leaned in, and said in a low voice meant only for her, "Save all your enchanting smiles for our dance."

Then he was gone.

The card room was predominantly occupied by men, although a couple of tables were composed of ladies, mostly older women, to whom a round of cards held greater appeal than capering about a dance floor.

William joined a group of gentlemen playing vingt-et-un. He took an empty seat next to Charles Townshend. "You're not dancing?" he asked.

"I did for a bit." Townshend nodded to the dealer to deal him another card, before giving William an oblique glance. "I don't have my own girl to dance with."

William made a sound of impatience. "I can only dance with her twice in an evening."

"I reckon that explains your presence in here," Townshend said. He made a face and pushed his cards away. He'd gone over twenty-one. "You won't be constrained by those unwritten rules once you're married, provided you still want to dance more than two dances with her in an evening."

William's cards added to nineteen, but the hand was won by a man seated across from them who smugly laid out his hand so all could see it totaled twenty-one. The dealer gathered the cards, the man gathered his winnings, and bets were offered for another round.

The players at the table weren't a chatty bunch, which suited William's mood. In his mind, he turned over what Charlotte had told him about Pemberton's odd regard of her.

It might mean nothing. Pemberton was an opportunist. It was possible he planned to strike up an acquaintance with her as a way to curry favor with William. On the other hand, if Pemberton was the party behind the false betrothal announcement, it could explain his fixation with Charlotte. He had to be wondering why they'd carried on with the engagement, since William was fairly sure the culprit, whoever he was, had expected him to disavow any connection to Charlotte.

But either way, William wasn't wild about the man's interest in her. He didn't like Pemberton, found him to be insincere, overly fawning toward those whose acquaintance he hoped would further his interests, and although William had never caught him in a lie, rumors of being less than honest followed the man.

After playing several hands, William tired of vingt-et-un and moved on to join a piquet game. He still had time to kill before he could rejoin Charlotte and claim his dance. He played a few rounds of piquet, before deciding to try his hand at whist. He joined a table of players, Townshend among them, and they were halfway through a game when Pemberton strolled into the card room. He didn't join in any of the play, just ambled from table to table watching the games, finally making his way over to William's table.

William acknowledged the man's presence with a brief nod, then turned his attention back to the cards. He could feel the man's stare on him but pretended to be unaware of it.

"Met your lovely lady, Norwood," Pemberton said at last. "Charming girl."

William played a card. "*I* think so."

Pemberton's fake-sounding laugh grated on William. "One would hope, given that you're about to be leg-shackled to her."

William flicked him a cool look before giving his attention to the card game once more.

"So when is the wedding?" Pemberton said. He smiled, but it came off more like a grimace. The man clearly wanted to draw William into a conversation about his engagement, and wasn't pleased by his short answers.

"We haven't set a date. There's a great deal of prewedding folderol to see to, but we'll be sure to insert a notice in the *Times* once it's taken place."

Pemberton's grimace-like smile was still plastered on his face. Whether he'd done it or not, William mused, he looked capable of villainy.

"Yes, she seems a busy lady by all accounts," Pemberton drawled. "Apparently, she's begun to help Lady Serena and her fellow do-gooders on their current project." William saw that Pemberton's comment had attracted Townshend's attention, who looked up at the mention of Serena.

"Oh?" William said indifferently, tossing a ten of hearts onto the eight of hearts Townshend had just played. "Did you speak with her about it?"

"No," Pemberton replied. "I saw her with Lady Serena in Bloomsbury visiting that house Beasley owned. It wasn't hard to figure out it must be related to another of Lady Serena's crusades." His nostrils flared and his mouth bent into an expression of distaste. "You might want to warn her about the company she keeps, Norwood."

Charles Townshend shot to his feet. "What are you saying, Pemberton?"

Pemberton took a step back. "Nothing to get upset about. Just that Bloomsbury isn't Mayfair, and it would behoove the ladies to remember that."

William pushed back his chair and stood. He sent Townshend a warning glance. Creating a scene would only play into Pemberton's hands.

"It might behoove *you* to remember Lady Serena's father is a good friend of Liverpool's before you so publicly criticize his daughter's behavior," William said in a low voice. "Or are you no longer interested in heading that reforms commission? Last I heard, yours was one of the names being bandied about as a candidate for the post."

Pemberton directed an angry glare at William. "Of course I am. Especially since some in the running are apparently prepared to do anything to get it."

He had to be referring to William's betrothal to Charlotte. William took a step toward the man. "I find that statement very ironic coming from you." He gave the man a look of implacable warning before turning back to the card table. "Gentlemen, you must excuse me. I should be getting back to the ballroom." Townshend joined him as he left the room.

"I don't trust that man," Townshend said. "And I definitely don't like him. You heard the disdain in his voice when he mentioned Serena. That he was right about her careless regard for propriety is just that much more galling. While I don't approve of everything she does, I admire that she tries."

"Someone should marry the girl," William said, giving Townshend a pointed look.

The other man snorted. "As if that would temper her actions."

"It wouldn't," William agreed. "But I'd worry about her less if she had a husband working alongside her."

Townshend didn't rise to the bait. "I've heard Pemberton has made unflattering comments about her in the past." His jaw tightened. "I know it's not my place, and she wouldn't welcome my interference, but someone ought to deal with him before he causes trouble for her."

"Do you think he intends something specific or … ?"

Townshend shook his head slowly. "I don't know, but there's something about his manner that makes my skin crawl."

"I'd say your instincts match mine. I didn't much care for his tone when he was speaking of Miss Hurst just now."

They re-entered the ballroom. William spied Charlotte dancing with Farrars again. He was so busy watching her that he didn't notice when Townshend's path diverged from his. He spotted Lydia and Chatworth talking with the Duchess of Rochester, and headed in their direction. It seemed likely this would be where Farrars would deliver Charlotte when the dance ended.

"Norwood," the duchess said. "I've been getting better acquainted with your fiancée this evening. She's truly a delightful girl."

William smiled and inclined his head. "I find her so."

"I gathered as much," the duchess replied, "I knew you were smitten when I heard she was driving your curricle. Any man can give a lady flowers; very few will hand over the reins to such a dashing vehicle." Her gaze was archly perceptive.

"Very true, Duchess. And I can honestly say I wouldn't have

done so for any other lady." He gave his sister a rueful smile. "Sorry, Lydia."

She pretended to swat his arm with her fan, but he knew she wasn't really offended.

"You're fomenting rebellion within the petticoat ranks, Norwood," Chatworth said, with a nod in his wife's direction. "Guess who wants to learn to drive a high-perch phaeton now?"

"You should have taught me sooner, James," Lydia said, giving her husband a pert glance. "It's time for you gentlemen to stop hogging all the fun for yourselves, and if it takes a few petticoat rebellions to achieve that, then so be it."

William felt his brows shoot up in surprise. He wouldn't have been shocked to hear Libby voice a similar sentiment, but Lydia? That he hadn't anticipated.

Lydia twined her arm around her husband's. "Come along, James. I'm positively famished. Let's visit the refreshments table."

After they departed, the duchess turned to William with a questioning look. "Is she?"

Perplexed, he asked, "Is she what?"

The duchess pressed her lips into a wry half-smile. "I think your sister and her husband are anticipating a blessed event in a few months. She has a certain look about her. Although I could be wrong. Perhaps she's just peckish."

Surprised for the second time in as many minutes, William said, "No, I expect you may be on to something. They've been married several months now."

"If I'm right, I'm sure you'll be hearing the news soon."

Farrars and Charlotte returned just then, cutting off any further speculation regarding the possibility of Lydia being pregnant. Farrars didn't hang around, probably sensing that

William was in no mood to share Charlotte's attention with another man, and the duchess wandered off soon after.

"Card room lose its charm already?" Charlotte asked, her smile teasing. "It's not time for the supper dance yet."

"Something like that." He wasn't going to tell her about his run-in with Pemberton. He didn't wish to let thoughts of Pemberton intrude on his time with Charlotte. Instead, he offered her his arm. "Let's visit the refreshment table. There's a gentleman approaching who looks intent on asking you to dance." He hesitated. "Unless, that is, you'd prefer to stay and dance with him."

"I *am* thirsty." She slipped a hand around his arm, then glanced at him coyly. "And if you like, perhaps we could linger over lemonade long enough to kill time until the supper dance."

He smiled down at her. "*That* I would like very much."

Chapter Fifteen

$\mathcal{A}$t half past ten on the morning after the Vandevere ball, Hopkins informed Charlotte that a young woman had arrived to interview for the position of upstairs maid.

"Good gracious, is it that late already?" Charlotte said, coming to her feet. She'd been kneeling down to rummage through the lower shelves of the linen cupboard, looking for items she could donate to help supply the house on Red Lion Square. She turned to the housekeeper, Mrs. Bridwell, who'd been helping with the task. "I'll leave you to finish up here, and if the girl seems right for the job, I'll let you acquaint her with the house and her duties."

"Very good, miss," the housekeeper said as Charlotte dusted off her hands.

"I put her in the small drawing room," Hopkins said.

Charlotte thanked him, took a moment to glance in the hall mirror to ensure she hadn't become disheveled digging through the household linens, then proceeded to the drawing room.

Waiting for her was a slip of a girl with a pair of large brown eyes set in a slender, pretty face. She sat ramrod-straight on a chair, her hands folded tightly in her lap, wearing an immaculate, but well-worn navy dress. The cracked tips of her leather shoes peeked from beneath her skirt, while a cheap straw bonnet completed the ensemble. She looked so earnest and nervous that Charlotte was tempted to give the girl's hand a reassuring squeeze to set her at ease. She refrained only because such a gesture wouldn't be entirely appropriate if the girl joined the household staff.

Instead, she directed a warm smile at the girl. "I hope you didn't have any trouble getting here." Maybe a bit of small talk would chase away some of the girl's unease.

"Not at all, my lady. Lady Serena gives us hackney fare to go to and from the interviews, and the driver delivered me to the address right enough." She smiled shyly. "It was tremendous to ride through the town in one. A real treat I won't forget anytime soon." Her eyes widened and one hand flew briefly to her mouth before dropping back onto her lap. "I do beg pardon if I'm talking too much, my lady."

Charlotte gave her a reassuring smile. "Of course you're not. I'm delighted you enjoyed the ride."

The girl nodded, but she held her lips pressed together, and Charlotte wondered if she still feared "talking too much."

"Before we discuss the position, perhaps you could tell me about yourself."

The girl blinked. "What would you like to know, my lady?" she asked cautiously, almost as if Charlotte had asked her to spill her secrets.

"Let's start with your name."

"Oh." She looked relieved. "I'm Rose Moore, my lady."

Charlotte suppressed a smile at this frequent use of "my lady," guessing it had been drummed into her at a former position. "Just so you know, I'm more often referred to as 'miss' or 'Miss Hurst' by our servants." At Rose's stricken look, she added, "Not that it's incorrect to call me 'my lady,' just that it's not my preference."

"Of course, my lady." She winced, then drew in a breath. "I'm sorry. I mean, Miss Hurst."

"No need to apologize," Charlotte assured her.

She continued to draw out some details about the girl. She found out that Rose was only nineteen, hailed from a small town in the Midlands, and had worked as a maid at a posting inn since her husband's death. The work, however, had been intermittent and, at times, nonexistent during the winter when weather conditions often prevented travel. Additionally, the wages Charlotte was willing to pay were roughly triple what Rose said she'd made at the inn. It was no wonder then, that these women were willing to leave home and travel to London in search of better opportunities.

There was nothing questionable in her background. Her only family consisted of a younger sister, who also worked as a maid at the same inn that Rose had. However, while she talked about her sister, Charlotte noticed that her hands, which previously had been loosely clasped in her lap, were now clenched together so tightly her knuckles turned white. Something about her sister agitated her.

She asked Rose if she were concerned about leaving her sister behind, but the girl immediately and emphatically denied that she was. However, the combination of the white knuckles and vigorous denial struck Charlotte as a bit similar to "the lady doth protest too much" line from *Hamlet*.

But then again maybe Rose was afraid to admit to worrying because Charlotte might think it would distract her from doing her job. It had been obvious so far during the interview that she'd pinned her hopes on getting the position.

"Well," Charlotte said at last. "I'm willing to hire you on a trial basis, say for two weeks. At which point, if your work is satisfactory, and you're happy here, we can make it permanent."

"Oh, thank you, my lady." Rose clasped her hands in front of her chest ecstatically. "I mean, my miss." She closed her mouth, took a slow deliberate breath, then said, "I mean, Miss Hurst."

Charlotte came to her feet. "Let me introduce you to our housekeeper, Mrs. Bridwell. If you have any questions concerning your duties, she can answer them, so don't hesitate to ask if anything is unclear to you."

"Yes, ma'am," Rose said, her relief at securing the job evident in her broad grin.

Charlotte turned her over to Mrs. Bridwell, who promised to show her the workings of the household and instruct her on the duties assigned to an upstairs maid.

She returned to the linen cupboard, where Mrs. Bridwell had left a stack of neatly folded sheets, towels, and tablecloths for donation. Charlotte tied them together in bundles, then went to her writing desk to compose a note to be delivered with the items. She called a footman and instructed him to see that they were delivered to the house at 6 Red Lion Square, and while she was at it, she wrote a note to the housekeeper at Chartwell, Phillip's country estate, instructing her to cull the household items there.

The soon-to-be-leased property that Serena had mentioned yesterday would need items to make it habitable, and the attics at Chartwell, like the attics of many estates, were stuffed with no-longer-used furniture, draperies, and other household items that might as well be put back in circulation. She'd check with Phillip, of course, to see if he had any objections, but she doubted that he would. He was more than happy to let her handle the household decisions.

Done with these tasks, she rang for a pot of tea, and when it arrived, fixed herself a cup and settled into a comfortable armchair with her feet propped up on a footstool. It felt heavenly to sip tea and rest a moment. Her thoughts drifted back to Rose, and she wondered how she and Mrs. Bridwell were getting on. Charlotte liked the girl and hoped she would fit in well here.

Offering the girl a position was a mere drop in the sea of problems facing the country in the aftermath of the Napoleonic Wars, but it was something nonetheless, and now that she was aware of their plight, she intended to do more to help women like Rose. Serena had opened her eyes and awakened her to the possibility of ladies effecting social change in their own way.

Not that she'd been entirely slack in that regard. She was sensitive to the needs of the tenant families around Chartwell, and always participated in local charity events, but she'd been blind to the needs of those outside her little sphere of orbit. Or if not blind precisely, had failed to see what she, Charlotte Hurst, spinster and bluestocking and no one of particular consequence, could do. But from now on, she was determined she would always, *always* do whatever she could.

After she rested a few minutes, she'd head up to the attic. She thought she remembered seeing some old carpets rolled and stacked up there. Surely those could be put to good use, either at the house at Red Lion Square or the new property Serena was leasing. As soon as she finished her tea, she'd go up and see what sort of shape they were in, and if they weren't moth-eaten from years in storage, have them brought downstairs.

She sighed, thinking she oughtn't to have sat down. Even though she hadn't gotten home from the Vandevere ball until the wee hours of the morning, she'd risen at seven o'clock and had been working steadily since eight. Her tiredness was catching up to her. She closed her eyes. Just a few more moments of rest and she'd get back to work.

She dozed off, and when she awoke there were two notes propped against the teapot where she'd be sure to see them. One was from William. With one finger she traced the now familiar handwriting that spelled out her name, imagining his lean fingers gripping the pen as he wrote out *Miss Charlotte Hurst*.

Her breathing quickened as her mind started imagining those lean fingers of his doing other things: sliding into her hair as he kissed her, tracing the curve of her jaw, following a trail along the line of her bodice, teasing her with a hint of naughtiness before slipping beneath the fabric to— She blinked away the mental image. He'd never behaved so improperly before, never taken such liberties. What was she doing harboring these thoughts? *Acting like a complete ninnyhammer*, she muttered to herself. Wanting to savor the anticipation of reading his note a bit longer, she set it aside. She'd open it last.

She reached for the other note. The handwriting was unfamiliar, but definitely feminine. She broke the seal and read:

Dear Charlotte,

If you're free tomorrow morning, why don't you come with me to the new property I told you about? I'm meeting Papa's solicitor there, along with the property owner at ten o'clock to finalize the deal.

*Mr. Drysdale will want to be on his way before
the ink is dry, but I want to stay and give it a
thorough looking over, poke about in the corners
and knock on the walls. Well, perhaps, not literally,
but you know what I mean. I want to imagine the
possibilities. And it would be much more fun to
have some company. I do hope you can come. I'd
love to show you around. I saw the way your eyes
lit up yesterday when we talked about helping these
women and their families. I think we're true kindred
spirits when it comes to extending a helping hand to
those who need it.*

    Send a reply and let me know if you can accompany me.

*Warmest regards,
Serena*

Of course she'd go. She wanted to become more involved
in this project of Serena's, to use her time and energy for the
good of others. She loved the way Serena put it…imagining
the possibilities. She wanted to have a hand in turning those
possibilities into realities. She'd send a reply to Serena after she
read William's note.

She picked up his missive and this time, without lingering
over it, broke the seal, but was disappointed to find it only
contained a few lines.

Dear Charlotte,

*Liverpool is determined to have the matter of how
to fund England's war debt settled once and for*

all with a comprehensive measure. Right now the Whigs and Tories are far apart on the issue, and I can see a great deal of contentious debate ahead in the coming week.

Which means (and I hope you aren't too happy about this!) that it's unlikely you'll see me for the next few days. Rest assured I will do everything in my power to bring about a swift agreement, but I don't hold out much hope that this will be decided quickly.

Ever yours,
William

P.S. In my dreams last night, we shared several delightful waltzes. I wish real waltzes could resemble my dream versions, which included holding you as close as I liked, and where kisses weren't frowned upon. You can lecture me about it next time we're together, if you want.

A sharp ache settled in her chest at the idea of not seeing him for a while. She probably wouldn't see Phillip much either, but this was a less distressing thought for her.

Resolved not to be ruled by melancholy, she reached for a sheet of stationery and dashed off a reply to Serena. Staying busy would help fill the hole of William's absence in her life over the next few days.

Not just the next few days, Charlotte. What about after you jilt him?

As it was wont to do, some aggravating corner of her mind insisted on pointing out truths she didn't want to face. If she felt empty at the prospect of William's absence while Parliament settled the war debt issue, how would she feel when they called an end to the betrothal?

Lonely.

Bereft.

Heartbroken.

All the more reason to find a worthwhile purpose to fill her life when that eventuality came. Because regardless of how much she enjoyed his company, the chasm between them hadn't narrowed, the type of life each wished to lead still diverged from the other, and she still didn't see how to overcome the differences between them in a way that ensured the happiness of them both.

Passionate kisses were all well and good, but they weren't a substantial enough foundation on which to build a life together. No matter how much her heart might wish they were.

The next afternoon, Charlotte arrived home tired, exhilarated, and more than a little sweaty and dusty from touring all five stories of the newly leased property with Serena. Afterward, they'd gone to Edwina's residence on Upper Grosvenor Street, and over cups of tea had discussed what renovations would be necessary to fulfill the vision they had for housing the widows and their children.

Intent and driven, Serena struck Charlotte as the commanding general of their quartet, while she'd been elevated to the role of aide-de-camp alongside Edwina and the duchess. She'd come home with a list of fifty-six names for which she was to write letters soliciting donations of household items as well as monetary funds for the day-to-day expenses of running the place. Writing that many donor pleas would occupy her free time for the next several days, but she was happy to have a worthwhile project to focus on.

To her disappointment, there was no new message from William waiting for her on the hall table, nor, when she hurried to her writing desk, was there anything bearing his familiar handwriting. Just a pile of invitations for which she could muster little interest if he weren't going to be able to attend them with her. She knew he was busy, but she'd hoped that he might find the time to dash off a quick note.

May as well get used to it, an inner voice taunted.

With a vicious tug on her bonnet ribbons, she undid the bow and tore off her bonnet, carelessly tossing it onto a nearby chair. With equal negligence, she pulled off her gloves, dropping them onto the chair as well, feeling not one whit better for letting her emotions get the best of her. She closed her eyes and drew in a long breath.

Calmer, she sat at her desk and studied the list of names. The first two on the list were Elizabeth and Lydia. She'd start with those, she decided. She pulled some stationery from the drawer, dipped her pen in ink, and…paused, her hand poised to write the salutation, when the name of a different recipient came to mind. After a moment's indecision, she began writing.

Dear William,

Strangely, I'm not thrilled at the news I won't see you for a few days, and am highly suspicious that it has something to do with avoiding the poetry reading at Lady Mortensen's tomorrow evening. I will be forced to soldier on without you, I suppose.

I accompanied Serena to the new property that's been leased to house the war widows and their families. I'm excited to help ready it for them. It's such a worthwhile endeavor... next time I see you I'll tell you about the plans we have for it.

Until then,
Charlotte

It wasn't the cleverest of notes, but perhaps it would draw an answer from him. And in the meantime, she had work to do. Busyness would help fill the void of his absence.

⌒

"How's tonight's speech coming along?"

William looked up from his work, surprised to see Lord Huntington entering his study. "It's done. Or nearly so. I'm just polishing some of the rougher edges." With his quill, William pointed to the pages spread across his desk. "Once I'm done, I can have Stevens make a copy for you, if you wish."

William's secretary had worked such long days this week as the parliamentary debates dragged on that William had insisted on putting him in one of his guest rooms rather than have the man trek home after midnight each day. He planned to give Stevens a few days off once they were past the intense pace of work demanded by the prime minister's push to reach a resolution on the war debt.

"No need." Huntington rested his elbows on the arms of his chair and steepled his fingers before him. "You've argued our position brilliantly this week. Just keep on doing what you're doing, and we'll have this wrapped up satisfactorily in a day or two."

William feared his friend was being too optimistic. They'd made some inroads in the last three days, and chipped away at some of the opposition, but there was still a wide chasm between the plan favored by Liverpool and the Tories and the proposals offered by the Whigs. With any luck, weariness with the process would draw the parties to a compromise solution.

Huntington leaned forward, a broad smile on his face. "I spoke with Tolliver this morning. He said Liverpool is impressed with your efforts on this funding legislation. I think that bodes well for your chances to lead the reforms commission. In fact, I think it's as good as yours."

"Did Tolliver say anything specific? Or are you merely inferring that my chances are favorable?" As one of Liverpool's trusted advisers, if anyone had knowledge of whom the prime minister intended to name to the chairmanship, it would be Tolliver.

"Tolliver's too wily to say anything definitive until they're ready to make an announcement, so I was forced to read between the lines. But there was a certain tone in his voice when he said he wasn't the only one in the inner circle who thinks you're on the cusp of a brilliant career in politics."

This was gratifying to hear, although William suspected Charlotte would be less than pleased by the thought of him seriously pursuing a life in politics. Truth be told, he wasn't entirely sure it was what he wanted, but neither was he sure he wished to rule it out. Beyond getting the chairmanship, that is, which he *did* want, although for reasons that had less to do with political ambition, and more to do with seeing it stayed out of the hands of men who would use it for their own gain.

"I thought you'd be more pleased to hear that," Huntington said when William made no response.

"I am," William assured him. "Being named to lead Liverpool's reforms commission is important to me. You and I both know how vital it is for the government to recognize the concerns of the populace, and enact the sort of policies that will address those issues. If it doesn't, we're going to have more unrest and strife throughout the country, and that serves no one's purposes in the long run."

"You are your father's son, my boy. Henry had the same strong sense of justice, the same desire to do the right thing. He'd be proud of you. What am I saying? He *was* proud of you, and he'd approve of the man you've become."

"I hope so." William wanted to believe that. Certainly, he tried to live up to the example set by his father. "I'll never measure up to the man Papa was, but I try to fill his shoes the best I can."

"Henry wouldn't want you to try to fill his shoes. He'd want you to choose your own path, but I know he'd be pleased if that path led you to the office of prime minister."

William shook his head. "I don't aspire to such lofty heights. You know that."

Lord Huntington's smile was indulgent. "Not yet, perhaps."

William returned the other man's smile with a wry one of his own. "Maybe not ever."

"That's your prerogative, of course. But don't close that door too hastily."

"I rarely do anything with haste. You know that."

Huntington chuckled. "Not usually. Although that engagement of yours happened rather suddenly."

"About that...," William said. "I feel badly it was sprung on everyone like that."

"Don't give it a second thought. Anyway, I'm hardly in a position to criticize. My Gwen and I shocked our families by eloping."

"I didn't know that," William said.

"It created quite a stir at the time, but these days it's largely been forgotten. So believe me when I say I understand that matters of the heart aren't always dictated by prudence. But in other areas of importance, one ought to be guided by reason and wise counsel."

"On that we concur," William said. "And I promise you that I won't make any decision concerning my role in politics without a great deal of reflection."

But now those reflections must include Charlotte, and how she figured into his future.

If she figured in his future.

It was becoming harder to imagine one without her, but he wasn't sure she felt similarly toward him. Until he sorted out his feelings for her and ascertained hers for him, it was hard to know what form his future would take.

He knew Huntington's ambitions for him; he knew Charlotte's reluctance to embrace a life centered in London. Less certain in his mind was what he wanted. Although perhaps the real question was more how to reconcile these competing interests.

He wasn't driven by a desire to attain a high office simply for its own sake, and he didn't want to be the sort of man who was. And he knew if his father were here, he'd agree with him on that. His father had always stressed service, but not ambition. But at the same time, he did feel a strong sense of duty to England.

He suspected gaining a sense of clarity on a potential future in politics would depend on whether or not he was named the commission chair. *And* whether or not he and Charlotte turned their pretend betrothal into a real one.

He missed her though. Missed her a great deal, and hoped she missed him.

She'd hinted that she might, in her note from a few days ago. Hinted for Charlotte, that is. She'd written she wasn't thrilled she wouldn't see him for a while. Maybe he was a deluded fool, but he'd taken that to indicate she longed for his company as he longed for hers.

Perhaps sensing his thoughts had turned to Charlotte—had it shown in his expression?—Lord Huntington said, "It's wonderful Serena and Miss Hurst have become fast friends. Especially if a career in politics *is* in your future. After acting as my hostess in the last few years, Serena can help ease your fiancée's transition into that role for you. With the shifting winds of politics, it can be a delicate balance, one which isn't easy for the inexperienced to navigate. I suggested she take your intended under her wing and ease the way."

"I'm sure Charlotte will appreciate Serena's assistance."

Huntington nodded thoughtfully. "I knew her father, Grenville Hurst. We were at Eton together, but I rarely saw him after that. He went to Cambridge, I attended Oxford. He came to London for parliamentary votes a handful of times over the years, but he was a scholar at heart. More at home immersed in ancient history, rather than taking a hand in shaping the present. Good man, but I admit I had some concerns when I first saw your betrothal announcement, concerns that she might share her father's reclusive tendencies. But she's a great deal like my Serena. I should have trusted your judgment."

William felt a little guilty at this praise, since his judgment had nothing to do with bringing Charlotte into his life, although it was leaning more and more in favor of keeping her a part of it.

"It's true she shares Serena's passion for the welfare of others." He refrained from adding that Charlotte's interest in social functions ran quite a bit cooler. "It's one of the things I admire most about her, in fact."

The hall clock chimed thrice, a reminder the afternoon was waning.

"Already three o'clock," Lord Huntington said, sliding forward in his chair and resting his hands on his knees, as if preparing to come to his feet. "I should let you finish your work. Are you still planning on coming to Bellamy's before tonight's session?"

"I'll be there," William affirmed.

Adjacent to the Palace of Westminster, Bellamy's was a favored gathering place for the members of both houses of Parliament before and after the evening parliamentary sessions. The delicious food and excellent wine cellar drew Whigs and Tories alike, making it a popular location to talk strategy, or rally support for a particular piece of legislation, or to celebrate a triumph if one's side prevailed in a legislative vote.

"Good enough then," Huntington said. He rubbed his hands together. "A juicy beefsteak and a fine claret will start the evening off right, and after dinner you can work your oratory magic."

"I'll do my best," William promised.

The other man grinned and winked. "It's as good as done then. I can feel it. We'll have you back to waltzing your fiancée around the dance floor before the end of this week."

William rose to see his friend out.

"No need," Huntington said, holding up a hand. "I can see myself out the door."

Once Huntington closed the door behind him, William picked up his quill again, but for a few minutes he let his mind wander to thoughts of Charlotte: her smile; her blue eyes alight with sparks of aggravation...twinkling with amusement...dreamy with yearning; the way she felt in his arms; the soft press of her lips against his...

He closed his eyes and drew in a long breath, savoring these remembrances. Finally though, he pushed them aside and returned his attention to the work at hand. Because the sooner they got this legislation passed, the sooner he could spend time with Charlotte and not have to rely on mere visions of her created from his memory.

With this thought motivating him, he quickly finished the changes to his speech. After instructing Stevens to make a fresh copy, he headed upstairs to bathe and prepare for the evening.

Chapter Sixteen

~

$\mathcal{S}$ince sending her last note, Charlotte still hadn't received any communication from William, which didn't entirely surprise her, since in that time she'd scarcely seen her brother either. Parliament was still locked in debate over a spate of new tax proposals to fund the war debt. Phillip left the house each morning by nine o'clock, and didn't return until after she'd retired for the night. That meant her only chance to talk with him was over breakfast. Or rather, because he disliked conversing while he ate, in those few minutes after he'd finished eating, but before he hurried out of the house. Admittedly, she was more interested in news of William than news of the parliamentary sessions, but the two were so inextricably tied, that news of one was news of the other.

According to Phillip, the Whigs and the Tories were slowly coming to a consensus, but apparently this involved a great deal of committee meetings during the day to draft legislative proposals, which were then debated in the evenings, resulting in more drafts and more debates as they tried to find a solution both parties would support.

When she asked how much longer he thought it would be until the matter was finally settled, he just shook his head and said, "Beats me. Soon, I hope. But with all the time wasted by idiots posturing and strutting about the floor of the chamber with nothing of value to add to the debate...Good gad, Charlotte, it's enough to make a Quaker want to knock a few heads together."

"That bad, is it?" she teased.

"Worse," he said, shaking his head as he buckled the clasp of the leather satchel he used to carry papers.

"What does William think of the proceedings?"

"Norwood is in his element. You should see him, Charlotte. When he takes the floor, people mostly pipe down and listen to what he has to say, so naturally Liverpool relies on him to make the case for the Tory position. Slowly, but surely, he's rallying the moderate Whigs to the Tory side."

A sense of pride welled up in her. She could just picture him standing tall and handsome before his peers, commanding their attention with his intelligence and ability to articulate his points.

"By the way, I almost forgot. He wanted me to tell you that he's sorry he's been too busy to see you, but that absence truly does make the heart grow fonder."

"And you're just now telling me this?" she asked with some exasperation, since she'd spent the last half hour in his company, and it did seem when one was entrusted with a message, one ought to convey it sooner rather than later. Still, a warm glow of pleasure suffused her from head to toe at the knowledge William had been missing her company just as she'd missed his. She'd rather convinced herself that, for him, it had been a case of out of sight, out of mind. It made her unspeakably happy to know this wasn't true.

"I only received the message from him last night," Phillip protested. "And you know my brain isn't at its best in the morning. At least I remembered to tell you now."

William missed her! Charlotte floated through the day on a cloud of happiness.

The knowledge that he yearned for her company just as she yearned for his made her giddy with joy and filled her with a shivery anticipatory fervor for their next meeting. Surely Parliament would reach an agreement soon.

Two days later, she was thinking much the same thing—Parliament *must* come to a consensus soon. It had been a week since she and William had attended the Vandevere ball together. A week that seemed so much longer than a mere seven days, though she took satisfaction in what she had managed to accomplish in that span of time. Thanks in part to her efforts, the house at Red Lion Square was almost ready for occupants. And there were the two afternoons spent shopping for clothes with Elizabeth and Lydia—shopping trips Charlotte herself had instigated. But with the Rochester ball around the corner, and Elizabeth still forging ahead with plans for an engagement ball, she couldn't ignore the need for new ball gowns any longer. Not that she confined herself to purchasing only ball gowns, because at the urging of William's sisters, she also purchased a new evening gown, three day dresses, and various accessories to go with them.

She sighed, staring at the swatches she'd ordered from the linen drapers. Working on the house at Red Lion Square had inspired her to do a bit of redecorating closer to home. The furnishings in Phillip's town house were adequate, but outdated. Reupholstering the sofas and chairs in the sitting room and replacing the drapes in all the first-floor rooms would smarten things up considerably without incurring a great deal of expense.

The late morning sun streamed into the sitting room as she studied the look of the different sets of swatches she'd draped over the sofa. She liked the hunter-green damask shot through with gold thread, but would it be too dark in the evening light? Maybe she should go with the royal blue. It was a brighter, more cheerful color, but she wasn't sure Phillip would like it. She could ask him which he preferred, of course, but he hated when she posed that sort of question. More often than not, he'd shrug and tell her to choose. Now if she were to ask whether he preferred roast pheasant or rack of lamb for dinner . . . *that* was a question he'd happily answer.

Her mental debate of the green versus blue question was interrupted when William unexpectedly walked through the sitting room door, looking so impossibly handsome that she drew in a sharp breath, almost afraid he was only a mirage conjured up because she'd missed him so. He crossed the room swiftly, took her hands in his, and for several seconds they just stood there, drinking in each other's presence.

"*You* are a sight for sore eyes," he said at last. Then he bent down and kissed her, warmly, but too briefly.

"What are you doing here?" Her gaze roamed over his familiar features, taking in the dark circles beneath his eyes and the careworn lines, which his smile didn't quite erase. "Phillip left two hours ago, and warned me it would likely be another late evening for Parliament."

"I expect it will be," he said, smiling down at her in a way that sent a tingling thrill of excitement through her. "But I stayed up all night drafting a new and, hopefully, final proposal to be brought to a vote this evening. I think I deserve a couple of hours to spend as I like."

"You look like you should spend them taking a nap," she replied.

One dark brow shot up and his eyes twinkled roguishly. "That might be a tempting suggestion…in the right circumstances." And from the husky tone of his voice she knew precisely what circumstances he meant. "But since I doubt you've abandoned your adherence to propriety in the past week, I have another idea."

"And that is…?" she prompted when he didn't immediately reveal what his idea was.

"Maybe I should keep it a surprise," he said, unable to resist teasing her. He'd missed teasing her, missed laughing with her, missed kissing her. He couldn't wait for Parliament to reach a resolution on the war debt.

"Tell me," she said, glancing up at him through her lashes, clearly trying to beguile an answer out of him.

"Resorting to feminine wiles, are we? This is a new tactic from you."

"Is it working?"

He laughed. "All right, you minx. A picnic. I know the perfect spot for it, and it's being set up for us as we speak. But don't think you'll flirt the location out of me, because that *is* a surprise. Now put on a pretty bonnet and let's be off."

"Bossy," she murmured as he tugged on her hands and pulled her toward the doorway where a smiling Sally waited, bonnet in hand.

At her quizzical glance, he shrugged and said, "I might have suggested that Hopkins have your maid fetch the appropriate headwear for you."

A short time later William drove his curricle into Berkeley

Square and they drew to a halt outside an arched wrought iron gate, the entrance to the private keyed garden in the square's center.

"Well? Does the location meet with your approval? I thought it might, given your comments about it that day we visited Gunter's."

"It's perfect," she said softly, and for a moment he found himself captivated by her happy, unguarded expression. This was the version of Charlotte he glimpsed too infrequently.

"I'm glad you think so," he said at last.

He handed the reins to a waiting groom, exited the curricle, and came around to help her down. Extracting a key from his pocket, he unlocked the gate, and they proceeded down a graveled path into the heart of the garden where a pair of footmen were just finishing laying out the picnic refreshments.

An assortment of platters with cold meats and cheeses, fruits and biscuits, and a basket of rolls sat on the snowy linen tablecloth. A pitcher of iced lemonade, the outside dewy with moisture, sat beside a pair of crystal glasses. Two places had been set.

Thanking the footmen, William dismissed them, then he reached for Charlotte's hand and brought it to his lips for a swift kiss before leading her to one of the chairs. "Shall we?" he asked as he pulled it out for her.

"I can't believe you arranged this on such short notice."

"I've had it in mind for a while, but there was no opportunity to put my plans into action before now." He settled himself in the other chair, which wasn't opposite her, but was more cozily placed on the adjacent side of the table, immediately to Charlotte's right. Around them the greenery grew thickly, providing a natural screen from the rest of the garden, as well as from the houses that ringed the square.

"It's lovely here…a peaceful oasis in the midst of a city block," she said. "Thank you for bringing me, although I still think you ought to be resting. You look as if you've been burning the candle at both ends."

"Sleep can wait." He took her hand in his, lightly stroking his thumb along her knuckles. "I needed to see you more. I've missed you terribly, and I felt all adrift without you there to keep me in line this week."

Adrift was putting it mildly. The truth was he'd felt her absence from his life more keenly than he'd have thought possible. There was more he wished to say, but he hesitated. Her eyes had assumed a guarded look, and he was afraid he'd pushed her into retreat yet again when her gaze shifted to a point past his shoulder.

"I missed you, too," she said at last, the words low and tentative, almost as if she were making the admission against her will.

"I think we should talk about that." At her frown, he added, "Not now. Our time this morning is too short. But later. When this war funding debate is behind us." He relinquished her hand. "Let's eat, and while we do I want to hear what you've been up to this past week. You already know what's claimed my time the last several days." He passed her one of the platters of food. "I gather from the swatches I spied this morning draped over your sitting room furniture you're thinking of redecorating."

"I am, although nothing too drastic," she said, putting some cold chicken on her plate before passing the dish back to him. "If Phillip ever marries, I expect his wife will want things to reflect her taste, so I don't want to make extensive changes. On the other hand, it seemed a good time to update things a bit."

"And what else have you been doing besides that?" he prompted.

She gave a little laugh. "Nothing particularly interesting, I assure you."

"Tell me anyway. *I'm* interested."

"Well, while you've been occupied with the weighty matters of government, I've spent quite a bit of time with Serena. She's put me to work writing dozens of letters seeking donations for a new property she's leased to house more war widows, along with their children. In fact, that's partly what inspired my redecorating project. It only seemed right to come up with a few useful items myself."

"Sounds as if you share Serena's passion for helping others."

"I do. Her enthusiasm is so infectious, one can't help but be inspired by it."

He shook his head. "I can tell you not everyone finds her actions inspiring, though that's partly because she occasionally defies convention in the pursuance of what she views as right."

"Sometimes defying conventions is the only way to change them," she said. "But don't worry. I'm not as bold as she is. Still, she's helped me discover a desire to do more, to live with more purpose than I have in the past." Suddenly, she looked self-conscious. "I didn't mean to turn so serious on you."

"I don't mind, and I understand the need to make a difference. What kind of world would we live in if nobody felt that way?"

"You do," she said swiftly. "Feel compelled to make a difference, I mean. It's why you were willing to risk entering into a temporary betrothal with a girl you'd never met. At that time, you couldn't possibly be certain I'd cry off."

He smiled at that. "After doing such a thorough job alienating you, I was pretty confident of it. But not risking my chance at the chairmanship wasn't my only motivation. Chairmanship or no, I wasn't willing to let you be hurt."

"I hope you get it," she said. "I truly do."

He thought she'd never looked so beautiful. Her cheeks were tinted a delicate pink, and the breeze had worked some tendrils of hair loose, softening her features as they lay in loose curls against her cheeks and forehead. In that moment he wanted to kiss her more than anything.

But before he could act on the thought, she spoke again, "We ought to eat some of this food before we have to leave. You said you only had a couple of hours."

"And so I do," he said. "If we don't linger over our plates too long, we could take a turn about the garden. There are some lovely flower beds at the north end."

Conversation lagged as they focused on the food. He hadn't had a proper meal since breakfast yesterday morning, so he ate with unusual gusto. She ate with much more decorum, and he found himself fascinated with watching her eat. Or more precisely, he was fascinated with those rosy lips of hers. Thoughts of kissing her again had never been far away from his mind even while his parliamentary duties had kept them separated this week.

"Why are you looking at me like that?" she asked, pushing aside her plate, then dabbing at her mouth with a napkin.

"Looking at you like what?"

"Like I have crumbs on my chin or something," she said. "I don't know. It just seemed like you were looking at me differently somehow."

"No, no crumbs. I'm just enjoying your company, that's all." He pushed his chair back and stood, then went and pulled her chair out for her. "I think we have just enough time for a stroll, and then we must head back."

Walking about the garden was mostly an excuse to remove some of the physical distance between them. With her hand tucked so snugly around his elbow, their bodies bumped together from shoulder to hip. They followed the meandering graveled path that crisscrossed the five acres that made up the square's parklike setting.

He wanted to kiss her again, to hold her in his arms, to bury his face in her rose-scented hair, but afraid that she'd erect that wall of reserve she threw up whenever he acted lover-like, he bided his time. A kiss could wait, though he did intend to take advantage of the privacy offered by some leafy-bowered corner of the garden before it was time to leave.

He asked her to tell him more about the war widows project and she did. He hadn't realized just how big Serena's plans were, but he was greatly impressed with the scope of her vision.

"I daresay you ladies have planned a much better program than if the government had been involved."

"Perhaps, but we don't have access to the type of funds the government could provide if they'd taken up the cause."

"The war debt has hampered the treasury's ability to fund much of anything at present beyond the essentials to keep the government running, which is why it's imperative that we find a way to pay it off. But once the state of England's coffers have improved, your efforts could provide the template for some governmental involvement. I'd certainly be willing to bring it up on the floor. And no doubt, Huntington would support it."

"Do you expect that will be anytime soon?" she asked.

His glance was regretful as he said, "Realistically, not very soon."

"In that case . . ." She tilted her head up to give him a saucy look. "You don't happen to have any extraneous household linens or furnishings you'd care to donate to a very worthy cause, do you?"

"As a matter of fact, you're in luck. Libby oversaw an extensive renovation of my town house a couple of years ago, and I'm sure there are items that went into storage that could be put to better use. I'll speak to my housekeeper about it."

"See that you do," she said with a mock severity he found adorable.

"I kind of like it when you turn bossy like that," he said.

They'd nearly returned to the picnic area, and since the foliage was obligingly thick here, and he'd waited long enough, *and* that saucy attitude of hers was so very seductively appealing, it was time to indulge his long-held inclination to kiss her. When he paused in the shelter of a leafy bower, she let go of his arm and turned to him with a questioning glance.

"Oh," she said, comprehending his intentions. "But we shouldn't. Someone might see."

"I think this spot adequately protects us from prying eyes, but so what if it doesn't?" he asked, pulling her unresisting into his arms. "What will happen? I'll have to marry you? We're already betrothed, remember?"

"But not actually betrothed," she whispered.

"Ah, but we *are*, though heretofore temporarily."

"But—"

"Charlotte, can we save the debate for another time? I'm desperate to kiss you."

She blinked, then nodded, and there was no more talking for the next several minutes. At last, William lifted his head and loosened his hold on her. Nearby church bells were ringing the hour, reminding him that this time with her was, by necessity, fleeting. Charlotte was looking at him uncertainly, her lips parted and with a rosy fullness that betrayed what they'd just been doing. He loved it when she looked like that...when she looked like *his*, marked by his kisses.

Had he been marked by hers? he wondered. For she had kissed him just as greedily, just as urgently, just as passionately. In fact, if they hadn't been in the middle of a garden square, he doubted that they would have confined themselves to merely kissing.

"I have a meeting in an hour, and I need to prepare for tonight's debate sometime. Would that we could stay here longer, but I'm afraid we can't."

She stepped back, and smoothed the front of her gown, while he retrieved her bonnet which had, at some point during their passionate embrace, fallen to the ground. William had a hazy memory of untying the bonnet ribbons, the better to kiss the sensitive skin of her jaw and throat.

"I know," she replied, setting the bonnet on her head. "I have plans this afternoon as well. We're meeting at Lady Beasley's to discuss an idea Serena has for a new fundraising campaign."

"Back to work then," he said. "But soon, very soon I hope, I can monopolize your time shamelessly."

Chapter Seventeen

Charlotte was jubilant. At breakfast, Phillip had shared the glad tidings that in the wee hours of the morning Parliament had finally passed the comprehensive measure to fund the war debt. Although she'd felt like dancing a jig right there at the table, she'd refrained, but inside she was exultant. Life could return to its normal rhythms, and that meant she'd have the pleasure of William's company tonight at a dinner party the Peytons were hosting.

She was bubbly with anticipation at seeing William again. Already this morning a large bouquet of red and yellow roses had arrived from him. The accompanying note had been brief: *Thinking of you and counting the hours until I can see you this evening. Ever yours, William.*

Her brother, in a celebratory mood, left for his club soon after their meal, declaring he was devoting his entire day to "larking about" and for her not to expect him before dinnertime.

She had the flowers put in a vase and brought it into the sitting room where she could enjoy the scent of the roses while she supervised a footman in taking the window measurements she needed so that she could order the new drapes. When a moving dray arrived to take some items to the house on Red Lion Square, she oversaw the loading of the furniture and rugs onto the bed of the dray, and then she sent the footmen along to help with the unloading.

It was nearly half past one before she had time to eat. Just as she finished a plate of cold beef and roasted vegetables, Mrs. Bridwell hurried into the dining room, accompanied by the downstairs maid, Jenny. Charlotte took in the young maid's ashen face and red-rimmed eyes and knew something was terribly wrong.

"I'm sorry to be the bearer of bad news," Mrs. Bridwell began without preamble. "But Jenny just came back from running an errand for me. I'd sent Rose along as well. According to Jenny, they'd only gone a few blocks when they were accosted by a seedy-looking fellow. But here, I'll let Jenny tell you." She drew the girl forward, and placed a comforting arm around the girl's thin shoulders.

Jenny blinked and swallowed. "Well, there was a man. He took us by surprise, coming up behind us and grabbing us each by the arm before he pulled us around to face him. Near scared me to death, and Rose, too, I think. He told us not to make a scene if we knew what was good for us. I was too frightened to say anything, but Rose said, 'What do you want?' And then he replied that the price had gone up. I didn't know what he meant by that, but Rose's face went white as a ghost and she said 'But she promised.' Then he shrugged all careless-like and said, 'She changed her mind, she has.'"

"Who is this she?" Charlotte cut in.

"I don't know, and that's for sure. Neither of them mentioned a name, just called her 'she' when they talked about her."

"And you have no idea who this man was?" Charlotte asked. Jenny indicated she didn't with a jerky shake of her head. "Go on then," Charlotte prompted. "What happened next?"

"Rose told him she couldn't give him any more money until she received her first wages. Then he said her sister could pay the debt right enough. And then Rose started crying and begged him to leave her sister be. He said she could take it up with her."

"Did he mean she could take it up with her sister or this mysterious woman?" Charlotte asked. "Because Rose told me her sister worked at a posting inn in the Midlands where Rose comes from."

"The woman, I think," Jenny said. "Rose said she'd talk to her, and then the man said, 'Well, c'mon. Mebbe she'll let you work it off instead.'"

Charlotte didn't like the sound of that. Somehow she didn't think they meant Rose could work it off by cleaning rooms or laying fires.

"What did Rose do then?" Charlotte asked.

"She said she couldn't go with him. That she'd lose her job if she did, but he just laughed and said 'So what? We can give you another job. Mebbe one you'll like better, eh?' Then he laughed again. Rose didn't say anything when he said that, just looked scared and hopeless. She turned to me and made me promise not to say anything to anyone. To go ahead and finish running the errand by myself and that with any luck she'd be back by the time I was done. And then she and that man walked away. Once they were out of sight, I came straight back here and told Mrs. Bridwell what had happened." Jenny glanced uncertainly at the housekeeper. "I hope I did right breaking that promise."

"You did the right thing, Jenny," Mrs. Bridwell assured her, putting an arm around the girl's shoulders. "There are times when it's more important to break a promise than to keep it."

"And they didn't say anything that would indicate where they went?" Charlotte asked.

Jenny shook her head. "No, miss."

She hesitated, and Mrs. Bridwell said, "Tell her what you found."

Jenny reached into her pocket and pulled out a slip of paper and handed it to Charlotte.

THE GOLDEN PINEAPPLE, CORNER OF BEDFORD AND MAIDEN LANE was written on it in an unlettered hand. Charlotte frowned and flipped the paper over, but there was nothing more. "Where did you get this, Jenny?"

A guilty look flashed across the girl's face. "I found it in our room the other day."

"She was snooping through Rose's belongings," Mrs. Bridwell said, "which I've made clear I don't approve of, although I'm willing to forgive it this time, since it might hold a clue about where Rose has gone."

"Do you know where this is, or what it is?" Charlotte asked. She didn't recognize the street names.

"It's near Covent Garden," Mrs. Bridwell said. "I know something of the area because my brother has a small shop a few blocks from the theater. I'd guess The Golden Pineapple is either the name of a tavern or an inn."

"Hmmm." Charlotte studied the note. "It appears Rose owes someone money, which really doesn't make sense to me, since she only recently arrived in London, and she was under Lady Serena's care before I hired her. I don't see when she could have incurred this debt, but I suppose that's a question for a later time. Right now the one thing that's clear is Rose has landed in a spot of trouble. It seems to me the only thing to do is to go to The Golden Pineapple to see if that's where Rose is, and then perhaps we can get to the bottom of this. The sooner, the better."

"I think so, too," Mrs. Bridwell agreed. "But we'll have to wait for the footmen to return. They're all out at present. The two you sent off to help with unloading the rugs and furniture haven't come back yet. And it's Hopkins's afternoon off. He's visiting his brother. So there's no one we can send after Rose. It might be best to wait for your brother to return from his club, in addition to a footman or two. That man Rose went off with sounds like bad news."

Mrs. Bridwell's suggestion made a good deal of sense, except that every minute they waited to go after Rose might (1) decrease any hope they had of rescuing her (and possibly her sister, if the sister were actually somewhere in London, as Charlotte was coming to suspect), and (2) even if they found Rose, by the time they did, she might already have been forced to "work off the debt," which Charlotte was fairly sure meant being forced to work as a prostitute. She could only imagine how frightened and desperate Rose must be feeling right now.

Charlotte shook her head. "We've lost enough time. Call for the carriage. I'll take care of this myself."

Mrs. Bridwell looked scandalized. "Good gracious, miss. You can't go running off on your own like that. And anyway, your brother took the carriage this morning when he left for his club."

"Oh, that's right," Charlotte muttered, aggravated by this setback. "Well, I suppose it's time to try something new." At the housekeeper's puzzled look, she added, "A hackney, Mrs. Bridwell. I'll have to take a hackney cab. Since I've never ridden in one before, it will be a first for me."

"But ladies don't ride in hackneys," Mrs. Bridwell said, making such a thing sound as improbable as if Charlotte had announced she intended to fly to The Golden Pineapple.

"They do in extenuating circumstances. Jenny, wait in the hall while I gather my things, and then we'll be off." Fresh tears welled in Jenny's eyes, but she nodded.

"Shouldn't you take Sally instead? Jenny's a wee slip of a girl. At least Sally has some size to her, in case..." Mrs. Bridwell left the rest of the thought unspoken, but Charlotte knew what she meant. So did Jenny, whose eyes grew round and saucerlike in her thin, tear-streaked face.

"Sally started her courses this morning, and was feeling so miserable I insisted she lie down with a warming brick against her back," Charlotte said, dismissing the idea. "Besides, Jenny knows what this man looks like, and that could prove exceedingly useful."

She spent the next few minutes getting ready. She went to Phillip's study, unlocked the desk drawer in which he kept a stash of ready cash, and extracted some banknotes. She didn't stop to count them; the amount would be more than Rose could possibly pay, even if she were to hand over her entire year's salary. It ought to be more than enough to satisfy whoever was threatening the girl, and Charlotte doubted they'd try to extort more in the future, now that they were dealing with the sister of a peer of the realm, and not just a frightened maid.

She collected her bonnet, gloves, and reticule, then she and Jenny departed. There were no hackney cabs to be seen on the street, but that wasn't uncommon, since the residents of the neighborhood owned carriages of their own.

"Come along," Charlotte said, heading up Berners Street, toward Oxford Street, a main thoroughfare with shops and, hopefully, some cabs for hire.

As they walked, Jenny continued to emit the occasional sniffle despite Charlotte's assurances everything would be all right. She only hoped they could secure a hackney before Jenny began crying in earnest.

Reaching their destination, Charlotte saw that, indeed, there were a few hackneys driving by. She raised an arm as she'd seen people do when hailing a ride. Despite Charlotte waving her arm in the air like a demented person, none stopped because every cab, it seemed, was already carrying passengers. After ten minutes of vigorous arm waving, she felt both idiotic and discouraged. Would an empty coach never come along? She let out a frustrated exhale.

"Perhaps we should go back and wait for your carriage," Jenny suggested timidly. She still had tears leaking from her eyes. Charlotte reached into her reticule and drew out a hand-kerchief, which she handed to the girl.

"We can't be discouraged," she said, with false brightness. She didn't add that securing a hackney was likely to be the easiest part of their mission, and so far they'd failed in that. Her own mood was rapidly heading toward tears as well, albeit tears of frustration.

They walked farther along Oxford Street in the hope of finding an empty cab for hire. As they passed a tobacconist's shop, Charlotte heard her name being called. She looked around to see who had hailed her.

"Miss Hurst," the male voice called again from behind them. She turned and saw, with no small relief, that Mr. Townshend was hurrying toward them.

"I thought that was you trying to hail a coach," he said as he drew up to them. He tipped his hat politely, then added, "But I can't for the life of me figure out why you're doing so. Surely your brother, and Norwood, for that matter, don't approve of your using hackneys to travel around town." He frowned as he took in Jenny's tearful expression. "What's the matter? And whatever it is, let me help you."

"If you wouldn't mind securing a hackney for us, I'd appreciate it. Time is of the essence."

"Of course. Naturally I'll help you in any way I can, but you must tell me what this is about." He stepped to the edge of the roadway and waved his arm while letting out a shrill whistle. "And it goes without saying, I'll accompany you wherever it is you're going."

"We need to get to a place called The Golden Pineapple. It's in the area near Covent Garden. I have reason to believe one of our maids has gone there."

Mr. Townshend shot her a quick, questioning glance when she mentioned the need to visit the area around Covent Garden, but he didn't offer any protest.

One hackney passed them by, but another slowed down, and when it came to a stop, he assisted Charlotte into it and turned to help Jenny, but the poor girl began shaking violently and crying harder. He glanced at Charlotte with a bemused expression.

"Jenny, it's fine. Just climb into the coach," Charlotte said. "We'll rescue Rose and everything will be fine."

Mr. Townshend frowned and his gaze sharpened at the word *rescue*, but again he didn't waste her time by demanding explanations.

"No," the girl said. "No, I'm scared."

"I'm sure there's nothing to be scared of. I won't let any harm come to you," Mr. Townshend said in a soothing voice. "Now come along like a good girl, so we can go."

"No, no, no," Jenny moaned. She pulled away when he reached for her arm to try to urge her into the carriage.

A crowd was gathering and someone shouted out, "Hey, wot's going on there, guvnor?"

"Oh, very well, Jenny," Charlotte said with some exasperation. This spectacle needed to end now before someone called a constable. "Can you make your way back home all right?"

Jenny nodded.

"Then go and tell Mrs. Bridwell that I'm not alone. That we ran into a gentleman acquaintance of mine and he'll see to my safety. Can you tell her that for me?"

"Y-y-yes," Jenny stammered, wiping her eyes with the cuff of her sleeve before loudly blowing her nose into the hand-kerchief Charlotte had lent her.

"Good," Charlotte said. "Come along, Mr. Townshend. We must go."

"Tell me again the name of the place where we're going," he said, "and I'll inform the driver of our destination."

She handed him the slip of paper Jenny had given her. He relayed the information to the driver, then he climbed in the hackney and thumped on its ceiling as a signal for the driver to go.

Looking out the window, she could see the receding figure of Jenny. The girl had turned back in the direction of Berners Street.

"Now then," Mr. Townshend said, "suppose you tell me exactly what this is about, why you're racketing around town without a proper escort, in a hackney coach, yet, trying to rescue someone named Rose, and whether or not Norwood knows what you're up to."

"To answer your easiest questions first, no, Lord Norwood doesn't know what I'm doing, but that's only because there wasn't time to alert him. Or the means, for that matter, since all of our footmen were off running errands when I left. Phillip's been gone all day, which is the reason for the hackney. He has the carriage." She stopped. Mr. Townshend had crossed his arms and was shaking his head as a slight smile played about his mouth. "What?" she asked.

"You're a redoubtable girl, Miss Hurst. I don't yet know what you're doing, but it's clear you weren't going to let anything stop you from doing it. However, I don't think Norwood is going to be pleased when he finds out you intended to visit the area near Covent Garden with only a maid for protection. Not to mention, one who appears to be scared of her own shadow."

"Jenny did prove to be a disappointment in that regard," Charlotte said. "But I've got you now, so that should make him happy."

He chuckled dryly. "I wouldn't be so sure. Norwood is a jealous fellow where you're concerned, and we're alone. I'll be lucky if he doesn't plant me a facer next time we meet."

She blinked. It hadn't occurred to her until that moment that some might look askance at the fact that they were riding alone together. "I do apologize. I didn't even think...I was so focused on getting to Rose, I didn't give any thought to the impropriety of going off with you. And now I've put you in an awkward position. I should have realized how it would look before I agreed to let you come instead of Jenny..."

He held up a hand to silence her. "There's no sense in worrying about that now. Indeed, I'm not worried about it. I thought about making the girl come with us, but I fear that would have involved hoisting her in here against her inclination, and with the crowd of onlookers that was gathering, I'm not sure that would have worked out so well either. I imagine the law might have been summoned and, well, things could have gone from bad to worse. The fewer people that noticed us go off together, the better."

"I shouldn't have let you come," she said. "Although, in truth, I'm glad you did."

"As if you could have prevented me," he said, in a tone that convinced her she wouldn't have succeeded in leaving him behind even if she'd tried. "However, I think it would be an excellent idea if you told me exactly what it is we've embarked upon and why it's necessary for you to visit the less-than-respectable environs of the theater district."

"The new upstairs maid I hired—Rose—is one of the war widows Serena is trying to help, and I don't know what she's mixed up in, but it appears she's being forced to pay money to protect her sister somehow. The details are fuzzy and were supplied by Jenny, who as you saw, is somewhat flighty by nature."

"Why does it not surprise me that one of Serena's projects is tangentially involved?" he murmured. "Was it Jenny who supplied you with the address we're going to?"

"Yes, she found that paper among Rose's things."

He nodded thoughtfully. "So we're likely to encounter some unsavory characters. I don't have a weapon on me, but I am quite handy with my fives." His smile held a hint of self-mockery. "And since I didn't have a gentleman's upbringing, I know how to fight dirty when the occasion calls for it. In other words, I'll do everything necessary to ensure your safety."

"Good heavens, I didn't think it was a question of ensuring my safety," she said.

She hadn't been worried up to this point, but now she wondered whether she ought to be. The extent of her thought process had been that whoever Rose was mixed up with would gladly accept a generous sum of money, and that would be the end of it. She hadn't considered that she might be putting herself in any sort of *real* jeopardy. True, these people had no hesitation about threatening a young maid, but she doubted they'd dare threaten the sister of a baron, especially one who was also the fiancée of an earl.

"I just intend to settle whatever debt my maid owes," she continued. "And to accomplish that I brought these. It should be more than enough, don't you think?" She reached into her reticule and held up a handful of banknotes.

His eyes widened in an expression of surprise and amused chagrin. "Whatever you do, don't pull all those out like that. People in that neighborhood would kill over a stash like that. At least, some would, and we don't know who we're dealing with yet. Although, if I were to hazard a guess, they'll turn out to be petty criminals, or they might not even be criminals at all in the strictest sense, merely individuals of low character trying to capitalize on your maid's vulnerability. But either way, criminals or not, I suspect we'll be able to settle the matter for the price of a few pounds."

Charlotte placed the money back inside her reticule. "I do wish Rose had confided what sort of trouble she was facing instead of trying to deal with it herself."

"Try to put yourself in her shoes. It can be hard for a widow to make an honest living, and that may be part of the reason she was so secretive. Or she may have been afraid you'd find her and her problems too bothersome if she told you about them, and so she tried to hide them rather than lose her job." He lifted one shoulder in a careless shrug. "Who can say why she acted as she did?" He looked out the window. "We're almost there. Who is it we're looking for at The Golden Pineapple?"

"Beyond asking about Rose, I don't know. This could all be a fool's errand."

"We're about to find out," he said.

The hackney pulled up in front of a building that sported a large painted sign in the shape of a pineapple. Mr. Townshend told the driver to wait for them, then he helped Charlotte down and they entered the establishment. Mr. Townshend demanded to speak with the proprietor in an authoritative voice that produced quick results. A balding man with a spreading gut plodded over to them and became instantly cooperative when Mr. Townshend identified Charlotte as the Earl of Norwood's intended bride. Mr. Townshend explained the nature of their errand here, and when he mentioned Rose by name, the proprietor, who'd informed them his name was Mr. Carter, shouted toward a back room for someone called Blade.

A man, presumably the aforementioned Blade, sauntered through a doorway wearing a sullen sneer, but his expression changed pretty quickly when Mr. Carter explained who they were and what they wanted. Especially when Mr. Carter mentioned Charlotte's connection to Lord Norwood, and added that he didn't want Blade to bring any trouble on their heads by messing with the wrong toff.

"Do you know this girl Rose who the lady's looking for?" Mr. Carter asked. His tone was genial, but the look in his eyes as they rested on Blade was hard and uncompromising.

"Yeah, I guess so," the other man replied.

"And the sister?" Charlotte asked anxiously. "Do you know her as well?"

Blade nodded.

Mr. Carter's eyes narrowed menacingly. "Does this business have anything to do with Mrs. Mast and her girls?"

"Not anymore," Blade muttered. "Not if you don't want it to."

"Are the girls nearby?" Mr. Carter asked.

"Yeah."

"Then go get'em," Mr. Carter barked. "And give the one called Rose her money back. Tell Mrs. Mast if she has a problem with that she can take it up with me."

Blade nodded and disappeared back through the doorway.

"I'm sorry 'bout this," Mr. Carter said, his tone and expression becoming more jovial as he addressed Charlotte and Mr. Townshend once more. "That's the thanks I get for tryin' to help that boy out." He shook his head ruefully, as if he were the victim here. "I hope but what you won't hold it against me. I run a clean business."

Charlotte felt Mr. Carter's innocent facade stretched credulity, particularly when the "boy" he claimed to be trying to help looked like a hardened individual who'd earned his moniker Blade in precisely the nefarious way one might imagine he would. If this man Blade was the same man who'd accosted Rose and Jenny on the street, Charlotte could see why Jenny was so fearful of seeing him again.

"We've no intention of pursuing this further as long as the matter comes to a satisfactory resolution," she said.

Mr. Carter nodded and returned to the spot behind the counter where he'd been standing when they entered the place.

She felt a rush of thankfulness that Mr. Townshend had spotted her and Jenny, and that he'd insisted on accompanying her today. Her naïveté could have landed her in a precarious position had she ventured out without him.

While they waited for this Blade to return with Rose and her sister, Charlotte looked around. The establishment wasn't as sinister-looking as she'd expected. There was nothing fancy about it, but it was on the whole clean, if rather shabby. She could see into the taproom, and it seemed to be filled with laborers, men who relied on strong backs and the sweat of their brows to make a living. Most were consuming plates of food and nursing pints of ale as they cast curious glances at her and Mr. Townshend.

Charlotte didn't feel threatened precisely, but neither did she wish to linger once their business was finished. Mr. Townshend, she noticed, was keeping an alert eye on their surroundings while he stood close to her side.

After about ten minutes, Mr. Carter slipped through the door that led into the back and quickly reappeared with a relieved-looking Rose and another girl, who bore enough resemblance to Rose that Charlotte knew it must be her sister.

"Here ya be," Mr. Carter said, leading the girls over to them. "We're squared up now."

"Are you unharmed?" Charlotte asked, the question coming out more sharply than she intended.

"Yes," Rose said. She glanced at her sister, then said again, "Yes."

"Did they give you your money back?" Charlotte asked.

"They did," Rose replied, sounding a bit stunned by this. "All of it."

"Do we have your guarantee that these girls won't be bothered about this in the future?" Mr. Townshend asked. His voice held a rough, steely edge so unlike his usual manner that Charlotte looked at him in surprise. She'd thought his statement about knowing how to fight dirty was more hyperbole than anything, but now she wasn't so sure.

Mr. Carter seemed to recognize that here was a man he didn't want to mess with. "You have my guarantee," he said.

"Then we're square," Charlotte told the proprietor. She put an arm around Rose and Mr. Townshend grasped the sister's arm and they departed. The hackney was waiting outside just where they'd left it. Mr. Townshend assisted all of them to climb in before taking a seat himself.

"All's well that ends well," Mr. Townshend said as the hackney cab left the area around The Golden Pineapple and headed to the welcome familiarity of Mayfair. As they made their way back to Berners Street, the whole story behind Rose's behavior came out.

"I didn't plan to bring Annie here when I came to London," Rose explained. "Lady Serena made it clear I couldn't bring family because there wasn't anywhere to house them. Annie was to stay back in Pentwhistle and keep working at the inn there until I could send for her. That's what we planned. But the inn was taken over by a new owner just before I was to come here, and we could tell that man wasn't the type to treat his employees well or to leave the maids alone, if you take my meaning. I couldn't leave Annie there all by herself with no one to protect her."

"We were told by one of the other maids that there was work to be had at an inn here in London. We thought it was cleaning work, but it wasn't. I begged Mrs. Mast to let Annie just clean the place, which heaven knows it needed. That she didn't even have to pay her, just feed her and house her until I could figure something out. She agreed, but then she demanded money from me, or she wouldn't keep her end of the bargain. I didn't know what to do."

"Oh, Rose, you should have told me," Charlotte said. "I'd have figured out some way to help your sister."

Rose shook her head sorrowfully. "I was afraid if I said anything, I'd lose my job. And anyway, you didn't need another maid."

Annie, who hadn't said a word to anyone yet, had fallen asleep, her head resting against Rose's shoulder. She looked very young and innocent. Charlotte hoped they'd rescued the girl in time, that she hadn't been forced to do the sort of work

Mrs. Mast had been pushing on her. She wasn't sure what they'd do with her yet. Let her stay with her sister for a little while, and then if they could bear to be parted, perhaps send her to Chartwell to work. A country estate always needed more servants than one in town.

"Well, it's behind us now," she told Rose. "Let's be thankful that it ended as well as it did."

Charlotte arrived home to find an anxious Mrs. Bridwell pacing in the entryway. "Oh, thank heavens!" the housekeeper said as they trooped into the front hall. She looked surprised to see that it was Mr. Townshend who was with them.

She gathered Rose to her in a motherly hug, before turning to Annie and giving her a warm hug as well.

"I'll see to these two now, miss. You must get ready to dine with the Peytons."

"Oh, good gracious," Charlotte said. One hand flew to her cheek as she realized that in the excitement of retrieving Rose and Annie she'd completely forgotten about having plans this evening. "Yes, Mrs. Bridwell, you see to Rose and Annie, and please send Jenny up. Since Sally isn't feeling well, Jenny can function as my lady's maid this evening."

"I already sent Jenny upstairs to lay out your clothes," Mrs. Bridwell said. "Now if you'll excuse me." She nodded to Charlotte and Mr. Townshend and led Rose and Annie toward the back of the house.

"After all you've done, I don't wish to chase you off...," Charlotte began.

"But you need to chase me off," Mr. Townshend finished with a smile. "I understand. Don't give it another thought. I'll let you tell Norwood all about this afternoon's adventure." He peered at her closely, and Charlotte silently cursed her inability to assume that carefully bland expression so many aristocrats had mastered to perfection. "You *are* going to tell him, aren't you?"

"I haven't decided if it's truly necessary to tell him. He was quite put out when I went to Red Lion Square, and that's a much safer neighborhood, so I know he won't approve of this jaunt to Covent Garden," she said.

"Maybe so, but I find honesty is always the best policy. Especially since we attracted that crowd on Oxford Street. Among all those onlookers I imagine at least one acquaintance of Norwood's was there to witness it, and if someone else mentions it to him, he's going to wonder why you didn't. And I wouldn't blame him."

"Of course," Charlotte said. "He might jump to the wrong conclusion. You're right. I'll have to tell him and suffer the scolding he'll surely deliver."

However, her confession of the escapade could wait a day or two. After so much time apart, she didn't want anything to mar this evening, and she knew William was bound to be unhappy with her actions.

Mr. Townshend smiled and gave a brief bow. "Adieu then, Miss Hurst. I hope you have a delightful evening. Give Norwood my best regards."

Chapter Eighteen

∽

The next morning Phillip brought a large paper-wrapped parcel into the small drawing room where Charlotte was once again studying fabric swatches with a critical eye.

"This just arrived. A footman was coming up the front steps as I was leaving. He said it was from Lady Peyton for you."

"Oh." Charlotte expelled a long breath. "At dinner last night she told me she'd send over a few things regarding the engagement ball. A preliminary guest list, menus, suggested floral arrangements and..."

A pained expression came over Phillip's face, much as it had last night at dinner when Elizabeth brought up her preparations for the ball. Like most men, her brother had little interest in these sorts of details. She went over and took the package from Phillip.

"And I don't really know what else," she concluded, untying the string that held the package together. She freed a leather folio from the paper wrappings and, briefly, flipped through the papers inside it. "I'll take a closer look at this later." She laid the folio on a side table.

"Well, I'll leave you to your work then," her brother said.

"Not so fast, Phillip. While you're here, tell me what you think of these colors."

"Honestly, Charlotte, you know I don't care. Decorate the rooms how you like."

"Yes, but it's *your* house. You should have a say," she pressed.

"Fine. I like the one on the left."

"Phil-lip! Be serious."

"I am," he said, sidling toward the doorway. "Besides if I don't leave now, I'll be late for my appointment at the tailor's." He gave her an aggrieved look. "An appointment, may I remind you, that you insisted upon in the first place."

"Because you haven't ordered new evening clothes in two years, at least," she protested, "and with all the invitations we've been receiving—"

"Yes, yes, I blame all that on Norwood's influence on our lives. Now, really, I must go."

He turned and slipped through the door before she could offer further protest.

She shook her head, then turned back to the selection of swatches draped over the sofa and a nearby armchair. "Was he referring to the left one on the sofa, or the left one on the wingback chair?" she muttered. Though it really didn't matter, she supposed.

By lunchtime she'd finished up with all the fabric selections for all the rooms she planned to redecorate. In the unlikely event Phillip cared enough to dislike them, he could embark upon his own redecorating project. After lunch, she'd make a trip to the linen drapers, place her order, and enjoy the satisfaction of having completed the task.

So it was a few hours later that Charlotte exited the linen drapers' shop, intending to head to a nearby sweet shop where her maid Sally was doing a little shopping of her own. She'd only gone a few steps when she was accosted by a young boy about ten years old.

"Miss Hurst?" the boy asked. He held out a folded piece of paper with her name clearly written across it. "If you're Miss Hurst, this is for you."

The boy looked like one of the many scruffy street urchins who ran errands or did odd jobs for pennies. What puzzled her was that someone had hired him to deliver a note to her, and rather than take it to her residence, had known she was at the linen drapers. The idea that she might have been followed raised the hairs on the back of her neck. Was this connected to the trip to Covent Garden? Or could it have something to do with Lord Pemberton? The man did seem to turn up in her vicinity with appalling regularity.

"I am indeed Miss Hurst," she replied, taking the missive from him. He started to dart off, but she called out, "Wait! Let me pay you for your trouble."

He glanced around before coming back to stand before her with a hand held out, palm up. Charlotte dug around in her reticule, trying to fish out a coin or two.

"How did you know that you'd find me here?" She continued to "search" for coins in her purse, afraid the boy would run off as soon as she paid him and she wouldn't get any information from him.

"A man tole me to look for a lady in a green dress with a blue purse coming out o' there." He pointed at the shop she'd just exited.

"I see," she said, keeping her voice friendly and conversational, even though she was rattled. Not only did the sender of the note know she'd been at the linen drapers, but the person also knew what she was wearing, and yet he didn't want to deliver this message himself. It was very odd, and more than a little unnerving. "Do you know this man? Does he have a name?" The boy shrugged and shook his head.

"Ah, here we are." She held up a shilling. "This is yours if you can tell me what he looked like."

"I dunno," he said, his gaze fixed on the coin.

"Well, you did see him, didn't you?" He nodded, still staring at the coin. It probably represented a fortune to him, and she knew it was the only thing keeping him there, rather than scampering down the street. "Did he have fair hair or brown or red? Was he a gentleman wearing fine clothes, or was he dressed less finely?"

"He weren't a toff," the boy said. "Didn't notice his hair, but he had a big scar here." He traced a line along his cheek with one of his fingers.

That didn't describe Lord Pemberton, Mr. Carter, or the man called Blade, and since it didn't, she doubted this information about the scar would prove all that useful in identifying whoever had directed the boy to give her the note. So she handed over the shilling. He grabbed it from her and was off like a flash, soon lost in the crowd.

She hesitated, wondering if she should read the note here, or wait until she got home. She looked around her, but she didn't catch a glimpse of anyone who looked familiar, or even anyone who looked unfamiliar, but who seemed to be watching her. Or for that matter, anyone sporting a noticeable scar on one cheek.

Making her decision, she slipped back into the linen drapers.

The fact that it had been delivered to her while she was shopping gave it an aura of immediacy and made her think it was meant to be read right away.

She smiled at the clerk who came over with a questioning look on his face. "I just needed a moment to check my...my list of errands for this afternoon," she said. The clerk nodded and went back to a counter that held several bolts of material.

Charlotte began to read. It was a short note, but the tenor of it sent a cold shiver of dread through her.

Miss Hurst,

It's been so heartwarming to see you and Lord Norwood together these last several days. Ah, young love. Or is it only a fraudulent portrayal of love? I think we both know the answer to that.

Nonetheless, real or not, your name is inextricably linked with Norwood's now. So how do you think the ton...or Lord Liverpool, for that matter...will react to the news that you went to a disreputable establishment in the Covent Garden area, alone, with another man. A man to whom you are not engaged.

Don't bother trying to deny it. I happened to be visiting my tailor on Oxford Street yesterday when that hysterical performance outside the hackney drew my attention. Imagine my delight when you were forced to leave the girl behind, and go off with Townshend...without any sort of chaperone. Naturally, I had my coachman follow the two of you. I hoped whatever you were up to, I'd find some way to bend it to my purposes, and frankly, you exceeded my hopes. Going to a seedy inn together? I could scarcely believe my good luck at being witness to that.

It's a scandal in the making, if you ask me.

But only if word of it were to get out. And since I'm a reasonable man, there's no need for word of it to leak out as long as we come to an understanding. An understanding between you and me, and no one else.

Meet me today at Hatchards. I'll be there at three o'clock. A bookshop seems an appropriate place to run into a bluestocking like yourself. If you fail to show up by four, I'll assume you don't intend to meet me, in which case...well, let's just say I'm fairly certain you will regret it.

Pemberton

Her hands trembled as she refolded the note and tucked it into her reticule. She was undone. *They* were undone if Pemberton talked. She blinked, trying to stave off the tears that threatened.

Pull yourself together, Charlotte.

She took a deep breath, and then another, willing herself to stay calm and *think*.

It was audacious of him to write her such a threatening note, and even more audacious of him to sign it. But he was probably confident she wouldn't show it to anyone, and he was entirely right about that. His note didn't say what he wanted in exchange for his silence, but it did practically confirm he'd been the one behind the false betrothal announcement.

There was only one way to find out. It was nearly half-past

two now. She'd best go collect Sally if she wished to make it to Hatchards by three.

Charlotte wandered among the display tables and tall shelves of books that formed the interior of Hatchards. It was a few minutes after three, but she saw no sign of Lord Pemberton. She idly picked up volumes and flipped through the pages, ostensibly looking for a new book, but in actuality keeping her eyes peeled for the vile man.

She found him—or rather, he found her—in the back recesses of the shop. "You're late," she said.

"No, I was early," he replied, smiling in a way that was eerily reptilian. "I saw you arrive and I've been observing you to make sure you weren't accompanied by anyone who might try to interfere with our business." He smiled again, a cold-eyed, menacing expression. She felt sick to her stomach.

"I only brought my maid, but I sent her on an errand to a shop a block down the street. If it's all the same to you, I'd like to conclude this before she comes in search of me."

"The good news is this won't take long because, as I said in my note, I'm a reasonable man. All I want is your help in eliminating Norwood from consideration for that appointment."

She stared at his gloating face a moment with a growing sense of dread. "I don't see what I can do to influence the prime minister's decision."

At her words, the sinister smile widened. "What I'm talking about is the whiff of scandal—which makes a man rather... undesirable for a position in Liverpool's administration. I admit, I didn't see it coming when the two of you pretended to be engaged to squelch the scandal of that betrothal announcement. I was so sure he'd deny there was a betrothal between the two of you. No offense, my dear, but marriage to a nobody like you was hardly in his plans. Yet, in spite of that, you somehow enticed him to honor a fake betrothal."

"I didn't have to entice him. He's an honorable man. He refused to allow me to suffer any damage to my reputation by honoring it."

"How very noble of him. In that case, my new plan may be doing both of you a favor." His gaze narrowed as he scrutinized her face. "Unless feelings have developed between the two of you?"

"But that would be ridiculous, wouldn't it? As you just said, he hardly planned to marry a nobody like me." She gave him a tight smile. "Can we please get to this plan of yours?"

She didn't want to talk about her feelings with him. If Pemberton possessed a scrap of honor, admitting what she felt for William might dissuade him from enacting whatever his new plan was. But clearly decency wasn't part of his makeup, and any such admission would probably be twisted and used against her.

"Of course. Let's get down to business, you and I. It's very simple, really. Are you familiar with *Tattles and Rattles About London*?"

She nodded, recalling the moment she'd spotted that particular gossip rag in the print shop the day she and William had gone to Gunter's.

"I thought you might be, since your name has appeared on its pages. I want you to supply them with some information. Damning information about your noble fiancé."

She started to shake her head, but he grabbed her wrist, grasping it tightly. "Damning information," he repeated, "to the effect you were coerced into this engagement, that he forced you to pretend it was real all because he was afraid to do otherwise would cause him to lose his chance at becoming chairman of the reforms committee."

"The only reason we agreed to pretend we were engaged was because of your scheme to cause a scandal that would cost him the post," she retorted. "All we have to do is reveal that you were the originator of the false betrothal announcement and your chance will be ruined as well."

He shook his head. "You're wrong about that and I'll tell you why." He smiled even as he squeezed her wrist harder before suddenly releasing it. "If you name me as the perpetrator of that bit of mischief, I will make sure that the tale of your trip with Townshend to The Golden Pineapple becomes widely known. I promise you, the version I'll have spread about town will be as lurid as possible. As I remember it, you and Townshend exited that inn looking considerably more tousled than when you entered. I seem to recall his arm around your shoulders, and that the two of you shared a lingering kiss before climbing into the hackney."

"You're despicable. Nothing like that happened. When we left, my maid was with us, and her sister. They can vouch for us."

He laughed. "Do you really think that will help you in the court of public opinion, the word of a maid in your employ? People love to believe the worst of others. It makes them feel better about their own failings."

"I expect you would know about that," she shot back. "But what makes you think I would agree to do this? Either way, I'm ruined. Why should I lie and say Lord Norwood made me do it?"

His expression hardened. "Look, I'm doing you a favor. One that offers benefits to both of us." He stepped closer to her, and leaned in confidentially. His looming presence was making her skin crawl, and it took all of her willpower not to step away. "I have nothing against you. You're merely a means to an end. As long as no one hears about that scandalous outing with Townshend, you'll come across as a sympathetic pawn in Norwood's quest for power. That ought to be enough to save you from complete ruination. You can always withdraw to the country until the gossip dies down."

His words unloosed a flood of rage through her. The man was despicable! He was exactly why William needed to gain the position, to keep it from going to a man like Pemberton. She wanted to tell him precisely what she thought of him, that he was the lowest of the low, greedy in the worst way, nakedly ambitious, seeking to enrich himself while those less fortunate than he paid the price. But she controlled the impulse. Better to let him think she'd cooperate with his demand. It would buy her time if nothing else.

"Let's suppose I do as you ask," she said, pleased that her voice sounded steady and cool, even though the man's threats had her quaking inside. Not from fear precisely, though there was that. Mostly she felt anger and disgust, and a great deal of regret that her actions had given Pemberton another means to threaten William. "What guarantee do I have that you'll keep silent about my trip to The Golden Pineapple?"

"You have my word of honor," he said.

"Your…word of honor?" she repeated. "I'm supposed to trust in your word of honor when you're willing to besmirch a man's character in such an unfair manner?"

"To that, I can only say life is rarely fair, Miss Hurst, which is why we must rig it in our favor. That's all I'm trying to do, you see. Gain a bit of an advantage for myself. It's why I had that ridiculous betrothal announcement published in the first place. I know your brother slightly, and I knew he had a bluestocking sister who'd come to London for the Season. And I knew Maitland still harbored hopes for a match between his daughter and Norwood. I definitely didn't want that to come to pass, or I'd never be able to pluck Maitland from Norwood's pocket. With Maitland and Huntington backing him, I'd have no chance for that chairmanship. Nobody would. Except for Norwood, who harbors those oh-so-admirable idealistic notions to help the common man."

"They *are* admirable and they're not merely idealistic," she said hotly.

He handed her a book and flicked a warning glance toward a pair of ladies who were perusing the shelves in their vicinity, and who were now regarding them with mild curiosity thanks to her impassioned response. "Here. You might enjoy reading this one." Charlotte took the volume and pretended to flip through the pages until the women moved on to another section of the shop.

"Let's not waste time arguing the point," he continued. "In any case, I thought my original solution rather brilliant. It would kill any chance of an alliance forming between those families and, I hoped, would create enough of a scandal to make Norwood an unpalatable candidate. In addition to the announcement, I fed a bit of misinformation to my paramour to further stir the pot." He laughed then. "I can tell from your puzzled expression you don't know who my paramour is. It's Lady Bohite. I hear there's no love lost between the two of you." He looked inordinately pleased with himself. "I partially succeeded in my goals, Maitland is withdrawing his support from Norwood, so even though your fiancé still has a number of supporters, this will deal him a blow in his quest for the post. Luckily, I also hired a man to keep tabs on you. I thought perhaps I could find a way to expose your engagement as a sham, but now you've handed me another means to knock Norwood out of the running. One even better than I hoped for."

She had. Inadvertently, but she had.

And now she must come up with a way to fix it as best she could. But how? Trying to persuade this man to behave decently would be a waste of her time, so she'd let him think she was cooperating. It would give her time to come up with her own plan.

"You look stunned, Miss Hurst. I'll take that as a compliment. Now do you and I have a deal or not?"

She drew in a long breath. "I suppose we have a deal, Lord Pemberton. I can't see any other solution." Not yet, but she intended to do everything she could to thwart this man's vile machinations.

"You can't know how happy that makes me," he said. "I can't wait to hear to see the next edition of *Tattles and Rattles About London.*"

"I'll need a few days to . . . to prepare. Especially since I think your suggestion that I leave London for a while has merit." She held her breath as she waited to see if she'd bought herself some time to come up with an alternate plan.

"Very well. You have until the end of the week. Don't make me regret my magnanimity."

"I understand. Now I should go. My maid will be wondering where I am."

She hurried from the shop and collected Sally, who'd been walking up and down the street looking for Charlotte.

That evening, after dinner, she pleaded both a headache and a stomachache as an excuse to spend the rest of the evening in her room. (She wasn't sure how long she'd wish to remain "ill," so it had seemed best to suffer from more than one malady.) Apprised of her condition, William sent over a lovely bouquet and a sweet note. In it, he wished her a speedy recovery, and concluded it with

You must rest and get better since the Rochester ball is in a few days, and I'm longing to waltz with you again.

Ever yours,
William

The Rochester ball. She'd forgotten about it, her mind consumed with one thing—how to counter Pemberton's blackmail. She sighed. She had the final fitting of her new ball gown in the morning.

She dismissed Sally for the remainder of the evening, telling the maid she'd ring if she needed her. "All I really need is to rest, and for that I don't need you sitting at my bedside."

Reluctantly persuaded that Charlotte would be fine without her, Sally helped her into one of the flannel nightgowns from Madame Rochelle's and left, but not before building up the fire and reminding Charlotte to ring if she needed anything or took a turn for the worse.

"A good night's sleep will probably put you right, but if you're still feeling poorly in the morning, we'll send for the doctor. The Rochester ball is in four days, and it would be a crying shame if you had to miss it."

After Sally left, Charlotte paced the room, thinking. When this absurd engagement scheme had been hatched, she'd eagerly awaited the day when she could rid herself of the boorish earl, as she thought of him then. Of course, the man had proved to be anything but boorish.

No, he'd turned out to be charming and amusing. Kind and thoughtful. He could make her laugh with a wry observation and make her pulse race with a soul-stirring kiss that thrilled her, that reached inside her and filled some empty place that she hadn't even known existed before he came into her life.

Was it any wonder she'd lost her heart to him? No matter how stubbornly she'd fought against it, she couldn't deny the truth of that any longer.

If only…

But there was no *if only*. Pemberton would have no qualms about trying to destroy William's chances for that chairmanship, but he wasn't going to do it with her cooperation.

She was resigned to being ruined, but there might be a way to limit the damage to William. She would call off their engagement, and let the weight of the scandal fall mostly upon her. Pemberton's claims that William had tried to coerce her would look ridiculous if she refused to back them up.

She knew what she had to do.

It was time to jilt William.

Chapter Nineteen

Once she decided that jilting William was the best—though far from perfect—option to save his chance for the commission chairmanship, it was then just a matter of deciding how to go about it.

Just a matter of...

The irony wasn't lost on her. She was *just* deceiving the man she loved. *Just* preparing to rip her own heart to pieces. *Just* about to set into motion a plan that, in the best case, might work out as she hoped, or might destroy everything they'd worked for with this pretend betrothal.

Just, just, just...

The word echoed in her mind, mocking her.

But she didn't dare tell William what she intended because she knew he'd never choose to save himself if he thought it would cause any harm to her. He would always choose to do the right thing as he saw it, even if she begged him not to.

So she wouldn't tell him. She'd do the right thing as *she* saw it, and that was to save him, no matter what it cost her.

But before she jilted him, before she did what she felt in the very marrow of her bones was the best way to deal with Pemberton's threat, she was going to throw caution to the wind, and do something for herself.

She was going to seduce William, or perhaps more accurately, allow herself to be seduced by him.

The details about how she'd pull this off were a little fuzzy in her mind, but they were attending an evening soirée at Lansdowne House tomorrow, and Lansdowne House was conveniently located (for her purposes anyway) on the south side of Berkeley Square, which would put them within a block of William's town house.

All she needed was a believable pretext, a logical reason that would get them from Lansdowne to William's residence. Perhaps she could plead some minor discomfort—a headache, a dizzy spell, a toothache...something that would allow her to request he take her to his residence for a little while to recover. As long as she could get them to the privacy of his town house, she was confident the rest would unfold as she wished.

One night. She just wanted one night with him, and after that she'd set him free.

A fat drop of rain fell onto Charlotte's cheek, before making a wet trail down her face. Another raindrop plopped onto the top of her head, followed by a third that landed wetly on her brow.

"I think we may have misjudged the wisdom of walking,"

she said, looking skyward to gauge the possibility of being caught in a rainstorm.

While driving to Lansdowne House, they'd gotten within four blocks of Berkeley Square when traffic had simply stopped moving, the streets too clogged with carriages for anyone to make progress. After half an hour, she and William decided to walk the rest of the way to the soirée at Lansdowne House, while his great-aunt Florence, playing chaperone again, elected to stay behind in the carriage.

"I can still see stars in the sky ahead of us," William replied. "Perhaps we're merely under an errant cloud. But walk faster, just in case."

"Is it too much to ask for twenty-four hours of fine weather?" Charlotte grumbled. "The afternoon was simply lovely." To protect her coiffure, she drew up the hood of her cloak so that it covered her head.

"In England?" he asked in an amused voice. "Need you really ask such a question?"

The drops continued to fall as they hurried along, Charlotte nearly trotting as she tried to keep up with his pace. "We should have heeded your aunt's warning that her achy bones predicted rain before morning."

"And we might have, if her aches had indicated its arrival was imminent," he replied. "The moon was still shining when we exited the carriage. Nor are we the only ones to grow impatient with the snarled traffic."

He referred to the other partygoers who'd also decided to make their way on foot, dressed in evening finery, hurrying to reach their destinations before the rain grew worse. The stars were no longer visible and the moon was only a pale smudge behind a thin layer of clouds.

"I expect this rain will put a crimp in the festivities at

Lansdowne House tonight," he remarked. "When the weather cooperates, the gardens are lit with torches and the guests are free to circulate between them and the house. If this rain keeps up, it will drive everything indoors. A shame, since the gardens are lovely in the evening."

"I looked forward to seeing them," Charlotte said.

"And perhaps you will. *If* it doesn't get any worse, and *if* it stops soon." Though he sounded doubtful this would be the case. "But if the weather doesn't cooperate, you can see them another time. The Marquess of Lansdowne often holds large gatherings."

She knew, however, if she didn't see the gardens tonight, it was almost certain she wouldn't in the future. Once she jilted him, her social life would return to its former state, and that had never included invitations from the marquess. She pushed back a stab of sadness at the thought.

The rain began to fall with more insistence, changing from intermittent fat raindrops to a light sprinkle.

"Can you run in your dress?" William asked. They were still more than a block away from the north end of Berkeley Square.

"I could," Charlotte replied. "But rain or no rain, I don't wish to make a spectacle of myself running through the streets of Mayfair."

"If it's any consolation, I expect we'll have company." He cast a glance heavenward. "I don't have achy joints like my aunt, but I have a feeling the skies are about to open up on us."

No doubt he was right. There were still a number of people making their way with urgency as the rain continued to come down. It was on the tip of her tongue to suggest they return to the carriage, when it struck her that this rain could be the answer to the question of how to get them to William's town house.

"Let's try to make it to your residence, at least. We could wait it out there."

"A practical, if not entirely proper suggestion," he replied. "However, I'm willing to skirt the bounds of propriety if you are."

"It seems the best course at the moment," she said, inwardly rejoicing that her plan was falling into place so neatly.

"Come on," he said, grasping her elbow. "Pick up your skirts. We'll make a run for it."

To the credit of William's household staff, they didn't bat an eyelash when they entered through the servants' back entrance of his town house. Not one eye crinkled in amusement at the sight of them, dripping onto the floorboards after their dash through the rain. Rather, a maid grabbed some toweling from a cupboard to clean the puddles, while the unflappable butler ordered another maid to build up the fire in the sitting room.

"I'll have a tea tray prepared and sent to the sitting room," the butler said, addressing William. "And towels for you both to dry off. Right now we should get you and the lady out of those wet outer garments."

"Thank you, Coates," William replied.

A maid bustled over to help Charlotte out of her sodden cloak and a footman helped peel the jacket off William. There was nothing to be done about his wet trousers at the moment. Surprisingly, his shirt and waistcoat appeared dry everywhere but the very front, as did her gown.

William turned to Charlotte. "Let's get warmed up, and then we can decide whether we want to try to attend the soirée."

"I think it's more a question of can we," Charlotte said. "During our dash here, I couldn't hold up the hem of my gown *and* keep my hood in place." She was sure her hair was beyond hope of repair.

William studied her a moment. "All isn't lost, though we need to get you dried off. I don't want you taking a chill."

"But what about your aunt?" Charlotte asked, suddenly remembering that Aunt Florence had been left behind.

"Coates, send a footman to find the carriage. When we left it, we were on Duke Street, a block away from Grosvenor Square. Unless the traffic has cleared significantly, I expect it's still north of Berkeley somewhere."

"There's no need, my lord," Coates informed him. "Your aunt dispatched a lad to relay a message here that she'd instructed your coachman to take her home. She seemed to believe, since you'd gone off on foot, that the rain would put an end to your plans for the evening, and that you'd possibly make your way here. A hackney can be hailed if you wish to leave before the coach returns for you."

"Well, that solves that then," William said. He took Charlotte's arm and led her up a set of stairs that in turn led to a grand entrance foyer.

As she entered this part of the house, her nerves threatened to get the best of her. Her knees went weak and her hands trembled ever so slightly. She was breathless and her cheeks warmed at the thought of the seduction she'd planned.

In the sitting room, they went over to the fireplace and stood before it, warming themselves. A maid brought in a stack of towels, and fast on her heels was another maid carrying a tea tray, which she placed on the sideboard. William dismissed them, and both maids offered a curtsey before hurrying from the room.

William moved an armchair before the fire. "Here." He indicated she should take a seat. "Let's see to that damp hair of yours." As she settled herself in the chair, he fetched her a towel. "For your hair," he said. "I'll pour you a cup of tea to warm you from the inside as well."

The funny thing was she felt quite warm already. They were the only two in the room, and her mind was well aware of the possibilities this presented. The *possibilities* she intended to set into motion. So while she appreciated his solicitude, she rather wished he were less focused on her welfare, and more focused on...well, just *her*.

"Thank you," she said. "I didn't realize earls were versed in the art of pouring tea."

He sent her a wry glance as he went about preparing her cup. "I've never learned the intricacies of serving tea with grace and elegance. Although I daresay my sisters know precisely how to cock their wrists just so while pouring, and how to stir in the milk and sugar to produce a musical tinkling of spoon against cup." He grinned at her. "But even if I don't do it prettily, I know how to create a drinkable cup. So what's your preference: Milk, sugar, or both?"

"A splash of milk, please, and one small lump of sugar."

"As you wish."

As he prepared her tea, she dabbed at her hair with the towel, but without unpinning it, her efforts were ineffectual at best. The warm fire would probably do the best job of drying it for now. She laid aside the towel to take the cup William brought over to her.

Taking a sip, she gave him a questioning glance as he continued to hover beside her chair.

"I'm just waiting to take your cup," he said, answering her unspoken question. "I can set it on the mantel and whenever you want another sip, all you need do is ask."

"Much as I enjoy having an earl at my beck and call," she said, with a teasing smile, "it isn't necessary. I'll just finish my cup while I sit here by the fire."

He frowned. "I really think you need to work on drying

that hair of yours. I meant it when I said I didn't want you to take a chill."

"And what about you?" she asked. "We should get you out of those wet trousers."

As soon as the words came out of her mouth, a fiery blush swept across her face, making it impossible to coolly ignore her poorly worded reply. "That is to say, we can't have you taking a chill either."

A more sophisticated woman would have made better use of that suggestive remark, but Charlotte lacked both the sophistication and the nerve.

His mouth quirked in amusement. "I was afraid that's what you meant. I'm fine. I can change later, while a maid attends to you, provided you still wish to attend the soirée."

"It's nice being here actually," she said. Not a bold declaration, by any means, and yet his gaze locked on hers with a questioning intensity that warmed and excited her, and ignited a certain hope deep within her. It was as if he asked, and she answered, and an unspoken understanding was formed between them. Familiar flutterings began to dance in her stomach.

"I'm glad you think so," he said at last. "But we still need to do something about drying your hair."

"We?"

"Yes, we," he said firmly. "Now, have some more tea, if you wish, and then I'll be your temporary lady's maid."

Before she could reply, Coates entered the room. "Is there anything else you or the lady require, my lord?"

"No, thank you, Coates. Tell the servants we'll ring if we need anything. In the meantime, I'm capable of seeing to Miss Hurst's needs."

Oh, I hope so, she thought, apparently able to be brazen in the privacy of her own mind.

He turned back to Charlotte, reaching out, as if waiting to take her cup. She took a sip to ease the dryness of her mouth, and handed it to him. He placed it on the mantel, and then surprised her by grabbing a cushioned footstool and bringing it over. He set it down beside her chair, and then, surprising her even further, took a seat on it.

"Now then," he said. "The only way your hair is going to dry properly is if you undo what remains of that lovely coiffure your maid created. I'll hold the hairpins for you."

"Is this what you meant by playing lady's maid?"

"For now, yes."

For now. What did he mean by that? Had he divined her intentions, or did he have intentions of his own?

She swallowed and reached up, slowly pulling out a hairpin and then another. Followed by a third and a fourth. His eyes, dark and unreadable, tracked her movements. Though she was only unpinning her hair, it felt a great deal like she was undressing before him.

◦⟋

William had never burned for a woman the way he burned for her just then. All she was doing was taking her hair down, but heaven help him, he wanted her, and she knew it. The knowledge was in her eyes, in the way she watched him watching her slowly pull out pin after pin, releasing section after section.

And yet, she wasn't drawing away from him, wasn't erecting that aloof wall of reserve that she always hid behind whenever he signaled any romantic desire.

As Charlotte handed him hairpins, the light touch of her fingers against his skin sent jolts of desire through him that were wholly out of proportion to the stimulus. But his passion was like a spring coiled too tightly, straining to be released and poised to be by the smallest change in force.

She placed another hairpin on his palm, and another, then another. One by one she pulled them out, and as she did, more of her damp hair came unmoored, unfurling in a brown curtain down her back.

Occasionally she ran her fingers through it, working to free the coils and plaits her maid had used to concoct the coiffure in the first place. The scent of roses wafted through the room. The pile of pins grew in his hand.

She worked silently, and he watched silently, but even so, he recognized a sort of unspoken communication between them. Perhaps it was his imagination, but she seemed to imbue the task with a sensuous quality, as if she deliberately wanted to stir up his desire. Intentional or not, she was doing an excellent job of it.

She reached for the towel and began drying her hair with it. Such a mundane task, but one that set his body aflame. He continued to watch her, too mesmerized to do anything else as she used her fingers to work out the tangles. When she finally finished, William's body thrummed from unreleased tension.

"I...I suppose that's the best I can do for now." She swallowed, and he followed the movement of her throat with his eyes, saw the pulse beating at the base of her neck. "Do I look a complete fright?" She worked her fingers through the long strands. "If I could borrow a comb, I could make myself more presentable." She gave him a rueful smile. "Lately every time I'm with you, I seem to need to put myself to rights."

"You look beautiful. I've wondered what your hair would look like unbound and loose. It's lovely. You're lovely, Charlotte. Don't ever believe I think otherwise."

She swallowed again. She was nervous. He didn't want to

scare her off, to see her once again mount those emotional barriers she always threw up whenever he expressed an interest in her.

"I don't—"

"Please don't,' he said, coming to his feet. He reached for her hand and gently pulled her from the chair so they stood facing each other. He smoothed back some wayward tendrils of her hair. "Please don't do what you always do and shut me out. I think you're beautiful, Charlotte, and I want to be able to tell you how I feel without worrying that you'll withdraw within yourself."

"You know why I do," she said.

"Because you think we're too different to make a successful match."

She nodded.

"But we're not that different," he insisted, ever so slightly closing the gap between them. "Not in the ways that truly count." He dropped his gaze to her mouth. "And not in other ways either. You can't deny when it comes to kissing we are very, *very* well matched."

Her lips twisted into a wistful half smile. "No, I can't deny that."

"Then let's discuss turning this pretend engagement into a re—"

She placed a finger on his lips to silence him. "Not now," she whispered. "Just kiss me. Sometimes you talk too much."

He drew her into his arms. "As you wish," he murmured.

He kissed her then, a slow, deep kiss that involved open mouths, and their tongues tangling together in a frantic dance of unleashed passion. He tasted the familiar sweetness of her, and knew he'd never tire of feasting on the exquisite taste of her mouth, but he wanted more. Tonight he wanted to kiss and nibble and explore her body, from her head to her toes, all the curves and valleys, and the hidden places in between, as far as she'd allow.

He pulled his lips from hers to trail kisses down her jaw, nibbling her skin as he moved on to her neck. A half-laugh, half-whimper interrupted the ragged sound of her breathing as he found a sensitive spot.

"Like that, do you?" he murmured. He nibbled, and kissed, and licked her skin before moving lower to the edge of her bodice. His hand cupped her breast as he placed a trail of kisses along the lacy edge, lingering at the shadowy vee of her cleavage. He pulled away, and she gave a little sound of protest, her hands gripping his shoulders now.

"There are so many ways I want to pleasure you," he whispered. "But I'll stop right now if you want me to." His eyes burned into hers. "Just tell me to stop."

She gave a jerky shake of her head. He reached out, and cupped her chin with his hand. "Say it, Charlotte. Tell me what you want. I don't want to misinterpret your desires."

Chapter Twenty

W hat did she desire? Her desire was for him to do every wicked thing he wished to do with her. Her desire was to spend this night with him, to make the sort of memories she could carry with her when she ended their engagement.

"I don't want you to stop," she whispered.

A slow, sensual smile crossed his lips. "I was hoping you'd say that." He brushed her hair back from her temple and placed a soft kiss there. "But are you absolutely sure? I don't want you to have any regrets."

"I won't." She wouldn't regret tonight. She wouldn't wish her virginity back in the morning. There was no reason to keep it when she'd already lost her heart to him.

"Then let's not waste another minute." He kissed her again, then swiftly bent and hooked an arm behind her knees, and swept her into his arms. His hard muscles encircled her, and the warmth of his body enveloped her as he tucked her against him. She slipped her arm around his neck, and leaned her cheek against his shoulder. For a second, he buried his face in her hair.

"Do you have any idea how that scent of roses has driven me mad?" he asked, walking toward the doorway. "Filling my mind with all sorts of naughty ideas, usually at the most inopportune times."

"Really? I'd no idea of the rogue you were hiding behind that staid, rather dull, exterior," she teased, twining her fingers into the hair at the nape of his neck.

He began to climb the stairs now. "Staid and dull, am I?" he growled, then nipped the ticklish spot on her neck, drawing a small shriek of surprise from her. "I take that as a personal challenge, my darling Charlotte. Let's see if you revise your opinion of me once I've..." He tightened his arms around her and gave her a kiss that left her breathless. "Once I've had my wicked way with you," he said, his voice husky with passion.

His broad strides were now taking them down a hallway with several closed doors that Charlotte assumed led to bedrooms. They stopped before a paneled mahogany door. Charlotte thought he had never looked so handsome as he did right then, his hair tousled, his eyes dark blue and heavy-lidded. He looked as if he wanted to devour her right there in the hallway. Her gaze dropped to his lips, and a hot flush swept over her as she pictured his sensual mouth exploring her body.

"Here's my bedroom, Charlotte. If this is what you want, reach for the doorknob and open the door. But if you have any doubts, tell me now and I'll take you right back down the stairs."

They studied each other for a moment, the sound of their unsteady breathing abnormally loud in the otherwise silent hall.

"Why would I have doubts?" she whispered, turning the

knob with a decisive twist. The door swung open, and for one brief second, while he held her poised on the threshold, she wished that everything could be different. That tonight could mark the beginning of their future together, not the beginning of the end of their charade.

Once inside, he pushed the door shut with his foot and carried her to his bed, gently lowering her legs so she stood beside him. "One moment," he murmured, then he moved toward the fireplace, adding coal to the grate so the flames burned brightly and hot.

She admired the movements of his tall, lean body as he attended to this task, was mesmerized by the sight of him unbuttoning his waistcoat as he came back to her side. He tossed it over a chair back, then loosened his cravat before his nimble fingers made short work of untying it. She swallowed hard as the thought of those fingers doing things—intimate things—to her sent a jolt of desire through her entire body. He sent the linen neckcloth over the chair back as well, but made no attempt to remove any more of his clothing. Instead, he bracketed her face in his hands, his thumbs softly brushing against her cheeks as he looked at her with an expression of wonder, as if he were amazed she was here, with him, in the privacy of his bedroom.

"Charlotte," he breathed. "You've no idea…" He leaned in and kissed her, his hands moving to her shoulders, where his fingers slipped beneath the fabric of her gown, pushing it down along her arms until it wouldn't go any farther without being unfastened. He trailed kisses down her neck to her collarbone, and along the exposed skin of one shoulder.

"I've no idea what?" she asked in a shaky voice, desperate to know his thoughts just then.

"How much I want you," he said, straightening again. "Now

turn around so I can attend to my duties as your lady's maid and get you out of this gown." She obeyed, lifting her hair to allow him to undo the buttons at the back of her gown. "I never thought I was the type of man to lose my head over a woman until I met you. At first you drove me crazy because... I don't know why. Probably because you didn't seem to like me very much."

His fingers continued at their task, sending shivers of delightful anticipation down her spine, along her limbs, and straight to the juncture of her thighs. "And then you were like an itch I couldn't quite scratch, which isn't very romantic, I know." He placed a lingering kiss on her neck just below her left ear before whispering into it, "I'll admit my feelings snuck up on me. I can't pinpoint the moment when I became captivated by you, but it's true. I am. Completely, thoroughly, irrevocably captivated. Lately, you've filled my thoughts day and night."

His words, so sweet and romantic, filled her with joy and a bittersweet longing, but she refused to rob this moment by thinking of a future without him.

He'd loosened her bodice enough to pull it down to her waist, exposing the light stays she wore over her petticoat and chemise. "Are there tapes at the waist?" he asked, and when she nodded, his fingers slid inside her gown, tugging at the ties until they gave way and her gown fell into a pool at her feet. Taking her hand, he helped her step free of it. "Don't move," he said. Then he strode back across the room and draped her gown over the back of an armchair by the fireplace.

"That should dry out any lingering damp from the rain," he said. It took him no time to undo her stays and remove her petticoat. These he placed on the same chair as her evening gown.

"You're awfully familiar with the art of undressing a woman," she remarked when he came back to her side.

"All in a day's work when I take up the task of being your lady's maid." He reached for her hand, and kissed its palm, then the sensitive skin of her inner wrist. "However, if you're implying I'm familiar because I've undressed many women, I haven't. I trust that doesn't disappoint you."

"Not at all," she whispered.

He smiled and then his gaze, hot and lascivious, traveled along her body. "I'm glad I didn't know you were wearing such lovely undergarments all this time. My imaginings would have been much more feverish."

"They're part of that trousseau I ordered at your sisters' insistence."

"I approve. Wholeheartedly."

"Yes, that's become rather obvious." She glanced at the straining fabric at the falls of his trousers. And then with uncharacteristic boldness, added, "Perhaps we should talk less and do more. One of us is a bit overdressed at the moment."

"I agree." His fingers trailed a path from her shoulders to the low-cut neckline of her chemise. "But there's no need to rush. I want to savor this first time with you."

The last time. But she refused to dwell on that now.

He pulled her against him. One hand cradled her neck while the other slipped around her waist, then moved downward, cupping her backside as he held her flush against him. His lips descended onto hers in a searing kiss that left her weak in the knees and, to remain upright, clinging to his shoulders. One of his hands traced a path up and down along her spine, and the light touch of his fingers felt hot through the fabric of her chemise, making her burn for him. His other hand kneaded her bottom firmly and with a growing urgency that stoked her own desires.

She squirmed against the hard ridge of his erection pressed

into her abdomen, feeling a surge of feminine power when he groaned into her mouth. He broke off the kiss saying, "You drive me to the brink of madness, Charlotte. I need you now."

And before she knew what he was about, he crouched down, untied her garters, and peeled her stockings off. Then he swung her into his arms again, and gently laid her onto his bed.

She raised herself onto her elbows, and watched him as, swift and businesslike, he went about the task of divesting himself of his own clothes. It would be more maidenly of her to avert her eyes, but she was feeling much more the wanton than the prim virgin. She wasn't going to let feminine sensibilities get in the way of her curiosity or her pleasure.

As he shucked off the last article of clothing, she drew in a sharp breath, her curiosity satisfied. He was magnificent, perfectly proportioned, lean and muscular, with a sprinkling of dark hair across his chest. His skin seemed to glow in the dim light of the room.

He stood a moment and watched her watch him, his eyes dark and shadowed. "Have you seen enough?" he asked, with a husky laugh. "I'm a bit impatient, and now you're the one who's overdressed."

Before she could answer, he was in the bed beside her, gathering her to him, raining kisses on her face, her neck, her breasts through the thin, nearly sheer fabric of her chemise.

She couldn't hold back an involuntary gasp of pleasure as his lips teased ripples of delicious sensations through her body. She'd never imagined a man's touch could make her feel this way.

So caught up in these new feelings, she barely noticed his hand as it slid down her side, her hip, the top of her thigh until he hooked his fingers around the hem of her chemise, and slowly began to pull it up toward her waist. The air cooled her exposed skin as he slowly and sensuously pushed the fabric upward, baring her inch by slow, tantalizing inch. Her breath was coming in soft little pants now.

He lifted his head to watch her as his hand made its torturous journey along her skin. Flames of desire flickered low in her belly at his hungry, almost harsh look as he studied her. His gaze held hers captive while his hand moved to the triangle of hair, exposed now that the hem of her chemise rested just below her waist.

She couldn't quite stifle the whimper that formed in her throat when he began stroking her with a light, sure touch. His nostrils flared slightly at the sound, and his eyes took on a possessive, self-satisfied gleam, but he didn't say anything. Just continued to ply his lover's caress, back and forth.

"Open your legs for me, Charlotte," he whispered, still watching her. She obeyed and his fingers began to work a new kind of magic.

His touch felt so very, very good, and the way he regarded her with such unwavering naked desire... it was erotic beyond anything she'd ever imagined. She wanted to lose herself in the sensations he was creating, the building, throbbing sense of anticipation that his clever, wicked fingers produced with each fluid stroke.

"I love watching you find your pleasure," he said. "You're beautiful, Charlotte. Perfect. Without fault."

Which, of course, wasn't true. She wasn't a great beauty and she had many flaws.

"I'm... I'm not perfect," she panted.

"You're better than perfect. You're exactly what I want."

With a swift movement, he sat up, and pulled her chemise over her head. He tossed it aside, then lay back down beside her, his fingers taking up exactly where they had left off.

She thrust herself against them in some instinctual response, wanting more of something she couldn't quite identify, but somehow knowing he could give it to her.

"Oh, yes, Charlotte," he murmured. "Do you have any idea how much I enjoy making you writhe like that?"

"It feels...so good," she said, barely able to talk. It felt so delightful, so wickedly delicious. "So good," she repeated, her teeth clenched against the low, throbbing pulse that had begun between her legs and now threatened to envelop her completely.

He quickened his strokes and her back arched as she thrust against his hand, reaching, reaching for something she couldn't quite attain. The pleasure continued to build, and she felt incredibly sensitive beneath his touch, but still something she needed was just beyond her reach and she didn't know how to get it.

He must have sensed what she felt because he changed his technique, focusing solely on her most sensitive spot. She felt herself being pushed to the edge of some high precipice of sensual satisfaction, lost in a haze of passion, almost, but not quite there.

"William," she gasped, trying to articulate the maelstrom of her feelings with that single word.

"I know, darling. Come for me. Let me see your passion."

"I'm...trying, but I can't...quite do it."

"Have you ever touched yourself this way?" he asked.

His words broke through the sensual fog that clouded her mind. She felt her eyes widen in shock at his question. She knew men sometimes took care of their own needs, but that was because they were men, and supposedly had little self-control when it came to lusts of the flesh. She'd never considered touching herself in the same way.

"No," she said, giving her head an emphatic shake. "Never." And then before she thought better of it, added, "Should I have?"

He let out a short bark of laughter and kissed her, first on her brow, then a languid kiss on her lips. "I only asked because I thought you could tell me what you liked best, but we'll just have to figure it out together."

"I liked that last thing you did...the way you touched that...that place..."

"I know what you mean," he said, beginning to do it again, sending her soaring once more to that torturous brink. But despite his efforts, she still couldn't quite tumble over into the complete fulfillment of orgasm.

"Maybe this will help," he murmured, leaning down. She thought he meant to kiss her again, but instead he placed his mouth on her nipple, flicking the hard peak with his tongue, sending explosions of pleasure through her.

"Ooooh," she moaned. "Oh, yes, William. Yeeesss."

He began to suckle, and something indescribable erupted within her, and she knew it wouldn't take much longer. Her hands came up, pressing his head to her breast, reveling in the pleasures he provoked. And then her release came in wave after wave after wave, the sensation so intense she could hardly stand it.

William felt a sharp stab of primal satisfaction when Charlotte shuddered beside him, her body convulsing with a climax he'd brought her to. There was no question now that they belonged together. She was his, and by the same token, he was hers. It had been all he could do to hold back his own desire to enter her and share in that thundering surge of completion.

But he was determined to take it slowly, to make sure it was as much about her pleasure as it was his.

"William?" Her voice, uncertain, tentative, broke into his thoughts. She shifted slightly, and he realized his hand still rested between her thighs. Reluctantly, he moved it to rest on her abdomen.

She frowned at him, and he almost regretted the impulse that had prompted him to delay entering her, because now he feared he'd given her time for second thoughts to settle in. But if they had, if she wanted to call a halt to it right now, he'd respect it.

"Yes?" he asked, steeling himself for the words he didn't want to hear.

"We're not stopping there, are we? I mean, don't you want to…finish what we started?"

"Yes!" Relief washed over him and he kissed her. "I very much want to finish what we started. I was just giving you a moment to recover."

"I've recovered sufficiently, I think." She smiled at him and her hand drifted down his chest to his abdomen. His stomach muscles clenched involuntarily as her fingertips brushed against his skin before drifting lower.

"Ticklish?" she asked, glancing at him through her long, dark lashes.

"No," he rasped as her knuckles lightly skimmed the length of him. "But none of that. I'm too close to the breaking point as it is."

"But shouldn't I reciprocate?" she asked. "I thought men liked a woman to touch them there."

"I would like it above all things, but not right now. I'm too close and I won't last if you touch me with your hands first. Later," he promised, bringing her hand to his mouth and giving it a kiss. He shifted, settling himself so that his body covered hers, his groin nestled against her thighs. "Right now I'm desperate to be inside you." He nudged against her, pressing lightly against her opening.

Her legs parted and he pushed inside her slowly, fighting his own impulse to bury himself in her quickly and deeply. He wanted to make this good for her if he could. He gritted his teeth, determined to minimize her pain as much as possible. Her lips fell open and her breathing appeared to accelerate.

"Am I hurting you?" he gasped. "Tell me if I'm hurting you." He was in paradise, entering her tight, slick heat. And as much as his male pride might wish otherwise, he wasn't going to last much longer.

"No," she said. "It feels strange, but not painful exactly."

"Good," he grunted. He kissed her as he slowly eased himself in, stopping abruptly when she winced and drew in a sharp breath. "Tell me when it's better," he said.

She nodded, and a few seconds later said, "It's better."

"I can give you more—"

"No," she said. "It *is* better."

He continued to go slowly until he was fully within her. He didn't move for a few seconds, except to trail kisses along her cheek to her ear where he gently nibbled the lobe, giving her time to adjust to him.

"Is there something I should be doing?" she whispered.

He smiled and kissed the tip of her nose. "More like something I should be doing, but I didn't want to rush and hurt you."

"You're not," she assured him. Her lovely blue eyes were large and trusting, and in that moment he acknowledged the truth of his feelings—he loved her.

He loved her.

It was on the tip of his tongue to tell her, and yet he was

afraid the words might ring hollow if the first time he uttered them was while he took her virginity. Nor did he want to risk declaring his love for her, only to have her retreat behind that wall of reserve once again. He'd speak the words later. Right now, he'd simply show her how he felt.

He began long, slow strokes within her, gritting his teeth as he tried to hold back the tide of his own pleasure, but he was fighting a losing battle. When she began to match the rhythm of his movements, he knew he wouldn't last much longer. "Bend your knees, Charlotte," he commanded, hoping this would help lessen any pain or discomfort she might feel. She did, and he thrust into her faster and faster until he reached his own shuddering climax.

He collapsed on top of her, his face buried against her neck. The scent of roses and the clean smell of her skin filled his nostrils, along with the faint musk of their lovemaking. He should withdraw. She'd been a virgin and her passage wasn't used to a man filling her, but he selfishly savored just a few more seconds of her warmth enveloping him. He still craved a few more moments of union.

Finally, he rolled onto his back and drew her close, cradling her against him. Her cheek rested on his shoulder and her arm was draped across his chest, a soft hand placed just below his collarbone. He grasped it in his and laced their fingers together before firmly placing a quick kiss on her forehead. She didn't say anything and neither did he. Somehow words didn't seem necessary. Before long he succumbed to the drowsiness overtaking him.

Charlotte stayed awake, trying to hang on to every moment. She wished she could expand time, or stop it. Just for tonight, just for a little while as she lay tucked securely in his arms, the heat of their bodies mingling, the slow and steady fall of his chest, the intimacy of listening to the thud of his heartbeat beneath her ear.

But she couldn't stop time. However much she wished this night didn't have to end, it would. Inevitably, morning would come, and she'd have to face it clear-eyed and resolute. She knew what she had to do: She had to jilt him now. Pemberton wouldn't wait forever to leak his damning information.

These were her stolen hours. One night with him before she called the betrothal off. He wasn't going to like her course of action, was going to expect them to marry now. His honor would demand it. Her sense of honor ought to, and if not for Pemberton's threat, she might allow the dictates of conscience (not to mention the desires of her heart) to guide her decision.

She thrust away thoughts of the future. Fretting about it now only robbed time in the present. She didn't want to diminish this time with William by worrying about tomorrow.

William awoke sometime later. The fire burned low in the grate, and Charlotte was snuggled enticingly next to him, one thigh thrown over his, her breasts pressed into his side, her face buried against his neck as warm puffs of breath tickled his collarbone.

It hadn't been a dream.

"Charlotte."

Nothing. She was sound asleep. He smiled to himself. It felt so right to have her tucked up against him, sharing his pillow. Sharing his bed. He raised his head enough to catch sight of the mantel clock. Only five past eleven. They still had a few hours before he'd have to take her home.

"Charlotte," he said again. Slowly he stroked one hand up and down her back.

She moved against him, making a small sighing sound, but her breathing remained steady. He wouldn't have guessed she was such a sound sleeper, but while she might not be waking up, his body was.

"Charlotte." He spoke louder this time, moving one hand to caress her bare breast.

"Ooh," she squeaked, awake at last. She moved to rise up onto one elbow, but he pulled her atop him.

"We can't be doing this," she said, obviously noticing his renewed desire. "What time is it? I've got to get dressed."

"There's no need to be hasty. It's only a little after eleven. That soirée we were supposed to attend will go until three o'clock, at least, so your brother is unlikely to expect you home anytime soon. Besides, I like your current state of undress."

"Stop that." She batted at his hand where it caressed her bare bottom. "Behave. I'm thinking."

"About?"

"About how much longer I can stay here without raising suspicion." She frowned and chewed her lip as she considered this.

"We have a few hours yet," he coaxed. "I promise to get you home in good time."

She still looked uncertain, so he decided to try a different method of persuasion. He rolled them over together so that he was now on top. In a swift motion, he lightly pinned both her wrists above her head with one hand, then ducked his head down so he could suckle her breast.

With a sigh, she surrendered to his plundering mouth, and

soon, as he continued to lavish attention to the taut tip, she began to writhe as a soft moan escaped her. Finally satisfied that she was sufficiently distracted from thoughts of leaving, he slipped a hand between her legs, stroking her as he'd learned she liked. It didn't take her long this time to make the climb toward ecstasy, but just before she got there she grasped his wrist tightly, pushing it away.

"No," she gasped. "I want you now. *Now*."

He needed no further invitation, entering her in one swift movement, then pausing to give her time to adjust to him, even though it taxed every ounce of his willpower. She, however, had other ideas—much better ideas—because she immediately began to move with a steady rhythm beneath him.

"Charlotte."

The single word came out rough and raspy, but he hoped she could hear in it everything that was beyond his power to say just then.

I want you so badly... You feel so, so, sooo good... Oh my God, I'm in heaven... Oh. My. God.

He matched her movements, and it wasn't long before they came together in the sweet oblivion of *la petite mort*.

They lay there for several minutes, bodies entangled in the aftermath of their lovemaking until, to his surprise, Charlotte began a curious exploration of his body.

"You've touched me everywhere, but I haven't had the chance to do the same to you," she said, running a slim finger across his chest, lightly teasing one of his nipples. "And since turnabout is fair play..."

He rolled onto his back, allowing her unfettered access to whatever part of him she wished to explore, which she did, slowly and deliberately, driving him mad with her touch.

Then when she'd taken him almost to the brink, and he was

just about to flip her on her back and make love to her once more, she murmured, "I once saw this illustrated in a book, and I've always been curious…"

Before he could divine her intentions, she straddled him, taking him inside her as she smiled down at him with the look of a woman enjoying the ability to exercise her feminine power.

"Have I ever told you how much I appreciate those bluestocking tendencies of yours? And incidentally, I heartily approve of your choice of naughty reading material," he managed to say, so aroused by this unexpected side of her that he could only speak the words as a series of breathless pants.

"I don't believe you have," she replied, her eyes studying him with a glint of supreme satisfaction. Then with a wicked smile, she added, "But I like the way you show your… appreciation."

He'd thought their lovemaking couldn't get any better, but the third time, with Charlotte acting as the aggressor, had taken them both to greater heights of passion than before.

"You're a revelation, Charlotte," he murmured against her neck. "But I'm not sure I can move from this bed anytime soon. Not for a week, at least."

"I know how you feel," she said, stirring from where she'd collapsed atop him. "But it's getting late."

"I know." Reluctantly, he withdrew and moved to lie by her side, his head propped up on one hand. "I'll go to Doctors' Commons first thing tomorrow for a special license. We can be married by the end of the week."

"What? No!" She struggled to sit up, drawing the sheet up to cover herself in a gesture of belated modesty. "You don't need to do that. Nothing's changed. I didn't come to your bed expecting you to marry me."

"I didn't bring you to my bed expecting anything else," he

said, sitting up himself. "Surely you didn't think I'd make love to you and then send you on your merry way."

She bit her lip and avoided his eyes. "I don't want you to feel obligated," she said.

"Not feel obligated? What kind of dishonorable cur do you take me for?" he demanded. "One without a conscience?"

"I don't think you're dishonorable at all," she said. "But the fact that we...did what we did doesn't change our agreement in any way."

"We made love, Charlotte, even though you can't bring yourself to say it. And it changed our agreement in every way," he shot back. "How can you think it doesn't? What if you're carrying my child?"

She stared at him a long moment, and he wondered if this possibility had even occurred to her. She swallowed. "If I'm carrying a child, then, of course, we must marry. But the possibility of that is slim. My own parents were married five years before my mother conceived Phillip. What are the chances it would happen after only one night?"

"I don't know what the chances are, but I'll tell you what I do know. We are getting married."

Her chin jutted out defiantly. "No, we are not."

He raked a hand through his hair in frustration. This was ludicrous. They were naked together, in his bed, after a glorious session of lovemaking, and they were fighting over whether or not they would marry. It was laughable, and yet the humor completely escaped him. At this point, a marriage between them shouldn't be a question, it should be an inevitability. And yet it clearly wasn't. Not to her, at least.

"Charlotte," he said, trying to sound calm and reasonable, "I don't know why you're fighting me on this. If it's some sort of postcoital regret, it doesn't make much sense to me. I'm willing to marry you. I *want* to marry you. Why—" But he didn't finish the question because she'd gathered the sheet about her and climbed out of the bed. She made her way over to her chemise where it lay on the untidy jumble of his own clothes on the floor.

She scooped it up, and turning her back to him, dropped the sheet before jerking the garment over her head. Then she walked over to the chair and donned her petticoat. She grabbed the stays and tried to fasten them, but failed.

She looked close to tears, and though he was frustrated himself, he said, "Hang on a moment, and I'll help you." Without attempting to cover himself—because really, after what they'd done together, what was the point?—he picked up his shirt and drew it over his head, then located his trousers and put them on.

He did up her stays, then helped her don her dress. She tied the tapes, but was helpless to button it without his assistance. She turned to him, "Please," she said.

He buttoned her up and then they finished dressing in silence.

"I'm sorry," she said at last.

"Are you going to tell me what this is about?" he asked. "Why you're so opposed to marrying me after what we just shared?" He stopped and closed his eyes, trying to contain his growing anger and hurt. "Is there something you haven't told me? Did I do something to offend you?"

She stared at him and it was obvious she was on the brink of tears, but he refused to drop the matter. He wanted answers. "Because I don't understand your response, and if it's something I did, tell me, so I can make it right."

She just shook her head sadly. "It's nothing you did. I didn't mean to mislead you when I agreed to come to your room with you."

"Then what was this about? Surely marriage is the obvious conclusion to what happened here. In my bedroom. *In my bed*."

"It was never about marriage. It was only about tonight," she said. "You know we're ill-suited—"

"Oh, that won't wash, Charlotte." He raked a hand through his hair. "That won't wash at all." He came to stand before her. "We are so well-suited, that as angry as I am right now, I want nothing more than to spend the rest of the night in that bed"—he flung his arm up and pointed to that particular piece of furniture to emphasize his point—"making love to you over and over and over until the morning comes, but I can't do that because we aren't married. Yet. Now if you're not willing to marry me, I think I deserve an explanation."

"I don't have one beyond what I already offered," she said, her voice soft and miserable. "But you refuse to accept it."

"Because I know it's not true, and I know that you know it, too. Whatever you believe makes us so ill-suited for one another can't be so insurmountable that it rules out a marriage between us. Surely you know there's nothing I wouldn't do to make this work. To make *us* work." She didn't respond, just continued to stand there, her eyes bright with unshed tears.

Something wasn't right, but he couldn't put his finger on it. He threw up his hands and began to pace around the room "I don't know what is going on with you, why you're being so stubborn and obstinate. If it's some crazy notion about sexual freedom planted in your head by Serena, or if it's something else, I wish you'd tell me, but I can see there's no reasoning with you tonight. We'll discuss this tomorrow. *Tomorrow*," he repeated, "right after I visit Doctors' Commons and get a special license."

Chapter Twenty-One

Surprisingly, Charlotte didn't cry that entire night. She didn't shed a single tear, even though she felt constantly on the verge of turning into a complete watering pot. For some reason, the tears refused to come, even when she was back home and Sally helped her out of her evening gown and she was finally alone in the privacy of her own room. She wished she could have cried, that she could have sobbed out all the heartbreak that had threatened to overwhelm her from the moment she told William she wouldn't marry him.

When Pemberton's threat of ruin had forced her hand, somehow she'd convinced herself it would be easy to end things between them. Or if not easy, precisely, at least not this hard. Not this *painful*.

She tried not to think of the hurt she'd seen in William's eyes, heard in his voice as he demanded she explain her refusal to marry him. Would it have made him feel any better if he'd known her heart was breaking into a thousand pieces? Would he have understood why she refused him in spite of that?

Sitting on her bed, her knees drawn up before her, her back resting against a nest of pillows, she closed her eyes and recalled the ghastly ride home from Berkeley Square. Neither had spoken to the other during that awful drive. William had sat stiff and angry, and she'd been seated across from him, remaining silent, since she knew there was nothing she could say to make him feel better. Not without telling him the truth, which she simply wouldn't do. Not when she knew he'd sacrifice his political ambitions to save her. Still it had been horrible, knowing she was the cause of his anger, knowing it was justified, knowing that she didn't blame him one bit for feeling it.

She'd been certain he'd offer to marry her, had expected him to insist upon it, because it was William and he would always do the right thing. But what she hadn't anticipated was how hurt he'd be at her refusal to accept his offer of marriage. Not that it had been much of an offer, just an off-handed remark that he'd get a special license the next morning. But after all that had preceded that moment, it would have been silly for him to go down on one knee.

Nonetheless, he'd been hurt by her repeated refusals. Deeply, deeply hurt. And *that* had surprised her. Shocked her, really, because he'd never—not once in all the times they'd kissed or when he'd brought up the possibility of considering a real engagement or tonight when they'd made love—not once had he ever mentioned the word *love*. Not once.

If he had, maybe she'd have chosen to handle Pemberton's blackmail differently. Or maybe not. She honestly didn't know, but speculation was pointless now. She'd set a course and she must see it through.

She just hoped that in the coming days at Chartwell she

could find a way to despise herself less. Perhaps if William received the chairmanship, she would feel her actions had been justified. If he didn't...well...she had to believe this was still the best course for both of them in the long run.

One good thing about being unable to cry out her misery and heartbreak in those wee hours of the night was that the notes she wrote to Serena, Phillip, Elizabeth, Lydia, and finally, to William, remained free of teary ink splotches. In them, she explained as best she could that she'd decided to end the engagement, but since she could hardly offer the truth, she justified it with the reservations she'd expressed to William earlier in their charade.

William and his sisters would surely be disgusted by her decision to end it so abruptly. Phillip would be puzzled and disappointed, but she'd give him the true explanation someday. Not now though, for fear he'd tell William the truth, and then William would insist on protecting her rather than himself.

For the same reason, she didn't reveal the whole truth to Serena, but she did ask Serena to break the news to Edwina and the Duchess of Rochester. Given the ripple effects of gossip, word of her broken engagement would likely be all over town by this evening, though she would be well away from London by then. She planned to leave for Chartwell at first light this morning.

It was cowardly of her to bolt like this, but it had taken every ounce of her resolve to maintain her refusal to marry William to his face. She wouldn't be able to repeat the process with her friends and family, much less the rest of the *ton*. She simply couldn't.

She piled the finished notes on her dressing table. It was nearly five o'clock. Dawn wasn't far off and she needed to choose some outfits to take with her to Chartwell. She pulled a valise from the bottom of the wardrobe and threw in some garments, not particularly caring what. Soon she'd rouse Sally to help her dress, and she wanted to have everything ready for her escape.

∽

Arriving at the Hurst home the next morning, William was met by Hopkins, who, after giving William the briefest of narrow-eyed glares in response to his request to speak with Miss Hurst, led him to the sitting room. Left to cool his heels, William paced about the room, wondering what had roused Hopkins's animosity.

Had Charlotte appeared at the breakfast table red-eyed from crying? Guilt pinched at him. She'd appeared on the brink of tears during their argument, but later, in the carriage, she'd been composed enough sitting across from him, holding herself so stiffly she might have been a statue save for the unavoidable movement of her body in response to the usual jouncing caused by rough pavement or the coach's turnings.

What a ghastly ride it had been. Even the memory of it pained him greatly. He wanted nothing more than to make things right between them—whatever it took—to bridge the emotional gulf that had existed between them on that ride. The ride had been all the more wrenching because of its stark contrast to all the other rides they'd been on together.

But to make things right, he had to know what lay behind her refusal to marry him after she'd come so willingly to his bed. On the face of it, it made no sense.

She was holding something back.

She had to be, because he was well aware of her resistance to the idea they could have a future together. She'd expressed her objections often enough. So why had she exhibited no reluctance to going upstairs to his bedroom, knowing what was about to happen? Knowing it must presage a marriage between them? She couldn't have misjudged him so badly that she didn't expect him to insist upon it, could she?

Surely not. So where was the logic of her actions? He couldn't see it. Couldn't grasp how one got from point A—they were too ill-suited to marry, and then arrive at point B—his bed, where she was an enthusiastic participant in the most intimate of acts between a man and a woman.

Which was why he didn't intend to leave this room until she told him—*truthfully*—why she refused to have him as her husband, but was perfectly amenable to accepting him as her lover.

He went to the window and stared out at the street below. The sun shone brightly now, glinting diamond-like off the few puddles left from last night's rain. If not for that rain, there would have been no quarrel between them, because there would have been no need to seek shelter in his residence.

Water under the bridge, he thought with bitter irony.

But the truth was, the only thing he regretted about last night was that it had led to this schism between them.

"Hopkins said you were looking for Charlotte."

William whirled around. Phillip Hurst stood in the doorway, looking uncharacteristically somber.

"Yes. I need to speak with her, and if she's asked you to dismiss me, I must insist—"

"She's not here, Norwood." Hurst walked farther into the room. "She's up and left."

William could only stare at the other man. A strange buzzing began in his ears and for a moment, he felt as if the floor tipped sideways. His heart thudded painfully in his chest, and he struggled to draw in a breath. He opened his mouth to speak, then closed it when the words refused to come, and opened it again, this time to inhale a ragged breath.

"So you didn't know," Hurst said, a look of concern coming over his face. "I'm sorry."

"What do you mean 'she's up and left'? Left for where?" he demanded.

"To Chartwell, my estate in Berkshire. At least, that's what her note said." He held out a small box. "In that note she asked that I return the betrothal ring to you myself."

William took the box from Hurst. The finality of her leaving it behind was yet another blow to his battered heart.

Hurst walked over to the sideboard. "No offense, but you look ghastly. Shall I pour you a drink?"

William brushed aside the offer of a drink with an impatient wave of his hand. "What note?" he asked urgently. "If she left you a note that she was dashing off to Berkshire, why are you here instead of going after her?"

"I admit, that was my first inclination, but she specifically asked that I not do that."

"In the note she left?"

"Yes."

"And you actually did as she bid? Are you daft? Letting a lone female travel to Berkshire?"

"She took our town coach and coachman, as well as one of the footmen and her maid, so she's hardly alone. Even so, I considered hiring some sort of conveyance and chasing after her, but there's no faster way to make Charlotte dig in her heels about something than to go against her wishes. I'm quite sure she's safe, and by not going after her, I hope she'll have the time she needs to cool off, and reconsider her actions." He shot William a quizzical look. "In the note, she said the two of you quarreled last night and that she'd decided to immediately call off the betrothal."

Hurst might have voiced that last sentence as a statement, but it was clearly meant to be a question. "We did quarrel," William said curtly. "But she never mentioned jilting me over it."

Phillip Hurst nodded, his brows furrowed as he waited for William to continue, but he offered nothing further. He could hardly tell the man he'd quarreled with Charlotte over the need for a hasty marriage after making love to her.

However, that wasn't the only reason he was reluctant to discuss what had occurred last night. He was barely holding his emotions in check. Part of him wanted to smash his fist into a wall to vent his frustration, to distract from the pain squeezing his heart into a painful knot. And part of him wanted to hole up in a room with a great quantity of whisky, and drink until he was well and truly foxed to dull the heartache. Truth be told, he considered it very probable he would indulge in both of those actions sometime today, but later, not now.

Breaking the silence, Hurst said, "Did you not receive a message from her this morning? I know for a fact she left notes to be delivered to you, your sisters, and Lady Serena two hours after she departed. According to the servants, a footman left around eight this morning to carry out the task. It's nearly ten o'clock. I should have thought you'd have received yours by now."

"I left home around eight to...attend to some business." Just as he'd promised Charlotte only a few hours ago, he'd made an early morning trip to Doctors' Commons to procure a special license that would allow them to marry within the week. "And then I came straight here to talk with Charlotte, and try to resolve our disagreement."

Hurst gave him a pointed look. "Must have been quite the

disagreement for Charlotte to decide to jilt you *and* flee town. I don't mind admitting I was shocked by her actions. Stealing off at first light isn't Charlotte's style. I can't recall her ever indulging in similar dramatics."

"It's my fault. I upset her. More than I realized, apparently." Frustrated, William ran a hand through his hair, at a loss for the best way to proceed. Like Hurst, his first inclination was to go after her, and make her tell him what lay behind her refusal, because he *knew* there was something. And once he knew, he could find a way to persuade her to marry him.

He had to find a way to persuade her because the thought of not having her in his life was too unbearable to contemplate.

"I don't intend to intrude on this lovers' quarrel," Phillip Hurst said. "But I will give you a piece of advice. And while I admit I'm not a man who knows much of anything about females, I *do* know my sister. Go home. Read her note. If she cautions you against coming after her, heed it. For a few days, at least. She can be intractable if she gets her back up about something, but once she cools down, she'll be willing to listen to reason."

"I'll take that under advisement," William said. "If she offers me no such prohibition, I intend to depart this afternoon for your estate and settle things between us. If she bids me not to follow her, I will consider your counsel, but I can't promise I will follow it."

"You must do as you see fit, Norwood. But let me offer another reason to delay following after her. You may need to stay and control any gossip that arises from her sudden departure. If you give the impression it's merely a lover's tiff, not a permanent break, it might blow over quickly, provided you *can* patch things up with her."

William nodded as a sudden weariness overtook him. The last

thing he felt like doing was putting on a brave face for the *ton*, to act as if this was only a little quarrel, a slight misunderstanding even, knowing it was anything but that. "I'll let you know what I decide to do. I'm going home now. If you hear from her…if you think of any reason to explain her actions…contact me. Even though we quarreled, I never expected her to do this. Refuse to see me this morning perhaps. Refuse to see me for the next few days even, but not leave entirely."

"If I hear anything, you'll be the first to know. As for her reasons, I expect they will remain a mystery unless she chooses to divulge them."

Phillip offered again to pour them both a drink, but William declined, eager to get home where Charlotte's note should be waiting for him. He made his farewells, again exhorting Hurst to share any news about Charlotte immediately, including her safe arrival at Chartwell.

However, watching the familiar streets of Mayfair roll past as his coachman drove him back to Berkeley Square, William's eagerness began to flag, replaced with a growing sense of unease. What *had* she written in her note to him?

Whatever it contained, he doubted it held any sort of explanation beyond what she'd offered last night, and it might very well be her attempt to irrevocably break the ties between them.

Two days later, still reeling from Charlotte's unexpected jilting, William was in his study going over his steward's report about needed repairs to the cottages of some of his tenant farmers. Or trying to. His concentration had gone all to hell, as had his appetite, and his ability to sleep in any way besides short, fitful stretches.

Based on Phillip's counsel, as well as opinions voiced by his sisters and Serena, he'd remained in London, and tried to quell the gossip, which thanks to the scandal sheets, had spread with impressive rapidity. He'd done his best to paint their quarrel as bridal nerves on the part of his fiancée, which had led to a minor disagreement.

"I'm letting her cool off, before I do the pretty and beg her forgiveness," he'd said more times than he cared to count in the past three days, often accompanying this statement with a wink or smirk of a smile. It was a nauseatingly jocular performance, to be sure, and if Charlotte were here to witness it, he'd no doubt she'd tell him so. But it seemed to be working. People appeared to view their separation with amusement more than anything else.

His patience with the situation, however, was fast coming to an end, since none of it amused him in the least. He *did* want to beg her forgiveness if that's what it took to end this estrangement between them.

Realizing his attention had drifted off again, he turned back to his steward's report, but he'd read only half a page before Coates appeared in the doorway.

"Mr. Townshend requests an audience with you. Shall I tell him you are in?"

William hesitated, not particularly in the mood for company, but he decided a diversion from his own thoughts might be a good thing. "Send him in, please."

A few minutes later Townshend strode into the study, a concerned look on his face. "Thank you for seeing me. I wasn't sure you would."

William gestured for him to take a seat. "We can commiserate on our troubles with the ladies in our lives. I hear you and Serena had a...disagreement."

"That's partly what I'm here to discuss."

"I'm afraid if it's advice to the lovelorn, I'm not the best person to ask."

Townshend's mouth twisted into a wry smile. "Lady Serena and I are merely friends. Or enemies. Depending on the day and whether I've rubbed her the wrong way."

"I'm sure enemies is too strong of a word. I think Serena secretly likes that she can't always bend you to her will. What was your disagreement about?"

"Miss Hurst, actually."

Even though she was never far away from his thoughts, just hearing her name caused his heart to twist in his chest. "Oh? What about Charlotte?"

"I wanted to make sure that whatever had come between the two of you, it had nothing to do with that trip she and I made together to The Golden Pineapple. But Serena told me I should mind—"

The statement brought William to his feet. A cold fury consumed him at the thought that she'd gone anywhere with Townshend and he was just now hearing about it. *What else didn't he know?*

"She didn't tell you, did she?" Townshend said, warily eyeing William. "I had a feeling she was reluctant to do so, though I advised her she should."

"No, she did not," William bit off. "Pray do rectify that."

"I knew you'd be angry," Townshend said. "And I don't blame you, but let me assure you there was nothing improper about our actions. The Golden Pineapple is an inn located in Covent Garden. We went there to rescue that new maid of hers, a widow she'd hired at Serena's suggestion."

William slowly lowered himself back into his chair. "Why did the maid need rescuing? Particularly in a neighborhood like that so far from the environs of Mayfair?" *Did this have anything to do with Charlotte leaving London?*

Townshend quickly relayed the events that had led to his accompanying Charlotte to The Golden Pineapple. William didn't say anything as he turned the information over in his mind, looking for some clue to connect it to Charlotte's later behavior. He'd known there was something she wasn't telling him, but was this it?

"I thought perhaps this had something to do with your broken engagement," Townshend continued. "I didn't want *that* to be what came between the two of you. But obviously it wasn't, if this is the first you're hearing of it."

"That wasn't what we argued over," William said. "But I'm not sure that it isn't the reason behind our argument after all."

Although if it had any connection to Charlotte ending their engagement, he couldn't see what it was.

"When did this trip to The Golden Pineapple take place?"

"A few days ago," Townshend replied. "When I accompanied them back to the Hurst residence, the housekeeper mentioned Miss Hurst needed to hurry and dress for a dinner party at the Peytons' that evening."

"So on Monday," William said grimly. He'd discovered she'd jilted him Thursday. Had something happened in between that visit to The Golden Pineapple and her flight from London?

"You said a crowd was gathering, and that's why you left the maid behind."

Townshend nodded.

"Did you recognize anyone in the crowd?"

"I wasn't really focused on those in the crowd," Townshend said. "We were on Oxford Street, so there were shoppers, some tradesmen, servants . . . just the usual assortment of people you'd see out and about. I remember Lady Biddle and her daughters were there, watching with mouths agape." He closed his eyes as if trying to picture the scene.

"Was there anyone else from our circles there?" William asked.

Townshend frowned and shook his head slowly. "No. I don't remember..." His eyes widened and he snapped his fingers. "I do recall seeing Pemberton's carriage. With those distinctive red spokes, it's hard to overlook. So he had to be in the area."

Upon hearing that, William was almost certain Pemberton had something to do with Charlotte's behavior. How he figured in the picture, he couldn't fathom. The evidence up to now was largely circumstantial, but that did nothing to dispel William's hunch the blackguard had a hand in this.

"Do you think Pemberton's mixed up with whatever provoked the argument between you and Miss Hurst?"

"Let's just say I strongly suspect he's tried to cause problems for us before." He came to his feet. "But it's past time I get to the bottom of this and find out if my suspicions are correct."

Townshend rose as well, clearly recognizing William's action as a dismissal. "I hope this leads to a reconciliation between you and Miss Hurst."

"That makes two of us," William said.

An hour later, William's carriage was pulling up to Pemberton's residence. On being told by the butler that Pemberton wasn't at home, William replied, "Really? That's odd. Because I saw his carriage being brought around from the mews, and the man himself peeping out from one of the front windows." He stepped around the butler into the entryway. "Obviously, he doesn't wish to receive me. Nonetheless, please be so good as to tell him, he *will* see me now. I'd prefer not to force my way in, but I'm perfectly willing to if that's what it takes."

The butler gave a stiff bow. "Very good, my lord."

Two minutes later William was ushered into Pemberton's study.

"Well, now that you've so rudely interrupted my morning, have the decency to state your business quickly. I was just getting ready to leave for an appointment."

"With pleasure. Time spent in your company makes my skin crawl. I've come because of what you said to my fiancée, Miss Hurst." This was a shot in the dark since he was still operating on conjecture alone.

A wariness crept into Pemberton's expression. "I should have known she'd come running to you rather than do as I asked. I warned her there would be consequences. If that's what you've come about, you're too late. The latest issue of *Tattles and Rattles About London* should be out later to—"

His sentence remained unfinished because William crossed the room and grabbed Pemberton by his lapels, hauling him from his chair and pushing him hard against the built-in bookshelves that ran across the side of the room behind Pemberton's desk. Some books dislodged and fell on the floor around them. Pemberton glared at him and made a futile attempt to free himself from William's grip, but William regularly sparred at Gentleman Jackson's boxing salon, and was far more athletic than the other man. A hint of fear crept into Pemberton's gaze.

"I don't know what trick you're trying to pull this time, but I suggest you make sure the latest issue of that gossip rag doesn't appear later today. Buy every damn copy yourself if you must. And henceforth, don't you *ever* approach her again." He gave Pemberton a long, hard shake. "*Ev-er*. Is that clear?"

Pemberton glared at him, but nodded.

William let him go, stepped back, and tugged the cuffs of his jacket back into place. "Then I won't keep you any longer. And make sure that not one copy of the current *Tattles and Rattles* goes up for sale."

Directing a last look of disgust at Pemberton, he turned and walked toward the doorway. When he reached it, Pemberton spoke. "After that I expect I'll be calling at Liverpool's office this afternoon," he said in a mocking voice. "It may have him questioning your judgment after he hears about the antics of Miss Hurst and a certain gentleman."

William turned back, and saw that Pemberton's bravado was fueled by the fireplace poker he now held in his hand. No doubt her trip to The Golden Pineapple was the threat he'd held over Charlotte to cause her to bolt.

"Don't bother. Lord Huntington and I have an appointment with him in half an hour, at which time I intend to tell him the truth about how my engagement started, and about your more recent threat to embarrass my future wife. It may, or may not, cost me any chance of receiving the chairmanship, but it will undoubtedly destroy any hope you have of getting it."

Charlotte wandered about the gardens of Chartwell snipping off dead flower heads, pruning back rosebushes that really didn't need to be pruned, jerking out any weeds she came across—although the gardener at Chartwell was annoyingly efficient at his job, so there weren't a great many weeds to pull. It was becoming increasingly hard to justify the time she spent out here, because, honestly, there wasn't much for her to do.

It didn't stop her from coming though. She needed to occupy her time somehow, and reading was presently a futile occupation because she simply couldn't focus her mind on the words. She'd quit trying to deal with her correspondence, since she ruined nearly every page with teary ink splotches because, while she hadn't been able to cry at first, the tears came frequently now.

That's why she sought refuge in the solitude of the gardens. At least here she could cry in peace without having to see the pitying looks on the servants' faces.

She blinked back the current crop of tears threatening to form.

If you can't think of him without crying, then don't think of him, you ninny!

Although she knew very well she might as well try to stop the sun from rising in the morning. No matter how hard she tried to put William out of her mind, it was impossible. He commanded all of her heart, so was it any surprise she couldn't excise him from her thoughts?

Her steps faltered as her hand automatically went to her abdomen. It was too early to tell, but she should know soon if a baby was a possibility. Her courses were fairly regular, and by her reckoning they were due next week.

She'd known before their night together there could be a risk of pregnancy. She wasn't ignorant of the facts of life, but she'd believed the risk to be a small one, given her parents' struggles to start a family, and since her parents had both been only children, it wasn't as if there was a family history of fecundity.

The funny thing was she wasn't quite sure whether she would view the coming of her courses (or, conversely, their absence) with disappointment or relief. She'd struggled with that question since she'd come home. There was a part of her that loved him so desperately that she would be overjoyed at the prospect of a baby.

But she also knew there'd be a certain relief if she weren't pregnant, because there was also a part of her that loved him so desperately that she was willing to do what was best for him no matter how painful it was for her. And she still believed in the depths of her heart that he was better off without her. If she hadn't believed it, she'd never have jilted him.

England needed men like William in positions of leadership, living their lives in the service of king and country. In a way, she was glad, really, that he hadn't fallen in love with her, because if she thought she'd captured his heart, she could never have denied her own.

But he'd never spoken words of love, and so far he'd respected her wishes not to come after her. It had been four days since she'd bolted. She was fairly certain that if he'd intended to come, he would have done so by now.

That he hadn't convinced her that her course of action had been the right one.

She'd been surprised though that her brother hadn't followed her to Chartwell. Even though, just as she'd done with William, she'd instructed him not to, and like William, he'd honored her wishes. She didn't *fault* him for not coming, but she'd have welcomed his familiar presence, even if he would have been woefully out of his depth dealing with this tearful version of her.

She felt a fresh bout of tears coming on, so she hurried to a secluded bench tucked well back among the greenery where it was unlikely she'd be observed either from the house or by anyone working about the grounds. She set the pouch containing her garden shears, pruners, and spade beside her on the cold stone seat of the bench, took off the old gloves she wore, and pulled a large handkerchief from the pocket of the apron she'd put on to protect her clothing, and cried until she was, for the moment, all cried out.

Naturally that was where William found her. Eyes undoubtedly red from all her crying, her face probably splotchy, not to mention streaked with dirt from her work in the garden, wearing an old housedress covered up with the shapeless apron. She had to look a fright.

While he…he looked marvelous. Her eyes greedily drank in the sight of his broad shoulders encased in a finely tailored navy jacket, that dear, handsome face, studying her gravely as he stood before her, looking more haggard and drawn than she liked.

She wasn't sure who moved first, but the next thing she knew, she was crushed in his embrace, his face buried between one side of her neck and her shoulder.

"You can't know how fiercely I've missed you," he said. Then he was kissing her with urgency—her neck, her throat, her jaw, her cheek. And finally, with a groan, he took her mouth in a hungry kiss, and she kissed him back with a desperate passion.

It wasn't until some time later that William drew back, still holding on to her in a loose embrace. "I meant to do this right," he said, giving her a rueful grin. "I promised myself I wasn't going to kiss you until we got a few things straight between us."

"William," she began, "there's something you should know—"

"Shhh," he said, placing a finger against her lips. "Before that, there's something I have to tell you. Something I should have told you earlier. I love you, Charlotte. Madly. Deeply. Desperately. I love you so much that I can't live without you, and I'm willing to do whatever it takes to persuade you to become my wife. Because nothing means anything to me, if I can't have you by my side."

It was the loveliest, dearest declaration, and her heart felt as if it might burst right out of her chest, so great was her happiness at hearing him speak the words. But mingling with that joy was the conviction that she had to confess all to him before she let him say another word. He deserved to know the reasons behind her actions, even if it caused him to take back everything he'd just said. When he released her and started to go down on one knee, she grasped his arms, preventing him from doing so.

"You...you don't know how precious those words are to me," she blurted out, "but before you go any further, there's something you have to know, something I should have told you before, but...but I'd no idea how you felt...not that that should make any difference, really, because I thought I was acting for the best...and I also thought I was the only one who...who was in love."

As she spoke, his blue eyes deepened to the color of dark sapphires. "If you love me, Charlotte, then that's confession enough for me. I already know about Pemberton. I know what he tried to do, and I think I know why you did what you did, and also why you didn't share your reasons for doing it. Do I wish you'd confided in me? Yes, because I've never been so miserable in my life as I was after you left. But all that is behind us now."

"You ought to hate me. It was cowardly the way I jilted you and quit London, leaving you to deal with the aftermath. I'll completely understand if you wish to heap wrath and censure upon my head."

"Shall I make you don a hair shirt as well? Really, Charlotte, give me more credit than that. How can I not forgive you when you were willing to sacrifice yourself to try to save me?"

"But did I manage to? Or were your chances for the post ruined anyway?"

One corner of his mouth quirked up in a rueful grin. "Let's just say I doubt I'm the front-runner any longer, although Liverpool has yet to make any formal announcement. But if it makes you feel any better, I have it on good authority that Pemberton has no chance of getting it either."

"Oh, William. I'm sorry. Everything was for naught then."

"No it wasn't." He cupped her cheek with his hand. "Because I've got you."

She began to tear up again, but this time they were happy tears. "I'm not at all the sort of girl you should marry, but I love you, and I'm not noble enough to give you up again," she said, dabbing at her eyes with her handkerchief.

"Thank God," he said fervently as his hand slid into her hair and his other arm tightened around her. He leaned in for another kiss that silenced all conversation for the next several minutes. "As delightful as all this kissing is," he said at last, "there is an important matter I wish to attend to."

He dropped to one knee before her, and now that the moment had finally come, her mind, perhaps too long refusing to hope against hope that he would ever propose, inanely thought the gravel of the garden path must make his position incredibly uncomfortable. He pulled something from the inner pocket of his jacket and held it out to her. "Charlotte, I want to offer this betrothal ring to you again, in the hope that you've revised your first opinion of me, the one in which you so justly declared that I was the last man you'd ever choose to marry. I love you, Charlotte. I think I started falling in love with you that morning when you didn't like me at all, because I knew even then, I'd found a woman whose good opinion was worth having. I hope I've been fortunate enough to earn it. Please, Charlotte. Make me the happiest of men, and say you'll marry me."

She couldn't say anything, couldn't give him an answer because emotion, like a cork in a bottle, kept the words from escaping her throat.

He reached out and took her left hand in one of his, and held the ring in his other hand, poised to slip it over her finger.

"Well, my darling? What do you say? Will you promise to marry me and wear my ring again?"

"Yes," she choked out at last. "Yes, yes, and yes! I love you, William. So very, very much!"

And with that he slipped the ring on her finger. Coming to his feet, he reached for her hand, and their fingers twined together. Hand in hand, they slowly made their way through the garden and back to the house.

"I brought the special license with me. We could be married today, if we wished." He gave her a hopeful glance.

"While that sounds lovely, I wouldn't want to marry without our families present."

He sighed. "I thought you might say that."

"You know you wouldn't be happy if your sisters missed our wedding." She giggled. "And we both know Elizabeth would be most put out to be excluded from the wedding celebrations. So what's another week or two?"

"Don't underestimate my eagerness to be a bridegroom. However, I guess we could put it off until tomorrow. You know, to give everybody a chance to arrive."

"What? You can't be serious. How did you...?" He was grinning from ear to ear, looking so supremely pleased with himself that she couldn't help giving his arm a light swat. "You were very sure of yourself, weren't you?"

"Not entirely," he admitted. "I could only hope you were as miserable apart from me as I was from you, and that no matter what objections you might still harbor, I could convince you being together would always be preferable to being apart."

"I still don't know about tomorrow," she said.

One of his brows shot up. "So I still have some convincing to do?" he murmured as his face slowly descended toward hers.

"I don't have anything appropriate to wear, and I refuse to

be married in a simple day dress. I only get to be a bride once, you know."

"Then set your mind at ease," he said, his lips a hair's breadth away from hers. "Libby is bringing one of your new gowns with her."

'You've thought of everything then," she whispered against his mouth.

"I've certainly tried to," he whispered back, following the words with a kiss to seal the deal.

Chapter Twenty-Two

Three weeks later…

I enjoy breakfast in bed, but it feels so decadent," Charlotte said as she dropped a spoonful of black currant jelly onto a piece of toast. They'd indulged in the habit of leisurely breakfasts in bed most mornings since their wedding the day after she and William had reconciled in the garden at Chartwell. Two days after that, William had taken her to his family estate for a short honeymoon. They'd just returned to London yesterday.

"I concur. Very decadent." William dropped a kiss on her shoulder. "Especially when you're wearing one of Madame Rochelle's creations."

"*I* only wanted to order a few flannel nightgowns, but she insisted she knew best what sort of nightwear you'd like me to wear." Charlotte giggled as he kissed the ticklish spot on her neck.

"And for that she has my eternal gratitude." He nipped her earlobe.

"Aren't you hungry?" she asked, trying to lean out of his reach as she took a bite of her toast.

"Only for you," he replied, his voice husky with desire. He scooted himself closer, reaching a hand around her back, and slipping it into the barely-there bodice of her night rail to caress her breast.

Halfheartedly she tried to swat his hand away with her free one. "I thought you had a meeting this morning. You don't want to be late, do you?"

"I'm considering skipping it altogether," he murmured. "After all, things appear to have hummed along well enough in my absence."

"I'm sure you were missed," she said, her own voice husky now in response to his knowing caresses. Her resistance was flagging and he had to know it.

His response was an indistinct "mmmm" as the hand not occupied with her breast began working its way beneath the hem of her night rail. She might as well admit defeat. Her appetite for food had vanished anyway, replaced with a more immediate need for *him*.

"You win," she said. "But you'll have to move the breakfast tray first."

"With pleasure," William murmured in her ear, before climbing from the bed to attend to the task.

Charlotte lay back with a happy sigh awaiting her new husband's attentions. Feeling lazy, she was content to let him take the lead, which he did with a concentrated enthusiasm that soon had them reaching a mutually satisfying conclusion.

A short time later Charlotte, more decently clad in a dressing gown, sat in bed with a plate of buttered muffins and fruit. William had already left after a whirlwind effort to get dressed and out of the house, because despite his words earlier, he was eager to get back to work. The reforms commission was scheduled to have its first meeting tomorrow.

To her regret, William had not been named chairman. During his audience with Lord Liverpool when he'd related the truth about their engagement's beginnings, the prime minister had expressed his sympathy that Pemberton had entangled them in his scheme to secure the post. But in the end, Liverpool had been unwilling to go against his advisers who were now reluctant to name William to the chairmanship.

However, Lord Huntington had used his considerable influence to see that a relatively benign candidate had been given the post, and that William was named as a commission member. So he'd still have a role in shaping the commission's recommendations.

During their time in Sussex, a single copy of *Tattles and Rattles About Town* had arrived by messenger along with a note that said simply *all others were destroyed prior to distribution*. Charlotte had been mystified by it until William explained Pemberton's hand in it—both in leaking the information of her visit to The Golden Pineapple and then, apparently, in seeing that all copies were destroyed rather than sold. Charlotte had then tossed that last copy into the fireplace.

It was not, all things considered, a bad outcome, and Pemberton was surely gnashing his teeth, because he was now effectively banished from the prime minister's circle. Liverpool had pronounced Pemberton's plans to undermine William's chance as "most unsporting and beneath contempt" and had given the man the cut direct the next time their paths crossed.

Sally came into the room. "Here's your correspondence," she said, laying a prodigious quantity of cards and notes onto the bed beside Charlotte.

"Thank you, I suppose," Charlotte said with a little sigh.

Sally grinned at her and fetched her lap desk from where it sat on a table across the room. "The water is being heated for your bath. I'll let you know when it's ready."

"Thank you, Sally." Charlotte sifted through the pile, not quite sure where to start. A large square envelope with *Open Immediately* written on the front caught her attention. She recognized Serena's handwriting.

Opening it, she withdrew an invitation and a small folded note. Written on the creamy card stock in Edwina's elegant script was the following:

> *Please join us for the inaugural meeting of the*
> *Wednesday Afternoon Social Club*
> *at half past one on the sixteenth of this month at*
> *12 Upper Grosvenor Street.*
> *No RSVP necessary*

She opened the note, which like the envelope, was written in Serena's hand.

> *We're pleased to hear you've returned. You were certainly missed, but our work continued while you were gone. We'd be delighted if you can join us today, but if not, we'll be meeting again next Wednesday!*
>
> *Welcome back, dear Charlotte. We have much to catch up on.*
>
> *Serena*

Today was the thirtieth; she'd missed the first two meetings of the Wednesday Afternoon Social Club. A sharp pang of disappointment dampened her mood, but she shook it off. She wouldn't miss the *third* one, and it was already a quarter to eleven. Charlotte hopped out of bed.

Though she'd been absent from London less than a month, life here had moved forward without her, and now she was ready to find out what she'd missed, *who* she'd missed at the first meetings, since the point of creating a more formal group was to grow their numbers of like-minded ladies.

Had there been brandy? Had the duchess worn breeches? She couldn't wait to see for herself.

"Sally," she called, hoping her maid was readying her clothes in the adjacent bedroom, which functioned as Charlotte's dressing room for now. They intended to have a proper one built soon, but for the present the bedroom was sufficient.

Sally poked her head around the doorjamb. "Yes?"

"As soon as some water is ready, have it sent up. It will have to be a quick bath this morning. I need to be somewhere at half past one."

"Yes, ma'am. I'll see to it."

Being addressed as ma'am still sounded foreign to her ears, but she was a married lady now. A *very happily* married lady, and for that reason alone she couldn't entirely hate Pemberton's intrigues concerning William.

As he'd told her when they'd met at Hatchards, he'd been their accidental matchmaker. And frankly, her happiness at becoming William's wife was the most satisfying revenge to Pemberton's troublesome efforts.

She smiled to herself and, since Sally wasn't about to witness it, did a little jig about the room. It was good to be back.

*Don't miss
Charles and Serena's
romance in the next
Unconventional Ladies of
Mayfair story,*
Say You'll Be My Lady
Available Winter 2022

About the Author

KATE PEMBROOKE is a lifelong reader whose path to becoming an author of Regency romance was forged when she first read Jane Austen's *Pride and Prejudice*. Kate lives with her family in the Midwest. She loves puttering around in her flower beds, taking beach vacations, and adding to her already extensive collection of cookbooks.

You can learn more at:
   katepembrooke.com
   Twitter @KatePembrooke
   Facebook.com/Kate.Pembrooke
   Instagram.com/katepembrooke/

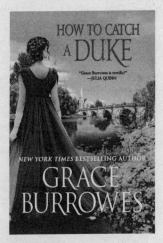
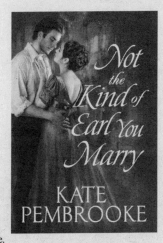

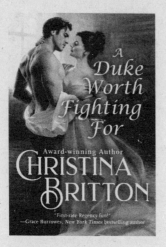

A DUKE WORTH FIGHTING FOR
by Christina Britton

Margery Kitteridge has been mourning her husband for years, and while she's not ready to consider marriage again, she does miss intimacy with a partner. When Daniel asks for help navigating the Isle of Synne's social scene and they accidentally kiss, she realizes he's the perfect person with whom to have an affair. As they begin to confide in each other, Daniel discovers that he's unexpectedly connected to Margery's late husband, and she will have to decide if she can let her old love go for the promise of a new one.

SOMEDAY MY DUKE WILL COME
by Christina Britton

Quincy Nesbitt reluctantly accepted the dukedom after his brother's death, but he'll be damned if he accepts his brother's fiancée as well. The only polite way to decline is to become engaged to someone else—quickly. Lady Clara has the right connections and happens to need him as much as he needs her. But he soon discovers she's also witty and selfless—and if he's not careful, he just might lose his heart.